TYCHE'S REBELLION

TYCHE'S REBELLION

J DEMOS

Published by Stygian Quill Press, Sandpoint, Idaho

Library of Congress Control Number: 2025922656

ISBNs: 979-8-9935955-0-4 (Paperback) | 979-8-9935955-1-1 (Hardcover) | 979-8-9935955-2-8 (ePub)

First Printing: November, 2025

Printed in the United States of America.

This is a work of fiction. The names, characters, places, and incidents are either the product of the author's imagination or are used fictitiously, and any resemblance to actual persons, living or dead, business establishments, events, or locales is entirely coincidental.

Titles may be purchased in bulk for educational, business, fundraising, or sales promotional use. For more information, contact Stygian Quill Press at rights@stygianquill.com.

Cover design by Selkkie Designs.

10 9 8 7 6 5 4 3 2 1

Για την αγαπημένη μου ελληνική οικογένεια—Χρήστος, Δήμητρα, Εύη, Τρύφωνας και Πάνος—των οποίων τα ονόματα δίνουν πνοή σε νέες ιστορίες μέσα σε αυτό το βιβλίο. Είστε ο παλμός της καρδιάς του Πικερνίου, που έχει γίνει το πιο αληθινό μου σπίτι. Μέσα από την αποδοχή και την αγάπη σας, διαγράψατε τις γραμμές καταγωγής, κάνοντάς με να νιώθω ότι ανήκα πάντα. Είναι η απέραντη ζεστασιά και το πνεύμα σας που φωτίζουν κάθε λέξη μέσα σε αυτές τις σελίδες, ένα ειλικρινές αφιέρωμα στις ρίζες που άνθισαν χάρη σε εσάς.

For my beloved Greek family—Christos, Dimitra, Evy, Tryfonas, and Panos—whose names breathe life into new tales within this book. You are the heartbeat of Pikerni, which has become my truest home. Through your acceptance and love, you erased the lines of origin, making me feel that I have always belonged. It is your boundless warmth and spirit that illuminate every word within these pages, a heartfelt tribute to the roots that have flourished because of you.

"*The strongest of all human bonds is the love a mother bears for her child. In its nature it is a permanent and unchangeable loyalty, the only loyalty we can call incorruptible.*"

—*Thucydides*

Acknowledgements

The final, polished form of *Tyche's Rebellion* would not have been possible without the skilled hands and keen eyes of a phenomenal professional team.

To my editor, Carol Craig of Editing Gallery: There is simply no adequate way to thank you. Your editorial instincts, tireless dedication, and razor-sharp grasp of structure elevated every single chapter. I'm especially grateful for the courage and shared professional kindness that underpins our unique working relationship. The fact that we are each other's trusted first reader and final polish is one of the greatest gifts of this journey. Thank you for making *Tyche's Rebellion* a stronger book.

To Selkkie Designs: Thank you for your artistry and vision. You captured the complex heart of this story and transformed it into a cover that draws the eye and perfectly represents Tyche's world within.

And to Sienna Arts of White Rose Publishing: Thank you for your work in making the interior of *Tyche's Rebellion* look as professional and beautiful as any book on the shelf. I deeply appreciate your dedication to turning an author's vision into a polished reality.

My inner circle, you served as the anchors that grounded me while my imagination soared.

To my daughter, Riley, and her fiancé, Joe: You are the deepest wellspring of my strength. Not only did you bravely dive into the earliest drafts of *Tyche's Rebellion*, providing the thoughtful, critical feedback that honed the story's edge, but you also stood as a fortress against the constant doubt. When imposter syndrome whispered that I was unworthy, you roared that I was enough. Thank you for sustaining my courage and affirming my dream.

To the countless friends who offered their optimism and cheer: Your consistent belief was a beacon when I was adrift in a sea of words. I owe you a debt of gratitude for the buoying encouragement that kept me moving toward the shore.

And finally, to the incredible people of Pikerni: Your support transcends encouragement; it is the vital thread of connection you so willingly cast out to me. Knowing the importance of this project to your community—and understanding what is at stake—inspires me every single day. Your love, appreciation, and belief in what I am attempting to accomplish for our village is the most meaningful acknowledgement I could ever receive. Thank you for making this journey about more than just a book, but about ensuring the roots of our children's heritage in Pikerni can thrive.

Finally, there are the emotions, the places, and the ancestors who breathed life into this narrative.

The origins of this story began with a powerful, unnameable longing that resolved itself only upon my many visits to Greece. To the ancient stones, the winding roads, and the sun-drenched earth that were instantly and remarkably familiar—thank you for giving me a home I never knew I lacked and for grounding my soul in the present moment.

To the unparalleled spirit of Greek hospitality, and especially to the relatives and wonderful people of Pikerni: You gave me the profound gift of belonging and the vivid cultural experience that fills the pages of this book. *Tyche's Rebellion* is a tribute to that connection and a promise to the future. It is my greatest hope that this story can, in some small way, honor your heritage and help ensure the heart of this incredible village beats on.

To the Fates, the Muses, and the myths that form the bedrock of this world: Thank you for your continued hold on the modern imagination.

Contents

1. Even the Gods Fear   3

2. Nightmares Gods Create   11

3. A Hunger for the Simple Joys   14

4. To Trade Starlight for Earth   22

5. The Sting of Mortal Sweat   31

6. In the Calloused Hands of Mortals   41

7. The Most Unsettling Truths   50

8. The Earth Remembers   57

9. Dreams are Whispers of the Soul   70

10. Justice is a Blade That Cuts Both Ways   78

11. Love is a Double-Edged Sword   84

12. A Balm Against the Storms of Fate   89

13. Secrets Are Heavy Burdens   103

14. Secrets That Bind   110

15. Bound by Love and Sacrifice   116

16. Steep is the Price of Power   125

17. Divine Fury Stains the Dawn   142

18. Human Compassion Anchors the Soul   149

19. Hope Forged in the Stygian Steel   160

20. The Fist of Mortal Rebellion   172

21. Tides of Justice, Threads of Hope   187

22. Hope's Ember Flickers   195

23. Whisper of a Daughter's Plea   208

24. Rebellion Flares Before Retribution   218

25. The Earth Claims Its Due   226

26. Fear Ensnares Even Gods   235

27. Fear Becomes A Cruel Design   254

28. Beneath a Mother's Heart   264

29. Love's Shield Births a Shadow   273

30. In the Heart's Farewell   281

31. Farewell's Eve   290

32. Herbs Scent the Dawn's Regret   297

33. Love's Choice Births a Human Soul   309

34. Dream Within a Dream   322

EPILOGUE   337

Even the gods fear what they cannot control. They build their cages of power, believing themselves secure, but fate is a weaver of intricate patterns, and sometimes, the threads unravel. Sometimes, love becomes a rebellion, and the greatest of powers are brought to their knees.

1

EVEN THE GODS FEAR

Love is a dangerous rebellion.

Backward, the Wheel of Fortune unspun her, even as her gilded cage screamed. A sea of grasping hands and warped mouths reached for her from the mosaics on the walls of her chamber. The tide of mortal need crashed against her. *I'm powerless.* The bitter words tangled on Tyche's tongue. She was a goddess of boundless fortune, yet now a Titan's fury simmered beneath her skin because she could do nothing to command her child's destiny.

Before she could process the unraveling of her world, the messenger god Hermes appeared in her doorway.

He gestured toward the grand hall, his gaze holding hers for a moment too long. "Lady Tyche," his solemn whisper caressed her ear, "your summons has come."

Gooseflesh prickled Tyche's arms. She knew what this meant. The silence of the halls, the whispers of the peacocks. Every shadow seemed to hold an Olympian eye. She was to face her judgment from the gods.

"Don't despair, Tyche." Hermes' smile was a fragile shield, his amber eyes a promise she couldn't yet grasp. "Apollo and I will be there, too."

But even his words couldn't quiet the fear in her stomach as she followed him past the whispering paintings along the deserted hallways.

As they approached the great hall, the murmur of voices and the rustle of robes raised Tyche's hackles. The bronze doors swung open to reveal a gauntlet of colossal statues of the Olympian gods and goddesses. Tyche paused at the threshold, where the stone faces glared at her with hostile judgment. Their immense size diminished the goddess of Fortune as she walked beneath their shadows, stony gazes impaling her flesh.

Hermes cupped her elbow and guided her between the towering figures. The stone groaned, and with a grinding screech, the statues' heads swiveled, their scrutiny locking onto her path to condemnation. Ancient, stony eyes tracked her with the weight of ages, as if reliving old battles for supremacy. Then she saw them. The faces of the Olympian gods came into view.

What have I done?

She swallowed the fear rising in her throat. On a raised dais at the center sat Zeus and Hera. Before the raised tribune, a shimmering, translucent platform awaited her. *Is this a trap?* Sweat slicked her palms as Hermes guided her onto the stage. A ward of arcane power shimmered into existence around her. *I'm caged,* she realized. *A golden prison to contain what they do not comprehend.* Her breath constricted in her lungs.

Tyche glanced at the faces of the watchers, hoping to find a champion among them. But Artemis offered no solace, her scowl deepening as she raised her hand toward the heavens. The Constellation of the Scales answered her command, its starry form igniting above the hall in a gyral display.

"By the power of Astraea," Artemis intoned, "let the divine will of Olympus shine upon the accused." With her words, a beam of silver light descended from the constellation and lanced onto Tyche, isolating her in its brilliant glow.

They're all judging me.

Tyche's heart wilted. The assembled gods radiated an oppressive power that pressed down on her. Some shifted on their thrones while others remained still, their haughty gazes fixed on her. Tyche glanced at the stoic faces and caught Apollo's discreet nod. She blinked in relief at the spark of compassion in his sunlit eyes.

The colossal figures of the gods and goddesses towered over the dais and the ring of thrones, their judgmental glares on Tyche. Others stared out across the hall, their faces impassive, as if observing the entire proceedings with detached indifference. Tyche's heart constricted under the vise of their stares.

Perched on the statues' encircled shoulders, Hera's peacocks fanned their magnificent tail feathers. Their enormous claws dug into the cold stone of their necks as thousands of eyes flickered to life. Their beaks clacked together like skeletal fingers, whispering GUilTyguILtygUilTY. Their eyespots, a host of watchful orbs, glistened with scrutiny and condemnation.

"Silence!" Zeus' voice boomed through the hall in a thunderclap of authority. "The Olympian Council is now in session." He gestured toward Tyche. "Goddess of Fortune, you stand accused."

Before she could respond, the stone figures flanking the dais began to speak. Their voices rang through the hall, stilted and unnatural.

"Balance, disturbed." A statue's golden face stretched against the words.

"Favor, misplaced," another blared. Its silver eyes turned to Tyche.

"Mortals, ascendant," a third hissed through its marble lips.

The ground trembled under Tyche's feet, and a bolt of fear erupted in her chest. *The gods fear the future the mortals' power has the potential to create.*

Tyche recoiled from the lithic giants' pronouncements. Their emotionless words warned of a divine overthrow, and an unnamed terror beyond mere threats seemed to build upon itself, escalating until the statues' voices grew hysterical in their insistence.

"Power, usurped. Chaos, unleashed. Order, broken."

A murmur rippled through the assembled gods, and Hera bolted up from her throne in fury. "And the greatest transgression of all..." Hera leveled her burning gaze at Tyche. "You, goddess of Fortune, have conceived a child who defies our dominion and corrupts the heart of our power."

Tyche's hand covered her swollen belly. A wave of hushed whispers swept through the hall.

Hera, the protector of mothers. The irony is a bitter sting.

"The child must be eliminated. Nemesis will be sent to carry out the decree." Zeus slammed his fist onto the arm of his throne.

The fatal proclamation for her unborn child stole the air from Tyche's lungs.

No! I won't let them kill my baby!

But even as the vow formed in her mind, she knew the futility of resistance. She was a goddess, yes, but she was also trapped in this realm, ensnared by the ancient laws of Olympus.

Hera gestured, and two guards approached Tyche. "You will be confined to your chambers until the order is carried out."

"I won't—" A strangled cry tore from Tyche's throat when the guards approached. But as their hands clamped onto her arms, she met Hera's glacial stare. The crushing weight of Olympian decree settled in her bones, and the fight drained out of her, leaving her limp and defeated as they led her away.

Once in her chambers, she slumped onto the divan and pressed a hand against her stomach. Tyche stared at the silent mosaic walls surrounding her, relieved they yielded no mortal need. She buried her face in her hands, then rose to seek the quiet of her private balcony. The palace grounds sprawled before her, but their beauty granted no refuge to her wounded heart. The garden's grandeur had become defiled, the flawless splendor a garish mockery of the untamed nature stirring in her Titan blood. She closed her eyes and attempted to connect with the life inside her, to draw upon it for strength in the coming battle.

She summoned the instruments of her power, the Wheel of Fortune and Horn of Plenty. The ivory and gold shimmered into existence before her. As they hovered nearby, a moan emanated from inside her chambers. Startled, Tyche returned to her room, where the mosaic danced across the chamber walls. The tiles expanded outward and then contracted as an image coalesced, transforming the mural into a window onto the mortal world. Tyche knelt before the portal and placed her hands around the frame. The image within sharpened, and a woman kneeling near a spring came into view, her head bowed in supplication. Tyche saw a child clutched to the woman's breast. A faint, desperate cry reached her, issuing through the mosaic's magic.

"Goddess of Fortune, please! This child has drowned! I implore you, grant us a blessing!"

Tyche leaned into the small form of the woman within the mosaic. She saw her in sharp detail, her roughspun clothes patched and faded, and her face creased with worry.

"I am here, daughter," Tyche breathed a whisper of maternal connection into the swirling colors. "I hear your prayer."

The goddess' heart clenched. The cry matched her wordless scream for help, for a miracle she could not perform for her unborn child, much less anyone else's. She hesitated. She had no heart for her duties, not now. But she knew she couldn't refuse. It was a small act of defiance, a way to cling to the remnants of her power.

She closed her eyes and focused on the distant, desperate voice. "What do you seek?" Her answer boomed across the mortal realm.

"Good fortune, Goddess Tyche," the woman's voice trembled in reply, "a blessing of life for this child."

Tyche studied her Wheel, and her heart ached. This mortal, so full of fear, so vulnerable, had no idea of the turmoil raging within the goddess from whom she sought help, who was lost in her own torment born of love, forbidden by those who wielded absolute power.

"Of course," her hollow voice carried on the wind. Her heart numb, she spun the Wheel of Fortune, its surface a ring of carved symbols, each representing a different fate. It slowed to a stop, and the symbol of misfortune rose to meet her gaze in a bitter reflection of her own unspun destiny.

The woman's desperate plea faltered. "Oh."

Tyche's heart twisted. With all that had happened today—the gods' cruel imprisonment, the threat to her child—she couldn't allow this woman to suffer as she had. Nor this innocent child. *No, not* this *child.* Fate, it seemed to Tyche, was a wandering tide, but it would not break this connection. She spun the Wheel again, each turn a gamble against the odds. Then, at long last, the Wheel granted her a symbol of good fortune.

"Thank you, Goddess!" the woman cried. The mosaic's tiles bulged in joy. "Thank you for your kindness!"

Tyche's heart clouded with sadness and resentment that she could change the destiny of a mortal but not the fate of herself and her unborn baby. The mortal's heartfelt thanks rose to Tyche on the sunset wind like a hot rebellion against the gods' decree.

"I have to escape." The desperate plea strangled Tyche's throat. She gazed at the Wheel of Fortune and sighed. "I have to protect my child. But how?" Tyche ran her fingertips along the mosaic wall. "This act of defiance for a mortal soul has ignited a fire in my blood."

Then a soft knock echoed through the chamber.

"Tyche?" Hermes whispered through the door.

"Come in," she murmured, not bothering to rise from the floor.

The messenger god slipped inside, his expression grave. "I witnessed it all. Every cruel word. Every threat."

Tyche exhaled, her hands caressing her swollen belly. "They want to take my child, Hermes."

"Yes." Hermes' shoulders slumped. "Zeus' decree is unshakeable."

"Then what am I supposed to do?" Tyche looked up at the god with sorrowful eyes. "I'm trapped." She flung her arm to encompass her chamber.

Hermes glanced around the room, as though checking for unseen listeners. "You're in immediate danger, goddess," he said. "They're going to... They plan to end this line." He paused, his words a sharpened knife against her skin.

Tyche grimaced, her gaze fixed on her mounded stomach. "I know," she whispered.

"It wasn't a warning, but a promise." Hermes stepped closer and touched her shoulder. "They'll come for your child tonight."

A rim of fire burned around Tyche's heart. "Tonight? But—"

"You need to be ready," Hermes interrupted with a conviction that defied Zeus' thunder. "I'm getting you out of here."

"But how can I escape?" Tyche clasped his fingers in a desperate grip. "They're watching. Every shadow holds an eye."

"I have a plan." Hermes' eyes glinted in the soft light. "A swift and silent one. Think... wings."

Tyche's eyes widened. "Wings?"

Hermes dipped his chin in affirmation. "When the time is right, and Olympus sleeps, I'll be waiting."

"Where will you take me?" Fear and freedom wrapped her heart.

"A safe place where their power has no authority," Hermes assured her. "Far from the eyes of Olympus. Where they won't find you."

She nodded, afraid. "I trust you. I'll be ready."

After the messenger departed, Tyche retreated to her bed, the silken sheets a comfort against her skin. Sleep claimed her, but it was a sleep of shadows. A descent into the heart of fear.

Some nightmares are born of fear, others of memory. But the most terrible nightmares are those the gods themselves create. They twist the fabric of existence, turning love into horror and hope into despair. And in those dark spaces, where the gods' cruelty reigns, even the strongest hearts can break.

NIGHTMARES GODS CREATE

The moment the child opened its eyes, twelve Olympian thrones trembled. No cry nor a whimper followed, only a silent wave of potential that could unmake worlds. Tyche's daughter carried chaos incarnate. The kind of birth the gods murdered to prevent.

In the nightmare, unbearable pressure tore through Tyche's stomach. Her hands clutched her rounded belly. Hot, fetid breath pushed into her nostrils, and she retched.

This isn't real. You're dreaming, a voice whispered in the back of her mind.

"Open your eyes!" A disembodied voice screamed at her. "Wake up!"

Tyche's eyes snapped open. Her hated enemy bent over her in a gross distortion of waking terror.

"Your womb carries a threat."

Nemesis, goddess of Retribution.

A groan escaped Tyche as another contraction seized her. "No!" She jerked and pushed away the phantom hand shaking her. "Get away from me!" Tyche tilted her head back and howled in despair and rage.

"Push, damn you." Nemesis pummeled her again.

Pain blurred Tyche's vision. Two figures pierced her fading sight, massive and terrible. Zeus stood rigid, power coiled beneath his skin. His eyes bled lightning. Beside him, Hera towered, her jeweled fists cradling oblivion. Their fury writhed against Tyche's flesh.

Then, the gods' faces melted from their skulls, and their skin flowed like liquid gold to reform into the cold, unyielding stone of the Olympian statues. Their dead eyes stared down at her in accusation. Tyche screamed as the stone cracked, and shards of marble morphed into the snapping beaks of Hera's peacocks, their eyespots burning into her.

Tyche clenched the sodden silk in her fists and howled into the hot bolt of the contraction as the irresistible urge to push surged through her body, and she bore down through clenched teeth.

Reality fractured. The nightmare swallowed her into its maw, while shadow-veined walls pulsed with hunger.

Bare feet scraped against cold stone. Slapdrag. Slap. Drag. A sharp scrape of fingernails clawed at the cave's walls and set Tyche's teeth on edge. Blood thundered in her ears. She lifted the candle, her fingers clenched tight around the wax. Its guttering flame wavered against the thirsty dark. Her heart burned cold as shadows circled her flame. The children's screams crashed and receded. The ebb and flow of their lament swallowed her scream whole.

Tyche thrust the stub of candlelight into the void. The flame's dying light carved monsters from the shadows. Her heart thundered with divine blood. Primal fear hollowed her bones.

The Nekrochim lurched toward her, a grotesque amalgamation of limbs and torsos. She recoiled, throwing an arm across her eyes, as their faces snaked and weaved through the darkness, flesh and bone unmade.

Recognition struck.

The monster before her, her own children. "Daughters!" Rage wept from her eyes.

Their heads snapped in her direction. A single word tumbled from their warped mouths.

motHERmoTHerMOThEr

She clasped her hands to her ears, but immortality offered no shelter from their screams. Their twisted arms unfurled like broken wings, some rigid with petrified anguish. Others reached with fingers that cursed the empty air, hungry, pleading, forever denied.

Tyche collapsed on the ground and rolled to her back. Their cries unmade her mind. So loud, a siren's song. She writhed and slammed her clenched fists into the stone. Her scream rose. Primal, unbridled. A curse against those who had stolen her children.

The Nekrochim's hands grasped at her, its puckered mouths wailing, "Mo tTh e r!" Tyche fought the nightmare's chains. Stone buckled beneath her as darkness pressed a scream from her lungs.

Then, the rush of wings.

Sometimes, the greatest acts of rebellion are born of the smallest moments of kindness. A touch, a breath, a whispered name—these are the threads that forge a new destiny. And in the heart of every goddess, there lies a mortal yearning, a hunger for the simple joys the gods themselves can never truly know.

3

A HUNGER FOR THE SIMPLE JOYS

The girl was already dead when she discovered her.

Where the Nekrochim's grotesque form had dissolved, the whisper of moving water brushed against Tyche's ears. She had awoken with a gasp, disoriented and confused. *They couldn't break me,* a bitter thought surfaced, *but even so, the scars remain.* Still, the nightmare scorched her heart, and cries of the monster raged in her mind.

Then, a blinding white light and the sensation of weightlessness as she had soared through the air. But here, the air smelled crisp, clean, the light less blinding. She looked around, bewildered, attempting to reconcile the horror she had experienced with the unfamiliar peace of this new place.

She pushed herself up onto her elbows, her gaze drawn to the shimmering water of a nearby spring. Kneeling at the edge, she dipped her fingers into the water, the icy liquid a welcome relief against the lingering heat of the nightmare.

Where am I?

Her body trembled, the remnants of nightmare still clinging to her skin. The water's whispers seemed to answer, drawing her gaze to the spring's surface. But the sun held no mercy in its flare, and she raised a hand to shield her eyes from the scorching daystar.

Then, relief bloomed in Tyche's chest at the reassuring flutter of life inside her, the quiet defiance against the gods' cruel decree. She leaned down to the water's edge, parched, and brought her lips to the surface.

Then she saw her.

The dead girl's hair swirled among the tendrils of water trickling from the mountain's side. The child's pale, lifeless face sealed her heart in sorrow.

"No!" Tyche's eyes hovered over the girl's lifeless form. "I shouldn't interfere. The gods forbid it." She drew back her hands and traced her fingers along the damp stone of the spring's edge. But then, the faces of her own lost children flashed through her mind. She tilted her ear to their silent plea for her to act, to defy the gods, to offer this mortal the compassion that had been denied to her own. Tyche rose to her feet with a loud groan. She gathered her garment in her fist and waded into the spring. With a trembling hand, she reached out to caress the cold, lifeless skin.

She cradled the girl's limp form, but a sudden flutter within her summoned waves of grief for her babies, who had been dispatched by the gods. But she had no time to dwell on past sorrows. This innocent human needed her. Now.

Tyche lowered the mortal to the ground and smoothed the locks of wet hair from her face. With tender care, she traced her fingers

over the staring eyes, frozen in a silent scream, and closed their
lids to shield them from the harsh light.

Tyche paid little heed to the rumble of distant thunder, but
the unmistakable snort and the rhythmic pawing of the ground
pulled her gaze toward the crest of hills overlooking the spring.
She glanced up and discovered a rider seated atop a winged
steed. The beast's coat gleamed white against the sparks of the
sun. Familiarity stirred. *Hermes.* Curious about his attentive
observation, she lowered her chin in acknowledgement before
returning to her task.

She collected nearby stones and assembled a crude altar,
placing the objects of her power—the Wheel of Fortune and
the Horn of Plenty—at each end. She lifted the girl's sleeping
form and rested her on the makeshift dais. Tyche blinked away
her hot tears and arranged the child's lax limbs. She cradled the
bulge of her child as she stroked the cheek of the mortal.

The goddess inhaled the world into her lungs as she prepared
to invoke the gods on the girl's behalf, but sorrow cut through
her. Her children cried out to her. Tyche's heart ached at their
loss. She seethed at the gods' selfish greed and their desire
to control human destiny, even as she caressed her writhing
stomach and soothed her newest child nestled within to sleep.

Tyche bent over the girl's form and tilted her head back. She
touched her lips to the child's mouth and breathed fortune into
the deflated lungs. Her arms raised skyward as she called upon
Ikelos, the god of Dreams, to guide the mortal's soul back from
the dark waters of the Styx, her sister, whose river marked the
boundary between life and death. Tyche pressed her hands to the
mortal's chest and hummed songs of fortune to affirm the child's

rightful place in the world. Then she stepped back from the altar and waited in quiet anticipation.

Just as Tyche's daughter shifted inside her, the girl coughed, alive once more.

"Mama?" the mortal rasped.

Tyche scooped the sodden child into her arms. "No, daughter. I'm not your mother. Let us find her together."

The girl's head bobbed in the crook of Tyche's arm as her new charge pointed her trembling finger to the road.

"This way, LittleOne?"

"Yes," snuffled the child. "I'm from the village that lies across this road."

"Then we will travel it together until we find her," Tyche assured her. "What's your name?"

The child's eyes turned upward. "My mother calls me Dora because she says I am a gift from the gods."

Tyche smiled at her. "You are a blessing, child. A fine gift every mother desires."

With Dora safe in her arms, Tyche turned her attention to the village beyond. Golden grasses parted like curtains to reveal a small town clinging to a mountain's ribs. The child, a fragile weight against her shoulder, drew warmth from her tunic's protective fold.

The squeal of pigs and soft mewlings of goats marked their arrival and drew them deeper into the village's embrace. Bent structures framed a cobblestone *plateia*, the square where the stones preserved generations of stories. Clusters of walnut and olive trees splashed green bouquets among the dwellings and along the village's aged walls. A sense of peace settled into her bones as she stepped into the mystery of Dora's origins.

Through the dying light, Tyche could make out the bobbing firefly lights streaming toward her. She halted her steps when the villagers converged around her. Their worried faces flickered in the glow of their torches. With gentle insistence, they pulled the child from her arms in relief and gratitude.

"Good day, stranger. I am Christos." A man, with skin the color of dried figs and eyes the deep blue of the Aegean, raked his eyes across Tyche. "Where did you find Dora? We've searched all day and had no luck. Her mother feared the wolves had taken the child."

"You have brought us good fortune today, my lady." A young woman stumbled forward, her dark hair pulled tight over her skull. With a desperate cry, she pulled Dora to her breast, her embrace steeling around the child like a cage. "Oh, Dora, my precious Dora," she sobbed and buried her face in the child's damp hair. "I thought I'd lost you."

Her gaze lifted to Tyche, brimming with unspeakable gratitude and lingering terror. "I am Althea, Dora's mother. Thank you from the depths of my soul. I was so afraid…"

Grief and hope intertwined like roots beneath Tyche's skin. This resurrected girl embodied her redemption. "Yes, the goddess of Fortune and Luck has passed through your village today. But now, I am ravenous. Will you be so generous as to offer me something to soothe my hungry belly?"

As she spoke, she glimpsed a sanctuary where her child could thrive, free from fear and the threat of sacrifice.

A life shared with these mortals, she mused. A *place where I can shed the burden of my divinity and enjoy the ease of human existence.*

The forbidden seed of hope planted itself in her heart, its roots desperate to seek nourishment in the earth beneath her feet.

Hope, a dangerous yearning. A rebellion against the nature of her being. But as she gazed at the faces of the villagers, she couldn't help but wonder if this was the path she was meant to follow, the destiny she was meant to forge.

"Come." Christos gestured toward the lights of the village. "We will honor you with a feast. A celebration for the return of our daughter." He winked at Dora and tousled her hair.

Tyche accepted the assistance of the village women, who guided her to a springhouse nestled under a walnut grove. Branches sighed as she passed beneath them. The steam rising from the bubbling hot spring swirled around Tyche as she entered the sanctuary enclosed by stone walls etched with deeds of the gods.

She cast off her robe and sank into the delicious folds of the water. Vapor rose like silken threads, and the tension melted from her tired muscles. Outside, the village settled into a hushed quiet, punctuated by the chirping of crickets and the distant bark of an animal she couldn't identify.

The mortals hummed as they scrubbed Tyche's body and rinsed her hair. Slapping fragrant oils in their palms, the women kneaded away her knots of tension. The goddess sighed and relaxed into their firm fingers.

Tyche closed her eyes in exhaustion, but soon the springhouse dissolved into the nightmare. Contractions squeezed her body, sharp as lightning. She thrashed and shrieked from the pain. In the hazy realm of her subconsciousness, the stern faces of Zeus and Hera hovered over her.

Hands stroked her bulging belly. Someone wiped the sweat from her forehead. She howled again and pushed until a searing pain cut through her, and the brittle cry of a baby pierced her ears.

"Give me my baby!" Tyche cried into the void of her nightmare. "Don't kill this one. I promise to—"

Hera jeered at her, the mewling child clamped in her rough embrace. "This child has no future, neither as an Olympian nor a Titan. It is a threat to our supremacy and control. It will be dispatched as were the others."

Tyche wept as she grasped her empty belly, her child stolen once more.

"My lady, wake up. You're having a nightmare." The village woman shook Tyche awake. Tears streamed down her face as the torchlight flickered across the worried faces surrounding her. She glanced at the stranger's tears, then down at her hold over her rounded middle.

She sat up with a splash, "my baby" on her lips.

"Your baby is fine, um..."

"Charis. My name is Charis," Tyche lied. A flicker of contempt burned in her chest. The name, a symbol of beauty and life, represented the path she sought, a future where her child could be safe. Perhaps, she mused, even the goddess Charis herself might offer a touch of protection to those who invoked her name as a shield against the cruelty of the gods.

These mortals need not know who I am.

"Welcome, Charis." The woman's twilight eyes sparked in the soft light. "I am Dimitra."

"Dimitra." Tyche offered a thoughtful smile in response to the woman's graciousness. "A name that honors the goddess of the harvest and the wellspring of abundance. A fitting name for one who tends to the land and nurtures its bounty." Tyche's gaze met Dimitra's.

Beside her stood two companions, whom she introduced as Melina, a young woman with hair the color of ripe wheat, and Kalliope, her weathered hands knotted in her tunic. The women dropped their gazes in embarrassment under the goddess' bold stare.

"Where am I?" Tyche asked. "I seemed to have lost my way before I found the drowned child."

She rose from the spring, and the water cascaded from her body. The women circled her and draped a rough cloak over her bare shoulders. Tyche rubbed her fingertips along its coarseness and recoiled.

So uncomfortable and prickly. How do they clothe themselves in such horrid garments?

"You're in the village of Pikerni near Mantineia." Kalliope gathered Tyche's robes and stroked their richness. "I'll wash your gown and return it to you tomorrow."

Tyche tilted her head in thanks and drew the scratchy chiton around her.

Dimitra beckoned to her. "Follow us. A feast awaits you for the fortune you bestowed upon us today."

To walk among mortals is to trade starlight for earth, to exchange the riches of Olympus for the simple rhythm of a human heart. It is a journey of contradiction, a dance between the divine and the mundane, where even a goddess must learn to find beauty in the ordinary.

TO TRADE STARLIGHT FOR EARTH

The prickling tunic chafed against Tyche's skin as she followed the women to the feast. Restored from the spring's dark clutches, a laughing Dora slammed into Tyche's knees when she stepped through the door of the *lesche*, the great hall, to the waiting villagers. For a heartbeat, the memory of the child's lifeless form in the water flashed through Tyche's mind—blue lips, still chest, death's shadow across her face.

Now those same lips curved in a brilliant smile, and her chest rose with vibrant breath. The child's eyes caught her attention, shifting from shadow to sea storm, like waves before a tempest. How had she not noticed before? She knelt and lifted the girl into her arms and hugged her to her breast, feeling the miracle of mortal life pulse against her immortal heart.

"I'm pleased to see you're safe, LittleOne. I believed the worst." Tyche released the child to the ground with reluctant fingers.

"Thank you, Mother Charis." Dora dipped like a flower in the evening breeze. "You saved me from the wicked spring that tried to drown me."

"Daughter," Tyche smiled and tapped Dora's nose, "you must take care near the springs. They are meant to give life, not death."

The girl raced into the crowd of celebrating villagers as the aroma of roasting meat and baking bread wafted past Tyche. Her stomach rumbled in answer.

She gazed around the shadowy room. A fire burned in a corner fireplace of stone, and the hall pulsed with chaotic energy. Torches sputtered in their iron sconces and cast writhing shadows across the rough-hewn walls. A thick haze of smoke clung to the rafters in a dark cloud. The air hummed with the clatter of wooden plates, the sloshing of ale in earthenware mugs, and the raucous laughter of men and women who seemed to find joy in the mere act of living.

Tyche watched as a child, no older than Dora, smeared pig fat across her cheek, her eyes alight with pure delight. A flare of envy, a sensation Tyche had never known in Olympus, burned in her chest. In the halls of the gods, such unrestrained delight was deemed uncouth, a sign of weakness. Here, it seemed the essence of life.

As Tyche scanned the room, taking in the sights and sounds of the celebration, she noticed a man across the room studying her with an intensity that made her skin crawl. His eyes, shadowed and unreadable, seemed to pierce through her mortal disguise, as if he saw the goddess beneath. Tyche noticed his hands, calloused and worn. But they moved with a subtle grace and quiet power. They were the hands of someone who knew how to use them, someone who held secrets. A prickle of unease snaked down her throat.

Who is he? Does he recognize me?

The man's face reddened as he lowered his eyes and turned to whisper to another. Tyche contemplated the stranger, her lips pressed into a thin line.

A sharp crash of pottery on the floor pulled Tyche's attention away from the stranger, followed by a boisterous chorus of "Ai!" Through the momentary lull, Kalliope, the woman who'd scrubbed her clean in the bathhouse hours before, danced across the lesche toward the bar. She bumped against Tyche's shoulder, and the goddess recoiled, her expression tightening with disdain. Kalliope grinned as she brandished a dented copper coin above the heads of the crowd. Tyche's eyes narrowed when the woman slid it onto the wooden counter, gesturing toward the spreading puddle on the floor.

"Another for Dimitra's loss!" she called to the barkeep.

Tyche watched, intrigued. *How different this is from home, where golden goblets are never spilled and the coffers endlessly replenished.* Yet here, to witness this mortal woman spend her coin on her friend's behalf seemed strange, extraordinary. Decent. The easy laughter of the villagers around her now seemed to carry a different weight, tinged with a genuine warmth she hadn't noticed before.

The men and women, dressed in simple chitons, feasted noisily. Their effortless laughter swirled around the smoke rising from the hearth. Worn sandals or scuffed leather boots encased their dirty feet. Some women, she noticed, wore jingling bracelets made of cheap metal. Her lip curled at their clawed fingers, weathered by sun and toil, tearing into chunks of meat and loaves of bread.

They are no better than animals. Their lives are as unrefined as their manners.

A rough voice broke the spell of her observation. "Charis. Come!"

Tyche remained silent when the man called her name. Charis, the name she had invented, pressed against her skin like a thin disguise that failed to conceal the truth. A hand on her shoulder startled her, and the man from the road stood before her. She cringed at the toothless grin puckered into his white beard.

"Welcome, Charis," Christos boomed. The odor of garlic and stale wine clung to him. "I met you on the road."

Tyche averted her gaze but managed a polite smile. "Yes, I remember. Thank you for your invitation."

Christos gestured toward a table laden with food, oblivious to her discomfort. "Come, sit with my family."

Tyche followed him, the clamor of the hall pressing in on her from all sides.

Melina grinned at her. She reached around Tyche and placed a plate before her heaped with pork and crusty bread next to a bowl of sliced tomatoes, cucumbers, and onions, glistening with olive oil and crowned with a generous mound of goat cheese.

"Help yourself, Lady Charis," Melina offered. "We're grateful for your kindness to Dora."

Tyche cringed as the villagers tore at their food with a crude ferocity, and a shudder of contempt ran through her as she cinched her cloak tighter, shielding herself from the boisterous atmosphere and the splatters of grease. A flicker of disdain drew her mouth into a pucker, but a new sensation stirred in her chest. Tyche's hand fluttered to her throat as she struggled to comprehend it. Disgust failed to coil in her gut. Instead of revulsion, a surprising hollow ache ruptured inside her.

This feels... human. I'm not mortal. I am a goddess. What is this that settles in my blood?

A shiver traced its way down her back at the sheer lack of refinement. Yet, a grudging appreciation bloomed within her at their open generosity. Confusion tugged her brows low.

As Tyche nibbled the edge of a crisp cucumber, a flash of movement caught her eye. Dora darted between the feasting villagers, her fresh wool chiton embroidered with tiny starfish, her mother's handiwork, no doubt. Her dark curls bounced free of their ribbons as she pushed through the crowd.

"Mother Charis, hold me!" Dora pleaded, her arms outstretched toward the goddess. Tyche's heart softened at the girl's earnest appeal.

She scooped the child into her lap. Dora's laughter carved a hole in her broken heart. "Have you eaten your fill of the pig, YoungDaughter?" Tyche poked the giggling girl's belly. "Tell me, LittleOne." Tyche smoothed the child's wild hair. "What drew you so far from the village today?"

The memory of a winged shadow on the hillside flickered through Tyche's mind.

Dora's eyes brightened. "I heard a horse squealing in the woods. But when I followed the sound," Dora leaned in to Tyche and whispered, "the spring sang to me."

Christos chuckled. "You must leave our guest alone, you imp." He lifted Dora from Tyche's lap and set her down. "You are well-fed, I can see. Now off to bed with you." He nudged her with his elbow and sent her scampering toward the shadows.

"She's no trouble at all. I enjoy her company." Tyche's face softened. "But I have yet to see her mother. Is she here? Althea must be so relieved to have her daughter at home, safe."

"Dora is the village daughter. Althea, the one she calls mother, has raised her since Lep discovered her hidden in the watchtower—an old, solitary lookout on the mountain overlooking Gortsouli Valley." Christos propped his elbows on the table and steepled his fingers. His sea-foam eyes flitted across her face.

Hidden... like I need to be.

"The watchtower," Tyche murmured. A fleeting thought crossed her mind about the circumstances of the child's discovery. *Why was Dora concealed there?* Her gaze flickered toward the distant hills before she refocused on the man before her.

"You seem out of place here, stranger. What brings you to these humble hills?"

Tyche dropped her eyes under his gentle scrutiny and wondered what she would tell him. The cries of her dead babies rattled in her ears, and she clutched her squirming belly. Should she divulge her true identity—Tyche, goddess of Fortune, Luck, and Prosperity? How would these mortals react if she told them she had escaped the gods to hide her unborn child?

"I... I became lost. I wandered from the path and found myself here," she lied.

"I see. But as we both know, there is nothing for miles around us. The village is remote and hidden from prying eyes." Christos breathed into her face.

He thinks he can see me. How quaint. He is blind to my truth.

"I am aware of its secrecy," Tyche said, heat creeping up her neck as she realized she'd been caught in her deception. She paused, scrutinizing the mortal before her. *How much truth can I risk?* "I wish to bear my child hidden from those prowling eyes you speak of. This appears to be an ideal location to raise my daughter in peace."

Christos leaned closer, his eyes narrowed. "Aware of its secrecy, are you?" He chuckled. "This village is hidden, yes, but not from the eyes of the gods if they choose to look."

The mention of the gods sent a jolt of fear through Tyche. She shifted in her chair, her hand poised to summon the Wheel. For a passing moment, she considered fleeing the village, but the fear of discovery held her captive.

"What do you mean?" she asked.

Christos smiled, a knowing glint in his eyes, then returned to his meal.

This mortal is more perceptive than he should be. It's unsettling.

A shadow fell across the table. Tyche startled at Melina's sudden reappearance and wondered how much of their exchange the woman had overheard. Melina's grin widened as she sat next to the goddess.

"Don't worry, Charis." Her voice soothed Tyche's anxieties. "Your little one will be safe and sound in my hands. I'm the village midwife, and I've helped bring countless babies into the world."

The scrape of sandals against the stone floor drew Tyche's attention. Kalliope joined Melina and slapped her shoulder in jest. "Except when you dropped *my* baby. You said she was very slippery. You pulled her by her cord from the ground and handed the swinging child to me. This is why I named her Aioropaia, the swinging child."

The women laughed together. Its sweet timbre calmed Tyche's nerves.

Dimitra bustled through the rowdy crowd, her weathered face pinched with concern. "Enough of your wild tales," she scolded the giggling women. "Can't you see our guest needs sleep?" She turned to Tyche and gestured for her to follow. "It's time for you to rest after your journey. We have prepared the barn for you. I hope you don't mind the animals for company."

Tyche's shoulders tensed at such a proposal, though she forced a thin smile. The woman led her to her humble lodgings.

I should be sleeping on beds of swansdown and silk, not in filthy hay. Certainly not with animals!

The straw was fresh.

A relieved smile crept across Tyche's lips. At least she wouldn't be forced to sleep in animal dung. The woman left her alone with a lantern and blankets.

The barn breathed into the warm space that defied the polished perfection she'd left behind. The eyes of the animals glimmered like scattered jewels in the lantern's light, and their steady gazes seemed to her a silent judgment on her fallen state. The rhythmic chewing of hay and the soft snorts and sighs created a lullaby of the mundane, reminding her of the distance she'd traveled from the heights of divinity. She shivered to find herself in such a place of inferiority. Her skin itched.

This poverty. It should repel me, yet it doesn't. Why?

Tyche arranged her bedding over the straw and lay down. She blew out the lantern's flame. From the open window, she gazed at Asteria's stars vibrating in the darkness and watched as Selini's chariot raced the moon across the sky. How she wished for her life to return to normal. For her child to be safe.

The memory of Hera's icy glare and Zeus' violent roar thundered in her mind as she nestled into the straw. She had refused their demands and fled from her cage, and now, hidden in the village with the ordinary mortals, she still feared discovery. Would Hera send a storm or a curse? Or would she send a deadly hunter? Tyche pulled the blanket closer, as if it could shield her from the eyes of Olympus.

She sighed and closed her eyes, willing Ikelos to keep her dreams free of nightmares.

A violent burst of wind hammered against the barn door, and Tyche held her breath. Was it simply the night's sigh, or had Fury tracked Tyche to this humble refuge? She strained her ears, listening for the rhythm of leathery wings and the rasping growl declaring her doom.

The gods believe they know the weight of the world, but they have never endured the calloused hands of labor or the sting of mortal sweat. To live among humans is to learn a new kind of strength, a resilience born of the simple act of survival rather than power. And in the humbling experience, even a goddess may find a truth she never knew existed.

THE STING OF MORTAL SWEAT

The clang of bells and the cries of the villagers woke her.

Tyche yawned and rubbed her belly as the restless baby squirmed. She stretched her arms and arched her back until she writhed in ecstasy, a hymn of gratitude arising from each unknotted muscle, unlike the effortless ease of her godhood.

A moment of peace, she thought, the unbidden worry already nipping at its edges. *Though Charis' luck rarely holds for long,* she thought with bitter amusement.

The peace can't last.

A whimper rose from her blanket, and she peered down at a young goat nestled into the residue of her warmth. Its wet nose tickled her leg. Tyche caressed its spotted coat and glanced around for its mother but saw none. *Like Dora. Motherless.* The thought brought a flash of sympathy, followed by a fresh wave of anxiety. *The gods could be anywhere. Watching. Waiting.*

"Am I to be your mother, too, goat?" She laughed at the absurdity, the sound high-pitched and strained.

Even here among these mortals, I'm not safe.

The village of Pikerni bustled with life as the rays of dawn careened across the horizon. Tyche stepped from the barn and cupped her eyes. She traced the familiar faces of the villagers as they went about their daily tasks, her nostrils flaring at the aroma of fresh bread and the earthy smell of plowed fields. Christos smiled and raised his hand in greeting. Tyche returned the gesture, and he turned back to his work.

Dimitra set down the jars of milk she carried across the road and rushed to her. "How did you sleep? Everything is okay?"

Tyche grinned as Dimitra pulled straw from her hair. "The animals and I had a peaceful rest together."

Dimitra retrieved the pair of *kadoi* pitchers and gestured for Tyche to follow her. "First breakfast, then work."

The goddess obeyed and kept pace with her new friend. The woman dropped the containers at a stall in the *agora*, the market where Kalliope and Melina baked rounded mounds of dough in dome-shaped ovens.

"Our friend here needs food to fill her belly." Dimitra jabbed her thumb in Tyche's direction.

Melina grasped the amphora's handles and poured the steaming milk into a bowl. She scooted it toward Tyche, then tore a chunk from the loaf she scraped from the oven. "Here you go, milk and fresh bread."

Tyche's stomach clenched in hunger at the pleasing aroma. She accepted the offering with a smile as she appraised the townspeople in the light of day. Everyone worked together, and they seemed cheerful. Their apparent contentment surprised the goddess. She had always assumed the humble mortals would be frustrated with their meager existence. Was this a lie she told herself when she and the other gods meted out hardship and misfortune to them? Or were they more resilient than she had given them credit for?

As she nibbled on the crust, children's laughter drifted from the walnut tree overhead. She spied little boys shimmying up the trunk and brandishing sharpened sticks at their companions, and her heart smiled at their innocence.

Tyche turned to observe young girls gather to braid one another's hair in gawpish designs, not yet skilled with the weave. She spotted Dora among them and approached to offer her assistance.

"Mother Charis, good morning!" Dora beamed.

Tyche laughed and pulled her around so her back faced her. "Come closer, children. Let me demonstrate the proper method to braid your hair."

The girls crowded around their teacher and watched in fascination as the goddess' fingers braided a pattern into Dora's hair. She pulled a ribbon from her wrist and weaved it into the design.

"There." She turned Dora by the shoulders for all to see. "What do you think? Now, would you be so kind as to braid my hair as I have shown you?"

Tyche sat on a stone bench in the square, surrounded by the giggling girls. Despite her fears, an unfamiliar warmth blossomed through her chest. She basked in their mirth and relished their touch.

When they had all taken a turn, Dora cocked her head at Tyche's braid. "Mother Charis, you may want to rebraid your hair. It doesn't... look very nice."

The goddess grinned and patted the awkward knots and weaves on her head. "I think it's perfect, and I'll wear it with pride."

Christos yelled from the barn, his outstretched fingers waving her over.

Tyche touched the uneven braids, a smile playing on her lips as she turned toward the barn with a new lightness in her step.

"I see the little women have been busy fussing with your hair." Christos laughed. "Now it's time for work."

Tyche patted her head but held her tongue.

"All who live in the village must lend their hands to it." Christos winked at her. "And you, my fine lady, will be mistress of the barn." He stepped into the ripe stench of the building. From the wall, he grabbed a rake and a shovel and held them out to Tyche.

She hesitated and then took them from his hands. "What shall I do with these?"

He chuckled. "Clean the animal droppings from the floor. What else?"

Tyche gagged and coughed. She pushed the tools toward Christos and shook her head. "No, I can't. It's disgusting."

"Life is unpleasant at times, woman. We do what we must, and this is your job." He pointed to a wheeled cart. "Shovel the manure into the cart, and the boys will take it away. If you want a clean place to bed, then do your job well."

Tyche prepared to dissent, but he had already gone.

"Now *I* am an animal." She tore a strip from her chiton and tied it over her nose and mouth and set to work.

At least I'm free.

The reek of the barn was a far cry from the ambrosial scent of Olympus. Here, her power was a dormant ember, hidden beneath layers of grime and mortal effort. A distant growl of thunder made her think of Zeus and the gods who had defied him and the punishments they had suffered. Exile, imprisonment, loss of power. She shuddered. The cost of defiance was steep.

Tyche set aside her rake. She groaned as she straightened, the muscles in her back protesting with a deep throb. Her hands chafed and burned. She called for the boys to remove the rubbish she had collected, the corners of her mouth twitching upwards in her shared commiseration with their complaints. But Christos' answering roar to "obey the lady" made her shoulders shake with suppressed laughter.

Outside, the women worked the communal gardens, pushing seeds into the soil until dirt darkened their palms. Tyche admired their effortless companionship and laughter. She sighed at the thought of her old life—these mortal surroundings so far from Olympian glory. Observing the villagers' interactions, she winced at the prick of guilt. What would happen to them if the gods discovered her presence? Would they be punished for their generosity?

I can't allow that to happen.

"Charis," called a woman she didn't know. "Will you join us? The earth welcomes all who wish to work alongside her."

Tyche groaned. She looked toward the barn, at the work she had been assigned. Hadn't she fulfilled her duty for the day? Her back ached, and she needed to find privacy to relieve herself.

"I'll join you in a moment," Tyche said.

She spied a stand of trees and hurried to take advantage of their privacy. She gathered her chiton with one hand and gripped the trunk for support with the other while she squatted. As she finished her business, the bushes rustled behind her. A man peered through the foliage as Tyche smoothed her garments.

Her heart stuttered in her chest. The man from the celebration stood before her, the same unsettling intensity in his glare. He froze, his hazel eyes dark with an unreadable expression. Beyond curiosity, something lurked in his gaze—recognition? Caution? Tyche's Wheel ground to a halt against her ribs. He had followed her.

"Apologies." The man pushed through the brush. "Did not mean to startle you. I am in pursuit of medicinal herbs." His lips curved in a gesture that held no warmth. A flicker of concern, or perhaps pity, crossed his face as he seemed to sense her unease.

The knowing glint in his starburst eyes prickled along her skin at the thought the gods sent him to return her to Olympus.

"Why are you spying on me?" Tyche spat.

"Spying? On you? I do not think so. I am in search of pharmakon, *medicine*, as I have said." The man patted his belt.

Her eyes hovered over his tall, broad-shouldered form, his dark hair pulled tight to reveal his face shifting like forest shadows. Vials and bottles clinked in the leather satchel strapped to his hip. Heat bent around his form, his bronze skin marked by the sun's fierce touch.

"What's your name? I haven't seen you in the village before." Tyche took in his simple chiton and worn sandals.

"They call me Lep in the village, for I am the Asclepiad here."

"So you're a healer?" Tyche asked.

"Yes, and I must be on my way," he grunted. "The earth holds both life and its undoing." Lep parted the bushes, his gaze sweeping across the forest floor like a predator sizing up its prey, and then the leaves rustled around him with an unnatural silence as he vanished into the thick undergrowth.

Tyche listened to the sounds of his departure and frowned, the absence of his question about her name humming in the silence he left behind. Was he a healer, or acting as one? The realization landed in her gut with a sickening lurch.

If they find me... The thought clutched at her. *If they find* her...

Tyche's thoughts raced, each possibility a fresh wave of terror. Imprisonment in Tartarus was a fate worse than death. Or better yet, they could take her child as they had promised, consigning it to the same fate as her others. She couldn't, she *wouldn't* allow that to happen again. The fear roiling beneath her skin threatened to burn her bones to powder.

A subtle tremor passed through the atmosphere surrounding her, and the Wheel of Fortune stirred. Its invisible spokes hummed a silent warning, matching the tension that coiled in her limbs. Tyche swayed, even as her fingernails bit into her clenched hands.

She had to appear calm, ordinary, a mortal woman concerned with the mundane tasks of village life. Anything less, and her carefully constructed facade would crumble.

She drew a shuddering breath and returned to the women working in the garden.

The woman she'd met earlier waved her over. "Come and work next to me, Charis. I can show you how to tend the plants." She patted the ground beside her. "I'm called Evy."

The goddess knelt between the women, her bare knees pushing into the rocky soil. Evy snapped a small cucumber from a vine and handed it to her. Tyche held the vegetable to her nose, then wiped it on her chiton and bit into its crunchy sweetness.

"This is delicious. I could eat a hundred of these."

But even as she joined in the easy banter, Tyche remained vigilant, the unsettling encounter with the village Asclepiad fresh in her mind.

"As the gods will it." Evy yanked weeds from between the vines. "But wait until you try the tomatoes."

Evy frowned at the paleness creeping across Tyche's face. "Are you alright, Charis? You appear a bit shaken."

Tyche didn't look up, couldn't let the woman see the fear scrawled in her expression. "I'm fine," she lied.

Her fingers tightened around a stubborn weed, yanking with a force that tore the delicate thyme. *Why won't you yield?* A sharp heat rose behind her eyes. This powerless existence chafed. She longed to will the weeds away and command the earth to submit to her divine touch, as she had done so many times before. But she couldn't. This wasn't Olympus, where a thought could move mountains. Here, she was simply another villager, her power muted beneath a layer of dirt and sweat. A wave of unfamiliar emotions washed over her—loneliness, frustration, and a yearning for the power she had so easily taken for granted.

Tyche's fingers sank into the dark loam. Her flawless nails blackened with earth, a mortal stain she both dreaded and craved. She thought of Lep's parting words.

"Evy..." Tyche glanced at her companion. "How long has Lep lived in the village?"

The woman paused, her head tilted thoughtfully. "Oh, dear. I couldn't say for sure. It seems he's always been here. He appeared one day, a stranger with a satchel full of herbs." She pressed her lips together and wrinkled her nose. "Now that you mention it, his face is the same as the day he arrived. Not a line more." She tapped her chin, a flicker of curiosity in her eyes. "It's... odd."

"He never ages?" Tyche's brow furrowed. "That's unusual, don't you think?"

Evy shrugged. "He's always been a bit of a mystery, that one. Some say he has a touch of the divine about him."

"Divine?" Tyche's fingers twisted in her chiton.

Evy chuckled. "Oh, just village gossip. But there's something about him, a stillness, a strength beyond ordinary men. He wanders through the world like a shadow." Evy stood and stepped away, feigning the need to stretch but instead using the opportunity to gather a handful of dirt.

Tyche sighed and broke a dead stem from a plant, but a smattering of dirt clods on her back roused the goddess from her musings.

"Hey!" She glanced over her shoulder to see Evy braced to throw another handful at her.

"Why'd you do that?" Tyche pushed herself from the ground. Her knees groaned, and her feet crawled with the sleep of ants.

"Sometimes, we have fun with each other. It makes for lighter work." Evy let the dirt she clutched spill through her fingers.

Tyche heard the snickers of the others aimed toward the mirthful woman. "Okay, then. Have it your way." She scooped up a handful of soil and aimed it at Evy. The woman screamed and dodged Tyche's aim.

"Come on," Evy laughed, "let's go to the spring and collect water for the crops. They thirst on such a hot day as this."

The day trapped Tyche in an endless cycle of labor, her body a prison of throbbing muscles and burning skin. But she would not yield. She would not reveal her discomfort, not to these mortals.

With the final sigh of the dying day, Tyche knew what she must do. She would learn everything about this village, every secret, every routine. She would become one of them so she could understand them and uncover the truth about Lep.

Fate whispers in the calloused hands of mortals, and a goddess, draped in roughspun cloth, finds strength in the earth beneath her feet. Secrets, like shadows, cling to the most familiar faces.

IN THE CALLOUSED HANDS
OF MORTALS

The rough earth beneath her hands vanished, replaced by the sharp bite of reeds. Over the next days, while the village moved to its familiar cadence, Tyche began her apprenticeship in the art of basket weaving. The old weaver's tutting followed her fumbling attempts like a dry rasp. Yet, his gentleness offered some relief against her growing irritation as he guided her clumsy hands. The reeds seemed to take pleasure in her awkward grip, defying her will with a silent, prickly defiance. She glared at the uneven pattern in consternation. The wide gaps and uneven weave displayed her incompetence for all to see. By midday, the lopsided proof of her mortality sat before her, a twisted parody of the weaver's art.

"Patience, Charis," he said, his rough hands demonstrating the subtle compromise between strength and gentleness. "The reeds yield if you respect their nature."

Tyche sighed, her gaze drifting to the other weavers whose fingers guided the reeds into place with their skilled hands. She picked up another reed and twirled it between her fingers, contemplating its brittleness. Tyche snapped the stalk in two and held up the pieces in her palm. *Perhaps I am a collection of fragments that I struggle to assemble.* She rubbed her eyes with balled fists and gritted her teeth, then willed her hands to strike a balance of finesse and rhythm. But time and again, her impatience flared, and the reeds bent against their will and broke. She closed her eyes, urging her irritable heart to steady.

"Even this trivial task frustrates me," she moaned.

She stared at the uneven weave, her hands stinging from the reeds' bite. For a goddess, perfection was a given, an instantaneous creation without a single flaw. But in the mortal world, the struggle to create *was* the point. Wasn't it? She tapped her chin in thought.

Perhaps my pursuit of perfection is the exact thing keeping me from it.

Tyche straightened and wiped her arm across her brow. She observed the people bent to their tasks, knowing they possessed a different kind of strength acquired from their common struggles. They wove their lives from the rough materials of their mortal stations.

Unlike Lep, who weaves nets of secrets.

Tyche picked up another reed, this time with a refocused motive. She knew she wouldn't create a perfect work of art, but she could create something that represented her belief in herself. She bent the reed, her tongue pressed between her lips in concentration, and with a surprise that made her laugh, it yielded.

With the finished basket before her, Tyche allowed herself a moment of satisfaction. She leaned back and grabbed her knees, giggling at its misshapen form. But even as she celebrated this mortal victory, the concerns about Lep remained. She sighed and stood up with a groan. She massaged her aching back as she made her way toward the river, the murmur of its current a pleasant relief to her troubled thoughts.

The silver ribbon of water sparkled in the afternoon heat. Tyche wiped the sweat from her brow and inhaled the scent of damp earth and river reeds. She sat and dug her toes into the cool, dark sand of the bank, the coarse grains a foreign but not unpleasant sensation on her skin. She pulled a torn fishing net into her lap, another one of the new tasks taught to her over the past weeks. With a grunt of displeasure, she began to work. In Olympus, her hands had commanded fortune and prosperity. Now they struggled to knot a simple fishing net.

Her arms trembled as the rope bit into Tyche's palms, the sun beating mercilessly against her neck. Her muscles screamed in ways her immortal flesh had never known. Each knot she tied in the net reminded her of the tangled web of questions surrounding Lep. Like the rough rope in her hands, his presence tightened around her like a trap.

The unchanging youthfulness of his face flashed before her inner eye. He'd been in the village for years, yet age never touched him. *Could he be a god?* The thought now reflected her own hidden nature. *Just like me,* a wry voice whispered, *he hides, but why this hidden life for him?* The unspoken question burned in her chest.

Lep might as well be hiding as many secrets as she was. The thought sparked a flicker of suspicion within her. Tyche sighed as the unanswered questions settled into a knot of worry. She had no answers, not yet, but she needed to remain vigilant. For her own sake and that of her child, she had to learn the ways of mortals. She had to be ready. In case whatever Lep hid from came looking for her.

Tyche pushed her concerns about Lep to the back of her mind—a seed of doubt to be dealt with when it sprouted. For now, the villagers' praise for her work soothed the hollow space where her powers had been, and though her hands might blister, their easy laughter and warm companionship helped her heart grow stronger.

As she made her way to the barn that evening, exhausted and sore, Christos waited outside. "Your hands are new to this work, Charis." He leaned against the door's frame.

Tyche's eyes traced the path of his gnarled fingers over the pattern of the wood grain.

"But I see how you care for Dora, how you teach the village children. The gods may have their grandeur, but here, among us mortals, we find something far more precious."

"More precious?" Tyche glanced at him as she picked the dirt out from under her nails.

Christos nodded at her dirt-stained hands. "The gods might boast about their wealth and powers, yet they know nothing of the bonds we forge through the loyalty and love that grow between us through our sacrifices to each other."

How do the boundaries between immortal existence and mortal life become blurred?

"The gods might not understand these bonds, I agree. But don't you ever wish they could be forged without so much hardship? Life seems so harsh here." Tyche waved an arm around the village.

Christos stared long into Tyche's face. "Easier? I must disagree. When people are idle, they lack purpose. They expect a share in the reward without the sweat of their brows. We wouldn't exist without our mutual need. To be honest, mistress, a man's true worth is in his toil and loyalty to his people. After all, the harvest does not grow on trees to pluck as one wishes. It requires favorable weather. Luck."

A flicker of irony creased her brow. *If only he knew.*

He patted her arm and stepped away, swept into the current of the village, the children dancing around him as he strolled through them. His hand cupped a boy's head, and he laughed at something she couldn't hear. Tyche's heart twisted beneath her ribs to see the love and devotion stamped on the boy's young face. How had Christos earned this love? Such devotion should belong to the gods, yet here it bloomed freely, without tribute or sacrifice. Tyche yearned to understand this mortal mystery. Christos wasn't wrong. The gods had much to learn from the mortals.

In the distance, laughter erupted from the market stalls down the lane. Tyche paused at the entrance to the barn and cast a glance at Melina and Kalliope, who were doubled over at Dimitra's words. Tyche's smile faltered as she decided to wend her way down the street and approach the women, curious about their laughter. The easy friendship between these women stirred a hollowness in her chest. In all her immortal years, she had never shared such simple joy.

"Hey, friends. What's so funny?" Tyche asked them as she neared.

"Oh, Dimitra told us how she slipped into the spring when she was soaking garments." Kalliope stifled a giggle.

"Yes, it's true. It wasn't pretty." Dimitra groaned and rubbed her back.

Tyche glanced at the bruise on the woman's leg. "I'm sorry for your misfortune. It looks painful."

"What misfortune? It was my carelessness that almost ended me." Dimitra chuckled. "We must remain vigilant, or the gods will make us pay."

"Hmm," Tyche replied. *Indeed.*

Melina gasped and grabbed Tyche's hands. She held them so the others could inspect them. "What have you been doing, Charis? Your hands are blistered and filthy."

"Thanks, Melina." Tyche pulled her hands away and hid them behind her back. "I've been using them to work."

"Well done!" Dimitra smiled and held out her calloused, stained hands.

"Listen, Dimitra. I want you to show me how to milk the goats sometime. As long as I'm here, I wish to be useful. Will you help me?" The goddess dropped her gaze at the astonished faces of the women.

"You don't know how to milk an animal? I don't believe it!" Kalliope snorted.

Dimitra grasped Tyche's arm and pulled her toward the barn. "Come on, Charis. I'll teach you how to do it. It's easy."

"Now?" Tyche pulled back on Dimitra's firm hold. "I meant sometime in the future. I'm exhausted."

"No time like the present."

Tyche groaned and followed Dimitra into the barn. She pulled a small wooden stool over to one of the goats, its udders full and ready for its second milking.

"Sit!" Dimitra patted the stool, then she placed a bucket on the ground under the animal.

With a hesitant nod, the goddess took a seat, her eyes on the goat before her. Dimitra positioned herself beside Tyche and guided her hands to the swollen udders.

"Now, grasp firmly and squeeze," she instructed.

The goddess' hands trembled as she grabbed hold of the goats' teats. Her fingers slipped on the smooth surface as she tugged at them. But after a few moments of squeezing and pulling, her hands cramped.

"You're doing well." Dimitra offered words of encouragement. "It takes time to acquire this skill. Try to be gentle yet firm with your hands."

Tyche took a deep breath, and she turned back to the goat. Her eyebrows formed a sharp V as she dutifully wrapped her hands around the teats. With each downward squeeze, a rhythmic hiss of milk struck the side of the pail.

The goddess glanced up at the woman, who stared at her with a narrowed eye. "What?" She blew stray hair from her face.

"You've never milked an animal before." It was a statement, not a question.

Tyche stared at the dirt beneath her sandals. "No, I haven't. Where I come from, such tasks were beneath me."

Dimitra tilted her head, her dark eyes searching Tyche's face. "Well, you're doing a wonderful job for your first time. With practice, your hands will grow stronger, and it will become easier."

Guilt tugged at Tyche as she listened to Dimitra's kind words. But as she straightened on the stool, she looked into the woman's trusting eyes and wondered how much longer she could keep her true identity hidden.

The woman retrieved the bucket and shooed the goat away. "Charis, you can trust me if you need a listening ear. In this village, we stand together." Her eyes dropped to Tyche's belly. "Everyone makes mistakes."

Tyche shot to her feet. The stool clattered to the ground, and she grasped her stomach with both hands. "This baby is no mistake, I can assure you, Dimitra."

The woman raised her hands and retreated. "I didn't mean the baby was a mistake. Just that, at times, we do things we regret. It's part of human nature."

Mistakes are of a god's nature, too! She screamed in her mind.

"Thank you for the lesson." Tyche winced and pressed her palm against her back. "Now I need to rest."

"Of course. Know I am here for you, for anything," Dimitra said as she walked toward the door. Then she was gone.

Tyche paced, fuming. The kid followed her steps. Finally, she bent down and lifted its fuzzy body into her arms, then buried her face in its soft hair. "What am I doing here? I don't belong with these people. And who is Lep, Kid? *What* is Lep?"

The young goat reared back its head and probed her with its rectangular pupils. "Baaa."

"I know, Kid. I'm not the goddess of Fortune here, revered and worshiped like I used to be."

"Baaa." Kid wriggled in her arms, and she set him down in the straw.

In Pikerni, she was another villager, her identity hidden beneath the guise of a humble peasant woman. A surprising sense of peace settled over Tyche at the realization. Since fleeing Olympus, she had worn tension like armor. Now her shoulders softened, and her breath deepened. Among these mortals, she discovered meaning beyond her divine nature.

But as she gazed out at the lolling sun, a nagging worry lingered. *Who is Lep? What is Lep?*

He doesn't even see me, Tyche thought, her jaw clenched. *He appraises me like a specimen. As though I were a rare creature to be studied.*

She couldn't shake the feeling she was being watched, studied, even hunted. A cold dread sidled into her veins.

Even in the stillest waters, reflections hold the power of deception.
A goddess may gaze upon her own image and find a haunting
question: Who am I now? And in the shadows of the night, where
secrets stir and wolves howl, the most familiar faces can hold the
most unsettling truths.

THE MOST UNSETTLING TRUTHS

The image of the healer's sun-sparked eyes lingered. Tyche
pushed the memory aside and returned her focus to the goat
she milked. The impatient doe shifted, her udder round and
warm, while one of the village cats sat beside the stool, its tail
twitching in expectation. A brittle laugh escaped Tyche's lips,
but the disquiet remained a constant hum beneath the surface
of her contentment.

Each squeeze of the udder sent a warm stream of milk spurting
into the bucket, the rhythmic sound dulling the unsettling
thoughts swirling in her mind. Before today, the barn had
become a sanctuary of sorts, a place where she could escape the
prying eyes of the villagers and find solace in the company of the
animals. She was proud of her work and the blisters on her hands.
She rubbed her thumbs over the tender mounds on her flesh.

I never knew labor could be so rewarding. I have much to learn
from these mortals.

Days fell to weeks and weeks to months, and still Tyche's belly grew. For the first time in her life, peace washed over her as she worked side by side with the villagers. Content with less. Yet she possessed so much more. People who loved her. *Mortals* who cared about her welfare and the well-being of her child.

The sun's guide had bid farewell, and the moon tugged itself from its perch in the mountains. She rested in her usual spot—a fallen tree affording her the perfect panorama of the Gortsouli Valley below. The rise and fall of the Mainalo Mountains rose behind the rounded mound of Mantineia's Acropolis. Tyche's breath caught at the beauty of the purple dusk descending over the land as deep green patches of agriculture blanketed the valley.

She bent to gather walnuts from the ground and cracked their husks open with a nearby stone. As she nibbled on the nuts, the image of the Nekrochim appeared, its grotesque figure of fragmented bodies melded together in a macabre mosaic of flesh and spirit. Tyche cried out and clutched her stomach to shield the baby from her memory. She would do everything in her power to protect this child, but would the gods ever relent in their pursuit of her? Had the peace of the village lulled her into a false sense of security, while fear carved deeper paths through her soul?

Tyche jumped when a hand fell on her shoulder. Dora cried out at the goddess' reaction. Tyche gathered the child into her lap and hugged her close to her chest.

"I'm sorry I startled you, Dora. I didn't know anyone had found my hiding place."

"Mother Charis," the girl said, "I know all your secrets. Do you know why?"

"Please, tell me."

"Children know things about their mothers that others don't."

"Dora, I'm not your mother. You have a fine one who loves you."

"But Fate and Luck have given you to me. Don't you see?"

A shiver rippled through her at the girl's words, even as a sharp fear of fate's inescapable grip taunted her. Dora's stormy gray eyes peered up at her with an expression of innocence and ancient wisdom Tyche couldn't understand. The naive curve of the child's lips belied the knowing glint in her eye. Dora wasn't wrong, but she wasn't ready to tell her. Not yet.

"Indeed, child. Luck has sent you to me as well. You are my gift from the gods, just as you are to your mother." Tyche squeezed Dora as she fidgeted on her lap. "Shall I braid your hair?" The goddess ran her fingers through the girl's dark locks.

"We haven't time. Christos sent me to find you. Supper is ready."

"Then let's not be late. This unborn baby is always hungry, and I'm a little hungry, too."

After supper, Melina called to Tyche when she rose from the table.

"Where do you think you're going? There are dishes to be washed." She stood with her hands resting on her hips. "It's not yet your time to deliver, so off to work you go."

Tyche stifled a groan. The weight of her pregnancy pressed heavily on her back, and the child within seemed to have drained every ounce of her energy. Surely, they didn't expect her to tackle the mountain of dishes alone, not in her condition. A flood of nausea swept over her as the greasy smell of the dirty plates wafted toward her.

"I can't." Tyche leaned back with a moan.

"I'm sorry, but we don't accept excuses in this village. No work, no eat."

"Ugh, fine. What must I do to earn my keep?"

Tyche eyed the stack of dishes, piled high from the villagers' hearty meals. Surely, someone could help. Perhaps one of the younger women, or even a child. But Melina's stern gaze quashed any hope of assistance. Was she being especially harsh on Tyche, the outsider, the *pregnant* refugee?

"The dishes, as I earlier mentioned. See this stack of plates and cups? They must be clean by morning."

"But—"

"Come, let me show you," Melina interrupted. "I will carry them to the spring for you."

"But, it's dark out. I'll need light," Tyche reasoned.

"Run along then. Fetch your lantern."

Tyche met Melina at the edge of the spring. In the shadows, the goddess made out the pile of dishes in need of cleaning. She groaned as she knelt over a rock and sat with an umph.

"Set them next to me. I'll do the best I can." She crouched over the water and began to scrub.

"Yell to me when you're finished, and I'll come collect them for you. I don't want you lifting heavy things now. Not when you're this far along," Melina said and faded into the night.

When the moon had climbed higher in the sky, the chill of the night seeped into Tyche's bones as she diligently scrubbed the dishes. She lifted her red hands to the lantern's light, then glanced at the stack of clean plates. Tyche paused, her back aching, and sighed. She gazed at her reflection in the still water. Was she Tyche, goddess of Fortune, or was it a title, a role assigned to her by the gods? Could she be more than that, something different? The warped image in the water caught her eye. She leaned down, her breath fogging the lantern's glass, and saw the familiar visage of her father wavering beneath her own.

O, Father, where are you now?

The image of Oceanus swam into her view, his flowing hair and beard, the arms that once held her. Oceanus, Titan of the waters, whose rivers flowed through both worlds. She thought of her sister's dark waters in the underworld—how Oceanus' other daughter, Styx, had chosen power over family, binding herself to the gods who now threatened Tyche's unborn child. She wished for her father now in the silence. In the dark. A wave of longing surged through her. She reached out, her fingers brushing the water's surface, as if to touch his face. The water shimmered, and a ring of ripples expanded across the surface—a tender message from home.

"Thank you, Father. I have missed you." A soft smile rested on her lips.

Tyche jumped when a rock skittered down the side of the hill and plopped into the spring.

"Who are you talking to?" A disembodied voice followed the stone's path.

"Who's there? Show yourself this instant!" Tyche yelled.

"Calm down, woman. It is me, Lep. I forage for nightshades when the sun no longer burns in the sky," the dark shape answered.

Tyche squinted her eyes to make out the features of the man as he made his way toward her. His height and raven hair matched those of Ikelos, but his hazel eyes held a different kind of wisdom.

"You're always sneaking around. Stay away from me," Tyche snarled.

Lep laughed, long and hard, which irritated Tyche even more.

"You think I follow the likes of you around, woman? I do not think so. You are of no interest to me."

He reached out his hand to help her up from her squatting position. Tyche slapped at it and struggled to her feet.

"I don't need your help, you... you... annoying man." She dusted her hands on her tunic.

Lep stood under the moonlight and glared at her. She watched his eyes travel from her feet to her head.

"There is something about you, woman. Something different, unnatural. I do not like it. Not at all." Lep's eyes raked across hers. "You are a strange one. I shall keep my eye on you."

"Keep your eyes to yourself and mind your own business. I am of no interest to you, as you have said." Tyche glared at the healer.

"Well, I cannot leave you here all alone. Beasts prowl and would love a tasty morsel. Allow me to carry your burden back to the village."

"I'm quite capable on my own. Thanks, but no. Melina will come and carry the load back," she retorted as she leaned to collect her bundle.

And yet, Lep's words sparked a dark thought in Tyche's mind. Was he a threat or a strange villager? And Melina, surely she didn't mean harm. She was simply firm, a believer in shared labor. Yet, sending Tyche alone into the night, knowing the wolves prowled—it was a risk. A test? Or thoughtlessness?

A hot tingle raced up her arm as his hand covered her own. He pulled the strap from her fist and hoisted it to his shoulder.

"Come, woman. We will return it together," he said and turned on his heel.

Tyche had no choice but to follow.

Lep led the way, the basket of dishes balanced on his shoulder. Moonlight glittered in his eyes as he turned to face her. "The air around you shimmers differently, Charis," he murmured. Then, he continued walking and disappeared into the village's lights.

Tyche's hackles rose at his words, but before she could ponder them further, a wolf's howl splintered the darkness.

The earth remembers, even when the gods forget. A goddess may hide her power, but the land itself knows the touch of divinity. And when shadows fall and wolves howl, the true measure of a heart is revealed in the fierce love of mortals and the choices they make to protect their own, a strength that surpasses even the gods.

8

THE EARTH REMEMBERS

The morning sun warmed her skin as she emerged from the barn. Straw and goat hair clung to her clothes. Tyche tried to push aside the unsettling memory of Lep's stare and his cryptic words as he walked away from her—*the air around you shimmers differently.*

When she joined the others in the barley fields, a subtle tension clung to the villagers. As they bent to their work, hushed murmurs punctuated the rhythmic scrape of sickles against the barley stalks.

Evy straightened with a frown, running a hand over a patch of pale, brittle stalks. "This doesn't feel right." She glanced at Tyche. "The barley is thinner than it should be. Look," she said, and bent the stalk closer for Tyche to see, "almost lifeless."

Across the rows, Christos paused to examine a handful of grain. "Aye," he agreed, his gaze sweeping across the field. "And the color has lost its richness."

An ancient harvest song rose from the people in a plea to the goddess of Fortune.

Tyche, hear our humble plea, (WHACK)

Guide our hands, our destiny. (WHACK)

Rich soil and skies so bright, (WHACK)

Bless our fields with golden light.

Tyche's eyes widened. *They ask for* my *blessing of bounty and fortune.* A knot tightened in her stomach. Had her withdrawal already begun to touch this land? The earth stirred beneath her feet, while the faint shudder sighed with a sense of depletion rather than the promise of abundance. Soil spiraled upward in listless eddies to reveal the earth's parched breath. The Wheel of Fortune inside Tyche, summoned by the mortals' desperate hymn, awakened and glimmered before her. She clutched at the Wheel as it spun wildly. Her lips shaped a desperate command for it to still.

Tyche glanced across the field, the tremors of her magic shaking her bones, only to discover Lep at the barley field's edge. The midday sun cast harsh shadows across his face, and his sickle gleamed like a sword. Tyche's limbs turned to stone. Could he sense her divinity? No. She pressed her palm against her pregnant belly. He must never know.

Dimitra paused in her work, wiping sweat from her brow, and then cinched the ribbon tight that held back her hair. Her gaze drifted over the pale stalks. "Enjoying the pitiful harvest, Charis?"

Her voice carried over the rasp of sickles, but Tyche caught her hint of concern about the yield. A deep ache pulsed in Tyche's lower back as she leaned on her sickle, a weary smile tugging at her mouth. "No, but the work fills me with something I never expected."

Just then, Tryfonas, Christos' son, approached with a shy grin on his face and held out a chipped cup toward Dimitra. "Take this," he offered. "I brought you water. And a fig." He palmed his damp forehead, his eyes sweeping over the sparse crop before meeting Dimitra's gaze.

Her eyes crinkled at the corners. "Why, thank you. How thoughtful." She accepted the cup and fig with a toothy smile. "You're a good lad." She took a long drink and turned to Tyche. "See, Charis? This is what I mean about our village. Always looking out for each other. Especially now... with the harvest not as plentiful as we'd hoped." Her smile faded. "Not to mention the prowling wolves."

Lep's shadow darkened the earth at Tyche's feet. His gaze swept over the bent backs of the people and then rested on her. "You're working too hard, woman." He thrust a gourd of water toward her. "Drink."

Tyche lifted the cup to her lips with shaking hands. The fresh water soothed her parched throat. "Thank you." A harsh cough burst from her chest. She pressed her palm against her mouth as a wave of dizziness rippled through her head.

Lep's eyes narrowed above his frown. "You look unwell, Charis. You should rest in the shade." His sun-struck eyes lingered on her pale face and the beads of sweat on her forehead. A flicker of concern, perhaps even pity, crossed his features, quickly masked by a look of indifference as he scanned the crops again. "Stubborn woman," he muttered. "You're carrying a heavy burden. You shouldn't overexert yourself, especially with the fields yielding so little."

"I'll be fine," she rasped without conviction. But when she straightened, the world swam before her eyes.

The land itself seemed to sigh beneath their feet. Tyche studied the villagers, their initial confusion giving way to quiet worry. Even Dora stopped her usual dance through the fields and stayed near her mother, her brow furrowed as she cocked her head. The Wheel of Fortune stirred and commenced with a sluggish rotation in recognition of the ailing earth.

Lep stood at the field's edge, his sun-forged eyes scanning the rows with an intensity that seemed to take in more than the state of the harvest. A knowing look sharpened his gaze, pulling his lips into a tight line as he observed the wilting stalks. Tyche's disquiet around him intensified. *Perhaps he senses the life drain from the land. Or maybe he sees through my disguise.*

As Tyche rested in the shade of a walnut tree, the workers' companionship struck her heart. She didn't belong here with them—she was a goddess, not a mortal like them. Her skin prickled at the memory of Olympus, where she had been threatened and forced to flee to protect her child, but then the gods had turned their backs on her. Now, among mortals, she found no solace, no connection. She floated untethered, homeless in both worlds, a goddess adrift, neither divine nor mortal, forever an outsider.

After her arrival in Pikerni, she had turned inward, seeking solitude in an attempt to escape this sense of rootlessness. But this retreat within herself led to consequences she hadn't foreseen. The shield of detachment she thought would protect her brought suffering to the mortals, and now the stain of death spread across the land as the creeping shadow of blight devoured Pikerni's harvests.

At the edge of the rise above the fields, Lep and Christos stood outlined against the desolate landscape. Tyche stepped to the shadows of the trees and turned her ear to their words, but the wind swept them away. No words were needed, though, as their worry was a clear language, spoken in the agitated flailing of their hands and the defeated droop of their shoulders.

Tyche turned to study the women's bowed backs as they knelt among the gardens. Their hands rested on the withered plants as though willing them to come back to life. Guilt pushed tears from Tyche's eyes, and she turned away from their grief. These were the mortals she had come to value and appreciate. The weight of her neglect had settled upon their shoulders. Tyche clenched her fists in a call to action. She had to act, to make amends.

Tyche stood apart at the edge of the square and observed the villagers' despair. Aioropaia jumped from Kalliope's arms and approached Tyche with hesitant steps. Kalliope's gaze met Tyche's, an unreadable expression flickering across her face, neither kindness nor malice, but a look Tyche could not decipher. Her heart crumpled at Aioropaia's haunted eyes, wide with hunger and confusion.

"Lady Charis," the child whispered, "why does the sky cry when we need it to smile? Why does the goddess of Fortune turn her back to us?"

The child's innocent question bound itself to Tyche's own unspoken agony. The gods wielded much power, yet they permitted such pain. While mortals starved, her Horn of Plenty lay unused. The awareness of her divine power stirred. She would make certain these mortals wouldn't suffer such hardship again.

From the square, desperate pleas rose to the unseen goddess of Fortune to save their crops. Tyche slipped behind the shadows of the walnut grove and summoned the ivory Horn. She gripped it in her hands and emptied it onto the ground. A surge of health and abundance raced across the fields, restoring the desolate soil. Thick shoots exploded through the replenished earth. Prosperity's energy bled up the stalks of the barley, turning them a lush viridian green. The land's bounty spread throughout Pikerni and the valley below.

Murmurs of a miracle spread like wildfire among the people, while a gentle breeze of blooming herbs brushed against their faces.

Aioropaia tugged on Tyche's tunic as the goddess returned to the plateia, a faint weariness settling in her bones. "Lady Charis," the child whispered with a budding wonder, "the plants look happier."

Tyche managed a strained smile. "Yes, LittleOne. Sometimes, even when we feel lost, help can find its way to us."

The cost of her healing the earth had been more than she anticipated. A jolt of panic ran through her as she sensed her divine connection weakening. The afterglow of the miracle lingered into the sun's descent, offering her a colder warmth. She wiped sweat from her brow and pushed limp hair from her shoulders. All around her, the villagers gathered their scattered tools and shepherd their flocks home, murmuring prayers of thanks.

It is time I rested.

As evening approached, the goddess left the barn and made her way to the plateia, where the trees offered welcome shade. She gathered nuts from the ground and perched on the low wall.

Children's shouts floated through the dusk, and Dora chased a butterfly. Tyche smiled, remembering the day she had saved the drowned child from the spring—the day that had changed the course of her life.

The villagers crowded around scattered fires when the shadows consumed the sky. Tyche rested her eyes and tuned her ear to the night's melodies. Insects droned their sundown lullabies, and animals howled in the distance. Wind stirred the leaves overhead. A warmth of satisfaction settled over her that she had been able to save these people. Contentment purred in the ginger cat winding around her ankles and drifted in the gentle laughter from the fireside gatherings. Centuries of divine solitude fell away. These mortals offered her what Olympus denied. Belonging.

A spirit of peace wrapped Tyche, carrying with it a hope this bond would stretch beyond all time. She sighed with the conviction that her past had finally receded. Perhaps the gods' pursuit had ceased, and this peaceful belonging had been her true destiny all along.

But the illusion shattered with a brutal cry.

A shriek pierced the twilight. A boy with a blood-stained tunic burst from the tree line and staggered into the firelight.

"Wolves!" The boy's throat constricted around the word. "Giant wolves with burning eyes! They tore through the flock!"

The village erupted. The men snatched spears and clubs from their doorways and rushed to gather in the plateia.

"How many?" Christos demanded.

"Six, maybe more." The boy's legs buckled. "They're not normal wolves. Their fangs drip green poison."

"Gods protect us." Kalliope yanked her daughter, Aioropaia, to her chest.

"Get the children inside!" Dimitra shouted above the uproar. "Bar your windows!"

Villagers scattered in panic. Doors slammed and metal scraped against wood as weapons were raised. The inhuman howls grew closer.

Tyche snatched a burning branch from the fire. The flames scorched her fingers, and she welcomed the pain. These mortals needed her protection now, not her complaints.

"Stay close, Charis!" Evy's worried cry pierced the chaos.

Tyche gripped her makeshift weapon tighter as she charged toward the danger with a cry of vengeance. She would not fail them again.

They reached the timberline, where massive wolves rippled from shadow and twisted in the torches' light. The alpha's eyes blazed gold—a gaze Tyche knew too well—now alight with a predatory cunning. Emerald venom bubbled and scored the earth beneath yellowed fangs that elongated and retracted with unsettling speed. Her heart twisted between recognition and doubt.

The villagers met the wolves' assault. Their torches flashed against the darkness, casting wicked shadows of the beasts as they shifted and blurred. The men's weapons smashed against bone with a sickening crunch, but the creatures' unnatural strength dismissed their blows. The villagers locked shoulders in a human wall against the horror that seemed to flow and reform with each attack.

"Hold the line!" Christos roared as he thrust his spear at a lunging beast. Blood sprayed and hissed in the torchlight as the beast momentarily recoiled, its form flickering as if caught between shapes, a fleeting glimpse of serpentine skin coiling beneath its fur.

"Father, behind you!" Panos thrust his javelin. The point punctured the wolf's skull with a sickening crunch, and the creature shrieked, its body contorting as bone and muscle seemed to rearrange, the spear momentarily trapped in its flesh before the wound sealed with unnatural speed.

Tryfonas dashed between the beasts with his torch held high. "Here! Face me, spawn of Tartarus!"

The wolves' eyes glowed with malice, and their howls froze Tyche's marrow. *These are no mortal creatures. The gods have sent their hunters.*

"Bind the wound tighter!" Lep bellowed as he knelt beside the injured. Blood coated his hands as he worked. "Stand firm! If they breach our line, our children will surely die!"

The wolves' snarls carried memories of the goddess' nightmares—ancient warnings or threats, she couldn't tell. The alpha's golden stare burned through the chaos while the villagers fought and fell.

Tyche thrust her burning branch at the snapping jaws, but the wolves surged forward in a wall of matted fur and fangs. Their hunger matched the gods' fury. A massive beast lunged for Tyche's throat. Her ankle twisted on a gnarled root, and she crashed to the ground, screaming when her torch cartwheeled into darkness. Hot, putrid breath scalded her face.

"No!" Christos' cry split the night.

The beast's muscles coiled as Lep materialized from the shadows, his spear flashing in a silver arc through the darkness. Bronze pierced matted fur. Bone splintered. The creature's momentum drove the weapon deeper until its point erupted from its shattered spine in a violent red blossom. Blood poured from the wound and sizzled across the decayed forest floor.

Lep pivoted to face Tyche. The sun's flames burned in his eyes—too bright. "Charis, can you stand?"

Tyche's heart thundered against her ribs as she sprawled in the mud. She peered at him and reached out her hand. "You saved my life."

His fingers closed around hers, calloused and strong. As he pulled her up, his touch lingered, and heat bloomed where their skin met. "These are no common wolves." His breath bathed her ear. "They hunt with purpose."

The battle surged around them as the villagers fought with mortal courage against immortal horror. Tyche staggered upright. The Wheel stirred within her chest, ancient power awakening divine energy that crackled across her skin.

A child's scream pierced the chaos, drawing her attention to a boy who cowered against a tree trunk as death approached on four legs. Yet as the wolf's jaws gaped, Tyche snapped, and her power engulfed her.

Twilight wrapped her like a cloak, even as the Wheel of Fortune materialized in her grasp, spinning faster than mortal eyes could follow. Golden constellations blazed along its rim, and fate itself bent to her will.

The Wheel flared in her hands, its light fracturing the darkness. The wolves stilled and turned their burning eyes on Tyche's power. A knowing glint intensified in the alpha's golden gaze—a flicker of dark satisfaction as her divine light surged. *It's as if the beast knows me and had expected me to openly display my powers. He orchestrated this.* The wolf seemed to smile as its lips stretched over pointed fangs, then the pack dissolved into tendrils of shadow that snaked into the forest and vanished.

The boy clutched Tyche's skirts. "The beast was going to eat me," he sobbed. His fingers traced the fading light still shimmering around her.

Tyche knelt beside him. Her heart thundered at the base of her throat as the power coursed through her veins. For the first time since fleeing Olympus, she had embraced her true nature—to protect, not to harm.

"You're safe now." She smoothed his tear-streaked face. "Go to your mother. Tell her the shadows are gone."

The villagers stirred from their shock as they gathered their wounded and herded the scattered goats to safety. Whispers rippled through the crowd, hushed questions and fearful speculation replacing their earlier cries of terror.

Tyche dusted the dirt from her chiton and faced the aftermath. *These humans, so vulnerable yet... invincible. What is this power they hold? Is it courage? Devotion? Or is it love?*

Then her power, radiant as the daystar, dimmed in her chest. The exertion of wielding her power had exacted a costly toll. A physical ache filled the void, and with it, her immortal strength ebbed like the receding tide.

Tyche shivered in the darkness, but the beast's eyes remained in her vision. The golden glare, so like those of a beloved face from a forgotten dream, held a message she couldn't yet interpret.

Sweat beaded on her brow, and the earth tilted beneath her feet. She clutched the rough bark of an olive tree in her palms. Her vision blurred, and the edges of the world softened. Mortality pressed against her skin, heavy as iron chains—the price of her exile and the cost of wielding her power for love.

Then a hoarse cry split the night. Tyche pushed off the tree and turned toward the commotion.

"My arm!" Christos staggered from the tree line. Blood streamed between his fingers. "The beast bit me!"

The villagers surged around the wounded man.

"Lep!" Dimitra yelled. "We need the healer!"

Lep shouldered through the panicked crowd and eased Christos to the ground, his hands already reaching for his medicine pouch. The venom spread in purple streaks from the wound.

"Hold him still!" Lep commanded. He uncorked a vial with his teeth, and the bitter scent of potent herbs lifted into the air.

Tyche stepped forward on shaking legs. "Let me help."

"Wolf venom works fast." Lep crushed dark, leathery leaves between his fingers, his gaze intent on the spreading discoloration. "Keep him calm while I work. This is potent... unnatural." Lep's eyes flickered to the shadows, then back to Christos.

His hands worked in a blur of motion as he applied the crushed herbs and a dark paste to the wound. The angry purple tint drained from Christos' flesh, replaced by an inflamed red blush.

"Our healer is a miracle worker," Dimitra breathed in relief.

Lep's mouth quirked in a wry smile, his gaze still resting on Christos' arm. "Luck and steady hands. And knowing what you're dealing with." But his eyes flickered to Tyche, holding a hint of a question in their depths. "Sometimes the gods smile on us, eh?"

Tyche stared at Lep but didn't respond. This close, his scent—herbs and sunlight—made her dizzy. Or perhaps it was the divine power ebbing from her limbs, leaving her mortal. Weak.

"Your skin burns." He pressed a palm to her forehead.

"I—" Tyche's world tilted. She gasped, her hands fisting in Lep's tunic as his arms banded around her waist before she fell. The press of his body sent a bolt of lightning through hers.

"I have you," he murmured.

But darkness crept at the edges of her vision, and through it weaved another voice, beloved and familiar.

That of the wolf. *Hold on, my love. I will be with you soon.*

Then, the world dissolved, and she followed.

Revelations are whispers of the dream's soul, where truths are spoken and horror takes root. In the soul of a goddess, virtue and malice clash, and even the most beloved faces can hide the secrets of the heart. For in the darkest hour, nothing is ever quite as it seems.

DREAMS ARE WHISPERS OF THE SOUL

Tyche awoke in darkness, the baby shifting beneath her ribs. The barn breathed its familiar scents—fresh straw, damp earth, and manure—mortal comforts she now called home. Moonlight sliced through the beam's cracks and painted silver threads across the floor.

She remembered collapsing after the wolf attack. Lep's arms had caught her, his touch awakening her ancient blood, his eyes, bright as Apollo's chariot, burning in her memory. Her fingers traced the spot where his hand had rested. A confusing heat lingered. Then, Ikelos' face rose in her mind, and her hand fell away. Yet, even as the healer's unexpected presence stirred a new affection within her, a deeper part of her yearned for the solace only one man had ever offered.

"Shhh shhh shhh," Tyche crooned to the sleeping child in her belly.

She turned on her side and drew Kid into her embrace. Shadows crept in from the corners of her eyes and drew the world inward.

"Tyche. Tyche," a voice whispered, silken and seductive, pulling her from the depths of slumber.

Her eyes fluttered open, and there towered Ikelos, the god of Nightmares. A surge of relief, of a familiar comfort in the darkness, snaked through her, though a tendril of unfamiliar warmth from Lep remained. *Ikelos.* He had come for her. His form shifted between shadow and substance. Moonlight caught the sharp planes of his face, while darkness pooled in the hollow of his throat. His golden eyes were her torch in the darkness.

She remembered their stolen moments in the shadowed corners of Olympus, where his whispers of dark promises had always seemed to find a way to calm her soul. Yet, even Apollo, his molten eyes filled with a rare concern, cautioned her about Ikelos, calling him shadow with a gilded tongue. But the god of Nightmares had always been a comforting presence to her in the midst of the gods' indifference.

Nightmare's dark hair cascaded across his brow like the black satin of a starless night. His lips curved into a smile holding twin daggers of promise and danger, and for the first time in what seemed like an eternity, peace settled over her.

Tyche reached for him, her fingers tracing the sharp lines of his cheekbones, the curve of his mouth. He yielded to her touch and sank onto the straw beside her, his midnight robes pooling around them. She breathed in his scent, darkness and starlight. Prickles of excitement strung along her skin at his exquisite beauty.

"Tyche, my love." His murmurs caressed her skin. He leaned closer, his lips brushing against her ear. Tremors of desire coursed through her. "I've been waiting for your summons, but you never called on me." A hint of worry laced his words. "What is happening to you?"

Before she could respond, Ikelos' tawny eyes flickered, and a surge of dizziness caused her head to spin. The barn's solid structure dissolved into fractured starlight and shadow, the familiar scents of straw and earth replaced by the tinkling of a thousand tiny bells.

When Tyche awoke again, she found herself in a plane of swirling mists and shimmering lights. The soft chimes caressed her ears. She lay on a bed of soft silks, where the scent of ambrosia tickled her nostrils.

Ikelos knelt beside her, his palm resting on her fevered forehead. "You are weak, my love." The song of the bells gushed from his mouth. "The journey has left its mark."

Tyche looked around, bewildered. "Where are we?"

His smile flickered, gone before she could read its meaning. "An illusion of peace, a place where you can heal."

The barn's familiar scents called to her. "But what about the villagers? Are they alright?"

Ikelos' smile faded. "They are safe for now. But the gods will not rest until they have what they desire."

Tyche's eyes widened. "What do you mean?"

"You know what they want, Ty." His gaze drifted away from her. "They want your child."

Tyche's breath caught in her throat. *A threat to our rule,* Hera's voice thundered in her mind. Fear, cold and sharp, pierced her. "But why? What threat does my child pose to them?"

Ikelos pursed his lips. "Our child"—he touched the mist between them—"is a force to be reckoned with. She is the offspring of Fortune and Nightmare and at the heart of unpredictable power. Her existence..." He paused, his gaze on the swirling mists. "It could disrupt the cosmos and its fate. The gods fear her potential and the chaos she might unleash." Nightmare paused and dipped his lips to Tyche's, murmuring, "If you give the child into my care, I will protect her from the gods."

The hairs on the back of Tyche's neck stood on end. She had feared this. The gods, always jealous of power, would see her child as a threat to their authority.

"We must defend her." His fingers traced protective symbols in the air. "We will find a way to keep her safe."

Tyche searched his eyes for reassurance and found concern, yes, but also a flicker of—possessiveness? Protectiveness? She couldn't quite grasp the emotions swirling in their depths, but they made her heart flutter strangely.

She pushed the unsettling feeling aside. Now was not the time for such distractions. The gods hunted them, and her child's safety depended on her. "What do we do? I'm not giving you my baby. *I* will protect our daughter."

For a fleeting instant, a shadow touched Ikelos' eyes, but it vanished as he stroked her hair. "We wait." His eyes gleamed. "We heal. And we prepare." He looked down at her with gentle affection. "But first we must guarantee no one disturbs us."

Darkness spun from his fingers, weaving walls of shadow around them. The barn's familiar sounds muted under layers of his power.

"Now," Ikelos' eyes twinkled with amusement, "we can talk."

She nestled into his side and pulled his muscular arms around her. His skin burned cold as a starless void against hers. Power rolled off him in waves, familiar as her nightmares yet somehow comforting. "Oh, Kelo. I longed for your comfort." She paused as a shadow fell across her face. "But I didn't want to trouble you. I don't know if the gods will make your life as miserable as they have mine."

Ikelos' fingers traced her cheek. "Shhh. All will be well, you needn't worry."

The rustle of animals caught the god's attention, breaking the spell of peace, and he glanced around for the first time.

"You are bedding with animals, Tyche? Is this the best these mortals can offer you, the goddess of Fortune? Have they lost the little sense they had?" Ikelos snorted wisps of smoke from his nostrils.

"Be calm, Lover," Tyche soothed him. "These are my people now. They have taught me much about life."

The rough hands of the village women flashed in her memory, accompanied by the music of their shared labor. They held a quiet power, a resilience that dwarfed Olympian might, revealing to her that life's true value wasn't in divine authority but in the warmth of community and the strength of human bonds.

"What is life without the opulence of the gods?" Ikelos retorted.

She smoothed her calloused hand over the softness of his cheek. "Lover, there is more to these humans than we ever considered." A vision of Lep sprung into her mind. "Have we ever given them a chance to teach *us* the importance of life? We curse them with nightmares and misfortune and don't concern ourselves with the consequences. And yet, I find comfort here among them."

"That may be true." Ikelos drew his fingers along the line of her shoulder. "You may *fit in* here, but you don't *belong* here."

Tyche flashed him a look of defiance. "There's a difference?"

"To fit in with these people would demand you change who you are."

"I haven't changed, Kelo. I am *still* Tyche."

Ikelos leaned over her and brushed his lips against hers. "No, Tyche. Here, you are Charis. You hide behind a lie in fear the villagers won't accept you for who you are. *What* you are."

She drew a sharp breath and hid her face in the heat of his neck.

"If you fit in because you change for their sake or yours, that's not belonging, my love."

Tyche remained silent, testing the truth of his words. The lord of Shadows drew her face into the light of the lantern, his golden eyes drinking in the dew of her own.

"True belonging doesn't ask you to change." His gaze held hers until she glanced away. "It demands you be true to yourself—Tyche, goddess of Fortune, Prosperity, and Luck."

She breathed into the space between them, then inhaled his essence into her lungs. "Must I tell them, then?"

"If you wish to belong with them, then yes, you must tell them who you are."

"I despise the gods. I don't *belong* with them." Tyche gripped his bronzed fingers between her own. She pulled them to her mouth and kissed them. "I'm spent. I can't run anymore. Will you stay?"

In response, Ikelos squeezed her in his embrace and hummed an ancient lullaby. The vibration of his chest soothed her.

The animals stirred at the god's tune and gathered around their modest bed of straw, while the kid tucked in at Tyche's feet. She rubbed her toes in its warm fur as the pigs snuffled and rooted in the straw before settling down beside them.

Ikelos moved to shoo them away, but Tyche drew his hand back and placed it on her rounded stomach.

"She grows," the god said, his eyes lamps in the darkness. "Have you given her a name?"

She smiled into the night. "Tychoneira."

"Ah, dreams of fortune. A name of power and purpose. It suits her, I think." The baby kicked into his palm.

"Yes, our daughter wields our powers. I already sense it. She'll be a formidable goddess born here in Pikerni, where she's safe." Tyche's voice broke in despair.

Ikelos kissed the mound of his child. "She will never be safe from them."

"I know. I'm scared. I can't let the gods hurt my baby. Not this time." She wrapped her arms around Ikelos and clung to him. "Stay," she pleaded. "Guard me from the Nekrochim tonight. I can't bear to see the faces of my children weaved into the monster's body." She shuddered and burrowed deeper into his chest. "They cry out to me, Kelo. Give me rest for one night. Keep my dreams safe."

The god of Nightmares relaxed into the bed of straw next to the goddess of Fortune and rubbed the tension from the small of her back. She sighed long in her contentment.

His spell wrapped around her like wolf's fur, both protection and trap. As sleep claimed her, yellowed eyes kept watch from the shadows, guarding or hunting, she couldn't tell, yet a sliver of fear pierced the warmth of Ikelos' embrace. Was it her child he sought to protect or a prize to be delivered to the gods?

He kissed her eyelids and her forehead, the tips of her silken ears. Then Ikelos settled deeper into the blanket next to her and closed his eyes, nestled in the warmth of the pigs and the goddess whom she knew loved her with all of his black heart.

Justice is a sword that cleaves two ways, and retribution hurls long shadows. In the presence of divine outrage, even a goddess must elect between the fate of her kin and the lives of the mortals she has come to love. For when the scales of fortune tip, the greatest burdens are often carried by the heart.

JUSTICE IS A BLADE THAT CUTS BOTH WAYS

Kid's terrified bleating shattered Tyche's dreams.

Bolting upright, torn from her restless encounter with Ikelos, she reached for him but found the space empty where he had been. Beside her, the Horn of Plenty convulsed. Tyche plunged her hand into its endless depths, where summer met winter, where seeds sprouted and fruits ripened in eternal cycles. But now Earth's abundance writhed and blackened within the Horn, nature's pulse fading beneath her fingertips. *What am I doing?* Her hand recoiled as if burned. *Am I corrupting everything I touch?*

The Wheel of Fortune roused without summons, its golden borders droning with an ancient power. The symbols etched along its surface blazed with an inner light, casting flickering shadows that danced across the straw. As it spun in her trembling hands, the air around her seemed to warp and distort, space bending and folding through its golden circumference. The constellations etched on its surface, fixed and familiar, now flared and parted, creating a swirling gyre of energy. A portal opened between worlds, and through its spinning rim, darkness converged over her village.

Tyche peered through the Wheel's gateway to observe a strong wind sweep through Pikerni, and with it, the scent of iron and the whisper of an ancient name—Nemesis. The tombstone moon convulsed upon itself with a shudder, plunging the world into darkness, as if holding its breath within the depths of the grave. The defiant howl of a wolf struck the stone, and it rolled away into the midnight expanse.

Nemesis. A chill settled on her skin. *Why now?* Then it struck her. *Ikelos.* The gods had used him. They knew he could find her, and they'd sent Nemesis to follow his path. It was a trap, a fulfillment of Zeus' decree. She shivered, the words—*child must be eliminated*—clawing at the chambers of her heart.

Through the Wheel's window, Tyche licked her lips and swallowed hard to see her enemy stride through the sleeping village. The ground shuddered beneath Nemesis, sending tremors through Tyche's limbs. Trees and flowers along the path twisted and contorted, recoiling from the goddess' touch. Their leaves rustled in a mournful dirge. Nemesis flicked her blade through the night. The breeze itself yielded before her and parted like a curtain to reveal the barn.

In her wake, the Scales of Justice shimmered with an ethereal glow, suspended by the fragile thread of fate. Tyche's heart thundered beneath her ribs, knowing no deed escaped Nemesis, goddess of Retribution.

Feigning sleep, Tyche stiffened when her crimson-robed enemy stepped into the barn in silent grace. She shuddered at the twin daggers of the woman's eyes searching for her in the darkness of the barn.

Tyche held her breath as Nemesis' footsteps halted. The kid burrowed into her side, and she placed a protective hand on its quaking head.

"So this is where the mighty Tyche now resides." Nemesis smirked with disdain. "With animals and mortals." She stepped closer. Her crimson robes swirled around her like a pool of blood.

Tyche glared at the goddess, her judge and executioner. Her marble skin glowed in the midnight hour, as her angular face, framed in a shroud of jet-black hair, wavered in and out of the shadows. Tyche's eyes traced the line of her stygian blade and the golden Scales hanging beside her.

"You are a merciless witch, Nemesis," Tyche retorted with a venomous edge. She pushed the goat aside and rose to meet her, stiff and disheveled from sleep. "Did the gods send you to retrieve me?" She held her unborn daughter in a shielded embrace.

Nemesis' lips curled into a cruel smile, her teeth gleaming predator-like. "Indeed they did." She leaned close, her breath hot against Tyche's cheek. "Your actions have provoked the contempt of Olympus." She advanced, her shadow swallowing Tyche whole. "You will return to face judgment." Her words shook dust from the rafters. "The gods demand it." She drew her blade, and starlight glinted on its razor-sharp edge. The night cried out as her sword sliced through the silence in sharp protest against the intrusion of her divine power. "Or face the consequences." The sword remained poised in a silent threat.

Ikelos.

"I am here, my love. Don't show her your fear. It'll give her satisfaction she doesn't deserve," his words whispered into her mind. "She doesn't belong here. She'll soon understand."

Tension melted from her shoulders. Yet, a flicker of doubt lingered. His words were comforting, but his absence reminded her that even in her dreams, she could not fully trust the lord of Shadows.

Ikelos.

Still, her fickle heart swelled with gratitude. *He came to protect me.* But then a flood of guilt—her resistance could endanger him. She knew that. But the thought of leaving the villagers to face Nemesis' wrath was unbearable. Tyche grasped his hand. She knew the consequences of returning to Olympus and the fate awaiting her child at the hands of the gods.

"I won't go with you." She clutched the spinning Wheel of Fortune in her grip and glared at the goddess of Retribution.

Nemesis' eyes dropped to the instrument of Tyche's power. "You wouldn't dare use that on me."

"Try me." Tyche lifted the Wheel, her finger poised to spin it. "The gods are murderers, and I won't sacrifice *this* child to their selfish jealousy. Never again, as long as I draw breath."

Nemesis drew the point of her sword across the Scales of Justice, the golden balance tilting precariously as she spoke. "If you refuse to comply, then the villagers will pay the price for your insolence." Her lips pulled back from her teeth. "Their fate is in your hands."

As if to punctuate her threat, a spectral image of the village flickered into existence above the Scales. Flames licked at the thatched roofs and consumed homes and fields in a fiery inferno. Twisted creatures with glowing eyes and curved fangs stalked the narrow streets. Their black claws dripped with the blood of villagers. The night crackled in screams of anguish.

Tyche's vision blurred, the flickering flames and spectral figures swimming before her eyes. These were not nameless mortals; they were her neighbors, her friends. She had witnessed their kindness and steadfast spirits. She could not, would not, abandon them to the wrath of the gods. *They will suffer,* she thought, her throat tightening with unshed tears. *They will die because of me.* Tyche understood the fate awaiting the innocent mortals. She wouldn't turn from them, even if it meant facing the consequences of her defiance.

Nemesis' voice dripped with cruel amusement. "Do you see, Tyche? This is the price of your resistance. These are the consequences of your weakness. You thought you could escape the will of Olympus? You thought you could hide among these insignificant mortals? You are wrong."

"Easy, princess," Ikelos whispered from far away. "She's bluffing."

Tyche's gaze locked with Nemesis' unyielding stare. "No. I will not be broken. I will not allow them to be harmed. I am Tyche, goddess of Fortune, and I will not yield to the gods' tyranny."

"You know the cost of your rebellion." Nemesis leveled the Sword of Retribution at her bulging belly.

For a fleeting moment, doubt gnawed at Tyche's bones. The specter of Olympus hovered inside her mind. Could she defy the gods' will and forfeit the security of the villagers she had come to respect?

Nemesis stepped forward at Tyche's hesitation, her voice a thunderclap in the barn. "You have until dawn of the third day.

You must choose—your child or the village." Her declaration left no room for negotiation. "If you refuse to comply, the consequences will be dire for you and for those you seek to protect."

Tyche stood mute. She understood the risks of defying Nemesis and the danger for her baby at Olympus' gates. The image of the Nekrochim wavered behind her eyes. Yet, the thought of abandoning the villagers to their fate filled her with dread. *GuiltyGuiltyGuilty.* The peacocks' bitter accusation burned through her veins and stoked the fires of her conviction.

They will not pay for my defiance. I will protect them, even if it destroys me.

There remains a resolution at conflict's root—a fracture of paths, or a clash of fate. When the gods' will opposes itself, the cosmos groans beneath the strain. For even immortal hearts know that love is a sword with two edges, a power that binds and shatters with equal force.

LOVE IS A DOUBLE-EDGED SWORD

The stands of trees sighed in their relief at Nemesis' departure as Tyche strode through their depths. A tangled canopy of walnut trees and oaks stood watch over her. The scent of wild thyme accompanied her footsteps while the moon's glare shot silver arrows through the dense foliage. She tilted her ear to the comforting whispers of the trees. Yet, the waves of disagreement building within her drowned out any hope of peace.

The pop and crackle of a fire disturbed the silence of the forest. A carpet of moss muted her passage, even as the smell of smoke drove her forward.

In the clearing ahead, the flickering flames of the fire revealed the god of Nightmare. His form shifted in the shadow, sometimes wolf, sometimes man, the firelight catching his golden eyes in every shape. Shadow wrapped him like secondhand skin, and the roaring flames carved menacing shadows across his features.

His molten eyes met hers on her approach. They held a wildness, a predatory gleam, reminding her of the wolves that had terrorized the village the day before.

"Tyche." Ikelos' melancholy voice sang in her mind. "These mortals you cherish, such fragile things. Like dreams, they fade with the morning's light. Perhaps this makes them precious. Perhaps it makes them... useful."

A mournful howl careened through the valley. Its lament sliced through the stillness of the night. Another followed, closer this time, a guttural cry, raising Tyche's hackles. Then, a cacophony of snarls and barks erupted, followed by a frenzied chase that echoed faintly from below. A desperate shriek pierced the sky, and Tyche held her breath. The growls and barks intensified, the sounds of the hunt growing more savage. An animal squealed. Then, merciful silence descended once more. She closed her eyes as a wave of nausea rose in her throat.

A life for a life. Is this the price of survival? Is this the fate awaiting my child?

Ikelos tossed a branch on the fire, and the light of the flames caressed his face. "Hear the song of the wolves, my love. Even now they dream of such delicious fears. Their nightmares feed the darkness, strengthen it, even as our child grows stronger with each terror they birth."

Tyche grasped his arm. "Don't dismiss the mortals!" She lashed the god with her scorn. "These *fleeting shadows* have shown me more compassion than any of the gods I've ever known. Their lives matter, Kelo, as do ours."

Ikelos' smile faltered. "I worry about you. You've grown soft, Ty. Remember who you are, the goddess of Fortune, not a guardian of *mortals.* You're losing yourself in their world, forgetting your own power, your purpose. We have our duties, responsibilities... to *our* kind. These mortals will drag you down."

"I am bound by the old ways, the lineage of Titans. Our worlds have never known peace. Here, I have found the belonging my heart desires. A peace I wish for my child." Tyche tilted her face to meet his eyes. "But you speak of duties and responsibilities to our kind, Kelo. You, one of the Oneiroi—the bringers of dreams—what about your responsibility to those less powerful? To those who suffer at the hands of the gods?"

"These mortals are not our concern." The god of Nightmares pulled his arm from her grasp. "They *are* fleeting shadows, insignificant in the grand scheme of things."

"I can't accept those words that came from your mouth. They are not *insignificant,*" Tyche retorted. "Their lives are precious. *To me.* And don't think I'll simply *stand by* and watch them suffer."

"How do you propose to save them, Tyche?" Ikelos stepped back with a smirk. "Your defiance will bring destruction to us all, gods and men. The Olympians will not tolerate your misconduct."

A cold silence settled between them, broken by the pop of the fire. Ikelos' expression darkened. "Tyche, how could you deceive me so?" Ikelos growled, low and dangerous. He paused, his eyes searching hers. "Did our love mean nothing to you? I would have protected you and our child with my life. Now, you intend to place us all at risk. The Olympians will not take this lightly, and neither will I."

Tyche took a deep breath. "What do we have if we live in fear of the gods' wrath? I can't stand by and watch the villagers suffer. If that means defying the gods, so be it."

Ikelos rose to his feet, his form towering over her. "Then you choose them over me? Over us? What of our child?"

"It's not about choosing sides." Tyche's voice cracked, and she turned away, unable to meet his gaze. "It's about doing what's right, protecting those who cannot protect themselves, our daughter included. The gods are jealous of our children." Tyche's words of acid flew from her lips. "They fear their power, their potential to disrupt their reign. They've taken my children. Twisted them into that... that *monster*." She shuddered, the memory of the Nekrochim vivid in her mind. "I won't let them do it again. Not to this child. She will never be a goddess, forced to live a life of immortal sorrow. I will make her human and give her a chance at a life free from their cruelty."

The hum of crickets interrupted the silence between them. Tyche shivered with the weight of their disagreement. Ikelos' gaze softened, and a flicker of understanding crossed his features. He drew the goddess into his arms.

"I cannot change who I am, my love," he whispered words of regret into her ear. "But neither can you. Understand that to belong with mortals demands a cruel ransom—the surrender of your eternal life and the descent into the pit of mortal death. Do you choose to allow the immortal light defining you to... fade? If you choose this path, know you walk it alone."

Tyche's hand rested against her throat as she considered the balance of outcomes. She knew if she were to lose Ikelos, she couldn't subject her child to the gods' tyrannical decrees as she had her other children. Someone had to stand for those who couldn't stand for themselves. Without that, they were no more than beasts, like the wolves howling in the darkness. "I must do what I believe is right, even if it means standing alone against the gods—for the sake of those I must protect."

A tense silence of unspoken challenge held them in its thrall. Tyche met Ikelos' eyes with a silent plea. She longed to yield and implore him to stay, yet she couldn't, not if those around her suffered. With a sigh, she steeled herself, her eyes glinting with contempt.

"So be it," Ikelos murmured.

A final, lingering look passed between them, a quiet acknowledgement of the paths they trod, then he vanished into the shadows, leaving Tyche alone.

Tyche scanned the midnight sky, its vast emptiness capturing the barrenness of her heart. Nemesis had given her three days. Three days to find a means to protect her child and shield these innocent people from the wrath of Olympus. But as she gazed at the stars, a troubling truth occurred to her. She wrapped her arms around herself and shuddered. Her unintended affection for these humans had become her Achilles' heel... her gravest weakness. The attachment to them was the perfect trap, the gods' means of binding her to a fate she could not escape.

Wounds to the flesh may renew, but bruises of the soul bear dangerous fruit. In the sanctuary of trust, secrets sprout like starving seeds, exposing the hidden depths of gods and men. For even the strongest among us crave refuge in the arms of understanding.

A BALM AGAINST THE STORMS OF FATE

Ikelos' bleak prophecy of her own undoing hissed in Tyche's mind.

These mortals you cherish, such fragile things. Like dreams, they fade with the morning's light. Perhaps this makes them precious. Perhaps it makes them... useful.

The abyss of despair swallowed her heart. Tyche caressed the bulge of her child. *Ikelos' words—are they true? Will my love for the villagers be my undoing?*

"Ikelos can't be right." Anger and doubt collided with her grief. She pushed herself off the tree where she rested and stumbled through the forest, the trees' gnarled fingers seeming desperate to hold her back. Crooked branches came alive and scored her skin with lines of fire, drawing golden ichor that tracked her path.

Her ragged breath sent a jolt of agony through her ribs, foreign in its sensation. *This mortal pain is not mine. Gods do not know such fragile suffering.* Her brow furrowed in confusion. Tyche stumbled out of the forest and collapsed onto the soft earth, her body convulsing with a wet cough. Her world swam as she studied the familiar outlines of Pikerni's thatched roofs and stone walls in the dull glow of the early morning sky. The distant murmurs told her the villagers were already at their chores. A rooster crowed the morning's welcome, and children's laughter struck her heart like an arrow's shaft. She sighed and picked her way through the brambles toward home.

Home.

A terrible thought slithered through Tyche. This sickening weakness, this physical disintegration, shrieked of deliberation. Was this the punishment of the gods, a gradual curse intended to break her? The thought sent a surge of nausea deeper than the fever raging in her veins. How could she rally the mortals and prepare them for the coming storm within the short span of days Nemesis had allotted if her own body betrayed her so utterly? She stumbled again, a desperate hardening in her spirit. She had to fight this. Had to recover. Only Lep, with his strange wisdom and forbidden knowledge, could possibly understand this divine unraveling. She must reach the barn. She must find him.

"What happened? Did wolves attack you?" Panos' breath came in gasps when he met her on the path. He reached out a hesitant hand toward Tyche, his brows knit with alarm at the bloody gashes covering her body.

"No." She flinched away from Panos' touch, her eyes wide with a desperate plea. "Don't come near me. You don't understand."

Tryfonas sensed her distress and placed a gentle hand on her arm. "Let us help you, Lady Charis," he pleaded. "You're hurt."

"You can't help me," Tyche choked out with a bitter desperation she didn't understand. "You're too kind, too good. I can't let you get involved in this." She clasped Tryfonas' hand. "I need Lep."

"Involved in what?" He released her hand and stepped back, his eye catching Panos' and tilted his head toward the village. "Let's go, brother, and find the healer to tend to Charis' wounds."

Tyche, bent from exhaustion, waved them away. "Tell the others I need no help from them!"

She watched the boys scramble away, yelling words she couldn't discern.

A treacherous warmth flickered within her at their concern, so unlike the cold indifference of the gods. *That's why I crave their aid*, a traitorous voice whispered. *Because they offer kindness, shelter—something the gods never did.* She shoved the thought aside, the familiar anger a more comfortable shield against the terrifying vulnerability that threatened to consume her. *If I let myself care, they'll be in danger.*

The goddess of Fortune dug her broken nails into the soil and pulled herself upward.

The barn's weathered timbers rose in the distance. Her gaze clung to the familiar structure. *Only Lep can help me now.*

Tyche gasped as she struggled toward the barn. As she neared the entrance, Lep burst from the shadows by the barn's doorway, Tryfonas and Panos panting a few steps behind him. He cast a quick nod toward the boys, dismissing them with a glance before his gaze returned to Tyche.

"Don't." She clenched her teeth. "Don't you dare pity me."

"Pity you?" Lep's mouth turned down in confusion. His eyes roamed over her tattered chiton and bloodied skin. "The boys rushed to tell me you needed me. I came as fast as I could."

"Heal m—" Tyche murmured, then crumpled to the ground.

"Charis!" Lep cried, then gathered her limp body against his chest.

Tyche drifted in and out of consciousness, the world a blur of pain and nightmare. She vaguely remembered Lep's strong arms carrying her. In her fevered dream, the tinkle of the bottles in the healer's belt became the cries of her lost children. Tyche drifted back to consciousness, and the room came into focus. *Where am I?* A gentle warmth settled beside her, the soft brush of fur against her skin, while the soothing song of wind in the beams of Lep's cottage lulled her awake. She inhaled a sweet, herbal scent permeating the room and turned her head toward the crackling fire. Then a gentle nudge brushed her hand.

Above her, the ceiling dipped and swirled in geometric patterns of old. Dazzling crystals garnished the whitewashed walls in the likeness of snakes and rods. Bookcases lined the room, stuffed with scrolls and parchment, smelling of ancient knowledge and forgotten magic. Through her hooded eyes, she observed Lep lean over a table strewn with wooden bowls where the pungent aroma of yarrow and wormwood folded together.

Lep glanced at her and noticed her wakefulness. "Welcome back." He sat next to her on the downy mattress where she lay.

Tyche rolled her eyes and looked away.

"How do you feel?" Lep cupped his hand over her forehead. "The fever still rages in your body."

As Lep spoke, a soft bleat sounded beside her. Tyche's hand fell onto a familiar, soft coat. Her eyes flew open. "Kid?" Her voice cracked into a question. "You brought him here?"

Lep nodded. "He wouldn't leave your side."

A warmth spread through Tyche in the quiet peace of the strange room. Groaning, she attempted to sit up, but the healer pushed her back into the blanket's folds. Kid mewled and scooted close to his mistress.

"Not so fast. Take it slow." Lep's words were guarded.

She lifted her arms to inspect the bandages wrapped around them. A spreading stain of ichor bled through the fabric.

"What is this? You are a healer. Why am I not healed?" She touched her face and examined the deep abrasions.

"I have given you herbs and potions, but your healing is far too slow. I must find stronger remedies." Lep stared into her eyes, searching for an answer he could not see.

Tyche sniffed the air, detecting the savory aroma that wafted from the hearth. A rich, delicious fragrance filled the space between them.

"I'm famished. The baby also." Tyche looked toward the boiling pot suspended over the fire.

Lep stood and dipped his chin. "I thought you might be. This is a very good sign, Charis."

"My name isn't Charis." Tyche groaned in her uncertainty.

Can I trust this mortal?

Lep said nothing. He went to the pot and ladled soup into a bowl, then pushed the warm stew into Tyche's hand and sat on the floor next to the bed, silent. Tyche's stomach growled as she lifted the stew to her lips. She savored the warmth of the broth as it slid down her throat.

After a few moments, she lowered the bowl and looked at Lep in confusion. "Wolf have your tongue, healer? Why the silence? Are you not curious about who I am?"

Lep met her gaze, amusement flickering in his eyes. "Curiosity can be a dangerous thing. Sometimes, it is best to simply observe and wait, *Tyche*."

She gasped. "How do you know my name? Who has betrayed me?"

Lep's expression remained unchanged, his gaze steady and calm. "I know many things, goddess of Fortune," he said. "I waited until you were ready to confide in me. Besides, your blood is the golden ichor of the gods. It was not difficult to see you are not mortal."

Tyche sank back into the pillows. "I have much to say," she admitted, "but I don't know if you're trustworthy."

Lep crossed his legs and rocked back. "Then let me tell you a story." A note of melancholy trailed his words. "A story about myself, about who *I* am."

The goddess handed him the empty bowl, its warmth lingering in her hands. She narrowed her eyes, her gaze on the healer's face to search for any hint of deception. Lep stared into the depths of the bowl, as though searching for the right words in its swirling patterns.

"I was born in Tricca." A shadow passed over his face. "And orphaned at a young age." Lep cleared his throat, his stare drifting toward the flames. "My father sent me to the centaur, Chiron, who raised me and taught me the ancient healing arts and the secrets of the land. My mother, Koronis..." His voice cracked, and he looked away. "She was burned alive while I was still an unborn babe inside her."

The whispers!

Tyche's eyes widened in a sudden flood of understanding of the stories drifting through Olympus over the years. *The infant saved from the pyre, the child of Apollo, rumored to possess extraordinary healing powers.* She had heard the tales, wondered about the child's fate, but never connected them to Lep.

"It was you!" She caressed his face with her fingers. "Apollo rescued you, didn't he?" she asked. "He saved you from the fiery grave, even though he killed your mother. But he was too busy, too caught up in his own affairs, to deal with an infant. So he gave you away to the beast." She paused and looked at him with sympathy. "Yes, I know. You are Asclepius, son of Apollo, the god of Healing."

Lep stood and returned with a cup of his own filled with stew. He drew a chair up beside the goddess.

"Asclepius, it was I who showered you with good fortune and luck all those years ago. You were a little boy. No child should be left without a parent to love him." Tyche reached for his hand in reassurance. "Chiron, the Centaur, was glad for it."

Lep stared at her with gratitude and wonder. "Tyche." His voice cracked with emotion. "I had no idea. I am in your debt as long as I have life." His fingers sought her hand, his touch sending a warmth through her that belied his cool skin.

"No, Lep." Tyche pulled her hand back and pushed the coverlet down. "I am in yours. You will learn of this sickness threatening my life and the life of my child and heal me." She paused, her gaze drawn to the snakes carved into the wooden bedpost. "Tell me," she leaned forward, "is it true what they say about the Gorgon's blood?"

Lep grinned. "Yes, the story holds truth. Medusa gifted me with the blood of the Gorgon from two of her veins. One to heal mankind, even from death, and the other to kill whomever I wished." A faraway look nestled into his eyes, focused on a memory where even the goddess was forbidden. "Few know the true source of my power. My life has been educational, to say the least."

Lep bent forward, his knees indenting the mattress. "Chiron taught me much of healing and choice. He elected to relinquish his life, although he possessed immortality. He understood true wisdom lies in embracing mortality, in experiencing the full extent of existence. Chiron demonstrated to me that even a being of great power can choose to walk a different path, even a finite road of existence. It was a lesson I have carried with me ever since."

Tyche's gaze softened. "I understand," she murmured. "If I knew my daughter would be safe, that she could live a life free of the burdens of my world, I would gladly give up anything." She trailed off as a strange premonition gripped her.

Lep met her gaze. "That is why I chose to live among mortals, in Pikerni. I am a son of Apollo, yes, but the politics of the divine realm is a world of endless power struggles and changing loyalties. Here, among mortals, I find true beauty. There is a depth of experience here that the gods, in their endless existence, can never comprehend. I have found my home here, in the heart of this village."

Tyche's eyebrows raised into a question. "But how did you, a son of Apollo, come to possess the Gorgon's blood? It's a powerful and dangerous gift, and not easily obtained, I would imagine."

Lep's expression darkened. "It is a story that still stirs my blood, even after all these years. You see, after Chiron was taken to the stars, I wandered, seeking a purpose beyond the petty squabbles of Olympus. I sought to heal, to mend the wounds of the world, but the gods' indifference clashed with my sense of justice. I could not stomach it."

"I found myself drawn to a remote cave, whispered to be the lair of Medusa. At the time, she was a beautiful woman trapped by the curse of Athena, not yet the monster of legend." Lep traced the carved snakes on the bedpost. "She was so filled with sorrow, Tyche, but she also had a hidden strength. We spoke for days, sharing our burdens, our hopes, even our fears. She saw in me a kindred spirit, one who understood the weight of power and the burden of choice."

"Then, she offered me a gift." Lep settled his hand on Tyche's knee. "A dangerous one. *To become a true healer,* she said, *you must understand the nature of both life and death.* She grasped my left arm, her touch surprisingly gentle, and then, with a sudden ferocity, she bit into my flesh. Her fangs pierced my skin, and the chill of the Styx flowed through my veins. I cried out when my body grew paralyzed and I struggled to draw breath. *This,* she whispered, *is the blood of destruction.*"

"As darkness closed in, my spirit drifted, separating from my body. Yet, I could still hear her voice, clear and strong. *Do not fear, Asclepius,* she said. *This is but a taste of the abyss. My other gift will bring you back, but first, you must understand what it means to die.*

And then, in the liminal space between life and death, we spoke. She taught me the fragile beauty of existence, the preciousness of every moment, and the impact of every choice."

"When the first spark of returning life ignited, she grasped my right arm and bit once more. This time, a searing fire ignited in my veins, and a burning vitality surged through me and banished the sting of death. *This*, she whispered, *is the blood of life*. I gasped as my body shuddered, but I was alive, with a more complete understanding of what life meant."

Tyche held his hand and drew it to her chest. "Please. Tell me what happened after you came back from death's embrace."

Lep squeezed her hand. "Medusa cared for me in her cave and nursed me back to strength. She taught me to control the power that now flowed through my veins. She advised me to use her gift wisely, to choose my path with care, for the blood of the Gorgon could be both a blessing and a curse. It was a harrowing ordeal, one that took me to the edge of my existence, but one of trust, placed in me by a woman who understood the true nature of power."

Lep smoothed the hair from Tyche's forehead and tucked it behind her ear. "This is the reason I have chosen to remain in Pikerni. Here, I can use my gifts without the interference of the gods, without the endless games of power and influence. I can be Lep, the healer, a simple man who chooses to use his gifts for the good of others."

He extended his arms, turning his wrists upward. "If you would see proof of my story, here it is." Two sets of faint circles marked his wrists, the skin discolored where Medusa's fangs had pierced him.

Tyche gasped and traced the delicate curves of the scars with her fingertips. "These," she said, "are the marks of your sacrifice."

"They are a reminder of the choices I have made and the paths I have chosen." Lep settled his hand over Tyche's.

A moment of silence stretched between them, then Tyche spoke. A greenish pallor had settled on her skin, and she coughed with a dry rattle. "Lep, you have the blood of the Gorgon, a power that can cheat even death. My affliction grows worse each day." She gestured weakly to the festering scrapes marring her body. "My powers wane, and I feel... strange, almost mortal. Would you—could you use your gift to heal me?"

Lep hesitated and took Tyche's hands in his. "You know I would do anything to help you, do you not? The blood is powerful but also unpredictable. I have never used it on an immoral before, and I cannot guarantee the outcome."

He paused, then cocked his head. "But I will try. For you, I will try."

Lep carefully prepared a small draught at his worktable, measuring each ingredient with meticulous care. He winced as he drew his knife across his right wrist. A single droplet of blood bloomed on his flesh. Tyche stared at the glistening wound with a sharp, anxious inhale. Lep steadied his hand and added the golden elixir to the mixture. He held the vessel up to the light and swirled the mixture with care. The liquid darkened as the Gorgon's blood tainted the draught with its potent vitality.

He offered the potion to Tyche, the vial cool against her trembling fingers. She sniffed it, then lifted it to her lips and drank it down in a single, desperate gulp, her eyes never leaving Lep's. Her nose wrinkled, and her stomach clenched in a knot of revulsion.

Seconds passed, then minutes, but instead of relief, a searing heat erupted in Tyche's belly. A shudder racked her frame, and her skin flushed crimson, then paled to a sickly pallor. Her fingers dug into her throat, and she swallowed hard in a desperate attempt to keep the venom down.

With a strangled cry, she lurched over the side of the bed and retched. Yellow bile gushed onto the floor. Her stomach heaved again and again, her body desperate in its attempt to expel the foreign substance.

Lep's eyes widened in panic, and he lunged forward. "Tyche!" He frantically dabbed at her brow with his sleeve.

Clammy sweat slicked Tyche's body, and her lungs quaked with rapid gasps. Her eyes darted around the room, searching for an escape from the torment burning in her veins. Then, their eyes met—a desperate language spoken.

Lep's brow furrowed. "What have I done? It should have worked! Why is it not healing you?"

Then, a memory surfaced of a lesson he had learned from his mentor. "Chiron," he said in sudden realization. "Even Chiron, the greatest healer, could not cure himself when he was struck by Hydra's poison. It was a divine toxin, beyond the realm of mortal afflictions."

He stared at Tyche with a dawning realization. "Your sickness is unlike any mortal ailment. It is different, something beyond even the power of the Gorgon's blood. It is as if..." He trailed off, as though unable to articulate the truth beginning to form in his mind.

The retching subsided, leaving Tyche weak and trembling. The acrid taste of bile lingered in her mouth. She glanced at Lep with a weary resignation. "It seems," she rasped, "my fate is not so easily altered."

Lep returned with a cup of water and offered it to her with a gentle smile, then adjusted the blanket around her shoulders. "Perhaps," he said, "perhaps some wounds cannot be healed with potions or elixirs. Perhaps some stories must be told before they can be understood."

He withdrew his arms and bent forward. "Now it is your turn to tell me what is troubling you. But only if you choose. Only if you are ready."

Tyche sighed and settled deeper into the pillow. "There's so much to say. So much misery."

"Little by little, woman. As you are comfortable with the retelling of it."

Tyche took a deep breath. Her gaze drifted toward the ceiling. "It's a long story. One filled with pain and betrayal." She sighed, her fingers tracing the patterns on the bedpost. "But I suppose it must be told." She met Lep's gaze. "I am the daughter of the Titan, Oceanus the Primeval."

Lep's eyes widened in surprise. "Why are you here, hiding among mortals?"

Tyche's voice wavered. "Since the beginning," she said, her words hardening in her memory, "I have wielded the Horn of Plenty and the Wheel of Fate, distributing fortune or misfortune among the world as I chose. But my power, my freedom, meant nothing to the gods. The Olympians resented my independence. But the *Olympians*..." She spat the word. "They have stolen my happiness from me time and again. My children—" Her voice broke, and she turned away, her shoulder brushing against his chest. The heat of his skin pressed against her, and a tremor vibrated through his frame. "My babies." Tyche buried her face in her hands. Sorrow crashed through her and left her gasping for air. Then, a gentle touch settled on her shoulder.

"Tyche." The soft cadence of the word broke through the haze of her despair, and in the space where their eyes connected, her spirit lay bare. He lay down beside her and caressed her shoulder, his touch a gentle comfort against her aching heart. "Let the tears flow, Tyche," he murmured into her ear. "They can cleanse the soul, even a divine one."

She nodded into the curve of his neck. "I love children, Lep. I have born many over the years, but the gods take them from me. They have turned them into a beast called the Nekrochim, a monstrous fusion of their stolen souls and a creature of nightmares meant to torment me for eternity."

Lep held her close, as though tasting the pain of her anguish. He hummed a melody of peacefulness over her, and she relaxed against him, molding into his body. Lep traced a finger over the delicate lines of her face and cradled it in his palm. He pressed his lips against hers in a soft kiss. Then, he brushed a stray curl from Tyche's mouth and gazed on her as she drifted toward sleep.

At last Tyche succumbed to the inevitable and began to dream. In the recesses of her mind, Ikelos answered her call.

You cannot hide from me, Tyche, he hissed. *You are mine.*

Even the strongest walls can collapse in the face of weakness. In the heart of a goddess, secrets are crushing burdens, and trust is a precious gift. For in the web of truth, every thread is woven together, and the past casts long shadows that shape the present.

13

Secrets Are Heavy Burdens

Tyche tightened her chiton, mindful of the bandages wrapping her wounds. Her head swam as she knelt on the stone floor, her fingers fumbling with the straps of her sandals. But the world spun out of control, and darkness spread across her vision. Strong arms caught her before she could crumple to the ground.

"You are not well enough to travel home. Who will care for you? Your little goat here?" Lep frowned at the billy.

Kid nuzzled Tyche's face, but instead of the usual playful nudge, a tingling sensation spread through her. A familiar voice whispered in her mind. "I will care for you, princess. You needn't worry."

Tyche's eyes flew open. "Ikelos?" she gasped and pushed the goat away. "What are you doing here? Get out of that animal right now! Stay in the Underworld unless I summon you."

Lep observed the exchange with a puzzled frown and rocked back on his heels. "Did you say Ikelos? The god of Nightmares?" He glanced at the kid, then back at Tyche.

A weary smile touched Tyche's lips. "Ikelos has a way of making his presence known, even when unwelcome." She patted Kid's side. "He's a shapeshifter and can take any form he pleases."

"A shapeshifter? But why the goat?"

"He has his reasons," Tyche said, not wanting to reveal the true extent of their relationship. "It's complicated." She waved him away. "There's much you need to know. But we can't stay here. We need to leave. Now," Tyche urged. "I'll explain everything on the way."

Lep opened the cottage door and stepped into the points of the sun. A warm wind tousled his hair, and he motioned for Tyche to follow along with the billy. He took the goddess' hand to help her over the high threshold.

Crash!

The door slammed shut with a resounding whump, and Tyche whirled around. But the dwelling was gone, dissolved into the landscape. An empty space sprawled before her where tall grass and wildflowers swayed in the breeze.

"What happened to the cottage? It disappeared. What magic is this?" She gasped at the absurdity of it.

Lep grinned. "I have woven an enchantment over my home so it remains invisible to humans and gods alike. One never knows how careful one must be."

He released Tyche's hand and turned in a slow circle, his gaze sweeping across the vast panorama. Tyche followed his gaze. The air caught in her lungs at the breathtaking beauty that unfolded before her.

"Is it not magnificent?" Lep murmured. "To think such beauty exists in this world, hidden away from the eyes of the gods." A smile touched his eyes.

The ascending sun bathed the landscape in a golden light and warmed Tyche's skin. Long shadows fell across the Gortsouli Valley below. To the north, the rugged peaks of Artemisio rose, their slopes cloaked in a robe of green and brown.

Lep pulled Tyche's arm through his, their bodies brushing together in a moment of unexpected closeness. They turned to look at Mainalo looming closer still. The mountain's barren summit towered above the lush foothills beneath it. To the west, the Arkadian Plain stretched out before her—emerald fields of grain, golden wheat, and deep crimson vineyards. And to the south, Mantineia's acropolis perched on Gortsouli Hill, watchful of its walled city sprawled below.

"This," he gestured toward the landscape, "is true beauty. Not the sterile grandeur of Olympus, but the ever-changing beauty of the mortal world."

Her gaze swept across the valley. "It is breathtaking, almost as though we stand on the balcony of the world," she agreed, then a violent cough erupted from deep within her chest. She doubled over, her bandaged arms clenched tightly against her ribs.

"Tyche!" Lep rushed to her side.

The coughing subsided but left Tyche gasping for air, her face pale and drawn. "I'm fine," she wheezed, but the tremor in her voice betrayed her words. She brought a hand to her lips, coming away with a smear of blood.

Lep's eyes widened in alarm. "You are not fine, Tyche. You are coughing up blood."

Tyche hid her hand behind her back. "You needn't worry. It's blood that seeped from one of the wounds on my arm." She pointed to the west, where a solitary lookout post stood sentinel. "What is perched on the hill over there?" she asked, eager to change the subject.

Lep followed her pointing finger. "You mean the watchtower? It was constructed there because it had a perfect vantage point to survey the entire valley," Lep said as he directed her to a narrow zigzag path.

"Is it the same tower where Dora was found, then?"

"One and the same. Come, woman. We will talk as we walk, or should I carry you?"

A quiet wind soothed their sun-drenched bodies as they descended. The scent of pine needles tickled Tyche's nose, and the earth beneath her feet whispered secrets of the forest. Cheerful banter of birdsong cascaded around her. The soothing melodies comforted Tyche, but she knew Lep waited for her to speak, to explain the Nekrochim to him, as she had promised earlier, so she began by telling him about the gods and what they did to her children.

"Oh, Lep, the Nekrochim is too horrible to explain." She covered her eyes and shook her head violently.

Lep stopped and faced her, grabbing her elbows. "Look at me, Tyche. If it hurts you to tell me about your past, I understand." He leaned down and plucked a red poppy from among the weeds and slid it behind her ear. His fingers grazed her cheek.

Tyche touched the flower and looked away. He lifted her chin with a finger and studied her eyes with a solemn expression.

"Shhh, shhh, shhh," he pulled her to his chest. "I will not allow any harm to come to you. I promise." His chin rested on the top of her head. "Tell me what is troubling you. We shall face it together."

Tyche gathered her courage and began. "The gods fear the power my daughter would wield," she explained. "With the combined heritage of fortune and nightmare, she could alter reality, bending luck and fate to her will, and even reshape the world with a mere thought."

Lep let out a slow whistle. "She could do all that?"

"And more." Tyche said. "She could influence events on a cosmic scale, bring about miracles or disasters, manipulate dreams, and even craft prophecies. Her power could warp the balance of the world and the lines between reality and illusion." She paused, her intent gaze focused on Lep.

"Whoa, slow down, woman. Breathe." Lep lifted Tyche into his arms and continued down the mountain, the billy close behind.

"I haven't even mentioned her ability to channel luck and fortune, to bestow blessings or curses to enhance the luck of allies against their enemies. To be truthful, I have used my power in this way many times."

"That is quite a bit of power your children have. I can understand the gods' concern." Lep pursed his lips. He cupped Kid's head in his palm as he walked. "It is a lot of power for one person to wield. You must be careful."

"I know." She rubbed her belly as if to soothe the baby within.

"You mentioned something about a Nekrochim?"

"Zeus and Hera have fashioned a monster from the bodies of my children after they were stolen from me. They call it the Nekrochim and use it to haunt my dreams and keep me in line."

She shuddered with the memory of the creature's grotesque form in the cave. "It's the worst kind of punishment to hear your lost children crying out to you. Especially when you are powerless to help them."

Lep closed his eyes in horror. "That is—" He struggled to find the words. "That is monstrous. Is this the reason you have come to Pikerni—to hide your daughter from the gods? Because I am sure the gods already know where you are. You cannot hide from them for long."

Lep stumbled on a protruding rock and jostled Tyche. She gasped, her free hand reaching to cover her belly.

"Are you alright? I am sorry I scared you. I will be more careful." He adjusted his hold and continued down the rocky slope.

"I came to no harm." She laughed, tight and short, but the incident had stirred a wave of fear in her. "Lep?"

"Hmmm?" Lep halted under the shade of a tree.

"Nemesis visited me two days ago. She gave me an ultimatum, threatening to destroy the village unless I returned to Olympus to face the gods." Tyche rested her head against Lep's shoulder.

"What will you do?" The healer's brow raised in question.

"I don't know. I have until tomorrow to decide. Ikelos has advised me to go to Olympus' gates and accept my punishment. He will abandon me if I defy him."

"Never will I abandon you." Lep hugged her to his shoulder. His touch sent a warmth through her that calmed her racing heart. "Let us speak to the villagers of this. They will help you decide what to do. I have faith in them."

"I don't want to risk their lives with the wrath of the Olympians." Tyche coughed into her hand. "But I can't let them take my baby either!" Tears welled in her eyes. "I won't lose another child."

"I will protect you both," Lep promised.

"Thank you for that. But now I need to rest," Tyche murmured into his chest. The Wheel inside her shuddered, and a sharp pain lanced across her chest.

Perhaps a touch of Fortune's favor would ease this discomfort.

She closed her eyes and pictured the golden Wheel. Tyche summoned its power, but silence answered her call. Sorrow flooded her heart. Her powers were fading, as was her body.

"It's no use," she moaned in despair. "I can't summon the Wheel anymore."

Lep shifted his hold, his grip more urgent. "Tyche, what is wrong?"

Her head lolled back. "My powers are fading."

He squeezed her body in his arms. "Shhh. It is alright," he crooned. "We will find a way to bring your powers back to you. Rest now. Let us speak no more and make haste to Pikerni." Lep gave her a worried smile as he hurried onward. "There, you will explain everything to the villagers, starting with your true name."

Within the heart of pain, transformation begins. The barrier between mortal and divine thins, and the hidden currents of power stir. In the bonds of community, even a goddess may find the strength to confront her true self and the courage to reveal the secrets binding her to destiny.

SECRETS THAT BIND

The fiery kiss of the sun dipped low on the river as the village walls came into view. Tyche swayed in tempo with Lep's hurried steps. Her fingers twisted in his tunic as he shifted her weight, the kid bleating an impatient "maa" against his legs.

"Easy, Kid." Lep's gaze flicked to the billy goat. "Do not make me drop her."

His blurred face swam above her in her fevered vision. "Ik-e-los?" she mumbled. "My ba-by... vil-la-gers..."

Lep's touch seared her skin and tore through the fever's haze. He pressed his lips against her forehead, cool against her fever. "I knew I should have insisted on keeping you at the cottage. Have I made a grave mistake?"

The villagers in the square grew silent at the sight of Tyche and Lep. Stone walls trapped the heat closer, and sweat trickled down Tyche's spine as whispers rose around her. Footsteps echoed against packed earth as they drew nearer.

"Lep!" Dimitra rushed forward, hands outstretched. "Is Charis ill?" She reached for Tyche.

"She looks..." Evy's hand fluttered to her throat. "What happened?"

"She requires a place to rest."

Christos stepped forward. "Take her to the lesche," he urged. "There's a small room off to the side, beyond the main hall, where she can lie down."

Dimitra and Evy rushed ahead of them to prepare a bed.

Lep shouldered past the villagers toward the wooden doors of the meeting hall. The movement jostled Tyche's wounds as Lep followed Christos. As they entered the lesche, heat from the hearth pressed against her fever-flushed skin. A curtain's shadow cooled her face as they entered a smaller, dark room, where stale air hovered still and close.

"Over here," Dimitra motioned. "We've made up a bed for her."

The beams above Tyche swam with shadows as Lep carried her toward a pallet on the floor, covered with woven blankets and soft furs. Evy and Dimitra were already smoothing the roughspun sheets.

"Lay her down here, Lep," Dimitra urged with a pat on the covers.

The wool's rough fibers scraped against Tyche's burning skin as Lep lowered her onto the bed. He pulled down the chiton covering her body to reveal a network of golden, oozing wounds marring her flesh.

Fever charred her thoughts to embers. The words "she burns" cut through the raging fire. A voice called for oregano and wormwood.

Pain shot through her flesh as bandages were peeled back. The touch of trembling fingers traced fire across her skin, even as the odor of blood and herbs stung her nostrils. She moaned when the poultice blazed through her torn skin.

Shadows blocked the candlelight as breath and body heat pressed closer. Whispers pricked at her awareness, sharp as spindle thorns.

A flicker of bright blue caught her attention—Dora's dress amid the dull colors of the villagers' clothing. The child pushed past the anxious adults.

"Is Mother Charis going to be alright?" Dora pressed against Lep's leg.

Dora. The child's face wavered in Tyche's mind, and a heavy weariness settled over her. Her eyelids fluttered shut, the room's edges blurring into shadow.

A shaft of sunlight fell across Tyche's skin. *Dora.* The girl's presence next to her quieted her pain.

The child's fingers were cool against Tyche's cheek. "Mother Charis?" she whispered. "Please wake up."

Dora's quiet call brushed Tyche's senses and drew her from the abyss' edge. "What has happened? Are the villagers... safe?"

"Hush, now. Everyone is fine. You have been very ill." Cool lips pressed against her forehead.

The goddess cringed at the scrape of shoes as the villagers backed away and left the room, leaving Dora and Lep alone with her.

"Dora," Tyche rasped. "Come closer, child."

The girl sank to her knees beside the pallet. "Mother Charis?" she whispered. "What can I do?"

A hot tear struck Tyche's skin. The droplet of memory sank into flesh and bone. Her baby's first cry, its fingers clutching hers. Fortune's Wheel stirred beneath Tyche's ribs, its hum pulling the Horn of Plenty from its slumber. The ancient powers emerged in an arc of silver light.

Through fever-blurred vision, Tyche beheld the Wheel materialize in the space between them. The Horn burst from her chest. Living water gushed from its mouth, setting the Wheel's grooves alight. Water thundered through the Wheel's spokes, while songs of mothers and daughters, of broken chains, and of rebellion swirled in light and shadow.

Dora's hand pierced the sacred waters. At her touch, divine words poured from her lips.

Τύχη μήτηρ προστάτης, δύναμίν σοι δίδωμι.

The ancient invocation burned Tyche's tongue as she mouthed the words.

Tyche, protecting mother, I give you strength.

The Wheel spun faster beneath Dora's fingertips. Power surged from the child's hands through the goddess' weakened flesh. The primal waters of creation poured into Tyche's open mouth, and she reared backward, screaming. She clutched for Dora's hands as the Horn drew its waters back into its depths. Fortune's Wheel slowed, then sank beneath her skin.

Power still crackled as Dora crashed into Tyche's arms in a tight hug, undisturbed by the ancient power. "Oh, Mother, I am so happy you're well."

Tyche clasped Dora to her breast. Her heart pounded with a fierce, yet unfamiliar love.

"Dora, child, Charis needs her rest now. Go ask old Christos for a refreshment." Lep eased the girl from Tyche's arms and scooted her out the door.

The goddess lay stunned, her divine power fading, but Dora's strength sang through her weakened flesh.

The healer eased down beside his patient and checked the wounds under the poultice wraps. "They are showing signs of healing. I must keep a watchful eye on their progress." His gaze met Tyche's. "What is it? What is wrong?"

"Did you see anything unusual between Dora and me?" The words scraped against her dry throat. "Anything strange?"

His eyebrow raised as a question. "Unusual? Like what?" His eyes darted to the door where Dora had disappeared. "I saw her hug you. She was clearly worried."

The power still thrummed in her blood, the peculiar connection with the child humming beneath her skin. She opened her mouth to speak, but the words caught in her chest.

"Never mind. We can talk about it later. While you rest, I will speak with the villagers," Lep said.

The rough-hewn beams above her wavered. Her limbs shook with weakness, but her mind sharpened as she heard Lep's footsteps retreat to the waiting villagers.

"She demands rest." His voice drifted through the curtain. "And she needs—she needs to be among friends."

The fire crackled in the silence.

"Please, everyone," his words struggled to reach her in her exhausted state. "Sit down. There are things you must know."

Silence crushed her chest. From beyond her room, voices rose.

"Why was Charis in the forest?" Tryfonas' voice cut through the blur of her confusion.

Questions erupted like thunder. Their vibrations pounded against Tyche's skull. Lep's command silenced them.

"I do not know why she spent the night in the forest." His lowered voice drifted through the curtain. "But I do know she needs our help."

Beyond the doorway, the villagers' murmurs melded into a low hum. The hearth's warmth carried their whispered comfort to Tyche's straining ear.

"Anything for the lady!" Althea's voice cracked with emotion. "She saved my little girl. I will never forget her kindness."

The gruff voice from the back of the outer chamber made her wounds ache with memory. "Aye, she saved my boy from those wolves. Fought like a lioness, she did!"

"And she helped us drive the monsters back." Panos' shout pierced her consciousness. "I've never seen anyone move like she did."

"She's a strange one, that Charis, but she's got a good heart. Never shirked her duties. She's one of us now." Tyche smiled to hear the old woman's words.

Christos' deep voice rumbled like distant thunder. "Everyone speaks true. Anything for the one who brought us such fortune and luck."

The outer room stilled. Her heart quickened at Lep's next words.

"Charis is not her real name."

The silence broke under his cough. "But before you cast judgment," he said, "allow me to explain."

The burden of truth can shatter illusions and forge enduring bonds. In the moment of judgment, the heart's allegiances are challenged. For even a goddess, bound by love and sacrifice, must confront the ultimate choice—to protect those she loves or to succumb to the shadows of her past.

15

BOUND BY LOVE AND SACRIFICE

Hours had passed since the villagers retreated to their homes, leaving Lep to stand vigil through the dark hours. Tyche thrashed inside her dream, where thunder and sulfur seared her flesh, and the gods' twisted faces towered above her. Blazing arrows rained down on the screaming villagers.

Ikelos materialized from the shadow, his wolven eyes burning with fierce protection. "Flee, my love!" His fingers brushed the softness of her cheek. "Abandon these mortals before it's too late."

Before she could form an answer, the Nekrochim emerged from the shadows, its twisted limbs reaching for her. The children's grotesque wails formed a dirge of despair.

Then, a slow, agonizing return. The chaos of the dream lingered with a phantom scent of brimstone and a distant scream. Lep's face wavered above her as her immortal sight faded to mortal eyes and power writhed beneath her skin, weaker with each breath.

Water touched her lips, and she closed greedy fingers around the cup. "Better than the nectar of the gods." The words clawed past her throat.

Lep's fingers lingered on her wrist as he steadied the cup, and heat blazed where their skin touched. His breath caught when she swallowed, his eyes fixed on her throat, the cup trembling between them. A warmth spread through her she hadn't known in centuries, even as his intense stare burned her heart. Desire flickered in his eyes, matching her own longing.

"Let me check your fever." His palm pressed against her forehead, thumb grazing her temple. Apollo's healing fire sparked beneath his touch. Their shared divinity ignited—his father's golden warmth meeting her ocean-deep power. A shiver of pleasure traced her spine.

Her fingers tangled with his. His pulse thundered against her skin, and soon the space between them thickened with immortal recognition as the healer's hand brushed the curve of her jaw, leaving trails of sunlight on her flesh. His feather-light touch sent jolts of electricity through her, and she leaned into his hand.

"Tyche." He breathed her true name like a plea. When she pulled him closer, his hands slid into her hair and cradled her head. The heat of their breaths mingled, and she breathed in his scent of herbs and sunshine, then closed her eyes. Hesitation flickered, and she drew a sharp breath. Could she trust this feeling? Could she allow herself to be vulnerable? Lep ran a hand over the line of her collarbone. She tasted the sun's rays on his lips and surrendered to her desire.

Time stretched between heartbeats. His touch anchored her failing divinity, while her power sang to his immortal blood. They balanced on the precipice of forever, caught between god and immortal, patient and healer, woman and man.

The afterglow of their bond fractured, and the starless current of Ikelos' darkness surfaced in the depths of her soul, forcing her to confront the choice between deadly passion and healing light. Two loves, two paths. Her heart twisted between them, the pull of her past and the promise of a different future.

He had stood by her and had honored her decision to remain with the mortals, even when the gods themselves sought to tear her away. On the other hand, Ikelos had bartered her and her unborn child and had offered them as pawns to the Olympians. But, unlike the god of Nightmares, Lep didn't hide in the shadows and had offered her his protection in her moments of weakness. He had proven his love with loyalty and quiet strength, not with grand gestures of power. This was true love, a willing sacrifice, a love that simply was.

She knew she had to choose. And in this moment, she chose him. A wave of tenderness flooded the chambers of her heart. She loved him. Would do anything for him.

Before she could ponder it further, footsteps thundered in the hall, and they broke apart as Dora exploded into the room.

"Mother Charis, how do you fare this morning?" the girl cried.

The goddess opened her arms, and the child folded into their embrace. The Wheel's strength sparked between them like the ghost of yesterday's healing. Power flowed through their joined hands, dimmer but unbroken.

"Dora. Dora. Who are you?" she murmured into the girl's ear. "How did you summon the Wheel?"

"I don't know, Mother." Dora nestled into Tyche's neck. "Strange things happen when someone I love is hurt."

A sudden stillness fell over her. *Mother?* The word pierced her heart like a delicate needle mending her soul. Tyche's mind reeled at the sudden surge of power from the day before and the unexpected connection she had discovered with the child. Love and bewilderment collided in the quadrants of her heart.

This child holds a power I can no longer fully grasp.

Lep disentangled Dora from Tyche's arms. "Dora. Child," he said. "Why do you not go and find out if your mother needs help with the afternoon meal?"

Dora's eyes narrowed. "But will Tyche be alright?"

"She will be," Lep assured her with a pat on the head. "But she needs time to heal. Come back and see her later."

With a final hug for Tyche, Dora skipped from the room.

Tyche watched her depart with a bittersweet ache. She longed to keep the child close, but she knew Lep was right. She needed to mend and regain her strength for the coming confrontation.

Tyche lowered her face into her hands as the weight of her decision pressed down on her. She had to tell them. She couldn't let them face the displeased gods unprepared. They must know the truth, even if it meant revealing her true identity, even if it meant risking their rejection.

"Lep." Her hoarse voice rasped against the walls. "They deserve to know."

"Know what, Tyche?"

"About the gods." Each word burned. "The danger is real. They must prepare."

"You are delirious. Sleep. We will discuss this later."

Her heartbeat thudded in her ears. "No, now! They must know. The Olympians—they will come."

Lep searched her earnest face and tilted his chin in agreement. "I will tell them everything."

Tyche pulled Lep's hands to her mouth and kissed them. "Thank you."

The healer stood and faced the doorway, then straightened his shoulders and marched from the room. Tyche knew the people loitered in the lesche to hear word of her condition. She heard Lep's sharp intake of breath

"Listen to me," he said. "Charis is not who she seems."

Disbelief rippled through the crowd. Their voices buzzed in her ears.

Christos stood from his bench and stepped forward. "What do you mean? Who is she?"

"She is not a stranger who came to our village to seek refuge. She is..." His words floated in the air. "She is Tyche, the goddess of Fortune, Prosperity, and Luck."

The villagers erupted in loud whispers. Their voices beat against her skull.

"Impossible," scoffed Tryfonas. "A goddess? Here, in our village?"

"Why hide among us?" Melina shouted.

"Is she dangerous?" Kalliope clutched her daughter in her arms.

Silence settled against Tyche's ears as Lep turned toward her doorway. His words pierced the chaos. "She is pregnant with a child of immense power. A child feared by the gods themselves."

A collective gasp snuffed the air from the room. Tyche staggered to her feet and gripped the doorframe.

"The healer speaks true," Tyche croaked as she emerged from the shadows of the doorway, her body swaying. "I am Tyche," she declared, "goddess of Fortune. And I am in grave danger."

A stunned silence fell over the lesche.

Her divine presence filled the hall. Prayers whispered through trembling lips and fists clenched protective amulets. The villagers bowed their heads before her as recognition dawned in their eyes.

"The gods fear my child." Her words rang with power despite her frail form. "The offspring of Ikelos and myself." His name tasted of darkness and desire on her tongue. Her hand pressed against her belly, where their daughter grew, Fortune and Nightmare intertwined. "Our child will possess powers beyond their comprehension, powers that could threaten their rule."

The villagers' faces paled. Terror seemed to freeze their hearts as realization took shape. She brushed their stunned faces with her scrutiny.

Evy's voice trembled. "Ikelos, god of Nightmares."

"They will come for me." Tyche's words carved fear on their faces. "They will come for my child. And they will destroy this village if they find us."

Christos' voice boomed across the silence. "A goddess?" His knuckles blanched around the ale horn in his hand. "And the gods would harm you? Harm your child?" His eyes flashed with anger. "Then they'll have to go through us first!"

A wave of disbelief surged through the room.

Panos pounded his fist into his hand. "They cannot take her," he shouted into the din. "We will protect her." He looked around the crowded room. "Even if it means defying Olympus itself!"

"We have little choice." Melina rose and faced her people. "We turn our backs on Tyche and face the wrath of the gods, or we stand by her side, even if it means risking our lives." Her gaze burned into each villager. "I, for one, will not abandon her."

"Aye!" Dimitra's voice cracked. "We will defend our own!"

Lep squeezed Tyche's shoulder. "We will not let them harm you. We will stand by you, goddess."

Silence crept over the lesche. Then, one by one, the villagers nodded in agreement with their newly formed covenant. Tyche threaded her arm in Lep's and gestured toward the door.

Outside, the evening sky bled into the faded light. Stars vibrated in the canopy over the square, and the usual sounds of the night grated on Tyche's nerves. The distant howls fueled her growing disquiet as she stared into the darkness lurking beyond the firelight.

Can we stand against the might of Olympus? Can we protect this fragile peace from the coming storm?

She knew a threatening storm brewed beneath the facade of this peaceful village, one that would engulf it and all its inhabitants.

Her heart clenched with fear. *And the gods, they watch. They wait.*

The ground swayed beneath her as Lep settled her onto a stone bench in the plateia. She closed her eyes in a moment of respite and sighed in gratitude to the people who loved her. When she opened them again, the ginger-striped cat curled around her ankles and then leaped into her lap, its fur still warm from the day's sun. A purr rattled through its body as she hugged it to her chest. Tyche stroked the animal's arched back and traced the delicate ridges of its spine with her fingers. She smiled at the staccato of its hum—a moment of peace before the coming chaos.

Her gaze swept across her people's stricken faces to linger on Dora huddled in Althea's arms. *They would die for me.* Dismay settled in her stomach. *And I would let them?*

Days before, she had yearned to stay, to find peace in their simple lives, and to build a future free from the gods' volatile moods. But now, witnessing their devotion, she understood if she was to become one of them, she must make a willing sacrifice.

The gods will never relent. They will hunt me, and they will find me. And when they do, this village will pay the price.

She knew the Olympians too well. They were not merciful nor forgiving. They were powerful, unyielding, and absolute. Divine purpose surged through her weakened form, and she rose to enter the hall. "I will return to Olympus. I will face the gods and plead for your safety and for the life of my child."

A wave of shock and disbelief crashed over the onlookers.

Dimitra scrambled to Tyche's side. "No! Please, you can't! It's madness!" But Tyche's friend was too late.

The Wheel of Fortune materialized at Tyche's side. Its hum vibrated through the stones under the lesche. A bottle of wine perched on the edge of a table teetered and then fell, shattering on the floor. Wine spread in a crimson pool as the Wheel's power built in a rising crescendo. With a deafening screech, the gears within the Wheel began to grind. The crowd buckled on the ground, hands clasped over their ears to ward off the agonizing wail.

Power blazed from Tyche's form as the Wheel spun faster, its ancient markings burning bright. She poured her strength into its grooves, claiming the price of mortal protection. The walls of the lesche trembled, and the ground shook in the earthquake of her remaining power.

"They must listen this time. They must see." A flicker of desperate hope burned within her. She'd pleaded before, for her other children, and the gods had turned away. But this time, it was different. This time, she carried a strength that blazed brighter than any she'd known. "For my child and the villagers, I will make them understand."

Tyche met Lep's eyes through the swirling frenzy. He screamed her name and clawed his way toward her. She saw in his face the connection binding them, his love demanding her ultimate sacrifice. Her eyes, two stars in the wailing chaos, pleaded for a rescue she knew was impossible.

Then the light winked out, and an unnatural calm fell over the hall. The flames from the hearth writhed and sputtered as if to gulp in the peculiar air. The villagers gawked, frozen in place. Nothingness claimed the floor where she had stood. Her plea whispered into silence.

Before the power of judgment, the thrones of Olympus tremble. For even among immortals, the cost of power is steep, and the boundaries between savior and destroyer dissolve in the face of retribution.

STEEP IS THE PRICE OF POWER

Ambrosia slammed against her senses as Tyche stepped through the glimmering portal into the vast hall of Olympus—the familiar aroma of a home that no longer welcomed her. The marble and gold breathed ancient tension while sunlight bled through stained glass windows. Epic battles warped the glass panes, and their distorted reflections clawed across their crystalline skins.

The goddess of Fortune held her head high, unmindful of the beauty of the hall. The current of hostility in the pantheon forged an iron cage around her heart.

Zeus paced before his throne even as the royal seat pulsed with the beat of his rage. Tyche blinked at his thunderous steps, and her breath caught as their eyes met. Lightning crackled in the depths of the god's electric blue glare, while a continuous rumble of thunder shook the floor under her feet.

Hera stood beside him, her raven hair framing narrowed eyes glittering with hate, while disdain carved icy lines across her face. The emeralds at her throat burned with a cold, primitive fire. Her lips curved into a blade-edged smile as Tyche's fortune unraveled in the glint of the faceted stones.

The queen's intent gaze fell upon the statue of her daughter, Eileithyia. Tyche followed Hera's stare and gaped at the goddess of Childbirth as it spun in a slow circle around Hera's throne.

Surely, the protector of mothers would understand.

But rage contorted Hera's features at Tyche's expectant stare, extinguishing the flame of hope in her chest. *Which face of the birth goddess will I meet?* Her hand strayed to her stomach. *The one who eases new life into the world, or the one who prolongs its suffering?*

Talon-like fingers stretched toward the pregnant statue of Hera's daughter. An aura of the goddess' dark curse wrapped the figure in spiderwebbed cracks across its marbled flesh. The figure released one shrill note of protest before crumbling to dust.

"I won't let fear cripple me," Tyche murmured to the residue at her feet. "I won't let them destroy what I love."

Still, her hands trembled as the statue's destruction seared her soul and left a burning imprint of the god's cruelty. She scanned the hall to take in the towering pillars and the triumphant tapestries. A rising anger flamed in her chest, fueled by a fierce protectiveness for the life she carried and the villagers who had become her friends.

In the eyes of the gods, her child was a threat, an immense power with the potential to unravel their carefully maintained order. But perhaps, just perhaps, she could make them see the potential for good. Maybe she could convince them her child could be a unifying bridge between gods and mortals. A foolish hope, she knew, after the way they had treated her other children, but a hope nonetheless.

Her eyes fell on the mosaic depicting the Titanomachy, the epic battle between the Titans and the Olympians. And in the image of her father's struggle, she found a strength she hadn't known she possessed.

Hera surged to her feet, electricity crackling around her form. "The Fates themselves tremble before this child's power. It will twist destiny to its darkest desires and *challenge our authority.*"

Tyche wiped the sweat burning her brow. "You're wrong!" A defiant snarl twisted her lips. "She will bridge the chasm between the heavens and earth. She will work for the good of both god and man."

Her knees buckled, and she crashed onto the marble floor, the cold certainty of desperation biting into her flesh. She reached toward them with trembling fingers. "I demand you spare her. She deserves to live!"

Tyche knew her words fell on deaf ears. She had pleaded for the lives of her other children, begged the gods to see reason, but they had never listened. They saw threats and power that required control. But this time, she had to try. For her child, for the villagers, for the slim chance the gods' hearts could change.

Zeus ignored her cries, turned toward the mosaic floor tiles, and placed his foot on the image of Oceanus. He ground his heel into the Titan's face with a ruthless smile pressed into his mouth. The god's blatant disregard for her father's image drew Tyche's mouth into a snarl.

"Ah, Oceanus," the god sneered. "Look at you now, old man. Defeated. Broken. Your legacy? Nothing but dust beneath my feet. And soon..." His gaze shifted to Tyche. "Others will join you."

He raised his hand, and a jagged scar of light erupted from his fingertips and struck the mosaic with a deafening roar. Oceanus' image shattered in Zeus' rage. Marble fragments exploded outward in a fiery rain of destruction—the Titan's sneering face vanquished once more.

"You dared to evade our control. To leave Olympus as if you were a simple mortal, not a goddess bound by our laws." Zeus glared at Tyche. "You will not escape us again. This child, this aberration, will be dealt with."

Tyche pressed herself against the floor and shielded her head as a shockwave ripped through the hall. Shards of her father's defiance scored her skin. The rivulets of blood coursing down her body screamed rebellion.

A wildfire of anger pulsed through Tyche's veins at the injustice to her father's memory. Her fingers tightened around her swollen belly, and she cried out against Ikelos' desire for her to relinquish the child to them. She staggered to her feet, blood and tears flowing in her rage. Her magic flickered in response to her fear. Her anger. But she forced it down, the embers of her hatred banked beneath a steely resolve. Rebellion could wait. She would find a way to pierce the arrogant hearts of the gods and force them to acknowledge her plea. But she also knew that pleading did nothing. She had to *show* them the truth. She had to show them their fears were unfounded.

But the fire burning within her grew brittle, replaced by a chilling weakness. The mortal affliction—a malignant predator she thought she'd defeated—sank its burning claws into her flesh. Bile rose in her throat as her magic cracked and faded, leaving her hollow and vulnerable. She fought for her own life and that of her child with a mother's love that fueled her defiance against the sickness ravaging her body and the gods who sought to control their fate.

A ragged cough tore from her throat, and she doubled over. A poisoned dagger of agony flared across her chest.

"I have come at Nemesis' insistence concerning my child and the village." Tyche clenched her teeth.

Was this it, then? Was this how it all ended? A lamb lured into the wolves' fangs, consumed by the same forces she sought to defy? No, not only for her child, but for the village that had become her home, she had to fight. Her heart hammered with the frantic beat of rebellion to escape its iron cage. Would the gods see the spark of divinity within her child? Would they recognize the potential for good, for creation? Or would they see a threat, a monster to be destroyed?

Tyche clung to the fragile hope, that tiny ember of dissent still flickering against the coming storm.

Hera's gaze drifted to the colossal statues encircling the hall. She turned to Nemesis and hissed. "Their pronouncements still echo in my mind. *Balance, disturbed. Order, broken.* The *goddess of Fortune* has underestimated us. To defy Olympus so brazenly, to slip from our grasp—it is an insult. This child, this threat, must be eliminated."

Power crackled around Hera. Her form shimmered and warped, then erupted in a riot of iridescent feathers. A majestic peacock rose before Tyche, its train rattling in a display of divine authority. Hundreds of *ocelli* blinked amid the swaying feathers. The eyes' intense gaze fell on Tyche—jury, judge, executioner.

The peacock's beak clacked together. "The Fates themselves tremble at the thought of this child's power and its challenge to their authority."

Tyche fisted her hands in the folds of her chiton. "Again, you are mistaken!" she cried. The ocelli squinted at her despair. "She will be a symbol of hope and creation. A link between the mortals and the gods!"

But the words rang hollow even to her own ears. How could they believe her when their fear was so deeply rooted? Her knees crumpled, and once again, she kissed the smooth marble floor. "Please." She reached out her hand to beseech the gods. "Spare her."

Nemesis raised her sword of retribution and admired her reflection in the blade. A cruel smile twisted her mouth as she swung it through the air. "And what of the child's potential for chaos?" the goddess of Retribution snarled. "Imagine a being capable of twisting hearts, of planting seeds of discord among mortals, sowing the seeds of revolution that could shatter our divine order."

Zeus cocked his head. His eyes hovered over Tyche's belly with a predatory glint. "Indeed," he rumbled. "And what of its power to shape reality? To defy the laws of nature? If we allow this abomination to live, it will be a storm of destruction we could never hope to control. The village that offered you shelter will pay for their disobedience to their gods!"

"No!" Tyche's scream ripped through the hall. She writhed amid her father's broken visage. "You heartless monsters!" Tears streamed down her face. "They're innocent!" Her fingers clutched at the unforgiving stone. "They welcomed me, sheltered me, *loved* me, and I betrayed them! Take *me* instead! Let my baby *live*! Punish me! But spare them! Let your punishment fall on me alone!"

"Do you believe your tears move me?" Zeus scoffed. "I am Zeus, King of the gods. I am the will of Olympus. Your pleas are meaningless."

Stricken by the god's pronouncements, a deathly calm fell over Tyche. Her carefully measured words belied the fury raging inside her. "Your power has become so great, it is *you* who should worry when the whole world rises up against you. She... she can save your lives, *all* your lives."

A flicker of surprise crossed Zeus' face. "How so?"

"Let her be the heart that beats within your laws," Tyche pleaded, her eyes searching theirs. "She will make people's lives better, which in turn will make your work easier because the people will no longer rebel against you. She will bring peace, not destruction."

"Foolish Titan," Zeus said, his eyes narrowing. "You dare to bargain with me? The fate of your child is not yours to decide."

Hera recoiled from Tyche's plea. "How is it possible for one with such power?" she cringed. "It terrifies me. A being with the potential to surpass even us."

Nemesis leaned in with a silken whisper. "We must act swiftly," she urged, "before this threat grows into something dangerous. We must eliminate it. We must feed it to the Nekrochim."

A guttural scream tore from Tyche's throat. The world spun violently, the faces of the gods blurring into grotesque masks of horror, followed by blessed darkness that swallowed her whole.

Then, a blinding burst of sunlight erupted in the hall, and in its heart, Apollo materialized, his hair a corona of fire. "HOLD!"

His command cut through the stunned silence. His golden bow—forged from the heart of the daystar—was already drawn, his nocked arrow aimed squarely at Nemesis' chest. Its steady point promised swift and decisive justice.

Zeus' face contorted with rage. "Apollo! Have you lost your mind? Stand down this instant!"

Hera rushed toward the god. "You fool! Put down your bow! This is madness!"

But Apollo remained motionless, his glare intent on Nemesis. His eyes, which had witnessed the rise and fall of civilizations, burned with the power of the ancient sun.

"You will not harm Tyche." His muscles coiled as he drew the fletchings of the arrow further into his cheek. "You will not touch her child. And you will not lay a finger on the innocent villagers who offered her shelter." The rays of the sun sparked from his skin. "I, who have healed the sick with a touch, will not stand by while injustice reigns. Do not mistake my mercy for weakness. Do not make me choose between family and justice."

Zeus' features twisted with rage at Apollo's transgression. He reared back and then flung his arm forward, and lightning snapped from his fingertips. But before the bolt struck its mark, Ikelos stepped from the shadows. He snapped his fangs and clapped his hands together, unleashing a void of darkness. The lightning bolt vanished with a hiss as the abyss' vortex swallowed it.

The foundations of Olympus groaned and trembled beneath their feet. Ikelos' form flickered between shadow and form. He braced himself against a nearby column, like a silent predator amid the chaos he had unleashed.

A pulse of dread swept through the hall, and the ground tilted. Zeus and Hera gasped and clutched their throats. Nemesis screamed, then stumbled backward, her sword clattering to the floor with a discordant clang.

Ikelos' nightmares, like ravenous wolves, stalked the chamber, their eyes burning with dangerous hunger as they hunted the halls of Olympus. They skirted around the forms of Apollo and Tyche, then lunged for their prey on the dais. Their fangs dripped with the venom of terror, and a snarl of dark joy twisted their muzzles as they sank their teeth into the gods' flesh to unleash a torrent of nightmares.

The gods' screams pierced marble and bone. Tyche curled around her swollen belly to shield against the divine terror. Colors bled from the hall as the gods' horror gathered in her lungs, her body trembling with a sudden rush of exhaustion and nausea. With a gasp, Tyche succumbed to the darkness. The world dissolved, and she fell, tumbling through a desolate void.

And then, a silken voice purred against her ear.

"Tyche, my love. You have fought bravely, but luck is against you. The gods seek to destroy your child and extinguish the spark of hope burning within you. But I offer you a choice."

Golden eyes pierced the inky blackness. Ikelos' form rippled between beast and man. Wolven fangs gleamed sharp behind his smile. She smoothed back the dark hair falling across his face and traced the sharp edge of his chin.

"Witness the gods' downfall," Ikelos whispered. "Their fear. Their pain." He buried his face in her chest. "Let their suffering strengthen you."

Words died in her throat, and the dream held her mute. She cradled his head against her heart while his touch burned hot on her hip.

"I guarded you from the wolves, Ty," he whispered. "To protect you. To protect her."

Tyche's blood surged to the chambers of her ailing heart and filled the void his absence had carved. Gratitude and love tangled in her chest as his protection wrapped around her.

"Now see." He tore her hands from his face. "See their true cruelty. Rise against them with this gift."

He gestured toward the swirling chaos, the fragmented images of the gods' nightmares flashing before her eyes. "Choose, my love. Surrender to darkness or wield it. Shape a new fate for you and our daughter."

Tyche hesitated, her mind a battlefield of conflicting emotions. Her hand trembled as she cupped his jaw, and then, in a silent plea, pressed her lips to his, a bargain struck in the language of the dream—protection for her baby.

The goddess drifted through Zeus' nightmare, her ethereal form brushing against the void where stars should burn. The King of gods stumbled before her, his breath ragged and shallow in the endless expanse of nothingness.

"See how it f e e l s." She whispered into the crushing silence. "To be powerless. To be nothing." Her words unfolded in the darkness and fell like dead worlds around him.

Zeus reached through her incorporeal form, grasping at empty air. His shoulders trembled. Tyche floated closer to study the fear etched into his face. "The mighty Zeus, reduced to this. A king with no throne to claim."

She watched him sink deeper into the shifting void. His form diminished with each desperate step. When the Olympians appeared, Tyche drifted among them. She caressed their faces as they turned away from their king. Their indifference cut deeper than hatred.

"L o o k," Tyche breathed into Zeus' ear as her daughter emerged from chaos. "Look what you feared to protect." The child's beauty pierced the darkness, her power warping reality itself. Her heart swelled with fierce pride as the Olympians bowed before Tychoneira.

Zeus' pathetic whimper drew her attention back. His attempts to summon lightning, to command the winds, withered in the chaos. Tyche hovered around him, watching his power drain away.

"Y o u, who devoured your own children." Her voice rang through the void. "You, who crushed my father beneath your heel. Now you understand true powerlessness."

The child's laughter echoed through the emptiness as Zeus' form shriveled. Tyche hovered above him to witness his complete undoing. "Remember this moment," she whispered as darkness claimed him. "When you were nothing. No one. Forgotten."

As Zeus crumpled beneath the weight of nothingness, Tyche drifted toward Hera's nightmare. The Queen of the gods thrashed against invisible bonds. Tyche beheld her proud figure bound to a grotesque Wheel of Fate.

"Watch carefully, dear H e r a." Tyche's curse frosted the air. "See how it feels to be bound and helpless."

Each turn of the jagged spokes revealed fresh horrors. Tyche floated closer to study the goddess' terror. "Y o u who bound so many in your jealous rage. You who cursed mothers and children alike."

The Wheel twisted and transformed into a blood-slick altar. Tyche's wraithlike form brushed against the stone, smelling of copper and decay. Above her, pregnant statues glided in endless circles. Their stone mouths chanted SAcRifcEsAcRIfiCeSaCRfiCE.

"Your greatest f ea r," Tyche breathed into Hera's frozen scream. "Not pain, not death, but the power of creation itself." She touched the queen's face with incorporeal fingers. "The strength that flows through a mother's blood."

The statues' faces melted into masks of agony. Their swollen bellies pulsed with unnatural life. Tyche grinned as monstrous offspring tore free from stone wombs, her hand pressed against her own child. "You fear what you cannot c on t r ol. What you cannot de s t r oy."

Clawed hands and hungry mouths descended upon the queen. Tyche drifted above the carnage, observing Hera's form shred beneath nightmare teeth. "R e m e m b e r, protector of childbirth. Remember this moment of powerlessness. Remember it when you think to harm my child."

The altar dissolved into a wasteland of fire. Broken statues clutched their twisted young, empty eyes fixed on their queen. Tyche hovered near Hera's trembling form. "L i s t e n well to my daughter's laughter, goddess. It heralds your downf a l l."

Her child's chortle rang across the barren plain, and Tyche's heart swelled with pride. Through the queen's terror, she glimpsed Nemesis thrashing in her own dark vision.

Tyche drifted through storm clouds. The wind's icy fingers whipped at her face as she watched Nemesis gasp for air. Jagged peaks pierced the rotting sky, and below, the pit of chaos churned and bubbled. Its fiery breath licked at the edges of their precarious perch. Tyche hovered over the spires as Nemesis teetered on the Scales of Justice balanced on the summit of a forgotten mountain.

Tyche heard the cries emanating from the links of the chain binding the trapped goddess' wrists. Her ear turned to the lost pleas of the gods and mortals Nemesis had condemned. Tyche followed the chain's curl into the wind and saw it had settled into the hand of her daughter, Tychoneira, who stood in silhouette on a distant peak.

"Feel the weight of your j u d g m e n t sss." Tyche's lip curled in derision.

Nemesis leaped between the Scale's pans, her footing teetering with each desperate jump.

"Listen to their voices, goddess of Retribution, the ones you condemned without mercy."

Tyche traced her finger along the omphalic line trailing from Nemesis' stomach and laughed as Nemesis clutched at the cord. She followed its length to the shadowy hand of her daughter, who stood across the world.

"Do you think this pitiful tether to Olympus will keep you safe from my child?" Tyche shouted into the rising storm.

With a sickening lurch, the child yanked hard on the chain, and Tyche watched the Scales tilt beneath Nemesis' feet. The goddess of Retribution scrabbled for purchase on her warped Scales. Her fingers grasped at the smooth, unforgiving surface, but it was no use. The Scales groaned and shuddered in their imbalance.

"Such a fragile connection," Tyche mused. "Such false security." She watched as Nemesis clutched her lifeline to Olympus.

With a sickening lurch, the Scales tipped.

"U n w o r t h y!" Tyche's verdict rang across the bitter landscape. A flash of blinding silver caught her eye as it carved a valley through the clouds.

Nemesis' frame plummeted as the child claimed her retribution against her accuser. The Sword of Retribution, in its final act of duty, severed her umbilical cord, and Nemesis sank into the endless abyss.

"R e m e m b e r this fall into the pits of your own making." Tyche trailed after the plunging goddess, whispering against her ear. "Remember what it means to face true j u s t i c e."

Tyche turned to the death toll ringing through the groaning halls of Olympus and left the dream. The hazy atmosphere warped and twisted as the mountain buckled in on itself even as the earth seized and shook Tyche with a violent spasm. With a bone-jarring crash, Zeus slammed against his throne, the marble armrest exploding into a thousand deadly shards. A cry of terror tore from his lips. Jagged fissures spread across the floor and grew wider as the struggle within the gods intensified.

High above, perched on the crumbling cornices of Olympus, Hera's sacred peacocks convulsed. Cracks, like veins of fire, pulsed across their perfect forms and shattered their elegant beaks and wings. Like iridescent waterfalls of sorrow, their trains of shimmering splendor sagged and cascaded downward to reveal the countless eyes hidden within. Blood streamed from the eyespots and stained the feathers crimson. A trail of dark ichor splattered over Tyche to the floor below. The shattered beaks lay scattered across the marble like discarded claws, their broken edges clacking together in a macabre chorus.

HElpmEHelPMeHELpME

Then, with a deafening crack, a blinding light exploded from the heart of the Pantheon. A storm of power consumed Tyche in its incandescent fury. The gods twisted and contorted on the dais before Tyche, and she clasped her hands against her ears to ward off their screams. For a terrifying moment, a searing light burned, and then—silence.

The stricken whimpers of the gods roiled over the stillness as the wind subsided. Bathed in a silver glow, Hermes appeared. Tyche stared through hooded eyes as the messenger glided toward the destruction's heart, pausing at the edge of the shattered scene. Then his attention fell to Tyche's limp form. The messenger scooped her into his arms and held her against his chest.

Beside him towered his magnificent winged steed—the same one who had rescued her from the clutches of Olympus so long ago. Hermes lifted Tyche onto the beast and then mounted Pegasus behind her. His arms encircled her waist and held her in position.

The creature flung its massive head and bared its teeth at the gods. The muscles beneath Tyche's thighs tensed, and a ripple of power vibrated through her weary frame as Pegasus' hooves struck the floor. Silver sparks erupted from the marble, showering the gods on the dais. With a leap, the creature unfurled its mighty wings and beat the air in a display of feathers and power, while Hermes' murmurs to the steed vibrated against her ear like a soothing song. Her hand settled on the beast's flank, stilling its trembling muscles beneath her touch.

Through waves of delirium, fragments of memory crashed over Tyche—Ikelos in the forest, firelight dancing across his face. "You've grown soft, Ty..." His words stabbed through her fever. "Remember who you are. *What* you are."

"Always the dramatic entrance, that Hermes," Ikelos purred from the shadows. His mouth curved into a grin to reveal rows of sharp teeth. He glanced at the stunned gods. "Nightmares," he growled, "can be quite contagious, wouldn't you agree, god of the Sun?"

Tyche's chest clenched. Ikelos' presence soothed her, but the feeling of disquiet persisted. His words from the forest whispered through her mind. "I would have protected you and our child with my life."

Apollo pursed his lips and fixed Ikelos with a steely glare. "You seem to enjoy this."

"Enjoy the chaos?" Ikelos arched his eyebrow in mock surprise. "Surely, you jest. I merely observe." He tilted his head with a playful curiosity. "Though I must admit, this little family drama has certainly piqued my interest."

"So, you have *merely* observed?" Apollo's scoff held summer's heat. "Or perhaps you've been guiding her dreams for years. These nightmares seem intimately crafted."

The amusement in Ikelos' eyes flickered and died. "And what vested interest could the god of Nightmares possibly have in the affairs of mortals and unborn babies?"

Tyche's breath caught. Through the fog of her illness, something clicked into place—all those years of torment, the Nekrochim's endless pursuit. Had he...?

"My son, Asclepius, seems quite attached to the mother of your child." Apollo's words pierced her delirium.

Tyche held her breath as Ikelos' form wavered between man and monster, his golden eyes burning with hunger. "It seems Asclepius has developed a rather *strong* affection for the goddess of Fortune."

Apollo's gaze hardened. "And you? What are your intentions? You seem rather... possessive."

A spark of surprise warped Ikelos' wolven expression. "Possessive? I simply admire her strength and resilience. And, of course, the intriguing nature of her child."

Through her fading consciousness, Tyche caught Ikelos' savage smile, familiar yet somehow wrong.

"Such delicious insolence deserves... *cultivation*. Her strength feeds our child's dreams so beautifully. Each nightmare I craft makes them both stronger." He stroked his chin with a sharp nail. "And of course, the child's particular nature. Such power shouldn't be left to chance."

Hermes' voice cut through the whispers. "Come, my lady. It is time to go."

His arms gathered her close as Pegasus' wings unfurled and beat against the dying light. They launched into waiting darkness, leaving behind the shattered remnants of Olympus and the gods' broken dreams.

Her final thought echoed Ikelos' words from the forest. "If you choose this path, know you walk it alone." Perhaps she already had.

Divine fury stains the dawn with dread, as the heart of the village beats a desperate rhythm. For even as the flesh falters, a hidden fire kindles, the revolt born of starlight and earth, ready to face the storm.

17

DIVINE FURY STAINS THE DAWN

The teeth of the gods' screams raked grooves across Tyche's bones.

Days bled into nights, yet the terrors of Olympus yanked her further into the abyss of heartbreak. She rolled her tongue over her cracked lips and grimaced at the taste of bitter fear. Her shoulders shuddered with a desperate groan, yet she remained a prisoner to the visions that refused to release their hold.

Tyche pulled her sleeve across her wet face and sniffled back her tears, the memory of Pegasus' broad back and Hermes' arms around her easing her despair. They had plucked her from the hands of the gods and delivered her safely back home. But where was Ikelos? The thought sent a fresh jolt of fear through her. She called out to him with her mind, but the cord of their bond was silent. Had the gods punished him for his defiance?

She choked on a mouthful of blame, and her chest exploded in an agonizing rattle. *My baby—their prize to be won or a monster to be slain.*

Tyche drew a shuddering breath and sank back into the straw's dry prickle. Golden shafts of light slanted through the rafters, catching dust motes as she watched the rise and fall of Kid's flank nearby. Yet, even here, the barn's walls seemed to tighten, becoming a cage built of her own fear. She squeezed her eyes shut. *They won't let this go. A storm is inevitable.* I will *not wait for the gods to strike.*

Determined to protect the children, her village, and the man she loved, she refused to allow them to dictate the terms of this conflict. She would fight for them all. But first she must rally the people, train them, and fortify the village's defenses. Then, they would stand together against the coming clash of wills. *I am no longer the victim, as they believe, but a warrior, a protector, and a leader. I will forge Pikerni into a bastion against the gods themselves.* Prepare. Defend. Defy. Tyche chewed over the bitter nourishment of her battle plan, then swallowed it whole.

She caught a hushed murmur of voices and the shuffle of footsteps outside the barn. Then, the door creaked open, and Kalliope's worried cry pierced the quiet.

"Tyche!" Kalliope rushed to her side. "You're awake! We were so worried!" Her eyes brimmed with tears. "We thought we'd lost you again. How did you get home?"

Lep pushed through the crowd. He knelt beside her and clutched her hand in his. "Woman," he searched her eyes, "you are burning up. It is as if your body is aflame."

Tyche winced as the barn seemed to spin. She closed her eyes and fought the urge to vomit. Kid bleated anxiously and nuzzled her side, and she managed a weak smile, but her voice was a hoarse whisper. "I... I don't remember how I got back from

Olympus," she lied. Her gaze flickered over their concerned faces. She swallowed hard while her throat tightened with emotion. "But I know one thing—the gods will never forgive me."

Apprehension rippled through the crowd. Anxious glances darted back and forth among the bystanders.

"Forgive you for what, exactly?" Dimitra demanded, her hands on her hips, her disheveled hair falling from its braid. "What did you do? Should we be worried?"

"For defying them." Tyche's heart sank with the weight of her secret. "For choosing to protect my baby and this village."

Christos' eyes widened. He looked away, then back at Tyche. "What should we do?"

"We must make ready," Tyche answered. "We must strengthen our defenses and make ready for battle."

Tyche laid her head back and closed her eyes, but the image of the gods, their faces contorted in rage, continued to haunt her. Terror threaded through her veins. Would they unleash a plague on the village and turn her friends into victims of their rage, or send monstrous creatures to ravage the land, leaving a trail of destruction in their wake?

A tremor ran through her. The gods, in their cruelty, would undoubtedly use her sorrow against her, unleashing those horrors upon the people she sought to protect. The thought settled on her soul, unbearable and suffocating.

"Don't worry, Mother Tyche."

Dora's hands rested on Tyche's brow. She stroked Tyche's hair and hummed a soft, melodic tune—a lullaby, the hymn of the stars, that a child of the gods could understand. Tyche stared at Dora as the notes rose to the barn's rafters, and a question took shape in her mind. *Whose daughter are you?* The power flowing from her touch was no mortal skill but the gift of a goddess. Tyche longed to understand, yet the words lodged in the base of her throat. Perhaps Lep knew and could shed light on the mystery, but right now, she needed to mend.

Yet even Dora's melody couldn't mask the tremors wracking Tyche's body. The mysterious sickness, which had subsided after Dora's touch days before, had returned with a vengeance. Despair whispered persistent doubts in Tyche's ear. Had she doomed them all? Were the gods already on their way, bringing fire and destruction?

The ancient melody seemed to weave its way through her troubled mind, but the pain chewed on her bones like a wolf feasting on its prey. It was a familiar pain, the same grip of dread that always came with the nightmares of the Nekrochim. Was this Ikelos' doing, then? Was he somehow responsible for the resurgence of her illness and the terrifying visions that plagued her?

A hush fell over the barn as Dora continued to sing. The villagers' murmurs grew silent, and they tilted their ears to the melody. Even the wind seemed to hold its breath. A radiant energy emanated from Dora and drove out the shadows clinging to the barn. But the light couldn't penetrate the darkness that clouded Tyche's heart. She knew the gods' wrath would not be so easily appeased.

A surge of power flowed through her. The child was not a simple village girl. There was something about her, something divine.

"Everyone out. Now." Lep commanded. "Tyche needs time to recover."

A fragile sense of renewal clung to Tyche as the evening deepened. But a hushed summons snaked through the village to convene in the plateia, interrupting her respite. Rather than the usual bustle, tonight an eerie silence clung to Pikerni. The houses seemed to huddle together for warmth, their windows dark and lifeless.

Tyche slumped against the stone wall outside the lesche. Lep's arm supported her as she addressed the villagers. Her hoarse whisper grated against the cobblestones. "The gods are angry," she warned. "They will unleash their wrath upon us. I'm so sorry. This is my fault. But we must prepare."

She spoke of the potential threats—earthquakes, floods, and plagues—but it was the mention of monstrous creatures that sent shivers down the spines of the villagers.

Her head spun, and she gripped Lep's arm. He drew her next to him. "Easy, woman. Save your strength."

A murmur of apprehension rippled through the crowd. "What do you mean?" Christos cradled his wounded arm. "What kind of monstrous creatures are we talking about?"

"They may unleash abominations born of their rage," Tyche warned. She turned away, a wet, raspy cough escaping her lips. "Monsters from our worst nightmares."

Kaliope gasped. "The Chimera?" she whispered. "Or something even worse?" She pulled her daughter closer as her protective instincts kicked in.

Tyche's face paled, and she swallowed hard, the word catching in her throat. "Worse," she gasped.

The villagers talked among themselves and exchanged anxious glances. No one dared to speak. The soft rustle of the wind and the distant bleating of a goat warbled over them.

Tyche's gaze swept over the crowd. "First, we must learn to fight."

Training began for the imminent conflict, though the villagers' maneuvers were clumsy with fear. The wind seemed to carry their desperation, as if it were seeking to summon a powerful ally. In a blaze of light, Apollo appeared among them. Gasps and whispers rippled through the crowd when the god walked in their midst, and a cautious confidence bloomed in his wake. He offered encouraging words and assisted them with drills and the harvest, his divine strength a comforting consolation to their fears.

Lep seemed to watch his father's every move. Tyche knew his heart was burdened with concern for the villagers. He wondered aloud if Apollo's presence was enough to shield them from the coming storm and what his role would be in the battles to come. Tyche had no answers, but whatever role Lep and his father played, it would be a welcome one.

Apollo eased the villagers' apprehension and smiled. "Have faith," he said. "I am here to help you. Know this. The gods' decree will be a difficult trial, but you will endure." With increased determination, the people continued to practice with sharpened spears and improvised weapons.

But as the days passed, Tyche's conviction wavered. The strange affliction consumed her, and a coldness gripped her bones despite the warm days. Her skin prickled with a clammy cold, while a persistent cough tore at her chest. Her eyes dulled and glazed over.

Ikelos had not returned. Was he in danger?

Where are you?

The villagers watched with growing concern as Tyche's strength faded.

"Tyche, you look pale. Your illness creeps, and I do not know how to help you." Lep held her by the shoulders.

"I'm fine," she insisted. "We must be ready. They're coming."

But even as she spoke, fear tore at her stomach. This unnatural disease drained her of her power. A deep ache wrapped her heart. The gods, she knew, inflicted these sufferings on mortals with terrifying ease. Plagues, famines, illnesses—all instruments of divine punishment. And now, the same pain tore at her that she'd inflicted on countless others.

A snake of dread coiled around her chest and squeezed. The memory of the gods' scorn, the image of her dead children. Was she strong enough to face Olympus and survive this wretched malady? Could she protect the people she had come to love, and what of Ikelos?

Her gaze fell on Dora, the little girl she had saved from the spring so long ago. Dora, the same child who had also rescued her. It was for this she fought. For this she would lay down her life to protect.

The fear continued to strangle her even as a spark of rebellion ignited within her. She would not succumb. She would fight. For the children and her people. For Ikelos and Lep. For the future.

Before the storm, courage was discovered in vulnerability's heart, forged by mortal love's flame. For in divinity's shadow, human compassion anchors the soul. Even a goddess knows the sanctuary of the hearth is a fragile ember before the gods' fiery descent.

18

HUMAN COMPASSION
ANCHORS THE SOUL

The scorching grip of fever burned through Tyche's body, and she shivered despite the woolen wraps the village women had provided. She sat huddled in the center of the village square, the somber murmurs of the villagers a distant drone. The sharp edges of their whispered words and averted glances raked fresh scars of guilt across her skin.

The bitter taste of terror coated Tyche's tongue. Then, a touch, warm and grounding, broke through the haze, and Lep knelt before her. "Your fever still rages. My cottage is a short distance from here, and I have medications that will ease your suffering. Your sickness is unnatural, unlike anything I have encountered before."

Tyche's lips trembled. "The village," she croaked. "What of them? The preparations."

Lep placed a comforting hand on her arm. "The villagers are capable, Tyche. They will continue without you. Besides," he added, "you need time to mend. And..." he hesitated, "I want to care for you. Away from the watchful eyes of the villagers and the burden of their anxieties. I wish to give you a moment of peace."

Tyche focused her eyes on his and admired the brilliance of the sun in them. Warm. Tender.

She turned her face to the sky and listened as the trees overhead rustled in the breeze, but their melody did little to silence her growing anxiety.

At the edge of the village, Christos mucked the stalls in the barn. Even from this distance, Tyche studied the play of his muscles as he labored on the task that should have been hers. Then, her attention snagged on a pile of roughly whittled branches leaning against the barn wall, alongside a few worn bows and arrows. *Good. They are preparing with what they have.*

Groups of people rushed back and forth, some carrying large woven baskets filled with fist-sized rocks. Children gathered more stones from the edges of the square, placing them in smaller pouches. The plateia vibrated with the clang of men sparring with their wooden practice swords while mothers and grandmothers were in the gardens, harvesting what they could. Some of the younger women, strong of body, trained with the men.

They have divided themselves, as they should.

Christos paused in his work, and his eyes met hers. She lifted her hand in greeting, and he nodded. He patted Kid and hung up his rake, then hastened across the square toward her with a waterskin in his hand.

"Christos," she said, "you shouldn't be doing my chores."

The old man bent and lifted the water to her mouth. "It's the least I can do. We all must help each other now."

Tyche sipped from the offered skin and glanced toward the barn. "Those branches leaning against the wall—are those the spears you're making?"

Christos smiled. "We've cut straight branches from the trees in the forest and sharpened them as best we could. And we've repaired any old bows and arrows we could find. They are stored within the barn."

Lep glanced in that direction. "Do you think it will be enough?"

Christos pinched his shoulders together in a shrug of uncertainty.

"How goes the grain harvest? Are the fields yielding enough in advance of the battle?" Lep asked.

"The men gather what they can. It's not a full harvest but enough to store for a time. Tryfonas and Panos have been a great help, and your father, Apollo, has been assisting the men in the fields as well."

Lep's expression tightened, and a flash of bitterness crossed his features at the mention of his father.

Tyche scolded him at his downturned mouth. "Lep, we need all the help we can get. We should be grateful for any assistance offered, especially from family."

She understood his resentment. Lep had confided in her during her fevered stay at his cottage, of Apollo's cold departure, leaving his mortal mother to die in childbirth. He had been born of fire and rescued by Apollo's knife in a brutal beginning. *But with war looming, now is not the time to allow such wounds to fester.*

A hint of shame colored Lep's cheeks. "You are right. My apologies, Christos."

Tyche turned to the mutterings of the women and waved to them. "The vegetable gardens and the fruit trees," she called. "Have you been able to gather anything?"

Dimitra and the others hurried to the plateia. "We've been in the gardens and collected all the ripened produce. We've stored as much as we can. The springhouse is filling quickly."

"We're preparing for the worst," Kalliope added, "but praying to the gods for the best."

Tyche smiled at their dirt-streaked hands. "My, my. You look like you've been wrestling with the earth itself. You're a sight to behold." A sudden coughing fit wracked her body, forcing her to pause. "But thank you," she gasped, "for your tireless efforts."

Lep turned to the women. "I intend to take Tyche to my cottage. Her fever is worsening, and I have remedies there that might ease her pain. I also have stores of medicinal herbs should the gods attack."

"That sounds wise, Lep," Melina said, nodding. "We'll continue our work here. Send word if you require anything."

"We will," Lep assured them. "I admire you all for your contributions. We must keep our minds to the tasks."

Tyche leaned back as the villagers spoke, their voices a comforting murmur. Even in the face of danger, the community remained steadfast. It gave her a sliver of hope amid the turmoil.

Lep pulled Tyche to her feet, while Dimitra and Kalliope clucked with concern as they steadied her.

"There you go," Dimitra murmured. "Easy now. Don't worry for your billy. We'll keep him safe."

Tyche leaned on Lep and inhaled a shaky breath. "I need a way to travel, but I don't want to be carried like a child." She quirked her brow at the healer, then looked around at the fallen branches. "We can build a litter."

Lep gestured to Christos and Tryfonas. "We will need sturdy branches and strong rope. Can you gather what we need?"

Christos stepped toward the edge of the square, where a scattering of fallen branches lay in the undergrowth. He selected sturdy limbs, snapping off smaller twigs and clearing away the debris, while Tryfonas rushed to fetch rope from the barn.

Tyche reached for a cord and attempted to pull it taut, but her hands held no strength. The earth spun, and she stumbled, catching herself on a nearby tree. Frustration and a sense of helplessness overwhelmed her. The men should be readying for war, not building a litter for her.

I should be leading them *instead of slowing them down. How can I fight a battle in this condition?*

Guilt washed over her to know she was a burden to the people she must protect.

I must regain my strength so I can ensure these villagers are ready for what lies ahead.

As if he'd read her thoughts, Lep guided her toward a shaded spot under a sprawling tree. "Let us handle this."

Tyche reluctantly allowed herself to be seated, her gaze following the men as they lashed the branches together.

Dimitra hurried toward her house and returned moments later with an assortment of soft furs and thick woven mats. When the litter was completed, she layered the matting inside the makeshift frame, then added the pelts on top, creating a comfortable and sturdy base.

"There," Lep said, "a litter fit for a goddess." He gestured toward the furs. "Now, if you would allow us?"

Lep and Christos helped Tyche on the litter with gentle hands and lifted her onto the furs. They arranged the blankets around her to keep her warm.

With a nod from Christos, Lep gave Tyche a final, reassuring glance and grasped the ropes. For a heartbeat, he paused, his gaze focused on the path ahead, then he braced his feet, settling into a firm stance, and took a deep breath. With a surprising strength that belied his lean frame, Lep pulled the harness taut and drove up the gentle incline.

Tyche held her breath as he strained, his muscles rippling beneath his tunic. She had never noticed the power in his movements before, the way his shoulders broadened and contracted with each step, the corded strength in his thighs.

As she settled into their journey, a biting wind tore through the trees and whipped Tyche's hair across her face, nearly sending the litter careening off the path. Lep's muscles bunched as he fought to maintain his grip. The litter lurched violently, slamming Tyche's body against the side. She yelped and dug her fingers into the fur.

Is this a sign? A warning?

Lep paused his stride and glanced back at Tyche. "Are you alright?" He stopped to adjust the blankets around her and tightened a leather strap on the side of the litter. "A passing gust. Nothing more. We shall be at the cottage soon." After looking around the eerily calm forest, its last sigh vanished, he continued on.

"The wildflowers are particularly vibrant this year," Lep remarked, his voice steady despite the effort. "See how the poppies bleed into the bluebells? It is quite breathtaking."

He's trying to act as if nothing is wrong, Tyche realized, *as if the gods' attack isn't imminent.* She knew he desired to shield her from the fear squeezing her chest, but the unnatural stillness of the forest, the hush that preceded a storm, amplified her panic. Still, she nodded, her gaze on his back, but her mind far from the wildflowers. To quiet the unsettling thoughts about what lay ahead, she forced herself to focus on Lep, to remember the taste of him, the sweet, earthy tang of his lips against hers. The welcoming sun of his eyes seemed to pierce into her soul, to read her thoughts before she even spoke them. Almost involuntarily, she compared him to Ikelos. Nightmare's dark intensity and brooding silence seemed a world apart from Lep's quiet strength and gentle humor. Ikelos was shadow, and Lep, the warm sunlight.

"The birds are migrating early," Lep hummed. "I wonder if they sense the change in the air."

Tyche stiffened at the thought of birds as a harbinger of death. No, she could not go there. Instead, she allowed her thoughts to drift back to the kiss she had shared with the healer, the way his hands had cupped her face, the tenderness in his touch. She remembered the warmth of his embrace and the feeling of safety it offered, so different from Ikelos.

"The path is a bit steeper here," Lep warned. "But it levels out soon."

Tyche closed her eyes and focused on the comforting cadence of his footsteps. She thought of Ikelos again, the way he had looked at her, the intensity in his gaze. She wondered if he thought of her now, if he sensed the same degree of dread she did.

The healer's steady drone pushed back her anxiety with a litany of ordinary things in a deliberate attempt to distract her from the impending tempest. Tyche blinked and pulled herself from her ruminations. She was caught between two worlds, two loves, two destinies.

Lep pulled the litter to a stop, and Tyche looked around in confusion. Tall grasses and wildflowers swayed lazily in the breeze around them. *This place,* a flicker of recognition stirring, *seems familiar.* She vaguely remembered a vast panorama, but the details were hazy, lost in the fog of her illness. But the cottage remained hidden.

"We're here?" she asked.

The air shimmered, and the ground beneath the wildflowers seemed to fold and rise, molding itself into the shape of the cottage. Thick vines with blood-red blossoms draped over the stone walls, blurring the lines between the cottage and the wild growth beneath it. A kernel of familiarity nestled in her memory as they approached. This was where Lep had stolen his first kiss, a tentative, almost reverent touch, believing her to be asleep. She had been awake, of course, her heart pounding in her chest as a burgeoning warmth had spread through her.

Lep pulled the litter to a stop before the cottage's weathered wooden door. "We have arrived," he announced. "A few more steps, and you will be inside, warm and safe."

Safe and warm, but for how long? Tyche shivered and nestled deeper into the confines of the litter. Well, she could not change the future, only the present, so she inclined her head and studied the cottage, but her mind was lost in a sea of recollections. She remembered the way Lep's touch had felt, the unexpected tenderness in his reserved demeanor—the way he had looked at her then, his eyes filled with a quiet adoration that had taken her breath away.

"The air is cooler here," Lep observed, his words pulling her back to the present. "I have spoken with Apollo, and the gods are still reeling from what happened before Hermes helped you escape Olympus again. He thinks we have a week to prepare to get you well enough so you will be ready for the conflict."

Tyche barely registered his words. The memory of their kiss consumed her thoughts. She wondered if he remembered it as vividly as she did or if he ever compared her to others he had courted. *Perhaps the kiss was simply a kindness, a gesture of comfort in a moment of fear?* A shudder of doubt brushed against her unexpected joy.

He's so different from Ikelos, she thought, her mind drifting to the dark god of Dreams. *Ikelos is a tumultuous whirlwind of passion and darkness. Lep is a gentle stream, a comforting warmth.* She considered Ikelos' intense gaze, laying bare her deepest desires. She thought of Lep's quiet strength and the way it offered a sense of security. *The unknown danger or the familiar comfort?* The stinging pain of uncertainty settled in her heart.

Oblivious to her inner turmoil, Lep continued his gentle monologue. Tyche, however, was lost in her own world, her mind a whirlwind of memories, desires, and the chilling certainty of war. *How soon?* she pondered, her gaze flickering across the distant hills that led to Pikerni. *How soon will they come?* She nodded absently as Lep mentioned the spring flowers.

But her thoughts were already consumed by the villagers' preparations, the sharpening of spears, and the hasty fortifications. *Are we ready? Can we withstand the gods' rage?* She glanced at Lep's serene face. *He trusts me. They all trust me.* Doubt challenged the precious moment of calm. *But trust could be dangerous, especially when built on the eve of battle.* She forced a smile as he turned to her with a lopsided grin, pointing out a bird perched on the windowsill. *How many will fall? How many will pay the price for my willfulness?*

A wave of weariness slammed through Tyche, and with a sigh, she shifted on the litter and raised her arms toward Lep.

"I am sure you are exhausted," he said, and lifted her from the litter.

His strong arms supported her as she took a few unsteady steps across the threshold and into the cottage. Lep guided her toward the downy mattress near the hearth. As if to mock her, the fire crackled merrily, casting welcoming light across the room. She breathed in the aroma of Lep's healing balms and smiled at his dedication to the earth's healing powers.

Then, her tranquility shattered in a surge of horror. *Many will die.* She closed her eyes, fighting back a tremor. *But I need this. I need this moment to recharge, to gather strength for what's to come.* The warmth of the fire eased the chill that had settled in her bones. *I must be ready. For them. For my daughter. And for Lep.* When she took a deep breath, the scent of chamomile and lavender filled her lungs, the essence of the precious life she fought to protect.

Her eyes settled on the carved snakes adorning the bedposts, recalling the story Lep had shared about the Gorgon. The blood still coursed through his veins, granting him the power to mend flesh and bone with a touch. She knew the serpents symbolized Medusa's blood, the duality within him—healer and monster, gift and burden.

Lep glanced at her, and a warm smile crinkled the corners of his eyes. "Welcome back." He sat beside her and touched her forehead. "How do you fare?"

Tyche groaned and attempted to sit up, but Lep pushed her back down. "Easy," he said. "Conserve your strength."

Lep rose and crossed to his work area at the far end of the room. Tyche's nose twitched as she caught the pungent scent of valerian and wormwood and a sharper, more acrid note she didn't recognize. She watched him work at the wooden table laden with dried herbs and tools. She knew this was Lep's *ergasterion*, the area where he practiced his strange form of earth magic, concocting remedies from the wisdom of the earth.

Tyche observed Lep stir a potion in a small clay pot, then check the fire, adding a few more logs to keep the embers glowing. Then, he disappeared out the door, leaving Tyche alone with her fears. *Tomorrow.* A shiver coursed up her spine. *Tomorrow, we face the dawn.*

Vulnerability is a forge where strength is tempered to Stygian steel, and even a goddess can discover her power in the earth. For in the face of divine judgment, it is the resilience of love that shields and the unyielding spirit of those who refuse to be broken. And in the moment the hammer fell silent and the weapons gleamed, a rebellion was born against the gathering darkness.

19

Hope Forged in the Stygian Steel

Tyche's gaze drifted to the empty doorway where Lep had disappeared. *Calm yourself, Tyche. He won't abandon you.* The thought was a small reassurance. She remembered the strength in his arms and the steadiness of his presence during the wolf attack. Yet, even his strength couldn't hold back what was to come. A moment later, she heard the soft crunch of footsteps at the cottage door, and Lep returned, carrying a crusty loaf of bread under his arm.

"Dimitra insisted I bring this," he said, a mischievous glint in his eyes. "She said you needed to eat something more than herbs." He placed the bread on a wooden board beside the hearth.

"She shouldn't have bothered," she murmured, though her stomach growled at the thought.

"Don't be ridiculous—it's a bit of bread. Besides," he teased, "I wouldn't want her to accuse me of starving you."

Lep stepped to a bubbling pot suspended in the hearth. "I've prepared lentil soup," he said, ladling the steaming brew into a clay bowl. Then he poured a cup of kykeon, a barley and herb drink that shimmered in the firelight.

The healer returned to the table and ground dried leaves in a small mortar. Tyche watched, her brow furrowed in apprehension.

"These will ease your fever," Lep murmured. "Willow bark," he explained, holding up crumbled leaves, "is known to ease infections." He added feverfew, its sharp scent hovering in the room.

Tyche's eyes widened at the unfamiliar, bitter scent. She had never known such earthly smells to heal. "Is that how mortals mend?" she asked with a hint of wonder.

"Indeed," Lep replied, "though I have used willow bark on you before, when your fever was at its worst, but you were unconscious then."

He shifted to another section of the table, where dried roots and berries lay spread out. "And this," he said, measuring comfrey, "will strengthen you." He held up the root for Tyche to see. "Comfrey repairs flesh and bones," he explained, "and fortifies your strength." He mixed it with elderberries. "And these stave off infection."

Tyche reached out a hesitant hand to touch the comfrey root. "Such earthly things." She watched him add honey to counter the bitter taste of the herbs. "Do mortals find strength in such potions?"

"They do," Lep confirmed. "Comfrey has aided in your wounds' healing, though you were unaware. And the honey provides a needed energy boost, especially when you are so weak."

He returned to the hearth and retrieved a clay pot filled with a dark, oily substance. "This is plantain and chickweed," he stated, holding it for her to see. "It will soothe your aches and pains. I'll apply it to your forehead and chest."

Tyche's breath hitched as he approached. The ointment smelled of the earth, unlike anything she had experienced. "Is this how mortals touch the divine?" She closed her eyes as he applied the concoction, its cooling sensation spreading across her skin. The poultice provided a moment's respite, but Tyche knew the true illness, the one that tormented her, would remain untouched.

"It is how mortals find comfort," Lep said. "The coolness of the plantain will lessen your pain and fever."

He rose from the bed and wiped his hands on a cloth, then went to the hearth to retrieve the lentil soup and kykeon. He returned to Tyche and sat beside her. "First, food," he said. "Then, the pharmakon."

"Lep," Tyche whispered, "what if... what if we can't stop the gods? What if they take my baby? What if they destroy everything?" Her hand settled over her bulge. "Should I have given her to them? Should I have spared everyone this?"

Lep cradled her chin in his palm. "No, Tyche. You made the right choice," he said. "They demanded your child out of fear, not love. Fear of what she might become. They would have used the child and twisted her to their own ends."

He leaned closer and covered her hand with his. "We will protect the village, no matter what. Apollo is here, and Hermes has shown you kindness. They may be Olympians, but they are not without compassion. So we will appeal to that and fight for what is just."

"But they are *Olympians*, Lep." Tyche's eyes filled with tears. "They are powerful. They are gods."

Lep squeezed her shoulder. "And we are not without our own power, Tyche," he reminded her. "Remember who you are—the goddess of Fortune and daughter of Oceanus, the Titan god of the Primordial Waters. I am Apollo's son, my own blood divine. And don't forget, they are not *just* Olympians. Apollo has Titan lineage, as does Hermes. This is not simply Olympians against mortals. It is a conflict where the blood of the primordial gods runs on both sides—where even those who call themselves Olympians have ancient roots.

He paused, the light of his eyes scorching hers. "I made my choice. I left the world of the gods to live among mortals. I chose this life and this village. I choose *you*. I will not abandon you now, not when I am needed. Sometimes, choices are difficult, but we must stand by them, especially when they are right."

"But what if we fail?" Tyche asked. "What if we lose everything?"

Lep's expression softened with a fierce tenderness. "Then we'll see this through. Let us not surrender to despair. We will fight until the very end, and even then, hope will remain."

He leaned closer and rested his brow against hers. "This darkness is not unknown to us. We have survived so far and will withstand whatever crosses our path. I promise you."

The warmth of the kykeon and the soothing herbs weaved their magic, easing Tyche's fevered mind and loosening the knots of tension in her body. Her breath came easier, her chest no longer tightened by the lingering cough. A calming warmth spread through her limbs in harmony with the peaceful intimacy of the cottage.

Lep drew closer and traced the curve of her cheek. His honeyed eyes, bright with sunshine, bore a depth of tenderness that set her heart ablaze. Then he leaned in, and their breaths mingled before he brushed his lips against hers.

The afternoon drifted in a current of whispered promises. His lips found hers again, urgent and lingering, tasting of unspoken dreams.

Tyche's fingers tangled in the dark strands of his hair in a desperate hold against the approaching dread. The fear and uncertainty that had plagued her refused to fade but became a dark pulse beneath their affection.

Lep cradled her pregnant belly, his touch reverent, almost worshipful. He lowered his head, pressing a soft kiss to the baby's swell, his lips lingering for a moment against her taut skin. The warmth of his mouth sent a shiver of joy through her body. Her gaze locked with his, and she recognized the shape of her own soul. She settled back with a sigh of gratitude, caught in the sensation of perfect completion.

In the whispered hours, Tyche and Lep laid bare their souls, their quiet murmurs a comfort to the growing disquiet. They spoke of the nightmares that haunted them, of the visions of ruin, and of the impossible choices ahead. A defiant spark against the gathering gloom, their love became their refuge. They held each other and found succor in their joined hands and synchronized hearts.

Through the cottage windows, twilight deepened, stretching shadows across the room that pressed a sense of urgency upon them. The village called—the coming battle a threatening gloom. With an anxious look, they prepared to depart, their hearts aching at the loss of their sanctuary, but they steeled themselves for what lay ahead.

Lep helped Tyche to her feet, guiding her to a patch of grass outside the cottage. "Rest here for a moment," he said. "I'll gather the remaining remedies."

Tyche settled onto the emerald swath, and the cool of the earth grounded her. Lep disappeared into the cottage to return moments later with an armful of dried herbs, vials, and small pots. He packed the items into leather pouches and a small wooden box.

A childlike impulse seized Tyche as she leaned to pluck a few blood-red poppies blooming nearby. She began to weave a garland with clumsy but determined fingers. She hummed a simple melody her mother used to sing to temper her childish fear when the battle between the Titans and the Olympians raged.

As she finished braiding her crown, Lep emerged from the cottage, laden with the last of his supplies, and placed them carefully on the litter before turning to Tyche with a soft, tender gaze. He helped her to her feet and embraced her in the circle of his arms.

Pausing near the cottage door to look over the valley below, Tyche noticed a figure approaching—a man who trudged his way up the steep hill. The stranger adjusted the pack on his back as he leaned into the incline. The glint of metal tools peeked from its worn edges. A coldness settled in Tyche's stomach. The unexpected arrival of the man and the threat of the Olympians tightened the knot of fear in her chest.

Lep pushed Tyche behind him to position himself between her and the approaching figure. "Who are you, stranger? And what brings you to my cottage?"

The man stopped a short distance from them. His gaze swept over the landscape, then settled on Tyche. "I have traveled far to speak with the goddess of Fortune," he replied. "I heard whispers on the wind, and I followed their call. I bring the skill of my hands and the knowledge of the forge."

Tyche leaned out from behind Lep. "Why have you come to speak to *me*?" she asked. "We are secluded here, not accustomed to visitors."

"The winds carry many things." The man's gaze shifted to the horizon. "News, rumors, and the whispers of those in need. Hermes sent a missive, and I have come in response."

"Hermes?" Tyche's brows raised in surprise.

The stranger dipped his chin. "He said you would require my services."

Tyche and Lep exchanged a look. "Very well," Tyche said, "but inside. We can speak more freely. If you were sent by Hermes, then I trust your intentions are good."

They entered the cottage, where the aroma of herbs and stew wafted toward the ceiling. Lep gestured to the table, and they all took seats.

"What are you offering?" Lep inquired with an air of mistrust.

"The skill of my hands and the knowledge of the forge," the man replied.

"You speak in riddles. Who are you?" Tyche pressed.

The man paused as his gaze swept over them. "You seek aid from the forge, and I am one who has long tended its fires, for I am Brontes, whose hands have shaped the metal of the gods."

A flicker of recognition crossed Tyche's face. *The Thunderer—maker of Zeus' own thunderbolts.* "Brontes, the cyclops? Did Hermes send you?" Tyche's brow furrowed.

"Yes, as I have said." Brontes' words sang from his lips. "He sent word with Pegasus. The Titans are not blind to your plight, Tyche. We see what the Olympians do."

"What do you mean?" Tyche asked.

"The Titanomachy." The flames from the hearth reflected in the depths of Brontes' ancient eyes. "The battle that shaped the cosmos. The war that tore the heavens asunder, leaving scars that still ache, even now, in the bones of the earth. Hermes believes the Titans must unite around you in this time of need and stand against the headstrong Olympians, who would repeat the errors of their fathers and reignite the old conflict."

Tyche's mind raced. "They fear my child. I fled Olympus to protect her and give her a chance at life. And then I found love here, a true life, not the prison I knew."

Lep reached for her hand across the table. "We will stand against them," he said, "as we always have."

"The Olympians would have me return to be their pawn." Tyche clenched her teeth. "But I cannot, I will not, I *refuse*. I have found a life worth living—a people worth protecting—and I will defend them with all my strength."

A deep crease on Brontes' forehead twitched as he spoke of Olympus' folly. "The Titans remember what it is to be cast aside, to be deemed a threat for simply existing. We will not allow the Olympians to repeat their crimes or to inflict such wounds again."

"So you will help us?" Lep leaned forward and put his elbows on the table.

"I will forge the weapons you require." The cyclops' eyes of fiery steel grazed the room and lingered on the hearth with a calculating intensity. "And I will lend my strength to your cause, to stand against the tyranny of those who would claim dominion over us all, even if they call themselves gods."

A bloom of hope unfurled in Tyche's heart. "Your support is our salvation, Brontes."

"This space," he motioned to the fire pit, "will suffice."

The stone beneath Brontes' feet liquefied, and the earth bound him to its strength as it pulsed in recognition of its own. A tremor ran through his bent frame while power surged from the ground and flooded his veins. His body uncoiled with unnatural speed, the illusion of age shedding away. His skin darkened, and coarse hair sprouted across his bulging limbs. Then, the deep crease across his forehead split, the skin receding like the petals of a grotesque flower to unleash a single, cyclopean eye. Molten flames erupted from its pupil, scouring the hearth before him. The stones seared white-hot as the hearth buckled, consumed by the earth's power, and transformed into Brontes' primordial forge.

"The earth provides," Brontes rumbled, "and the forge answers."

"So it does." A knowing smile touched Tyche's lips as she regarded the cyclops. *A power we both understand,* she thought, *the power of our ancestors.*

Brontes pulled some ingots from his pack and held them out in his hand. "These are gifts from the earth and the depths. They were forged in the heart of volcanoes and quenched in the waters of the Styx. They are Stygian iron, imbued with the strength of the Titans and the blessing of your sister. They will hold an edge that no mortal steel can match and strike with the force of divine retribution."

Tyche touched one of the ingots in his palm, its smooth surface cool under her fingers despite the inner fire that shimmered within. "Stygian iron quenched in the waters of grief. You bring weapons, and with them, the strength of the Titans."

"What do you need from us?" Lep asked.

"Strength." Brontes' stare locked with the healer's. "And courage. The forge can create the weapons, but it is you who must wield them."

The cyclops' massive eye slid to Tyche. "And you, goddess. Your power will be needed to imbue these weapons with the blessing of fortune and guide their path to victory."

Confidence surged through Tyche and quenched the last of her fear. She glanced at Lep, then Brontes, with sharp, clear eyes. "Then let us begin," she said. "Beyond weapons, let us forge hope."

Brontes gestured toward the furnace. "The ingots must be heated, and the bellows worked with strength and rhythm." He nodded at Lep. "You have the strength, son of Apollo. Can you feel the sun's fire in your blood?"

Lep stepped forward and grasped the handle of the bellows, his muscles coiling and bunching as he pumped. The flames in the forge roared and licked at the ingots with hungry tongues.

The hint of a smile played on Brontes' lips. "Good," he said. "Now, goddess," he turned to Tyche, "your touch is needed. The weapons must be blessed with fortune, that they may strike true."

Tyche approached the forge and brushed back her hair as the heat radiated against her skin. She closed her eyes, focusing her will, and summoned the fading strength of her power. A faint light flowed from her fingertips, bathing the ingots in a warm glow.

"These weapons will devour with the might of Styx' dark waters," she murmured. "They'll be guided by the hand of fate to shield the village and its children from the gods' wrath." The golden light intensified, leaving the ingots shimmering with a faint, otherworldly radiance.

Brontes' single eye blinked with approval. "The blessing is given," he said. "Now, the work of the blacksmith can begin."

Tyche's hands itched for the forge as Brontes seized a pair of tongs and yanked a glowing ingot from the flames. The anvil met white-hot metal with a hiss, and the cyclops swung the Ironheart. The cottage shuddered with the rhythmic clang as sparks erupted in a constellation of fire. Tyche glanced at Lep, whose eyes burned with the splinters of the sun.

Brontes swiped a hairy arm across his dripping forehead, mallet in hand. His massive eye swiveled toward Tyche, then Lep, and he reared back and brought the hammer down on the hot iron with a clang. Lep pumped the bellows, urging the flames to leap like hungry beasts, and Tyche held her breath, watching as the shape of their future solidified on the anvil. Then, the final strike rang out with a victorious clang, proclaiming the birth of their rebellion.

Tyche ran a reverent hand along the gleaming weapons laid out on the table. The spears' points shimmered like captured starlight, and the swords' edges seemed to drink in the shadows. She traced the metal tips of the arrows nestled in their quivers, caressing their sharpened teeth ready to tear the enemy.

With the weapons complete, Lep and Brontes hoisted them onto the waiting trestle outside.

"Brontes, we must depart for the village," Tyche said. "Would that I could bestow upon you blessings worthy of your aid, but my strength wanes."

The cyclops' gaze, ancient as the dawn of creation, lingered on Tyche, assessing her with an age-old understanding. "The Olympians will not yield easily. But neither will we. Bear in mind, goddess, the true might of the Titans. It is not just power. It is the unyielding spirit of our resilience. Our refusal to be broken. That is our true might." He paused, and his great eye narrowed. "I will remain here, at the forge within the cottage. Should you need me, call upon the primordial fire, and I will answer."

"Let us make haste," Tyche urged, turning to Lep. "To the village."

Lep settled her amid the herbs and steel—a cradle of life within the shade of death.

Tyche's gaze flickered back to Brontes, whose dark silhouette lingered in the cottage's doorway. A tear of farewell traced her cheek. Her heart beating with dread and hope, they set out on the road, village-bound.

Though the gods let loose their ruin, the earth concedes to the fist of mortal rebellion. A song of starlight weaves through the storm's heart, and a goddess' resolve stands as a fragile shield. For it is in the face of divine wrath that the true measure of courage is revealed.

20

THE FIST OF MORTAL REBELLION

The litter lurched forward as Tyche and Lep descended the hill. Although Lep's pharmakon eased the symptoms of her strange affliction, a tangle of anxiety remained, fueling her worry about the sickness' return. She swallowed the knot of dread that tightened in her throat as she regarded Brontes' fading silhouette. She had urged haste, and now, with every jostling step, the safety of Lep's cottage receded as the danger of the village grew.

The hours dragged on, and Tyche cringed at Lep's ragged gasps and straining muscles as he pulled the litter down the steep path. No words passed between them, their descent bearing the import of their mission. Shadows of rocks and trees rose through the darkness as they hastened forward, forming monstrous shapes like those the gods intended to unleash on the village. Tyche's grip tightened on the mound of weapons surrounding her. Her fingers curled around the hilt of a Stygian blade, its weight pressed against her hand like a promise and a curse.

The villagers' fearful faces flashed in her mind, their hopes resting on her. Would she be enough? A cluster of flickering torches marked the village against the darkening sky. Soon, they entered the plateia, which hummed with tension. Then the voices stilled as the villagers turned to watch the litter's approach, their eyes drawn to the mound of Brontes' weapons. They drew around her in silence and inspected the treasure Tyche and Lep had brought them. She climbed from the platform and stood back, her heart pounding with relief when the apprehensive faces of the villagers gave way to enthusiasm.

Tyche sighed in satisfaction as she watched them handle the weapons. "Friends, your attention. We will meet in the lesche." Her command silenced the murmurs.

One by one, they stepped back from the litter and released the weapons they held, returning them to the mound. With Lep at her side, Tyche turned and led the way to the large wooden doors. The villagers followed behind, their murmurs and footsteps scraping across the cobblestones. Tyche flung open the doors, directing the people inside to settle on the benches around the tables.

"Christos, drinks for everyone," Tyche ordered. "Panos, light the torches. Tryfonas, add wood to the hearth."

Tyche stood before them as the lesche filled with the warm glow of firelight and the comforting aroma of barley. Lep stepped forward and placed a sword into Tyche's waiting hand. The torchlight shimmered along its blade and held captive the villagers' gaze.

"I thank you for allowing Lep the time to take me to his cottage, where his pharmakon eased the symptoms of my affliction. I don't know how long this first siege will last, but for now, we must prepare." She lifted the blade high, its steel reflecting the light. "You've seen the weapons forged with Stygian steel, my blessings bestowed upon them." Her level gaze scanned the crowd. "These are not just blades but points of reckoning forged by Brontes, a master smith of the Titan cyclopes. Hermes sent him to Lep's cottage to aid us against the Olympians." She raised the sword higher. "These weapons are born of volcanic fire and Styx' dark waters. They have been imbued with power, capable of harming even the gods."

Tyche stepped to the hearth and plunged the sword into the heart of the fire. The flames erupted as the crash of a hammer vibrated through the lesche. The fire writhed and knit into the shadowy image of the old man, Brontes, his grey eyes flickering in the firelight. Then, the crease on his forehead parted, and his massive eye swept over the crowd. Brontes' gaze met Tyche's, and he bowed his head in deference. Then his voice boomed through the lesche. "From forge to fight, we rise." The image flickered and vanished, leaving the sword glowing faintly in Tyche's hand.

A hush fell over the assembled villagers. In awe, they gawped at the cold hearth where Brontes' image had vanished.

Tryfonas spoke up, his eyes wide with wonder. "My lady, Tyche, may I hold the sword the cyclops forged?"

Tyche smiled warmly. "Of course, Tryfonas, but be careful. It's sharp." She handed him the sword, and he grasped it with reverence, testing its weight.

"It feels powerful," he whispered.

Dimitra spoke up as she stepped closer to Tyche. "What if we fail? What if we further anger the gods?"

Tyche's spine stiffened even as her gaze softened. "We will not fail," she declared. "These weapons are forged from the earth's heart and the Styx' depths. They will wound those who would harm us. But more than that, Dimitra, you are not alone. Although Brontes remains at the cottage, I will be here with you."

Christos' lips pressed into a rigid line, and he glanced at Dimitra. "We have faced hardship before. Do not fear."

"What about our children? What if they are harmed?" Kalliope shouted.

Tyche spotted Althea in the crowd and noticed Dora's absence. "Where's Dora?"

Althea replied with a mother's calm. "She is safe and asleep in her bed, my lady. I made sure of it."

Lep stepped forward. "And we will *keep* her safe," he stated, side-eyeing Tyche.

"We will protect them all," Tyche agreed.

Murmurs rippled through the crowd.

"These irons of war are our opposition." Tyche declared. "They are our assurance. They are the tools we will use to protect our home and our children."

Christos lifted his cup of barley drink, and others followed suit.

Lep's gaze swept the crowd. "Are we ready to defend our homes?"

"We will not cower." Tryfonas stood with his cup raised. "We will fight."

Tyche studied the boy's innocence. "Now, return to your homes. Rest. The morrow will test our resolve, and we must be ready."

The first sparks of dawn glistened over the valley when the villagers descended into the fields. The air, still cool from the night, vibrated with the urgency of their task. They wielded scythes, their honed edges glinting sharply in the soft light, and bent to the task of cutting the last of the barley stalks with desperate strokes. Sweat beaded on their foreheads and dripped into the dust that rose from the earth. Dimitra and Evy held open sack after sack and urged the others to fill them with grain. Once they had collected the last of the barley, the men hoisted the heavy bags onto their shoulders and hauled them to the barn.

The clang of stone against stone rumbled against the mountains' flesh as the sun climbed higher. Tyche regarded Apollo, who stood at the edge of town, his attention on the half-built barricades.

"Heave!" Christos grunted as the men's muscles strained against the boulder.

Tyche grimaced at the straining cords of their muscles as they struggled. The heavy stone shifted, groaning against the earth, and a collective sigh of relief spread through the men when it settled into place.

Tyche surveyed the assembled villagers in the square, the weapons laid out before her, dark and gleaming under the morning sun. Before she could speak, the village weavers rushed into the square, displaying their handiwork—woven reed targets, sturdy and tightly bound. Tyche's mind flashed to the misshapen basket the weavers had taught her to make, and she prayed the targets would be stronger than her basket had been.

She accepted one of the targets, then turned it in her hand and smiled. "Well done. These will prove useful for our training."

Then she motioned to the weapons. "We must learn to wield these. These blades, these spears, these arrows—they are our defense."

She turned to Christos. "Have Panos fetch the sackcloth bags from the barn. We will fill them with the leftover barley stalks for the *skiamachia* forms." She paused to consider the villagers. "These will be our training figures, representations of our enemies, where we will practice our strikes. Meet me in the cleared fields," she commanded, "where we will learn to fight."

Driven by Tyche's command, the villagers collected the sacks and woven targets. They streamed toward the cleared land, where the scarred earth would soon bear witness to their desperate preparations against the gods.

The field buzzed with anticipation as Tyche turned, her hand grasping the hilt of a long, dark sword that rested point-down in the packed earth beside her. With a fluid grace, she swept the blade upwards. A rippling darkness advanced along its honed edge, drinking the sun's light. A low hum vibrated across the field as she settled into a balanced stance and glared at the woven skiamachia, her enemy in practice. Tyche gripped the hilt tighter and advanced with the steel fang canted over her shoulder. A terrible cry exploded from her throat as she surged ahead, her arms a blur of power as she brought the sword around in a devastating sweep. The woven skiamachia shrieked when the blade tore through its packed barley heart.

Fortune favors the keen eye and the steady hand. Perhaps the currents of fate themselves guide my aim.

She stood among the shredded stalks, the sword still humming. "The gods will not yield, nor will they falter. Only through such decisive action will you survive their wrath. This I know." She hefted the weapon before them. "Remember, my friends, this is your survival. Let this lesson be written in your hearts."

Tyche planted the sword in the earth beside her and reached for her bow and quiver, resting against a nearby training post. She selected an arrow and nocked it to her bow. The cord thrummed as she drew it taut against her cheek. Then the arrow streaked across the field with lethal grace. The mournful groan of souls bound for Styx' shores hummed, then was struck silent by a sharp thud as it pierced the distant target dead center.

"Set aside your bows for now. We will practice together after I have demonstrated Bronte's weapons to you. So, grab one of the spears, and watch closely." Tyche passed Lep her bow and quiver and accepted the spear he offered.

"Your skill with the weapons is remarkable," Lep murmured.

She nodded and grinned. "It's called necessity, Lep, and perhaps a touch of my own nature. Fortune isn't always passive. Sometimes, you must be swift and decisive to seize it or protect it. And in the days following the fall of the Titans, it was wise to be able to stand your ground, so I learned to fight. My father saw to that."

Tyche hefted a spear, and its bronze tip gleamed, hinting at the volcanic fire that birthed it. "These weapons," she announced, her grip firm on the shaft, "carry a fragment of the earth's darkness, cooled in Styx' waters." With a swift thrust, she launched the javelin. A trail of viscous darkness clung to its flight and dissipated when the point slammed into the skiamachia with a muffled whump. "Observe how this energy clings to the enemy." Tyche paused and glanced at the villagers, then back at the spear vibrating in its mark. "It weakens what it strikes, drawing strength from primordial power. Now," Tyche announced, wiping her hands on her tunic, "some of you show me what you have learned."

Tryfonas nudged his brother and nodded toward his bow. "Pay attention, brother, while Tyche is here to help you. I will go practice my swordplay with Father."

Panos collected an arrow from his quiver and adjusted his grip on the bow with a frown of concentration. Tyche followed the arc of the boy's arrow, then stepped forward to demonstrate the proper form. She stood rigid and tilted the bow higher so the point of the shaft kissed the corner of her steady gaze, her draw hand a firm anchor against her cheekbone.

"Feel it in your back, not just your arm, Panos." She smiled at the boy and tapped her cheek. "The same point, every time." She eased the tension in her draw hand, the bowstring inching forward without a sound. "Hold the tension until the moment is right. Control is power."

Panos nodded. "Control is power." He peered at the distant target. "So, even when they move?"

Tyche's smile faded. "*Especially* when they move, Panos. Precision will be your shield."

"Did you train to be a warrior before you became a goddess?" Panos' wide eyes studied her face.

"Fortune favors those who are prepared. And in times past, even a daughter of Oceanus learned the value of defending herself." She winked at the boy. "The currents of fate are not always gentle."

As Tyche offered this final piece of guidance to Panos, the sharp clang of metal rang out across the valley. Flashing steel caught the sunlight as Christos and Tryfonas tested their sword strikes at the edge of the training grounds. With the pulse of the ongoing drills, Tyche turned her attention to the next demonstration.

"Lep," Tyche called, her attention focused on the targets. "Call your father. Ask him to demonstrate his skill."

The clang of practice swords faded, and the thud of distant arrows ceased as all eyes turned toward Lep. He nodded, a flicker of something unreadable in his expression, and turned on his heel. A moment stretched before Apollo stepped forward, his silver sling gleaming from his shoulder. He seized the single golden shaft from the quiver, then nocked and aimed it at a distant fallow deer grazing at the edge of the field.

Panos piped up, his brow furrowed with curiosity. "Lord Apollo," he asked, "why is there only one arrow in your sheaf?"

Apollo grinned, a flash of sunlight in his expression. "I need only the one, boy."

Before the villagers could register his words, Apollo's arm moved in a blur. Arrows, too swift for the eye to follow, streaked across the field, thudding into each of the targets with pinpoint accuracy. Then, with a fluid turn, he aimed once more at the distant deer. The golden arrow flew in a streak of light against the sky, and the deer fell dead.

Effortless. A prickle of envy stirred in Tyche's chest.

Apollo turned back to the astonished villagers, his eyes sparkling with a playful light. "You see? One is all I need."

"Women," Tyche shouted toward the village, "fetch the deer. Let us share a meal tonight, a moment to gather our strength and spirits before the darkness falls."

Tyche caught Lep's grimace at his father's casual display of skill. He turned away, his focus shifting to the soil beneath his feet. Her eyes widened as his hands glowed with a faint, earthy light, the luminescence flickering with what she thought might be frustration. He seemed to wrestle with the earth's elements and his attempts to bend them to his will. She gasped at the subtle vibration of the ground as he struggled against a force unseen to her.

Curious, Tyche approached him. The air around Lep thrummed with the energy of his effort. "What magic do you weave now, healer?" she asked, her fingers lightly touching his arm.

Lep glanced at her, resentment flickering in his eyes shadowed by strands of fallen hair. "What does it look like?" he retorted. "I'm learning how to use my elemental powers—to stir the earth under my command."

He turned back to his task. "See?"

Lep closed his eyes, his muscles bunching with the strain, the light in his hands intensifying. Then, shoots broke through the parched ground and advanced toward Tyche, their vines ending in succulent tubers. *Food or defense?* Her heart pounded at the unsettling sight.

"Stop, Lep! Save it for later." Tyche stepped back, her hands flying to her mouth at his power over the earth's elements. *We need that energy for the fight.* The grasping vines hovered in front of her and then retracted.

Apollo clapped Lep on the back. "You have your father's touch, son." His eyes sparkled with a fleeting tenderness.

A thin smile touched Tyche's mouth when she glimpsed the affection on Apollo's face. *Now is the time for it,* she thought, and turned her attention back to the training field. "Christos, your stance is too wide. Tryfonas, balance the sword's weight. Let it guide your strike. Panos, draw the string back. Further. Feel the tension."

She praised a well-placed shot and corrected a clumsy form, her instructions pushing the villagers to their limits. Children sent stones flying from their slings, the sharp snap of the leather slapping against their wrists. Tyche relaxed as renewed confidence sparked in her veins now that the promise of defense replaced the uncoordinated maneuvers.

Amid the clang of steel and the thud of stones, Tyche's gaze drifted upward to the edge of the square. There, within the flurry of activity, Dora remained calm, her demeanor unlike the villagers' tense rhythms. Tyche noticed a group of younger children gathered around the girl, their fingers clutching at her skirts. Dora patted the air, and the little ones sat around her in a semicircle. Then a soft melody drifted through the valley. Dora's voice, clear and pure, wove through the chaos, and the villagers' features lost their hard edges, replaced by a look of quiet peace. Even Christos paused, she noticed, his sword lowered as he listened.

Tyche's heart swelled with awe. The girl's melodies of power and strength, songs whispered by the stars themselves, braided themselves into their defiance.

There's a familiarity in her, something I should know, something I must know, yet it slips through my grasp like mist.

A tear carved a glistening line down Tyche's cheek as she regarded Dora, the village's wellspring of strength. Her powers had waned to a mere ember against the child's blazing presence. The creeping fear of failing when the villagers needed her most settled dark upon her heart.

Tyche smiled, her heart bursting with a bittersweet love. Dora was a force of light in the advancing storm. But Tyche understood that the gods had the power to destroy the child's tender spark. And not only her light, but that of all the children in Pikerni—they were all precious, all vulnerable, and she would shield them as long as she drew breath.

She left the training field and climbed the path to the market. Kid ran to greet her with a plaintive mewl. The animals grew agitated, and Tyche frowned, attributing their unrest to the villagers' mounting tension. She cupped Kid's chin and tilted his face toward her. He stared at her with his peculiar eyes, wide and unblinking, and clung to her legs, his playful demeanor replaced by a stillness that unnerved her.

Tyche straightened and stood still, listening, watching. Nervous grunts rippled through the pigs as their hooves pounded a frantic tattoo against the earth. The dogs huddled around her with their tails tucked between their legs. Even the birdsong had stopped.

The storm clouds cast ominous shadows and stretched like grasping fingers across the village. The wind wound itself around Tyche with anticipation—an imminent countdown to the storm's arrival.

Lep stood nearby, his eyes closed, his face slack with concentration. Tyche studied him, her unease tightening her chest. The earth beneath her feet pulsed with a subtle rhythm, and a heartbeat of terror slid up her spine. The faint but continuous vibrations of power growing in the distance could mean one thing. *They come.* A chill coursed down her arms and raised a rash of gooseflesh.

Lep stepped toward Tyche and circled her waist with his arm. "They approach," he murmured. "The earth itself trembles before their arrival."

"Come," said Tyche. She clutched Lep's hand and led him to the village's edge. They stood side by side, their gazes held by the horizon. A solid wall of darkness roiled above them. "They're close." Tyche glanced at Lep and drank in his pale face. "I can feel their presence clamping my chest in their grip."

Lep turned to stare at the storm. "The earth agrees," he replied. "But are we ready?"

Signaling him to follow, Tyche crossed the square to survey Apollo among the villagers.

"Fortify the west wall!" The god's command rang out. "The Geryon will target the weakest point." His sharp gesture sent the men scrambling to shift the heavy stones, reinforcing the incomplete wall against Geryon's predicted assault.

Lep stepped to his father, his eyes narrowing. "What right do you have to command here?" he asked. "This is my village, my home. You abandoned me, left me to be raised by Chiron, and now you return to give orders?"

Apollo's radiant face flickered.

"Asclepius... son." Apollo turned to face Lep's anger. "I know I have failed you. I carry the weight of my past mistakes." A flicker of humility bloomed in Apollo's eyes.

Tyche's breathing stilled as she watched Lep search the map of his father's face.

"Convenience..." he muttered with bitterness. "You gods are so quick to act when it suits you but nowhere to be found when we need you."

Apollo reached out, his hand hovering over Lep's shoulder. "I know words are not enough," he said quietly. "But I will try, Asclepius. I will try to be the father you deserve. I am proud of you, as I have always been."

A distant rumble of thunder rolled through the village, and Lep stepped back. "We have no time for this now," he said. "The village needs us."

Apollo answered with a curt nod and returned his attention to the men. "Then let us defend it together."

Tyche observed from a distance, her heart aching for Lep's pain. The regret in Apollo's face was clear, and hope for a truce between them flared in her chest. She turned her attention to the villagers' weapons, still dirty from the training, gripped tightly in their hands.

"Where will we hide the elders and the children when the time comes?" she heard a villager ask.

"The springhouse, as it's the most fortified building," Tyche responded.

A violent tremor rippled through the village. The peoples' faces paled as they clutched each other and exchanged anxious glances. Howling winds raked across the thatched roofs, launching scrabbling debris across the cobblestones. Dark-edged clouds crept closer, and the sky buzzed with electric energy.

"They're coming," Kalliope cried. "The gods are angry."

Despite her rising panic, Tyche swallowed her fear and moved among the villagers to offer words of comfort. "We're strong," she reminded them. "We have the weapons, and we have each other."

Words did little to suppress the rising tide of fear. The villagers crowded together, their faces slack with terror. Their whispered petitions caught in the wind and swept away.

What have I wrought upon these innocent mortals? What right did I have to decide their lives were less than my own?

Rain lashed down in a relentless torrent, and the sky crackled with lightning. The villagers knelt before the lesche, placing their weapons on the cobblestones, their lips moving in wordless prayer.

Tyche stood next to Lep and clenched her hands. "They are upon us," she murmured into the storm. "There is no turning back."

Lep's gaze met hers. "Then we face them, Tyche," he replied. "We hold this ground, or we fall together."

A final, deafening clap of thunder rumbled through the valley, and the last sliver of light vanished behind the storm clouds. Darkness claimed Pikerni. The village glowed in a momentary outline in the lightning's burst, like a fragile rebellion against the gods' fury. Then a lethal hush consumed the land, swallowing the storm's rage and birthing the dread of anticipation.

Even the mightiest storms do not yield to the tides of justice. Instead, in the aftermath of divine wrath, it is the quiet strength of resilience that weaves the threads of hope and the lingering shadows that whisper of battles yet to come.

21

TIDES OF JUSTICE, THREADS OF HOPE

The silence shattered.

Tyche crushed her palms against her ears as a shockwave of air compressed her skull, stealing her breath and drawing a panicked kick from her baby. Her immortal senses prickled with warning when the sky above Pikerni rippled like disturbed water. A shadow detached from the storm clouds, darker than the night itself. It moved with deliberate malice, circling the village square in tightening spirals. Tyche bent, her fingers closing around the cold hilt of a blade from the pile of weapons in the square. *The gods have sent their first assault.* Her chest heaved in terror as she raised her sword. *This is only the beginning.*

As she scanned the villagers' faces, their fear a bitter taste in her mouth, she knew she must be strong. But her legs buckled as her eyes lifted to the sky, where a monstrous aberration descended, its form a grotesque fusion of woman and bird. *A harpy!* The stench of rotting flesh trailed the beast and burned Tyche's eyes with acid tears. The foulness coated her tongue with death's promise, a warning that Pikerni now stood in the shadow of divine vengeance.

The creature's tangled hair whipped in the wind like serpents and framed a face contorted with ancient rage. A guttural shriek tore through the valley, and Tyche knew annihilation had come.

Its vast wings shimmered with scales of iridescent obsidian, plucked from Nemesis' own Scales of Justice, and flashed with an unforgiving light. The beast clasped a sword in its talons, forged from the fires of retribution and thirsting for vengeance.

"What is that?!" Panos pointed upward.

Melina and Kalliope cowered in each other's arms and cried in unison. "It's a monster!"

The villagers responded to Tyche's unspoken command and rushed to gather their weapons and shields. With the clang of steel and the thud of wood, they armed themselves, their eyes fixed on Tyche.

Once they were ready, Tyche raised her voice, her command cutting through the chaos. "Villagers, to me! We must form a circle. Shields up! Protect the center!"

Althea held her daughter, Dora, to her chest and moaned as the shields raised over her head. "The beast bears the mark of Nemesis! We are cursed!"

"Cursed?" Tyche echoed. "No! This is a warning, an omen of what is to come!"

"Look!" Evy pointed to the pulsating markings on the bird's feathers. "Those are the Scales of Justice! This beast is a harbinger of reckoning!" She clutched the amulet around her neck and whispered a prayer of protection against evil.

The creature's screech clawed at Tyche's ears as she followed its slow, predatory circle above them. The molten embers of its eyes, eyes that held the blood of the Titans, burned in the deepening gloom. Tyche's heart sank as she recognized the harpy, Nikothoe, her sister Elektra's daughter. How had she fallen so far, to become a weapon of the gods?

"Nikothoe, blood of my blood," Tyche's voice rang out, "why do you torment my people? What have they done to deserve your wrath?"

The harpy glared at Tyche as she passed overhead. "I am an instrument of the gods," she snarled, "a bringer of *their* justice, the deliverer of *their* vengeance. These mortals have defied them by harboring you and your child, and they will pay the price. Even one of my blood must obey, *Aunt.*"

"But the villagers are innocent!" Tyche retorted. "They don't deserve to be punished for my defiance."

"Rebellion is a transgression, goddess of Fortune." Nikothoe's wings beat faster, and a storm of feathers erupted against the darkening sky. "And the gods do not tolerate disobedience, even from their own."

"Then I will defy them again," Tyche declared. "I will protect this village and my child."

Lep rushed to stand at her side. "Tyche! Let me get the people to shelter! The gods have sent destruction upon us!"

"It's too late. They are already here." Tyche stepped in front of him, her eyes locked on the hovering monster.

"Then we face them!" Lep shouted, shoving a vial into her hand. "Drink it! Pharmakon. Let it ease the illness for a few minutes."

Tyche hesitated but swallowed the potion, feeling the familiar surge of strength coursing through her limbs. She stepped before the villagers to see each face turned upward as the beast screamed overhead.

"We have a choice to make," Tyche shouted. "We can step up to face the challenge, or we can run, and the beast will chase us down! Do you not tire of the gods' meddling in your lives?"

A unified roar answered her.

"This is *our* village," Tryfonas cried. "The gods will not have it!"

"Then let us meet death on our feet." The line parted, and Tyche strode forward, her blade raised.

Tyche sensed the villagers' eyes on her, their hopes now pinned to her skill. She could not fail them.

The harpy dived, wings shrieking through the air.

"Now!" Tyche cried, and the front ranks of the villagers raised their shields again.

Nikothoe screamed, the beast's talons grazing the gleaming metal barricade as it passed over them.

Lep grasped her arm. "Tyche, do not allow the tip of the sword to pierce your skin. I have blessed it with the power of the Gorgon's blood, coated in curses that can pierce darkness!"

"Medusa's blood?" Tyche swayed backward on her heels. "You have no faith in Brontes?"

"It is not a matter of doubt but one of wisdom. Brontes' weapons are powerful, but this creature is divine. The blood of the Gorgon will guarantee the weapon finds its mark." Lep stepped forward, then back.

Tyche nodded and whispered a prayer as she glanced skyward. "Oh gods, which ones remain to hear me? Grant me strength, even as your fury descends upon our village!"

She bent down to kiss Dora, who clung to her chiton.

"Be brave, my lady." Dora placed a hand on her cheek. "May good fortune protect you."

Tyche pulled the child aside and strode forward as Dora's blessing coursed through her blood like a divine shield. She squared her feet in the cracked earth and hefted the weight of the blade. *Fight to win, or all will fail and die.* She glanced up at the rustle of feathers and the rapid beat of the harpy's wings as it swooped down for the second time. Its talons glinted like flashing swords.

Another of my blood, twisted to their will.

Her raised steel, the dark Stygian edge rippling with an unnatural fire, met the Sword of Retribution, and a shower of black sparks erupted, casting eerie shadows across the terrified faces cowering under the protection of their shields.

"Nikothoe wants to play at gods and monsters. Well. So can we!" Tyche cried.

The creature pulled back and laughed, and Tyche took a step forward. "With my blade, I call to those who suffer under the gods' yoke. I say rise up to defend yourselves."

Nikothoe's eyes burned with rage. "Foolish," she hissed. "Your insolence is a futile flame against the gods' might." The harpy screeched and dove, its talons extended outward.

Tyche's blood pulsed in her veins. The dark magic of the Gorgon's blood hummed a mournful dirge as she raised her blade and parried the first strike. To her dismay, Nikothoe's talons scraped against the steel, sending a shower of sparks into the gathering gloom. Tyche cried out as the force of the blow nearly wrenched the sword from her grasp.

"You cannot win, goddess of Fortune!" Nikothoe howled. "The gods' will is supreme!" She swooped in again, her wings beating like thunderclaps, claws aimed for Tyche's throat.

Tyche rolled as the harpy's talons screamed past her, the wind of their passage a sharp whistle in the air. A jolt shot through her as she scrambled to her feet. *I must find an opening.* Then, a flash of movement overhead caught her attention just as the creature dove.

With a rush of wind, the creature closed on her. Tyche raised her blade, Medusa's dark blood hissing in time to the Stygian steel's scream as she parried the attack. Nikothoe swooped in again. Tyche ducked as the creature's talons scraped across her chest and cut lines of golden ichor. With a desperate cry, she pivoted and drove the sword upward, the blade plunging into Nikothoe's side. Tyche recoiled as the curse of the Gorgon's blood took hold.

Nikothoe howled in surprise, her claws raking the air inches from Tyche's face. The beast hit the ground in a heap, its roar twisting into a gurgling wail. Tyche stumbled back when a violent shudder seized its body.

"Victory!" Tyche screamed, though she knew this was only one of many such battles. Nikothoe shuddered, her wings beating the air in a panicked frenzy as Medusa's poison swirled through her veins.

Tyche's hold tightened on the hilt as Nikothoe's body writhed in a final attempt to free the weapon. With a swift thrust, Tyche pushed deeper into Nikothoe's heart. A tremor ran through the beast as disbelief flooded her widening eyes.

Then, Nikothoe's expression softened, and she met Tyche's gaze for the final time. Tyche knelt beside her, a trembling hand brushing a stray feather from her niece's cheek. "I remember when you were a fledgling, Nikothoe," Tyche murmured. "Playing in the waves with your mother..."

"The darkness... it calls to me." Nikothoe's eyes glazed over as her lifeblood seeped into the earth. "But it also whispers your name, Tyche. Beware the shadows... They hold secrets that could destroy you."

"What a cruel fate, my niece." Tyche raised her blade into the dying light. "Aren't we all beasts in the end?" *Forgive me. There was no other way.*

The gurgling wail died in the creature's throat as its body erupted, a shower of scales and ichor sending Tyche stumbling back. She raised an arm to shield her face, the stench of death filling her nostrils. As the debris settled, a grave silence fell over the square. *They use our own against us,* her heart cried with grief and anger.

Panting, she lowered her blade. "I killed a beast," she whispered, her eyes meeting Lep's pale face before dropping to the fallen harpy. Her grip tightened on the hilt of her sword, still slick with Nikothoe's blood. "But it took another beast's poison to do it."

"Tyche!" The healer rushed to stand before the defeated monster.

Nikothoe lay dead at Tyche's feet. Its wings lay broken and stained. The spark of revolt flamed in her chest. Yet, as she regarded the fallen creature, she understood Nikothoe had no free will to choose her fate. Tyche's hand slammed against her chest in a fierce declaration of self-possession. "I am mine own." When she drew it back, her fingers were slick with ichor, and the world fell away.

She collapsed into Lep's arms, a bloom of golden blood staining her chiton.

Titan blood stains the lamenting earth, as wails of grief shatter the dawn's resolve. Though gods unleash their kin's cruel fate, mortal hearts rise in defiance. For it is in the shattered heart of the soul, a glimpse of forgotten faces, that hope's ember flickers, even as nightmares claim their due.

22

HOPE'S EMBER FLICKERS

Ichor and burnt feathers choked the air. Hushed whispers pressed in around Tyche as she lay cradled in Lep's arms. Even now, the harpy's attack raged in her mind. She clenched her teeth against her body's savage tremors, causing the flayed skin of her wounds to sear with renewed intensity across her chest.

Nikothoe.

Tyche closed her eyes, and the image of her niece, wings still soft and eyes full of innocent mischief, flickered behind her eyelids. The laughter of her sister, Elektra, splashing water at her young daughter, brought a stab of sorrow.

They used you, as they will use us all.

Lep's arms tightened around Tyche, his lips moving in a silent, frantic language lost in the tempest of her grief and pain.

Drifting in the shallows of unconsciousness, the truth of Nikothoe's death hit her—the first strike of the gods' fury.

"Wraps! Someone bring me clean cloths to bind her wounds!" Lep's urgent words cut through the darkness of Tyche's regret.

Pushing through the villagers surrounding the fallen goddess, Dimitra stumbled to Tyche's side. Her eyes widened in horror at the sight of blood staining the chiton, and she pressed a shaking hand to her mouth to muffle a cry. "Gods... Tyche!"

Evy followed Dimitra through the crowd, dropping to her knees beside the goddess. Her face blanched at the blood seeping from Tyche's chest. A soft gasp bubbled from her lips, and her eyes, wide with horror, darted from the gashes to Tyche's pale face.

"Oh, my precious girl... what have they done to you?" She brushed a stray lock of hair from the goddess' forehead, her fingers shaping a line of desperate comfort.

"The medicine pouch! Quickly!" Lep's frenzied shouts wrapped around Tyche like distant alarm bells she couldn't quite place inside the chaos of her mind. He spoke to no one in particular, but the women rushed to obey.

A flutter of awareness registered his frantic tone and the sharp edge of fear beneath it. She grimaced as another tremor shook her body. *Villagers... safe. I can't... too weak.* The activity around her coalesced—Lep's sharp commands, the hushed whispers of the crowd. Her eyelids sagged, but she managed to crack one open, registering the shadow of worry tightening Lep's eyes as he barked orders.

Tyche hissed when Lep pressed firmly on her chest. "The lacerations are deep. I must prepare a salve and bind your wounds!"

"No time," Tyche gasped. "The gods... will send another. You must... stand in my place until you can mend me." She glanced up at him and winced. "Protect them, Lep."

Lines of worry dug into Lep's brow as he bound Tyche's injuries. "Even your kin are not safe from the gods' wrath. They twist many of those with Titan blood to serve their ends."

They will use every weapon, every soul, to break me. How many more of my kin will I be forced to face?

The villagers' earlier relief faded into the earth's sudden silence, their eyes riveted on their goddess. Tyche trembled in fear as the earth's heartbeat pulsed beneath her body. The rhythm grew into a thunderous drumbeat, and a final, violent tremor tore through the ground. The earth split open with the squelch of breaking bones, and from hell's throat rose the Geryon.

Lep shielded Tyche with his body just as the crowd was knocked off their feet. Tyche's blood froze at the sight of the behemoth. She stared up at the beast and saw a shudder of horror and regret in its many eyes, and a sudden dread fell over her.

Geryon. Nephew of my blood, what cruel fate have the gods forced upon you?

Tyche tried to rise, to stand before the villagers once more, but her limbs refused to obey. The world swam before her eyes, and a rush of nausea sent a rush of bile to her throat. As she watched in helpless horror, the shadow of the monstrous Geryon loomed against the darkening sky.

Three heads, crowned with manes of blood-red fire, loosed their burning gaze on the villagers. As the Geryon's form twisted up from the chasm, Tryfonas and Panos seized their weapons, their faces pale in the dark gleam of Bronte's steel. The creature's torsos followed, fused at the waist, and six arms rippled with strength that defied nature. Serpents writhed beneath its flesh, their undulations creating a sickening churn beneath the surface.

"Tryfonas! Panos! No!" Tyche cried. "That creature is a force of primordial power, beyond your weapons. You cannot win."

"We may be victorious," Tryfonas said, his accusing eyes on the Geryon, "but we will not cower. We will meet it with courage."

Panos drew a deep breath and raised his bow. "We will show it the strength of our hearts."

The stench of brimstone scorched Tyche's throat and turned the air to poison.

They rushed forward, Brontes' weapons raised high. "For the village!" Tryfonas surged ahead to meet the monster.

"We fight together!" Panos drew his bow and ran beside his brother.

"By the gods, I will not let you face this alone!" Lep roared, racing to join them.

Tyche and Christos bellowed their names as the villagers retreated behind the fortified sections of the wall to shield against the monster's assault.

The Geryon's charge tore the sky, the ground trembling beneath its shuddering stride. Tyche swallowed a scream and shrank away from the living monument of muscle and rage. A grotesque fan of limbs churned with blinding speed, its bronze shields and swords shimmering under the moon's cruel eye. In a flash of steel, the monster carved paths of death through the darkness. Tyche's blood thundered as Tryfonas and Lep wove between the deadly blades.

Molten sparks screamed Styx' wrath as the spears struck the monster's shields, but the Geryon didn't flinch as its swords whistled past Tryfonas' head. Lep stepped beside the boy and leveled his spear at the creature, calling upon the earth. Roots erupted and tripped the Geryon's massive legs.

A cry tore from Tyche as Panos loosed his arrow, the shaft's flight humming with mournful groans. It flew past Lep's ear, piercing one of the monster's burning eyes. The creature howled, stumbling back as its clawed hands pulled the barb from its ruined orb with a sickening squelch. Tyche clasped her hands over her ears as its roar shattered the night.

Fire blazed in the beast's remaining eyes, its heads turning toward Panos with savage hunger. Tryfonas rushed forward to stand in front of his brother, who scrambled backward in retreat. He reared back and launched his spear into the creature's scaly side, but the point found no hold in the hell-formed skin. Lep cried out and cast his weapon, but it clattered uselessly to the ground.

The Geryon snatched Tryfonas in its grip. Panos clung to his brother's leg to anchor him, but the monster swung Tryfonas' body high in the air. Lep roared and rushed the Geryon. He leaped and rolled under the creature's massive body, then snatched Tryfonas' spear from the ground and thrust it into its stomach.

Rage swelling his chest, Panos threw down his bow and snatched a sword from the ground, following Lep and swinging wildly at the beast's legs. Blood sprayed from his brother's lips, and Panos screamed. The Geryon's three mouths split into savage grins as its grip tightened. Tryfonas kicked and wailed, struggling to get free.

Tyche knew she must act, wounded or not. Her sole hope was the Wheel of Fortune. She lurched forward, her fingers clawing for the Wheel, only to find empty air—her power refusing her summons. "Dora!" she cried. But it was too late.

"Geryon, I see the pain in your eyes!" Tyche screamed in desperation. "Fight against the gods' control! Remember who you are!" For a heartbeat, Geryon's grasp hesitated in a moment of terrible indecision. The villagers gasped in horror. Tyche prayed her words hit home, but then the Geryon blinked and flexed its claws.

Tryfonas gasped. His eyes bulged as the creature's talons constricted around him. The Geryon's claws sank deep into his flesh. Then his body gave way with a wet rip, and the beast tossed him to the earth.

A cry of rage tore from Christos as he seized his spear and rushed the monster. But the earth shimmied and split beneath his feet, and the Geryon sank into Tartarus' maw.

Christos collapsed over his son's broken form, and Tyche rushed to them with a howl of despair. A question trembled in her heart as she looked upon Tryfonas' maimed body.

Is my daughter's life more valuable than the life of Christos' son?

Doubt stole Tyche's breath as the gods' cruelty carved hollows in the flesh of her heart. But before she could make sense of it, the shadows twisted into nightmare flesh, and the darkness took form.

"The Nekrochim," Tyche hissed.

As if they'd heard her cry, a surge of power rippled through the air, and the night sky split with a golden light.

Apollo and Hermes! "The sons of Zeus dare to defy him?" Tyche's whisper caught in her throat.

Apollo descended through a tear in the darkness. His bow blazed like a captured sun. Behind him, hoofbeats thundered across the sky. Hermes sat astride Pegasus, the immortal steed's wings carving the moonlight into ribbons.

"We stand with you." Apollo's arrows burned holes into the shadow.

Pegasus screamed in agitation as Hermes guided him to earth. "The Olympians forget the ones who came before." His curved blade flashed in a silver arc. "But we remember the Titans and their fate."

The villagers fell to their knees before such divine glory. But darkness swallowed their awe. The faces of Tyche's daughters writhed beneath the Nekrochim's skin, their mouths stretched in silent screams. The monster rose on its grotesque tangle of limbs.

"MoOTthhHerR" The word tore from a hundred twisted throats.

Tyche stumbled back, her children's faces pressed against the creature's flesh from within, hands reaching, grasping.

Apollo's arrows blazed through the darkness. "Face me, creature!" Golden light scattered off the Nekrochim's twisted form. Each shaft passed harmlessly through its nightmare flesh.

"yoUR wEApOnS cAnNOt HArm Me." The voices of her dead children pealed with cruel laughter. "I aM bOrN Of dEEpeR daRKneSS."

Hermes swung his sword above his head as he urged Pegasus forward. But the blade found no purchase in the monster's ever-shifting form. "What sorcery is this?" he cried.

The Nekrochim's limbs stretched toward Tyche. Its groping hands brushed her skin. She screamed as their fingers sank into her flesh, tearing at her swollen belly.

"YoUr CHilD wILl joIN uS." The creature's voices rang with hunger. "aLL yoUR chILdReN fEEd THe dARknESs."

Wicked satisfaction masked the faces of Zeus and Hera as they descended into the nightmare. The gods' laughter swallowed her children's cries as Tyche collapsed, thunder cracking overhead.

Tyche huddled beneath the Nekrochim's shadow, her daughters' hands still reaching.

Then, the nightmare loosened its grip on Tyche, who lay spent on the ground, but her children's screams still vibrated in her bones. Her tears fell unheeded as she rocked back and forth, the pain of her lost children fresh after all these years. A wound, she knew, time could not mend.

But she had no time to recover before a terrible scream tore a gash in the sky. Tyche's head snapped back as Medusa, the Gorgon, descended through the rift. She landed with a thunderous crash in front of Tyche. A nest of hissing vipers crowned the creature's ruined face. Her stone scales shifted and slid beneath the skin of her serpentine body. A thousand captured stars blazed on her wings, scattering the darkness with their reflected light. Tyche's hands clenched the earth for purchase against the terrible beast who was the darkness before the dawn.

"Shield your eyes!" Tyche's warning tore through the square. Villagers dropped their gazes. Some grabbed shields or polished spear points to view the monster's reflection. Even with her gaze lowered, Tyche risked a fleeting upward glance.

The Gorgon slithered toward her, stone scales rasping against the dry earth. Its body carved furrows in the dust. The whispers of its thousand hissing snakes pierced Tyche's skull. She threw her arms around Dora, shielding the girl from the Gorgon's gaze, even as her heart slammed against her ribs.

Gods, send someone to help, Tyche pleaded, her gaze darting around the square. Her instinct screamed to flee, to snatch Dora and run, but then her eyes locked with Lep's across the crowd. The subtle shake of his head—a silent command, *Stay*—held her rooted, and a fierce protectiveness for the child knotted in her gut, answering his unspoken plea.

Then, with a roar ripping from his throat, Lep exploded from the crowd, throwing himself between Tyche and the Gorgon. He raised his spear and pointed it toward Medusa.

"You seek to mend flesh, little healer?" The Gorgon hissed. "I will mend it for eternity—in stone."

As Lep met the creature's gaze, Tyche's eyes were drawn to the terrifying reflections of his face, miniaturized and multiplied across the shimmering surface of the Gorgon's wings. Each tiny image seemed to scream in silent horror. But what struck Tyche was the absence of the swift petrification she had feared. Instead, the Gorgon's gaze seemed arrested. A shudder of disquieting recognition in its depths hinted at a search for an answer, questioning Lep instead of petrifying him.

Medusa flinched, her gaze breaking for a fraction of a second. "Impossible!"

Tyche's heart stuttered as Lep's finger traced the scar on his wrist, the dark legacy that bound him to Medusa. *Fear not,* she read the words forming on his lips, *the blood is mine now.* Her stomach twisted with a knot of fear.

Then he straightened in a defiant challenge. "The blood of the Gorgon flows in my veins," he declared. "Your power cannot turn me to stone."

Please, Lep. Let it be true.

The polished point of Lep's spear reflected the Gorgon's gaze, forcing her to see the monstrous image staring back. Uncertainty blossomed across the beast's face. Then, Medusa's tail uncoiled with explosive force. The monstrous eye at its tip swirled in a storm of emerald and gold.

Gods, he's too close, Tyche screamed in her mind.

A pinpoint of malice, the eye's pupil rotated with predatory slowness, then locked onto Tyche. She flinched when the monster's tail whistled past Lep's ear, missing his face by a hair's breadth. The air reeked with a rotten stench when her tail whipped past again. Tyche's blood shrieked in her veins as Lep dodged with a desperate roll, narrowly escaping the deadly strike.

Please, let him be safe, she prayed silently. *But what about Dora? And what about my child?*

Tyche swayed, her legs trembling beneath her. White-hot agony flared across the torn flesh on her chest, and she gasped as her strength ebbed with each pulse of dark heat. She fought the rising nausea, her eyes locked on Lep as he faced the towering Gorgon. A surge of fierce protectiveness tightened her throat.

Where is Ikelos?

Doubt flared into a wave of terror. "Brontes," she whispered, longing for the strength of his forge, for a weapon to turn the tide.

"You cling to these mortals, little healer, while your divine blood cries out for its rightful place." The Gorgon stalked Lep. Her serpent's body weaved a menacing circle around him.

"My blood compels me to *heal*, Gorgon," Lep said, his voice steady despite the tremor in his hands. "It does not demand *dominion*."

A wave of power radiated from the beast. "What do you want, little Asclepius? Have you come crawling for my blessing?" Her voice dripped with venom and mockery. "Or have you come to beg for more of the blood that should have been your undoing?"

"I do not require your power," Lep said. "My power comes from a different source."

Medusa's eyes narrowed. "You bear Apollo's legacy, yet you cling to these humans, these fleeting shadows. A god among mortals, a mortal among gods—you belong nowhere. Do you think such insubordination will go unpunished? The pain of longing will consume you."

"You say I belong nowhere." Lep's hand tightened on the shaft of his spear. "Perhaps you are right. But I belong *with* these people, with those I love. And that belonging is stronger than any claim Olympus can make. My heritage is a gift, and I will use it to protect them, not to rule them." He raised his sword. "Your blood grants me the power to heal and to kill, a gift from you, yourself. Do you now scorn the very power you bestowed? The bond we share is broken. Your power over me is no more."

The Gorgon's snakes hissed in her laughter. "You wield Titan blood, little healer, but your heart remains mortal. Do you not feel the pull of your weakness?" She slithered closer, her gaze never leaving Lep's. "Those monsters manifest the Olympians' will. In this battle, you will be as much a target as those you wish to protect."

"Enough of your lies!" Lep leveled his spear at the beast. "Let us end this, here and now!

The Gorgon launched herself at Lep with a flash of deadly speed. Stripes of blood appeared across his shoulder as the Gorgon's claws struck. Even before the pain registered, his divine heritage surged, mending the wounds. Lep flowed to the side, focusing his will on the earth. The soil beneath Lep's feet roiled. From the cracked surface, tendrils of wood exploded upwards. The grasping hands of the roots surged forward, their wooden claws seeking purchase on the Gorgon's body. Her tail lashed, smashing against the branches coiling around her torso and arms.

The Gorgon's forked tongue spat out deadly ichor that blackened the binding cords. The roots blackened and withered where the poison touched, but more surged to replace it. They snaked around the Gorgon and bound her in a cage of writhing wood.

Tyche's eyes widened in horror as the woody strands, like serpents themselves, tightened around Medusa. Her scales shimmered, then dulled, as wood grain spread across her skin. Soon, her sleek form contorted, sharp angles emerging where smooth curves had been, as wooden threads furrowed her flesh. Agony contorted her decaying face as the woody growth consumed her features and reshaped them into the rough texture of bark. The Gorgon screamed her final rage, the transformation complete—a twisted tree—its branches rising toward the sky in supplication.

Tyche stood next to Lep as he hacked a branch from the twisted tree. It writhed in his hand for a moment, then stilled. He raised the staff, and Tyche saw it clearly—a length of wood around which a serpent coiled. Its scales shimmered even in the dim light. Before Tyche could react, Lep drew his knife and sliced his right wrist. As the drops of his blood fell, the serpent on the rod opened its mouth and accepted the offering. The blood glowed briefly as it touched the serpent's tongue before being absorbed. He placed the rod, warm and alive, into Tyche's outstretched hands. She slid her finger along the Staff of Asclepius, surprised by the life that pulsed from it.

Tyche whispered in awe. "From the Gorgon, healing is born."

An unsettling peace settled over the ravaged square. For a moment, Tyche believed the horror had passed, the gods appeased. Then, a low tremor snaked through the earth beneath her feet. Above, the dangerous sky churned in a coiling maelstrom, and her heart stuttered as gargantuan forms converged, promising a fury yet unknown.

As gods descend on stormy wings, rebellion flares against divine fury. Though lightning strikes, a flame of hope blazes in the mortal soul. For it is in the heart's courageous stand, where the authority of Titan blood holds command, that even Olympians must yield to love's decree. And shadows whisper of a daughter's plea. And shadows whisper of a daughter's plea.

23

Whisper of a Daughter's Plea

The darkness recoiled before the onslaught of a god-forged dawn, and for a fleeting breath, relief washed over Tyche's seared wounds. Her body throbbed with the ache of victory. The terror of her encounters with the gods' beasts settled into her bones, and before she could mourn what she'd lost, a fresh peal of thunder rolled over the mountain.

A wave of apprehension crashed over Tyche as Zeus tore through a gash in the heavens. Lightning flickered in his eyes, etching his rugged face of granite carved from the swirling clouds. He clutched a scepter of blazing lightning in his fist, its bolts of white energy shooting outward to paint the storm-wracked sky in streaks of fire.

Hera followed close behind, her tempest of dark hair cascading around her shoulders. The silken noose of her glare settled around Tyche's throat.

"You dare defy us? Kneel before your king!" Zeus thundered, and before his words faded, Tyche's blood ran cold.

I'm no longer battling a beast. I'm fighting a god.

Hera's voice sliced through the chaos like a stinging whip. "Your rebellion will be your children's grave," she hissed, and a frozen breath of annihilation brushed against Tyche's skin.

Tyche stood before them, king and queen of the Olympian gods, and trembled. Before the paralyzing fear could take root, Lep's voice rang out.

"We refuse to live in fear!" Lep raised the rod, the serpent coiling around it, writhing against the gods' fury. "We choose our fate, not you!"

Then the thunder cracked again, and Zeus' furious glare cut through the storm. His face, contorted with rage, blazed with lightning. "You dare oppose my will? Taste of my lightning!"

His words hit Tyche like a physical blow, and she clutched the bindings around her chest with a grimace. She stepped forward, her feet planted wide in the ruined square, and words rose in her throat as a shield against their fury. "We will not be pawns in your game!"

The square shook with the villagers' trembling. Tyche looked over her shoulder to see their faces pale and drawn. They cowered on the ground, their teeth chattering in the sudden bitterness gripping the air. Many clutched at amulets, their only hope against the divine wrath hovering in the sky. But amid the petrified masses, Tyche's eyes rested on Lep, his feet braced, the Rod of Asclepius held high.

"You will not break their spirits!" Tyche's hands clenched into fists at her side. "You will not break mine!"

Zeus' lightning hammered the earth, its white-hot light splitting the sky. The ground bucked and heaved, throwing Tyche off balance. Then the wall beside her imploded, and a wave of debris billowed outward from the point of impact.

Villagers scrambled for cover, their screams lost in the thunder's roar, as Tyche stumbled, her arm scraping against the jagged edges of a broken wall. She hissed at the pain, the image of Tryfonas' broken body swimming in her vision, and choked on the fear knotting in her chest.

Not like this. It cannot end like this.

Bolts of lightning blasted craters into the earth around her. A hail of rock fragments stung her exposed skin, the smell of her singed hair stinging her nostrils. She rolled her tongue over her split lip, the taste of blood in her mouth. She whispered a silent plea, then called on the Wheel within, but the familiar surge of power did not answer. Tyche cried out as the ground gave way and threw her to her knees, her mouth gaping at the jagged crack crawling across the square toward her.

Tyche stumbled to her feet, her words tearing from her throat. "No more shall we cower!"

Beside her, Lep swept the Rod of Asclepius in an arc, pushing back the panicked villagers, who formed a circle of defiance around them. "We are not animals to be slaughtered! We are people! We are the heart of this village!"

A murmur rippled through the crowd. Tyche glanced around the ring of her protectors and saw the fear stamped in their faces, but something else flickered there now—a spark of insurrection.

"No more!" Althea stepped from the crowd, Dora clinging to her side, and a chorus of voices shouted after her.

"We will fight for our homes! For our families!"

"For Tryfonas!" Christos bellowed.

The villagers surged forward, tightening the circle around Tyche and Althea. The goddess clenched her fists even as her heart swelled in gratitude. "We will not be slaves to the gods any longer. This ends now!" She raised her fists skyward.

Then, she heard them. "We stand with Tyche. We choose freedom!" The villagers' roar merged into a single declaration of power.

The villagers' proclamation clashed with Zeus' thunderous laughter. "You dare...?"

But before Zeus could unleash his fury, Tyche charged forward.

"For our freedom!" she bellowed.

The villagers swept forward, their fear replaced by a surge of righteous anger. And then, as the first clash of divine and mortal forces shuddered across the valley, a whirlwind of speed appeared. Hermes descended from the heavens on Pegasus, the steed landing beside Tyche. The messenger god dismounted with a leap, his eyes locked on the faces of the gods.

Zeus' roar ripped through the valley, and lightning clawed the earth, forcing the villagers to dive for the shelter of the walls.

Christos hunkered behind a wall and gathered the collected rocks into his fists. "For my son. You killed him, you tyrants!"

A cry tore from his throat, and Tyche held her breath as he stood and flung a stone that smashed into a diving gryphon's face. Armed with slings and stones, the villagers pelted the gods and their beasts. Their small attacks stung, but they were enough to distract the gods' fury from Tyche and Hermes.

A searing bolt of lightning split the air as Hera's power shimmered, conjuring hellhounds from thin air. The villagers stood behind a wall of spears and braced for the charge, but the hellhounds vanished, Hera's illusion a cruel trick. Even as they gasped with relief, monstrous serpents plunged from the sky, their translucent scales gleaming in the lightning's flash, their hisses mingling with the crackle of Zeus' wrath.

The serpents struck, fangs bared, as the ground bucked beneath the villagers' feet. Lightning blazed across the earth beside them, and Tyche heard Lep's scream as he pushed his way among the wounded. His hands glowed with a faint, golden light, and as a monstrous serpent lunged toward a group of terrified children, he raised his hands. The earth trembled, and thick roots erupted, snaring the serpent's tail. The creature shrieked, thrashing wildly, but the roots held fast.

Hermes perched atop a crumbling wall and pointed toward a narrow path next to the lesche. He launched a spear at a swooping gryphon, shouting, "To the springhouse!"

In a whirlwind of motion, Apollo appeared between Tyche and a diving sphinx, his bow a blur. A silver arrow sang through the air, sending the eagle-feathered lion crashing to the earth. He directed the villagers to reinforce the west wall, using the fortified sections as a chokepoint.

Face streaked with dirt and blood, Tyche rallied the villagers. "For our home!" Her voice rang out amid the tempest. She charged toward a group of serpents, her Stygian sword a flash of deadly steel.

The gods' attacks lessened. The beasts' shrieks faded, and the serpents seemed hesitant to strike. The lightning still flashed, but less frequently. As the sounds of the battle dwindled, a roaring silence settled over the valley, more terrifying than the storm.

Tyche stumbled through the wreckage. Everywhere she looked, she saw the faces of the fallen. Her throat choked on a sob. She saw Althea, wounded but cradling Dora, her face streaked with tears. A burning timber tilted near them. Tyche shouted, pushing mother and daughter aside as the tree struck the ground, sending a spray of burning embers into the sky. Dora cried out and buried her face. A searing pain shot through Tyche's arm, and she crumpled to her knees.

Tyche's ribs rose and fell in her anguish. *No. More.* The thought thundered in her mind like a desperate mantra. She raised her trembling hands toward the storm-wracked heavens. "Zeus! Hera!" Her voice tore through the battlefield. "Styx herself would call this slaughter unjust! You swore by Styx, yet you show no mercy! Look at them!" She gestured toward the fallen. "Take your vengeance on me! Spare my daughter, spare my village!" Her words crashed through the ravaged square.

And then, the heavens answered. A single drop of rain landed on Tyche's cheek. She flinched as a shiver ran down her spine. Then another drop, and another. The sudden deluge slammed the ravaged earth. The lightning paused, and the thunder stilled. A hush fell over the battlefield in a moment of breathless anticipation.

"SoMEthINg VaSt aNd POweRFuL cOMeS," her sister's presence whispered through the icy downpour, chilling Tyche. Even Styx seemed to question the gods' wrath.

Then, the rain parted. From the heart of the storm, the Titan rose, Oceanus, god of the Primordial River. His form coalesced from the rain itself in a towering wave of turquoise and emerald, shimmering and shifting with the earth's energy. The ground trembled beneath his immense weight. In a cascade of white foam, his beard roared down his chest. His eyes, twin abysses of the deepest springs, burned with righteous fire. He was the lifeblood of the world—vast, ancient, and unstoppable. Tyche gasped, her heart leaping in her chest. *Father.* The cry tore through her mind like a desperate lifeline.

Oceanus roared from the storm's center, his voice a thunderous decree that mastered the elements and brought Zeus' thunder to a trembling halt. "Zeus! Hera! You dare attack my daughter and her people? You dare reignite the flames of the Titanomachy? Have you forgotten?" He paused, his eyes boring into Zeus. A deep rumble boomed from the earth beneath the Olympians. "Have you forgotten the oaths you swore by Styx? Have you forgotten the cost of Titan blood? You ignore what binds you to justice!"

Zeus thundered back, his voice ringing across the valley, but Tyche heard the tremor in his tone, the edge of his desperation. "Oceanus, this is about *her.* Stand aside." His hand flashed with lightning as he gestured toward Tyche.

Oceanus towered over the battlefield in a wave of turquoise and emerald against the storm clouds. "Justice?" he scoffed. "You call *this* justice?" He gestured toward the fallen villagers, his gaze sweeping over the devastation. "You have overstepped. You harass mortals, but your threat extends to the oaths that bind us all. You threaten *my blood*, and you defile the very river that gives you power."

The tension radiated from Zeus and Hera and reached Tyche on the ground. As the rain intensified, a surge coursed through her, raising the hairs on her arms. A fire burned hot in her veins, a sense of rightness. She saw Hera's eyes narrow, a flicker of fear crossing her face before she schooled her features into a veneer of anger.

"Lord of the Waters," Hera hissed, "do not interfere."

Oceanus' attention remained fixed on Zeus and Hera. "These mortals are under my protection." His outstretched arms embraced the village. "Harm them, and you will face the wrath of the Titans. And not my fury alone. The foundations of Olympus will tremble. And *she*," he gestured toward Tyche, "will not be harmed. Styx herself witnesses this transgression."

Tyche caught Zeus and Hera exchange a look from the corner of her eye. The glance was brief, almost imperceptible, but Tyche observed the subtle shift in their posture, the almost imperceptible tightening of Zeus' jaw.

Icy shards of rain lashed Tyche, each one a decree from Styx. The Titan's ancient power coursed through her in a frozen tide. Then, silence.

Tyche held her breath as Zeus and Hera turned, their forms dissolving into the storm clouds. The softening rain comforted her after the gods' fury. A towering pillar of water, Oceanus stood before her, his liquid form a paradox against the inevitable flow. Then, as the storm's energy receded, Oceanus' gaze lingered on Tyche with adoration in his eyes. His outstretched arms flowed back into the wave. Tyche reached for him as his powerful torso yielded to the water, his form shimmering and ebbing. Until only his gaze lingered, pools of ancient wisdom and love, before they too dissolved into the wave that cleansed the village with its passage.

The soft, heart-wrenching sobs of the survivors broke the lingering silence. Tyche smashed her hand against her mouth to crush a rising scream. Kalliope, her face streaked with soot and tears, clutched her child close. Evy offered a ghost of a smile and hugged her bandaged arm to her chest, while Christos stood statue-like beside his dead son, tears of grief lining his cheeks. Lep leaned heavily on Dimitra, who held him close.

Is this the price of my insolence?

She tilted her face toward the faint light piercing the clouds and the sliver of moon chasing the retreating storm. The rain dwindled to a soft drizzle. Victory. They had defied the gods. She placed a protective hand over her stomach and spoke a silent prayer for the life within. But the villagers' moans and screams muted the joy of her triumph. A cough wracked her body, and she wiped a trembling hand across her brow. Tyche shivered as she turned her ear toward her people's lament and her eyes to the gnarled silhouette of the Gorgon's tree.

Devastated by the destruction, Tyche staggered across the battlefield, stars exploding in her vision. She stumbled and crashed against the rough trunk of the disfigured tree. Beneath her fingers, the bark writhed, the snake-like scales shifting and hissing against her hands, and an icy chill rippled across her skin.

A scream tore from her throat as she tried to pull away, but her feet tangled. She stumbled backward, her back slamming against the knotted trunk, and then slid down its length. The sharp scales tore at her flesh. The branches stirred and descended around her to form a prison of darkness.

The nightmare constricted around her as though the Gorgon herself exhaled terror into existence. The tree pulsed—a dark heart beating beneath the bark. The scales, slick with a cold sweat, pressed against her skin. A hiss rose from the depths of the wood in a promise of eternal imprisonment. Then the branches coiled, and the horror engulfed her whole.

Fear and betrayal test the heart, yet rebellion flares before retribution. For the void whispers secrets that unmake fate.

REBELLION FLARES
BEFORE RETRIBUTION

Tyche's world dissolved. Fragments of a burning village. Screams. Blood. Terror.

Then... nothing.

The darkness inhaled her as if a living thing drew her into its suffocating embrace. Her body drifted, weightless and lost, suspended in a viscous fluid that pressed against her like congealed blood. Tyche thrashed against the violation of her being. Pain lingered at the edges of her awareness, but here, in the heart of the void, sensation abandoned her. An absence of her physical body. The negation of existence pressed in, leaving a bitter taste of what might never be.

"Lover?" The fragile word slipped from her lips.

No response. Only vast, consuming darkness.

The goddess' mind, untethered from her physical form, wandered through flashes of destruction—burning homes, Tryfonas' lifeless eyes, then Christos' grief-stricken face. The children's laughter cackled around her in a mocking chorus of betrayed innocence. The village—her sanctuary she had sworn to protect—reduced to ash and memory.

They trusted me, and I failed them.

She thrashed against the crushing weight in her chest and gasped for air that offered her no sustenance. Dora's eyes hovered in the murky blackness, huge and damning. Dimitra's rough laugh, Evy's kind words, and Lep's soothing hands—all gone. *Because I dared to defy the gods.* Where was Ikelos? Captured? Destroyed along with everything else she held dear?

The darkness writhed with familiar patterns. *His* patterns. Shadow-wolves stalked the edges of her vision. Their golden eyes burned with his particular hunger.

"Ikelos?" A braid of hope and terror curled from Tyche's mouth. "Are you here?"

Shadows swayed. Waiting, watching.

Tyche clawed at the darkness, her nails scraping against the unseen substance that surrounded her. She needed him with a desperate urge that overrode the growing unease in her heart. Needed to know he survived, that the destruction she had witnessed wasn't the end.

The void split like a wound, and his form stitched itself together—wolf, then the threads unraveled as serpent, then knitted anew as man. The fire in his golden eyes tore through her with a searing heat. And then he was there—Ikelos.

"You're here," she breathed, fingers already straining for him.

"Always," he murmured. His hand cupped her cheek in the bankrupt landscape surrounding them. "Did you think I would abandon you?"

His touch was real, solid, yet the void around them pulsed with an unsettling rhythm. Tyche leaned into his hand, her senses surging at the familiar warmth of his skin like a fragile anchor in the swirling chaos. "I needed you." She breathed. "Where were you?" Her fingers traced his face. "During the battle, when everything burned—are you alright?"

"I am here now." His tongue tasted the curve of her lips. "You need not fear for me. For fear serves its purpose, my love." His fingers traced possessive designs across her skin. "As do nightmares."

She leaned into his touch, straining against him. "I was afraid. I thought—"

He silenced her with a gentle finger against her lips. "Shhh." He traced the line of her shoulder, her neck, his touch both comforting and unsettlingly intimate. "The Olympians have no power here."

He whispered promises of a world crafted only for her, but the yellowed fangs behind his smile held a glint of a possessive hunger that sent a shiver down her spine. His words were honey, but his gaze was steel. The darkness seemed to press closer, whispering secrets she couldn't decipher, promises of forbidden knowledge.

"Tell me." She pulled him closer. "Tell me what the gods did to you."

"They tried to bind me," he murmured against her ear, "to chain the essence of nightmare. But they cannot hold me, not when you call."

Then, his body stretched, elongating like molten glass drawn into strings of shadow. A low, guttural growl sprang from the darkness around him. Tyche gripped him harder, panic rising as he pulled away.

"Kelo? Don't—" Tyche trembled with desperation.

His flesh rippled between forms—lover to predator, protector to hunter. Each shape held a fragment of truth she dared not name. Tyche's heart beckoned him in her desire and shrank from him in her doubt. His fingers lengthened against her skin. She flailed, trying to find a hold in the shifting darkness, but her hands found nothing.

As she stared at his fading smile, a thick line of crimson tore across his cheek, and then Lep's face pushed through the wound and glared at her in silent accusation. *What does this mean?* Tyche screamed into the void. *Is this a warning? A betrayal?* The image glimmered, leaving her with a sharp pang of guilt and a sense that she had betrayed something precious. Someone precious. Then, Lep's bloodied face flickered before dissolving back into Ikelos' handsome features. Before her, two hearts beat in a sickly rhythm. From one spouted the crimson blood of mortal man, and from the other, the golden ichor of the gods.

"Stay!" Her hands passed through him like mist.

Then, he melted into the blackness before her eyes. But his smile remained—a wolfish grin—as he faded into the shadows that coiled around him.

His laughter echoed, then died away to leave behind a boneless chasm in her chest. The void around her rippled, and a faint drone replaced the oppressive silence. The murmur grew and resolved into the thunderous judgements of the gods. The cold, unyielding stone undulated beneath her feet. She turned toward the Olympian thrones towering above her.

"Let Ikelos go!" she cried.

Zeus sat at the center of the dais. Tyche cowered under his fierce gaze. Hera, regal and cold, stood beside him. Nemesis hovered at the edge of their council, her booted foot pressed onto the Scales of Justice.

"Please!" Tyche's desperate plea went unnoticed—a ghost haunting the edges of their reality—visible yet unseen.

She screamed and clasped her hands to her ears, her eyes as visions crashed into her—blood, screams, destruction.

The memories fractured and spun, sharp edges of horror and guilt. Disorienting. Brutal.

Panic erupted into a flame of protective instinct, its tongues twisting and burning brighter than the destruction around her.

"Ikelos!" She clawed at her throat as she spun around in search of him once more.

But all that remained was despair's cruel whisper and shadows that bled secrets she could not grasp.

The gods' voices rose around her like thunderclaps, their words springing from their mouths into the dreamscape.

"He must be punished for his audacity," Zeus growled. "His nightmares have threatened our dominion."

"Let him hang suspended until he understands true despair." Hera's voice trumpeted in the darkness. A chorus of murmurs and screams rose from the warped mouths of a thousand shattered statues.

Tyche swallowed the hot bile in her throat, sickened by their words—the collective decision forming like dark clouds above her—and yet she could do nothing but watch, helpless, as the gods plotted Ikelos' fate.

"His power must be bound, for the Scales of Justice have made their decree." Nemesis leaped from the crumbling edifice of retribution in a storm of wrath and righteous condemnation. Her claw-like hands wove sigils into the air designed to suppress Ikelos' ability to cast nightmares or dreams.

"No!" Tyche gasped. "Kelo!"

And then a velvet cord of Nightmare's words wrapped itself around Zeus' neck. "Did you enjoy your little nap, *my lord*? I hear my brother, Morpheus, has been quite busy of late."

The gods fell silent. At Ikelos' sarcasm, lightning snarled and spat, tearing fiery cracks across the dream-spun abyss. Tyche wondered if Ikelos' words were meant to silence Zeus.

An unexpected surge of pride swelled in her chest at his brazenness, yet fear crushed her heart—the knowledge that this might not end well for him or for their child.

She turned to find Ikelos hanging suspended in midair—no chain nor any visible means bound him. He floated in the black expanse, immobile, suspended within a swirling riptide of shadows, his own creations turned against him. Malevolent energy throbbed around him. Bitter darkness seemed to seep from his soul.

"You dared to defy us," Zeus roared as he stood to face the god of Nightmares. "You have unleashed chaos upon your own kind. You, *Nightmare*, have subverted our order!"

Ikelos' eyes gleamed with a rebellious sparkle. "Chaos," he smirked, "is the root of existence, King of the gods. It is the force from which order itself arises. You cannot ignore it, for it is the lifeblood of the cosmos."

"You meddled in affairs that did not concern you, demon of the underworld. You sowed discord and rebellion among the gods, and for that transgression, you shall pay." Hera's form expanded and crowded the void.

Ikelos laughed long and hard into the oppressive silence. "Fear," he hissed, "is the most potent of all weapons, dear Hera. It can crumble empires and shatter the will of the gods. And you, it seems, have experienced the sting of your own wrath."

"Your arrogance will be your undoing. But you have underestimated the power of the Olympians." Nemesis' sword elongated and pressed into Ikelos' neck, drawing a thick line of putrid ichor.

Nemesis pointed a long finger at the suspended god. The shadows around Ikelos intensified, growing denser. Suffocating. He gasped and struggled against the magic that bound him. The shadows pressed in, whispering insidious thoughts into the maelstrom around him.

As Zeus scrutinized Ikelos from his throne, Tyche caught a flicker of—unease?—cross his face before he masked it once more.

Tyche turned her attention to Hera as her eyes followed the path of Ikelos' struggle. The Queen of the gods flinched and rested her hand against her throat. She glanced at Nemesis, who stood rigid with her hands still outstretched from the spell she had cast. The goddess of Retribution stepped back and into the shadow of Hera's throne.

Ikelos' head hung low. Through her tears, Tyche glimpsed a flash of satisfaction on his face. Even in defeat, his eyes concealed a secret.

The gloom surrounding him vibrated with ambition rather than despair. Beneath his right foot, the earth revolved, and under his left, a dark maelstrom of chaos churned. A sense of misgiving surged in her blood—he straddled two realms, possessing a power she didn't understand.

"Ikelos!" Tyche screamed. "Fight them! Do not let them win!" She leaped into the oily blackness to reach his side, but her hands pushed through the penumbra of his form.

As quickly as it began, the vision dissolved—the marble hall, the looming gods—all fading into nothingness. Tyche beat her chest and cried out into the barren landscape.

Then, a different sensation of strong arms lifting her, the rough fabric of a tunic brushing her cheek, and a familiar voice whispering soothing words, their meaning just beyond her grasp. Her body swayed through the shadows, no longer crushed by the weight of nightmare, absent the whispers of terror but filled with the quiet rustle of straw. Her thoughts drifted and found no shore. Where was she? The darkness was different—a softer, gentler dark. But where were the villagers? Had they escaped? Or were they all dead?

In the heart of sorrow, truths long buried creep to the light, and the burden of secrets threatens to unravel the brittle bonds of trust. For even as the earth demands its due, the sighs of the past can sometimes unveil a shocking truth, and the shadows of horror stretch long across the dawn, declaring a darkness yet to come.

25

THE EARTH CLAIMS ITS DUE

Tyche's scream tore through the barn's stillness. Straw pricked her skin in a brutal reminder of her mortal form. Kid's warmth was solid against her body, but Tyche's heart vibrated under her flesh in a drumbeat against the silence. She clutched at her chest, her fingers pressing against its frantic rhythm. Was Ikelos' acquiescence a performance for the gods or something more sinister? The question vexed her like a thorny vine tightening around her heart.

She clutched the goat's bristled coat. "Oh, Kid. What have I done?"

The first light bled across the sky in accusatory crimson from a divine gash across the heavens. Tyche pushed through the barn door and peered outside, her shoulders slumping as her steps carried the burn of betrayal to those she had failed to protect. All around her, the village lay destroyed, and the breeze stung her nostrils with the bitter perfume of burnt offerings. The coppery scent of blood merged with the rising smoke while muttered accusations scraped against her ears. Buildings grasped at the sky in skeletal ruin.

Among the rubble, an orange cat crouched, its plaintive howls soaring through the destruction. Tyche's face fell at the sight of the cat's amber eyes, wide with grief, as it hunted for a familiar face, matching her desperate search for Lep.

Then her gaze settled on a familiar figure amid the chaos. Lep knelt beside the wounded. Sweat and grime streaked his brow as he pressed yarrow into deep gashes and smoothed salve over burns, while the lives beneath his hands seemed to carve new lines of weariness onto his face. His deep sigh broke her heart as the flames of empathy, unexpected and fierce, coursed through her. She knelt beside him and pressed her knees into the rough ground.

"What can I do to help them?" she asked. Her hands once held the power to bestow fortune or misfortune, to weave destinies with the turn of her Wheel. Now, she made an appeal for direction, her power useless against the truth of mortal suffering. The irony stung and left a bitter taste on her tongue. Yet, beneath the sting, a new desire stirred within her—a yearning to connect, to heal, to endure the pain as one of them.

Lep glanced at her, his eyes heavy with a sorrow that matched her own. "Here." He placed a poultice of crushed herbs in her hand. "Apply this to the wound with a gentle touch. Imagine the breath flowing from your hands to draw out the pain and restore balance." The brush of their hands sent a pulse of tenderness to soothe her shattered heart.

But even as she worked beside him, her mind was elsewhere. Tryfonas' death—a blade twisted in her chest. She rose, leaving

Lep to tend to the wounded. Her gaze drifted toward the open doorway of the lesche, and for a fleeting moment, she saw it—the still body beneath a rough blanket on a makeshift table. *Tryfonas.* Grief ambushed her, swift and brutal. The son, lost in defense of her daughter. The choice between one life and many carved her heart deeper with each breath—a mother-to-be tormented by decisions made before all this began. She pulled herself back from the pain and swept her gaze across the ravaged square. The barn, miraculously untouched, stood behind her like a sentinel against the ravaged village. And the lesche, now a silent tomb holding Tryfonas' hushed form, still reached toward the sky.

They buried Tryfonas beneath a weeping sky in a rain of tears Tyche could not shed. Generations of sorrow lined the village women's faces, their lament weaving centuries of grief into the dirges on their lips.

Christos stood before his son's bier, his grief as unyielding as the stone of the Gorgon's gaze. As the villagers gathered to prepare for the procession, Tyche approached the bier and placed an olive branch next to Tryfonas' body.

Peace, she thought, *can it ever bloom again from this ravaged earth?*

Rough and calloused from a life of toil, village hands prepared the boy's final journey. Then the mourners formed their procession beyond the walls. Olive groves bent overhead to witness their loss. Mud tugged at their feet as they carried their burden to rest.

Tyche walked with Lep at the rear of the procession with her head bowed low over her chest, the healer's hand resting on her back as he led her forward. Tears fell from her eyes like stones, each a piece of her shattered heart.

"I should be the one lying here." Christos' sob ripped through the quiet. His fingers lingered on the cold curve of his son's cheek, as if to recapture the lost warmth, the vanquished laughter, the extinguished light.

Tyche averted her eyes at his sorrow, the brutal reality of mortality a sharp ache in her chest.

Christos blinked at the copper coins in his hand. "A poor offering for such a loss." He closed his red-rimmed eyes.

Tyche read his despair and placed her hand over his clenched fist. He looked up, surprised.

In her open palm lay gleaming gold coins. "For his journey," she whispered.

Christos stared at the gold, then back at the copper, and he hesitated.

Tyche slid the coins into his fingers and wrapped her hand around his. "These are for him." She motioned for Christos to place the coins on Tryfonas' eyelids.

A murmur of gratitude rippled through the gathered villagers. "May the gods bless his journey," Dimitra choked out.

With a cry, Panos stretched out his hands toward Tryfonas. Christos wrapped his arms around him to offer the only comfort he could—the closeness of a father's embrace.

"Brother," Panos wept. The word held all he could not say.

"Remember Tryfonas, whose life was sacrificed for our people." Christos' bloodred eyes met Tyche's. "And our village."

Climbing into the fresh grave, Christos waited for his son. The healer gathered the boy's form from the bier and lowered him into his father's arms as Christos offered his child back into the earth's eternal embrace.

Evy and Dimitra passed clay vessels filled with honey and barley wine to the grieving man. He placed them within reach of Tryfonas should he require them for his journey to the underworld. And as the earth thudded against the shroud, Christos poured the remainder of the honey over the fresh mound as a golden offering to the earth.

Tyche stumbled from the gravesite, away from the accusing silence and Christos' inconsolable grief.

Lep found her collapsed against the barn wall and knelt beside her. Her curled body shook with reckless sobs.

"I'm here, Tyche. You don't need to bear this burden alone." The healer pulled the goddess into his arms.

"His son." The words stung her throat. "Tryfonas died protecting my child. My secrets." Her daughter stirred in her womb, and her fingers clenched with the painful reminder of the life Tryfonas had saved—a life now tainted by his death. "How many more must die for my choices?"

"He died a hero, Tyche. I know the guilt is heavy, but do not let it consume you. Honor his sacrifice by living, by protecting the life he saved." Lep smoothed the hair back from Tyche's wet cheeks.

"A hero?" Bitter laughter cut from her chest. "Tell that to the father who cradled his son's lifeless body, who will never hear his laughter again."

Lep's expression grew somber. "There is more. I did not want to burden you further in this moment, but you deserve to know.

Althea... She did not survive the clash with the gods. She fought bravely to protect the village and Dora, but..." His voice trailed off.

Tyche's breath hitched. "Althea? No—" Her hand flew to her mouth. "She is... she was Dora's mother."

Lep nodded and looked away. "She loved that child as her own. And now, Dora is alone."

Tyche's heart clenched. Dora, a child twice abandoned by fate. The weight of this new loss settled upon her in a crushing mantle of guilt. "Oh, Dora," she whispered, tears streaming down her face. "What will become of you now?"

"Come." Lep offered his hand and pulled her up, then guided her inside the barn. "I will bring Dora to you. The child needs you now more than ever." Then he spun on his heel in search of Dora.

Tyche sank against the hay bales, ashen and drained. Hay and dust wrapped around her, offering a brief shelter from the grief and guilt that ravaged her soul.

She reached out a trembling hand toward Lep as he returned moments later with Dora. The child stirred in the healer's arms, a faint whimper on her lips. In the soft light of the lantern, Tyche studied her face and wiped away the tracks of dried tears on her cheeks.

Lep lowered Dora into Tyche's arms. The child's hands clutched at Tyche's tunic, her body trembling with suppressed sobs. A keening wail escaped Dora's throat that tore at Tyche's heart. She held Dora close, the child's tears soaking into her skin. A fierce protectiveness surged through her. *This child needs a mother's comfort.* Tyche bit her lip, glanced toward Lep, then back at the sleeping child. *I will be her refuge now.* She tugged the ribbon from

Dora's hair she had given to the child long ago and clutched it tightly in her hand.

Tyche looked up, startled, as a shadow fell across the barn's entrance. Then, hoofbeats thundered outside, and Pegasus landed in a sweep of wings. Hermes dismounted and entered the barn, all traces of his usual quicksilver grace gone.

"The price of defiance comes due." His words struck anvil-hard. Ancient grief lined his face—the same sorrow Tyche remembered from that day at the spring when he had observed her breathe life back into the drowned mortal.

Tyche's fingers dug into the straw and crushed it beneath her grip. "And what of Ikelos?" His name tasted of fear.

"They've enslaved him." Hermes' voice was tight with anger. "They force him to weave nightmares so real they bleed into the waking world."

Tyche pushed off the ground with a cry.

No. He wouldn't—

"They left him no choice." Hermes interrupted and knelt beside her, placing his hand over hers. His eyes glimmered with centuries of watching, of secret-keeping. "Just as I had no choice but to spirit away your firstborn before the gods could."

The sharpened dagger of truth slammed into Tyche. Her gaze fell to Dora's face, and she saw what had been there all along—the delicate curve of her brow, the otherworldly light in her eyes. *Mine.* A surge of recognition flooded her senses. Love and terror wrapped thorns around her heart.

"My daughter?" The word splintered. "All this time..."

"The watchtower, where I found Dora." Lep's voice broke. "When Hermes brought me to her, the moonlight bathing her seemed to emanate from within, a clear sign of her mother's blood. Yet, as I looked closer, I noticed the way her dark hair framed her face, the almost unsettling intensity in her expression—traits that implicated a different lineage."

Tyche squeezed her eyes closed. "Ikelos." She whispered her secret into the stillness of the barn. "He's Dora's father."

Lep's eyes narrowed in disbelief. "Ikelos?" He whistled and stepped back.

Tyche nodded, tears streaming down her cheeks at Lep's blanched face. She sobbed as the comprehension dawned in his eyes, the pieces falling into place.

Then the barn flooded with the foul scent of terror. Monstrous shadows swayed on the walls, their fangs snapping and claws extended toward Tyche. She threw her hands over her face and stifled a scream. A hollow moan, tangled in a thousand screams, vibrated through the ground—the voice of Ikelos, twisted and tormented, forced to give shape to the villagers' deepest fears.

Dora whimpered in her sleep. Tyche pulled her daughter close, her heart aching with fierce love. But even that love, she knew, was powerless against the nightmare that was about to engulf them all. Lep lifted Dora from her arms and laid her down on the straw, his gaze lingering on Tyche, then raised a hand in a silent farewell. He turned and slipped into the darkness.

Hermes followed close behind, his expression grave. "I'll accompany him." He glanced at Tyche. "We will investigate the source of this disturbance."

Tyche nodded to him and lay down beside Dora, her eyes heavy, fighting to stay open. The tormented wails of minds unmade by terror echoed from beyond the barn walls. Her eyelids fluttered, then fell, and the nightmare took root.

Nightmares twist desire into obsession, blurring creator and destroyer. For fear ensnares even gods, and obsession whispers their undoing.

FEAR ENSNARES EVEN GODS

The nightmare's roots reached to hold Tyche's eyelids fast and enveloped her in the rich, black earth of their terror. As the shadows of horror sought purchase in her dream, the cries of twisted minds formed a cacophonous hum that vibrated against the walls of her sanity.

"Hush, Mother," Dora whispered, her voice a low, soothing melody. "Sleep now. I want to show you something. A truth you must witness for yourself." She placed a firm hand on Tyche's temple. "I will weave a path through Ikelos' shadows, allowing you to see as he sees, to know his thoughts as if they were your own." Dora's eyes, old with the wisdom of her lineage, studied Tyche's face. "This is a gift of my blood, Fortune and Nightmare entwined."

Show me? Tyche thought in the twilight of half-sleep. The knowledge of Dora's lineage sent a torrent of hot dread through her. *Something horrible is about to happen. I can feel it.*

Dora began to sing, her tune blending a melody of shadow and light, of a darkness that lurked beneath a peaceful surface. As she sang, the ordinary world shifted and bent around Tyche. The lantern's flame flickered, casting perverse forms on the barn walls, and the steady moan of the earth vibrated through the floorboards.

What is happening to me? Tyche's body convulsed as her spirit twisted from its moorings. *This isn't just a dream... it's a nightmare* he *has crafted.* A wave of nausea rose in her throat. *Dora, what do you want me to see? What horrors are you about to unleash?*

"Listen," Dora murmured. "Do you hear them? The villagers. Ikelos has begun his work."

The screams—I can hear them. He's already started. I have to stop him. But how?

Dora's lullaby deepened, forming a melodious song that flooded Tyche's mind. The barn dissolved around them, the walls melting away into swirling mists of song. Reality buckled in its savagery, dragging Tyche into a stretch of sickening distance from her mind and body, hurling her sideways into a maelstrom of swirling color and half-formed images. The torn cosmos seized her and knit her spirit into a shadowed union, then plunged her into the heart of another's nightmare.

Dread ripped the certainty into her mind. She was not alone.

He's here. Ikelos is here, and I sense his dark excitement.

Screams of the villagers, Ikelos' wailing growls, and Dora's constant, hypnotic singing battered her from all sides. The images sharpened, coalescing into a horrifying scene. Tyche was no longer in the barn but standing in the ruined village, the air writhing with the stench of smoke and fear.

The reek of terror clung to her skin like a sickening miasma that choked her lungs. His foul delight in their terror coated her throat with revulsion. The sharp bite of their fear violated her mouth.

This is unbearable. A knot of revulsion rose in her throat. *Is this what he's become? A monster who feeds on the villagers' suffering?*

She stared down at his hands, his claws, his form and recoiled in horror. The devastated village spread before her eyes like a feast for her senses and a playground for her dominion. His pointed muzzle grinned in a forest of deadly points. Wolven eyes surveyed the wreckage. His form rippled in fevered sequence—wolf, beast, man. Nightmare leaned back with his claws clenched into fists. The blackened talons dug into his palms as his jaw unhinged in a pit of endless night.

His dark ecstasy mounted at the thrill of their torment and surged through her veins, making her want to retch. *He's savoring this. He's a monster. How can this be the god I loved?*

The screams echoed in her skull and fueled her power as Ikelos' gnarled form bled and shifted. Serrated scales rippled beneath cracked, pallid skin. Molten eyes raked the wreckage with a predator's appetite, his hunger clawing at her insides, sending tremors of revulsion down her back. He prowled with his nose in the air and inhaled the aroma of nightmare.

She hunted them—a predator in pursuit of its prey—and she couldn't escape. She was trapped, forced to look on as he cursed them through her own eyes. Tyche struggled with a silent scream building in her throat, frantic to pull away, to escape the horror.

Dora's hand tightened on her shoulder. "Watch, Mother," Dora whispered with a firm command. "See what he has become."

"Such exquisite fear." His unsettling murmur vibrated through her bones. "A harvest of terror."

This is what he is now. A monster. Completely adrift. The man I loved is gone.

The lingering taste of terror drew him onward, to where a flash of movement revealed a cat, its fear a sharp, enticing scent in the ruined alley. Tyche recoiled in disgust as Ikelos' back arched, and his matted hackles rose at the feline's delicious fear. His tongue rolled across her lips, savoring the cat's sharp bite of dread. His foul violation scalded her spirit, and a violent retch tore from her chest. Nightmare's monstrous body cracked and shifted into his true form, then he knelt and extended his hand. The cat hissed, but he stroked its fur with a deceptively gentle touch.

"Even in fear, a flicker of warmth." He purred at the cat's panic. "A tender terror."

Nightmare's pleasure surged through her, the animal's frantic pulse a dark thrill in his grasp, then the terrified submission beneath his hand.

This is how he will treat me. Tendrils of ice bloomed through her veins. *Gentle until the moment he strikes.*

"No!" she cried out, her voice trapped in the dream, unheard. "I won't let you turn me into a weapon. I won't let you destroy everything I love."

He rose and swept his cape back. The cat's lingering fear left a tantalizing taste on his tongue with the promise of more to come. His pleasure, the delight of instilling fear, surged through her veins in a sickening wave of emotion.

It's sick. It's twisted. This is who he is. A monster who hides behind a mask of tenderness.

"Such fragile creatures," his voice intruded into her mind, "easily bent to my will."

Drawn by tormented cries, the god of Nightmare stalked onward, and Tyche was forced to follow. The moon's weeping eye followed her course through the village. She detected the barn's skeletal frame in the distance. A single lantern flickered within, marking where she now slept. At her feet, a broken scythe reflected her distorted image—man, wolf, beast. She stared at his reflection and recoiled. Her eyes stormed with the war of his natures.

"Tonight, I will not add to her torment." A flicker of mercy burned in the sparks of his eyes.

Liar! You're already tormenting me! By hurting them, you're hurting me! You're tearing me apart.

His anticipation burned with a dark hunger that consumed her senses and violated her spirit. The dreamscape twisted, and the lord of Nightmares stood before Christos' ruined home, her body forced to mimic the ripples between wolf to man, man to beast, the dizzying sequence a prelude to his dark pleasure. She fought against the transformation with a silent scream trapped in her throat, but his control was absolute.

Ikelos' jaw clenched, and his lips curled into a snarl as he conjured the nightmare, the ancient curses rumbling from his throat. Dark power surged as his form unraveled, beasts flickering beneath his skin. He howled in ecstasy as his bones splintered and muscles unknotted. Tyche cried out at the agony of his transformation, the searing pain threatening to shatter her mind. Ikelos forged the herald of Christos' deepest fears—a predator woven from nightmare. Ikelos reveled in the power to unleash the dream's terror as a wolf, whose eyes burned with the Geryon's molten gaze.

The old man huddled beneath a tattered blanket like a fragile island of sorrow in a sea of fear. Tyche winced, experiencing the waves of his grief as her own, pulsing with the harsh rhythm of her breathing. The ruined village made her stomach turn as she studied Christos' figure, broken and defeated. She watched him thrash in his sleep, stripped bare, left with only the tattered remnants of the destruction.

Oh, Christos. Tyche hovered over the old man, her spirit recoiling from the monstrous form she was forced to wear. She tried to reach out, to warn him, but her hands were bound by Ikelos' will. *What horrors await you now? What fresh hell will he drag you through? Please, be strong. Don't let him break you.*

Ikelos released the nightmare itself, wolf-shaped, through the ruined door, and the dark beast implanted its fangs into Christos' sleeping mind.

"No! Christos!" Tyche screamed, her voice lost in the nightmare's din. "I have to stop Ikelos! This can't be happening!"

Tyche cried out as the seed of Ikelos' venom took root in the twisted reality of Christos' nightmare. His wolf's poison shaped the darkness and gave it form, becoming a dark gateway for the true horror to come—the monster that stole Christos' son.

Within the nightmare, Tyche gasped in confusion as a distorted figure of herself towered on a hill, her grin stretched too wide, and her eyes glittering with an inhuman brightness. Then, the focus of the nightmare warped, and Tryfonas, Christos' son, appeared, his form vibrating like a possessed specter. Ikelos grinned as he shaped the Geryon from shadow and imbued it with his own burning madness. The beast's three heads lunged, snapping and gnashing, its fangs burrowing into Tryfonas' flesh. His screams rippled through the dreamscape, and his blood stained the ground.

Tyche tried to look away, but Ikelos' stare forced her to watch. She gasped as, within the dream, Christos lurched to his feet, grabbed his spear, and charged the beast. The point struck the Geryon with an empty thud, and the creature cackled with wicked joy.

"No! It's not real!" Tyche cried in silent entreaty. "It's a lie! He's trying to break you, Christos! Don't let him! Fight it!"

"Fool!" The dream Tyche shrieked, her words distorted by Ikelos' malice. "Do you think that spent toy can save you now?"

That's not me speaking! That's not who I am! He's twisting his perception, turning him against me! She tried to wrest control, to scream a warning, but her body behaved like a plaything in his hands.

Nightmare paved Tyche's twisted laughter with his own bitterness as he forced her to spin the Wheel of Fate with cold indifference. Christos crumbled and wept in horror to see his son die, again and again.

He's reliving his worst nightmare. Tyche sobbed in her sorrow. *It's cruel. How can Ikelos do this?*

"Tyche... why?" Christos' bitter accusation threaded into the nightmare and tore at Tyche's heart. She recoiled from Ikelos' will as a bitter, invasive tendril wormed into Christos' thoughts, shaping his words into venomous accusations. *"You betrayed us all. You are the one who killed my son."*

Tyche yearned to scream, to shatter the illusion, but her voice was a phantom, her body a prisoner of Ikelos' malice. Just as her spirit threatened to break, a faint thread of Dora's song, fragile against the terror, protected her in its shield. Hymns of defiance, of endurance, wrapped her soul.

The last of Christos' screams ripped through the night, then abruptly ceased. The wolf paused and licked its salivating muzzle.

In the dreamscape, a dark morsel of nightmare quivered beside the elder's curled form. He lunged, his jaws snapping shut around the fragrant flower of torment. Tyche gagged at Nightmare's growls of pleasure at the viscous substance palpitating in his mouth.

Trapped within his gaze as a prisoner in Ikelos' flesh, Tyche watched the wolf turn from the ruined dwelling, its fangs dripping with the nightmare's foul ichor. The wolf lowered his snout to a nearby puddle of water stained crimson with the residue of Christos' horror. A wave of disgust lashed her throat as Ikelos lapped at the tainted liquid, the taste of nightmare, thick and coppery, coating her tongue.

His reflection floated in the puddle as he drank. The hideous wolf snarled at her reflection, which was his reflection, its snout streaked with blood and its yellow eyes blazing with a predatory fire. Tyche recoiled, her stomach clenching in a violent urge to tear herself free from this unholy union.

The vileness of his desire threatened to unravel her. His pleasure in their torment swept through her in a disgusting wave of satisfaction, clashing with her own rising outrage. She rebelled against it, desperate to regain control.

Is that what you see when you look at yourself, Ikelos? A monster?

Driven by a frantic need to stop him, Tyche struggled against Dora's hold, desperate to escape. "Stop! Ikelos, stop this madness!"

The dreamscape warped, the stench of blood replaced with the foul odor of corruption, as the ruined village dissolved into a haze of swirling shadows. Driven by the need for more, Ikelos' form shifted, and he left the waterhole to stalk toward the slumbering Kalliope, who lay within the skeletal remains of her home, her young daughter clutched tightly in her arms. Tyche jerked forward as if her limbs belonged to another, every forced footstep a battle waged against her will.

Dark gore dripped from Ikelos' fangs as he approached Kalliope's makeshift bed of straw.

"No..." Tyche whispered, her plea lost in their shared mind. "Please, not her. She's suffered enough."

The scent of Kalliope's terror coated his tongue in sweet poison. His hands flowed with disturbing grace and wove nightmares imbued with vile design. Tyche rebuked his control, his deliberate cruelty and fought against it in an agonized struggle for her own sanity.

Ikelos' form shifted, and a forked tongue flicked from his lips with a hiss. His skin glistened with an unnatural sheen. With delicate malice, he shaped the sleeping woman's dream. The sickening thrill of Ikelos' dark desire surged through Tyche, threatening to shatter her. She choked back a sob, the forced intimacy a violation of her nature.

He's lost all sense of decency. How can I ever reach him again?

As the dreamscape beneath Kalliope buckled, an avalanche of dread buried Tyche, and the foul atmosphere ripened with the stench of rotting seaweed. A screeching hum rose from the rising water and engulfed her, its vibrations setting her teeth on edge. The mother tugged her child closer as the nightmare's twisted reality flooded the dreamscape. A wave of dark, glassy water crashed over Kalliope, and she choked on its thick, tainted dread. The woman screamed, her voice echoing strangely within the dream, as she thrashed against its wicked current.

"Where's my daughter?" she cried, her empty hands slapping against the water's skin.

Then, she threw her arms across her face when the water rippled and distorted, and Tyche's corrupted image oozed from its depths, cradling Aioropaia like a venomous offering.

"What are you doing?" Kalliope's voice pulsated, distorted and thin. "Give me my baby!"

The mother fought against the nightmare as Tyche's wavering image held her child beneath the surface. Ikelos grinned and wove ancient curses into the illusion's whispered words, threads of corruption, infusing the god of Nightmare's venomous promise of death as the child's struggles weakened. Kalliope's body thrashed on the floor with a silent scream trapped in her throat.

Tears rolled down Tyche's cheeks, her will enslaved by Ikelos, as her face committed the unforgivable. "This is a perversion of my being!" Tyche cried in anguished denial. "I would never hurt a child!"

He's twisting everything, turning me into a monster in their eyes!"

A feral howl rose from the depths of the forest and threaded through the silent village. Nightmare slithered around Kalliope and nudged her side with his snout. A hiss escaped his mouth when she groaned. His forked tongue flicked out, greedily tasting the woman's intoxicating terror.

His feeding on her pain—his thriving on it—surged through her with a vile thrill that made her want to rip free from this depraved fusion.

He's become everything I despise.

The world around Tyche dissolved into a jumble of distorted images and echoing wails. She screamed as her grip on reality loosened, but then, a familiar melody cut through the madness—Dora's song, her steady foothold in the storm. The dreamscape, ever changing, shifted once more.

Then, a blinding white flare erupted from the night's orb, and Ikelos lifted his face to its warning. In the star-dusted void, the moon glared back with a pale, indifferent eye.

"Let them watch." A cruel smile twisted his lips. "Let the gods witness how I embrace their intended punishment."

His defiance, his revelry in darkness, hardened Tyche's anger into rebellion. She wrestled against the rising tide of his will.

He thinks he's untouchable. But he's wrong. I won't let him win.

Against the violent rage of her own spirit, Tyche endured the horror through the windows of his eyes as their form buckled, bones cracking and muscles writhing, reshaping into a monstrous aberration. Scales receded, and black velvety wings unfolded from his back with a soft rustle. He rose, transformed—a winged monster—his fiery eyes raking across the landscape in the pale moonlight.

With a piercing screech, he spread his wings and launched himself into the night. The wretched wind tore at Tyche's face as they soared toward the Gorgon's tree. The scattered collection of flickering lights and charred ruins shrank below them as she followed his path toward the ancient goddess.

The Somnium—even the name sent a shiver down Tyche's spine. She knew it was dangerous, the heart of nightmares. And now, Ikelos flew straight for it.

What dark purpose drives him there? What new horror awaits the villagers in that place of twisted dreams?

The wind howled its dark symphony in her ears as Ikelos lurched through the sky. Tyche strained against his mind, desperate to break free from their bond before it was too late.

Dora's voice sighed in sorrow. "Mother, now he's changing—the beast and man are strangers."

The dreamscape warped and shifted around her as she flew, the lesche materializing from the swirling shadows. Forced to descend, she landed with a soft thud on the worn stone steps of the meeting hall. She paused at a darkened window and peered inside. His reflection wavered, his golden eyes widening as she witnessed the war raging within him—love and hatred, twin serpents, their fangs locked in a venomous conflict.

She recoiled, then shook her head in a frantic attempt to regain control, his internal conflict momentarily forgotten. Inside, the hall's wooden beams loomed in the darkness, the cold fireplace harsh in its absence of warmth. Beyond, in the depths of the hall, Dimitra lay sleeping, her form a pale silhouette against the shadows.

His wings folded into his back, and his body shifted once more. The god of Nightmares rose and wrapped his cloak around his form. He pushed aside the dark hair that tumbled from his brow and squinted an eye as he peered into Dimitra's dream.

You can't stop, can you? Tyche's silent accusation echoed in their shared mind. *Even after torturing Christos and Kalliope, you still need to inflict more pain.*

Nightmare peered into the depths of the sleeping woman's mind, his mouth turning down at the sight of Tyche and Dimitra working side by side in the sun-drenched fields of her dream. His shudder surged through her, and Tyche gagged in revulsion. The women's laughter, rising with the rustle of golden barley, tasted bitter on his tongue.

Ikelos' stare lingered on the image of Tyche's pregnant form, the gentle curve of their child. He snarled, and the dark power of his nightmare wove itself into the dream. Dimitra watched in alarm as Tyche's belly swelled, the skin stretching and contorting in grotesque waves. Dimitra recoiled, her hands flying to her mouth to stifle a scream.

"No!" Tyche cried in an unheard plea, trapped within the confines of his mind. *He's using our child to twist her into a symbol of horror.*

"See how she betrays you." The dark echo of his curse floated through her thoughts. "See what your goddess truly is."

His hand reached into Dimitra's dream and tore open Tyche's swollen belly. A monstrous serpent, black as Tartarus, unfurled from the gaping wound. The serpent's muscular body pulsated, each undulation sending shudders through the nightmare. Dimitra stumbled back at its orbs of molten fire burning with the nightmare's rage. The beast's fiery breath devoured the innocence of the village, reducing dwellings to ash and crops to blackened waste.

Atop the serpent's head, Ikelos crowned Tyche's figure in flames, her form a twisted mockery of divine power. Her broken wails ripped through the dream. Then, her form melted and reformed into a perverse monster. Ikelos' laugh cut through Dimitra's horror while she backpedaled into the roiling darkness.

"He twists me into a hideous parody!" Tyche screamed in denial, lost in the storm of his thoughts. "This isn't who I am! He's trying to turn them against me, to make them fear me!"

"They will fear her." His hiss snaked through her mind. "They will cast her out."

He'll destroy everything. I must break free.

Ikelos grinned and plunged deeper into the hellscape he had woven, and the scene flickered, as though a reflection within a reflection. The landscape warped and rippled, revealing a deeper, more unsettling layer, as if the dream itself were dreaming, a nightmare within a nightmare. A dark river's waters churned with unseen power through the profaned landscape where Ikelos' will reigned.

This is what he wants? For me to be a monster? Tyche thought, her eyes fixed on the scene before her, the forced observation a torment in itself.

The bubbling river loomed, and her form shimmered on the opposite bank, bathed in deceptive moonlight. Around her image, the village children played at her feet. Lep stood close, his hand resting around her waist in a gesture of love and protection. The villagers themselves worked with a quiet acceptance, their faces turned toward her with smiles of admiration.

Ikelos' hatred surged through Tyche in waves of dark emotion.

"You hate this." The ethereal Tyche glared at Ikelos from across the water. "You despise their love for me. That they accept me. That I can be content without you."

In his despair, Nightmare howled at the illusion. "Why them over immortality?" His form undulated into a cacophony of monsters in a grotesque display of his inner turmoil. "Over me?"

Tyche tasted his desperation, and a flicker of pity warred against her anger.

You're breaking, Tyche thought. *You can't stand it. You want me to be as miserable as you are.*

In the dream's impossible logic, the image of Tyche smiled, lifting the child she would soon bear into view, her gaze a silent challenge to Ikelos. "Your daughter, Tychoneira," she proclaimed. "This is what you desire to corrupt." Her serene voice carried across the impassable divide of the rushing waters. "You said they would cast me out. They know I am the goddess of Fortune, and yet they defy the gods for me, for our child."

That's what hurts him the most. Tyche stared at her illusion across the river. *That I am with them without anything to offer. They are drawn to me, not my power.*

"You would live with the mortals?" Fangs gnashed against his forked tongue. "You would keep my daughter from me?"

"I belong where I choose." The sharp blade of the phantom Tyche's words cut through the dreamscape, revealing a dark wound to his unraveling control. "I will protect the villagers and this child from you." Tyche held the baby in her arms as if to say, this child, her Tychoneira, would not be Ikelos' weapon.

I won't let you have her, she vowed, her spirit a burning defiance. *You will not use her. She deserves better than this.* A phantom ache of longing gripped her for the child she could not yet hold.

They held each other's gaze across the churning water as a mute battle waged in the depths of the nightmare he had unleashed, now turned into his own condemnation. Tyche's spectral form wavered, the dreamscape twisting in a manifestation of his own deepest terrors. As the nightmare warped around him, Ikelos stepped back from the roiling water, his eyes wide. Tyche's mind lashed out, savoring the dark justice as Ikelos recoiled from the nightmare's rage.

Ikelos' gasp shuddered through Tyche as her image across the river raised a hand to summon Styx. "Sister. Come. I need you. Ikelos must pay his due!"

The river surged with a jet-black pulse, and a frigid exhalation spread across the water's surface. Styx' midnight shadow unfurled from the fathomless depths, ribbons of darkness forming her shape. She towered over Ikelos, radiating a frozen hatred—the goddess' anger given form in summoned wrath.

Demanding payment for Ikelos' intrusion, the river goddess stretched her dripping, elongated fingers across the water's surface. "You corrupt the boundaries between sleep and waking." The words swirled across the water's surface in an unsettling pronouncement that echoed in Tyche's mind. "Pay your toll in blood or soul."

Ikelos dipped his paw into the water's edge, and it recoiled from his touch. "I have already paid. My heart bleeds for what I destroy."

Liar! Tyche's anger flared in a rage that was both hers and his. *You revel in destruction. You enjoy their suffering.*

The dreamscape grew thick with dread, and the River Styx towered before them, its dark waters roaring with primordial authority. Then, a faint whisper of Dora's melody reached Tyche's ears in a call to strength.

Styx' fingers curled into a fist of relentless judgment. She leaned into Ikelos, her eyes burning with cold fire. "Your heart bleeds for yourself. You twist dreams into weapons, and you would steal my sister's child for your own dark ambition. I offer you one chance, god of Nightmares. Swear by the Styx that you will leave Tyche and her daughter untouched. Swear, and I will let you pass."

Take it, Ikelos! Tyche pleaded silently, her voice trapped in the shared mind. *Please! Just let us go!*

Ikelos' monstrous form rippled with rage in a display of his unchecked power. "I swear by nothing. Tyche and her child are mine to command. You have no power here, River Witch. This is my domain."

Styx' eyes burned with fury. "Then you will know the true meaning of nightmare." Her curse rippled on the water like a dark promise of retribution. "Your dreams will become your prison. The Styx will claim you, Ikelos. You will drown in the nightmares you create."

Oh, gods. No! Tyche's heart pounded with dread. *She's going to destroy him, us. Wait, sister, until I am freed from his fetters!*

The river surged, its oily blackness rising like a tidal wave, and consumed the dreamscape. The water flooded the nightmare, filling his lungs, her lungs. He screamed—her scream trapped in his throat—an animalistic cry of rage. Then, he cursed Tyche. Cursed her sister. His monstrous form writhed as the Styx engulfed them, pulling them into its depths. The words of Styx' prophecy surged into their lungs with a final, damning promise. "You will drown in your own darkness, Ikelos. Forever."

The curse unraveled Ikelos' sanity, and a surge of horror struck Tyche as his perceptions warped. He witnessed impossible things, she knew, an evil that would later become the foundation of his own terrible dream and trap her within it.

"No! No, please!" Tyche cried, her voice breaking in a frantic appeal for mercy. "Don't let me be trapped in this hell forever!"

Then came a violent shift. The crushing blackness of the Styx melted away, and Ikelos' fractured mind resurfaced, dragging himself toward the dawn like a doomed beast. Fragments of depraved hellscapes pulsated in his vision—roots that gnawed at flesh, grins stretched too wide, the air ripe with the stench of fear. Yet still a dark excitement burned within him, within her. He would weave these horrors, she knew, into a cage for his wayward goddess. A prison where she would learn to fear him.

He coughed and then retched, the phantom burn of the Styx searing her lungs. A thick dread settled in her stomach.

What is he planning?

Then, the gentle tug of a familiar melody began to draw her back. The suffocating darkness of the Styx receded, and the chaotic visions of Ikelos' fractured mind blurred and faded.

Sickly purple and grey fingers gouged the sky with the coming dawn. Ikelos' strength diminished, forced to retreat from the light as his nightmares completed their dark work. The villagers would awaken to fresh horrors, their trust in his beloved irrevocably poisoned.

What have you done?

Tyche's heart raced as his dark thoughts twisted through her, but the gentle pull of Dora's song grew stronger. Soon, Tyche unwound, a thread pulling free from a dark spool, guided toward release. The spindle turned, and the threads, binding her to him, loosened. His dark satisfaction dulled to a static hum in her mind, rather than the previous sharp sting, as his wolves gathered at his side. The nightmare had served Ikelos' purpose well—isolating Tyche and poisoning her bonds with the mortals—all to prepare for the moment he would claim their child as his own.

He still thinks he can win. Even after all this, he believes he can control me and our daughter.

She choked on his unwanted ache for love and belonging, the weakness a foreign intrusion into his spirit. He cursed the lingering emotions that made him hesitate.

He believes our child would prove his strength, as if she is his ultimate masterpiece. Tyche understood now—Ikelos didn't love Tychoneira. *He wants to control her. To exploit her.*

The spool of Dora's melody spun freely, the threads loosening Tyche's tether to Nightmare.

"The gods play their game." Nightmare murmured in the pre-dawn light. "But I play my own."

And what game is that, Ikelos? Tyche's mind screamed, still bound to his. *What is your endgame? And how much more will you destroy to achieve it?*

But no answer was forthcoming as Dora's song soothed Tyche, and a gentle release from the shared mind was complete. "Sleep now, Mother. You are strong. I have shown you Ikelos' true nature. I must go now, but do not fear, for you are safe."

As the nightmare dissolved, a deep weariness settled over Tyche. The residue of Ikelos' treachery and obsession spilled into her uneasy sleep. His shadow stained her with the assurance of trials to come, for her soul, for her daughters, and for those she had come to love.

Nightmares battle the mind, testing the soul's truth, as fear becomes a cruel design. For despair's trial reveals love's light, and lost innocence reshapes belonging.

27

FEAR BECOMES A CRUEL DESIGN

Dawn's fangs tore through the sky and smeared the heavens in scars of crimson and ashen yellow. The mountains beneath Pikerni shuddered, their stone bones groaning with the aftershocks of Ikelos' nightmares. Twisted shadows clung to the peaks as the unnatural hues spread across the waking world.

The barn door creaked open, and Lep and Hermes stepped inside. They returned from their search of the perimeter, their eyes downcast at the horrors they had seen.

The morning's light offered Tyche no relief, only the torment that still clung to the edges of her vision. Guilt and sorrow burned Tyche's heart as Hermes paced in frustration, while outside, the soft moaning and shuffling feet revealed the villagers' suffering.

Still trapped in the aftershocks of the nightmare, Tyche stared into the distance, but her eyes couldn't seem to settle on anything in particular. The shapes of Lep and Hermes blurred, and their voices became distant, muted.

"We should get back out there." Lep peered from the doorway. "Maybe we can help anyone in need."

Lep held out his hand to Tyche, and together they stepped out into the village square. To her dismay, Pikerni's ruins spread before her in a grotesque panorama of shattered stone and charred timbers. The stench of destruction lined Tyche's nostrils with a renewed sense of Ikelos' treachery. She meandered with a strange detachment, her body obeying Lep's guidance, but her mind remained trapped in the nightmare's labyrinth. The shadows writhed in a macabre dance of the prior night, and every distorted wail of torment rang in her ears. She fought the urge to scream, to tear herself away from the horrific vision she had been forced to witness.

"The village is so quiet." She strained her ears for the familiar sounds of children's laughter and birdsong but found an unsettling stillness.

An orange cat brushed against Tyche's legs, and she knelt to pet its back as it arched into her palm. The rotten stench rising from the animal triggered a flash of Ikelos' twisted smile, and she stumbled, momentarily lost in the nightmare's grip. Tyche's gut twisted. *He did this.*

The smell of fear and the blank looks on the villagers' faces warned of a new horror. A black feather, oily and bright, caught her eye. *Ikelos was here.*

Hermes offered his hand and pulled Tyche upright. "The barn is the safest place for you. We must return."

Without another word, he turned and strode back toward the barn. Tyche and Lep followed, their footsteps a grim procession through the village. Once there, Hermes pushed open the heavy door, its hinges groaning in protest, and the trio stepped inside. Kid rushed to Tyche with a soft, questioning bleat. She grimaced as Hermes slid the large wooden bolt into place, the solid thunk resounding in the barn's stillness.

"I warned you, Tyche," Hermes said as he stood before the door. "The gods have given Ikelos no recourse. They force him to curse the village. I tried to prepare you, but failed."

She shuddered at the memory of her dream—Ikelos bound before the gods.

"And they will not stop there," Hermes added. "They will take your child, as intended."

Lep's hand tightened on Tyche's shoulder. "We will not let them." He kissed her temple. "We shall find a way to protect her."

Tyche breathed hard and stared at the splintered wood of the barn door with a vacant expression. "Ikelos has made his last mistake," she said.

"The village..." Hermes barred the door. "They suffered greatly last night. I heard their cries, even from here. The nightmares—"

"They were not mere nightmares," Lep interrupted. "They were calculated and cruel. I fear what they have done to the peoples' minds."

"It was Ikelos' work." Tyche buried her face in Lep's shoulder. "He knows how to distort dreams and turn them into weapons." Tyche's voice rose. "Dora... oh gods, Dora! What has he done to my daughter? Where is she?" The villagers' approaching voices cut short her concern.

"They are here." Lep glanced at Hermes and stepped between Tyche and the barn entrance.

A wave of angry shouts crashed against the doorway. Then came the heavy, rhythmic thuds, sending tremors through the floor. *Christos*. The thought made her stomach clench. The sickening crack of splintering wood grew louder with each impact. She braced herself as the door groaned in protest, then a final, earth-shattering crash vibrated through the barn, and the door gave way. Lep raised his staff, his eyes darting between the villagers and Tyche. Hermes rushed to stand beside Lep as the villagers surged through the gaping hole in a torrent of anger.

Tyche gasped at their wild and bloodshot eyes. Christos pushed to the front, his face lit with a dark fire.

"She laughed." Christos broke from the crowd and lunged at Tyche. "She didn't just laugh—she *cackled* when my son was ripped apart." Lep pushed Christos back, and he fell to the ground with a curse.

Tyche's stomach clenched as Christos spoke, the memory of the nightmare battling with the horror of his accusation. *How could he think...?* "Please," she cried out. "You have to understand. Ikelos is manipulating your minds and using your grief against you. I would never..."

Tears choked Kalliope's accusation as she stumbled forward. "I saw her at the water's edge." Rage spilled from her eyes. She pointed her finger at Tyche. "The spring was tainted." Kalliope's eyes widened at the memory and then narrowed as she glared at Tyche. "The water turned black like death itself and seeped into my bones. She chanted in a tongue I didn't understand, invoking gods that made me want to retch. Then, she held my daughter under the putrid water until she... drowned."

Tyche's heart shattered, and her legs loosened. "No," she whispered. "It wasn't me. It was him, Ikelos. He forced his nightmares on you to see things that weren't real."

Lep's jaw tightened as he gripped his rod. Hermes' brow arched, his gaze darting between Tyche and the villagers.

"The serpent!" A shriek cut through the barn as Dimitra pushed forward. "She births a monster to destroy us all!"

A chorus of accusations swelled around Tyche. Lep and Hermes stepped toward the villagers still steeped in the clutches of the nightmares' debris.

A strange stillness fell over Christos, then his voice shifted, and a purr growled from his throat. "Why cling to mortals, my love? They are unworthy of you." The sun burst in the man's ocean eyes, and a wolven glow burned. The dark tang of putrid nightmare grew stronger as Christos seized a pitchfork from the wall of the barn. A shadow rippled across his form, and a shock of raven hair tumbled over his forehead. He leveled his molten gaze at Tyche, and with a menacing growl, the man-god raised his weapon and charged Lep. With a sharp crack, the Asclepian Rod intercepted the pitchfork's blow. Lep whirled away, the rake's prongs hissing past Lep's ear and whipping his hair in a trail of displaced air.

Tyche stumbled, her attention locked on Lep's desperate defense. Kid's bleats rose to a frantic pitch, and his hooves stamped the ground, sending tremors through the barn floor. The goat positioned himself between Tyche and Ikelos.

She stepped around Kid and faced the frightened villagers. Her voice rose above the chaos. "Please." Tears of sorrow streamed down Tyche's face. "You have to listen! He's twisting your minds. Look at Christos, at Kalliope! He's used your love, your grief, and your deepest fears to make you see things that aren't real, to turn you against me."

Her plea settled over the barn. Dimitra's shoulders trembled, and Tyche saw a glimpse of comprehension flooding her eyes. The woman inhaled a deep breath and directed her hardened gaze to the goddess.

"You're right," she said. "I won't be his puppet anymore. *We* won't! The god of Nightmares deceived us. This anger is his poison, not our own." Dimitra faced the crowd, and Tyche sighed with relief when the other villagers nodded.

Tyche approached Christos and pulled the pitchfork from his shaking hand and handed it to Lep. "Christos, will you look at me?" She lifted the old man's chin with her palm until their eyes met. "Ikelos punished the village with his nightmares, with visions of drowning and death. I'm so sorry, Christos," she said. "The vision you saw of Tryfonas wasn't real. It was the weapon he used to try and divide us, you and me." Tyche pressed a kiss to the old man's forehead. "But he has no power here among us," she murmured as the fragile beat of his heart trembled against her lips.

Silence descended on the barn as the villagers absorbed the truth. In the quiet, a surge of panic clenched Tyche's chest. *They believed the nightmares,* she thought, her stomach twisting. *They believed the monster Ikelos made me out to be.* Their accusations cut her with blades of doubt. Had her divine power changed her so much? Was she capable of such cruelty?

No, of course not!

She shook her head to dispel the dark thoughts, but the villagers' expressions, sharpened by suspicion and fear, raked her heart. *Dora.* The name became her salvation in the swirling chaos. *I have to find her. I have to prove to them—to myself—that I'm not a monster.*

"Dora," she gasped. "Is she with you? Where is Dora?"

Confusion swept through the villagers. They exchanged glances of blame and dread.

A faint whimper rose from the back of the crowd. "I saw her last at Tryfonas' funeral." The crowd parted to reveal Evy. "She was with me then." A sob ripped through her. "I thought she was with you last night, Tyche. I believed she was safe."

"What of the wolves?" Melina's cry rang out. "The child should never be alone after nightfall!"

Tyche's heart seized. "She *was* with me." A flicker of fragmented memory surfaced. "She wanted to show me something, then said she had to leave. I was exhausted and caught in the nightmare's thrall. I didn't understand." *My daughter. Gone. The wolves and the nightmares.*

Ikelos. He has her.

"Dora!" Her name tore from Tyche's soul. "We must find her before it's too late. She's the child of my flesh and bones!"

The barn fell deathly silent at her confession. Lep's arm tightened around her shoulders to ward off the shock that rippled through the villagers. They turned to the goddess in disbelief. Tyche's heart hammered in her chest, the revelation still fresh. Days before, in the aftermath of Tryfonas' funeral, Hermes had revealed the truth to her. Dora, the child Lep had found in the watchtower, was her daughter. A secret kept by the gods and a truth she had barely begun to comprehend.

Tyche gasped at the memory of Hermes' words. *I had no choice but to spirit away your firstborn.* The knowledge that Dora was hers, a child born of forbidden love and divine manipulation, squeezed the breath from her lungs. She saw the confusion in the villagers' eyes, the unspoken questions. How could this be? How could the child the village raised, the girl they knew as Dora, be the daughter of a goddess and the Nightmare god himself?

"I know this is difficult for you to hear." Tyche's voice trembled in the silence. "I only learned the truth myself after we buried Tryfonas. But Dora—she's mine. And she's in danger." She struggled to find the words to explain the impossible, the divine forces that had shaped her life, and the guilt that ate at her for keeping this secret, even from herself. "I need your help. We have to find her. Before Ikelos..." She trailed off in unspoken fear.

Lep squeezed her against his chest. He had carried the burden of this secret with him, and now he would stand by her. The villagers stirred as their sense of urgency replaced their stunned silence.

Tyche's haunted gaze swept across their faces. "Please," she held out her hands to them. "Help me. Help me find my daughter."

"We all love Dora no matter her parentage. She may be your child, Tyche, but she is the daughter of the village, too." Lep raised his voice for all to hear. "We will bring her home, no matter the cost."

Tyche closed her eyes and prayed to any power that hadn't turned its back on her. She strained to summon her Wheel of Fortune, but its silence shattered her willpower, and she fell to her knees.

The sight of their fallen goddess ignited fierce protectiveness in the villagers. They surged forward, lifting her, hugging her with love and promises. They would find Dora, they would face the wolves, and they would defy the gods, for she was their Dora, and she was Tyche's daughter.

Tyche regained her footing and clenched her fists. Her fingers brushed the ribbon tied around her wrist and caressed a strand of Dora's hair bound within.

"Hurry!" Kalliope urged. "What is everyone waiting for? We don't have time to waste!"

Within minutes, the barn emptied, and the village soon erupted with frantic activity—ropes snaked through calloused hands, waterskins gurgled as the women filled them, and the sharp, rhythmic clang of metal reverberated as the men sharpened their spears.

"Let us not lose another child of Pikerni to the gods. We must move with haste," Christos commanded the people gathered in the square. "We find Dora before nightfall.

"We'll search the forest, the spring, and the fields." Dimitra hugged Tyche, then motioned to the villagers, ready to depart.

A sharp snort cut through the barn door, and Hermes backed away, his lips pressed into a thin line. "Pegasus," he said. "I'm needed elsewhere." He gave Tyche a reassuring nod before vanishing in a flash of light.

Lep leaned into Tyche and wrapped an arm around her waist. "The watchtower," he murmured. "It overlooks everything."

She gripped his hand and pulled him forward. "Yes, the watchtower."

Christos wrapped a coil of rope around his shoulder and lifted his spear. "Then we move!" He turned to the crowd and pointed toward the spring. "Kalliope, Dimitra, you take the spring. The rest of us will spread through the forest and fields. We meet back here at midday."

Pikerni's scorched ruins marked their departure even as the gods' wrath still smoldered. A dank breeze swept through the plateia, and Tyche shivered. *He's watching.* Her fingers tightened around the ribbon on her arm. *The watchtower*, she thought, her daughter's name a silent mantra on her lips.

Ancient power stirs beneath a mother's heart as destiny's balance teeters over the abyss. What force will birth from love's protection when the scales of fate tip?

28

BENEATH A MOTHER'S HEART

"Dora," Tyche exhaled the name in a plea to calm her rising dread.

Lep steadied her as they began the trek toward the watchtower. "We will seek every path and every corner." He drew her into his arms. "I know you are upset, but we need to think about the baby." He pressed his lips to her forehead, then her temple. "Your time is near. Have you suffered any contractions?"

Tyche hugged him tightly, the swell of her stomach a frustrating barrier. "This child has to wait until I find my other one. Oh, Lep, what if the wolves took her? Or Ikelos?"

Lep kissed her lips with a promise. "Shh, we will find our daughter."

Tyche's breath hitched as she absorbed his words. "*Our* daughter?"

"Yes, woman." Lep smiled. "I've loved her since I found her." He guided Tyche forward. "Come."

Tyche struggled to focus, to push aside the lingering fear and the tightening in her belly. Loose stones shifted beneath her feet, and the steep incline intensified Tyche's labored breath. She clutched Lep's arm for support as the sting of nausea burned her throat. She leaned over and clutched her knees, gasping for breath. Each step sent a sharp twinge through her abdomen in a warning she endeavored to ignore. Tyche clenched her teeth, her stubborn will refusing to yield to the pain.

"You are not well." Lep halted and took Tyche's hands in his. His eyes dropped to her belly. "We should stop."

Tyche offered a tight smile. "I'm fine." She pressed her lips around the bitter lie. "I need you to listen. If anything happens to me, you have to guard the baby. You must protect Dora."

"Nothing is going to happen. We will find Dora. Together. I can go alone if this journey is too difficult."

"She's my daughter! I will search for her, no matter what it takes." Tyche pulled away from his hold. "Don't you dare underestimate me," she hissed.

"I apologize." Lep steadied her. "I did not mean any offense. I worry about you."

"I know." Tyche's anger subsided as she leaned against him. "But I need to go. I must know she's safe."

"I understand. Say no more." He smoothed the hair from her sun-drenched face.

"Do you remember when you first found her?" Tyche wheezed. "At the top of the watchtower?"

"It seems a lifetime ago." Lep kept a firm hand against the small of her back.

"She must have been so small." Tyche's brow furrowed. "Did she cry? Was she scared?"

Lep shook his head. "No, the babe did not cry. She looked at me with her strange eyes like she already knew."

"Knew what?" Tyche asked.

"That we were hers." Lep's gaze remained on the path. "When I found her, there were wolf prints near the base of the tower."

"Exactly as I feared." Tyche glanced at Lep, then at the trail. "We must hurry."

With each step along the steep climb, the Mantineian watchtower pulsed into view. Its white stones glowed like an anchor against the valley's swirling disarray. At first, only the tower's peak pierced the horizon in a sliver of sunlit bone. Then, as they ascended, the entire structure materialized, its form shifting as if shaped by the hands of forgotten gods. Lep's eyes narrowed as the air around the tower hummed in a shimmering curtain between worlds.

A primal current drew Tyche toward the tower, stirring her mother's heart with the vision of her daughter's safe haven. "It's alive," Tyche breathed in awe.

They reached the tower's base. Its white stones thrummed with an inner light under the sun's golden fist. Tyche leaned a hand against the weathered marble to catch her breath. The massive wooden door beside her stood ajar like an unspoken invitation. Tyche's gaze met Lep's, and he pushed. They entered the tower's cool darkness. Dust and damp stone choked the air, while silence pressed against their ears, broken only by their breaths.

Ragged groans marked Tyche's ascent of the narrow spiral staircase. Lep followed, his hand a supportive presence against her back. When they reached the top landing, they stepped through an arched doorway into the circular chamber. The sight before them stilled Tyche's breath.

Dora knelt before a stone altar. Her fragile frame was bathed in a silver glow that pulsed from within. Tyche paused at the doorway, her hand pressed against the tightening in her belly. Dora's eyelids fluttered, her lips moving in a silent incantation. Lep gripped Tyche's arm, and together they crossed the threshold.

Tyche's hands flew to her throat. "Dora."

The child opened her eyes, and a knowing smile touched her lips. "Mother."

"What are you doing here? We were so afraid." Tyche rushed to Dora and clasped her daughter against her chest.

"I came here after I left you in the barn." Dora gestured toward the altar. "I wanted to ask the gods to bring Tryfonas back. But they didn't answer." A shadow of sadness crossed her face.

"And why the tower?" Lep cupped the child's head in his palm.

Dora looked from Tyche to Lep, her eyes filled with an old wisdom. "My heart led me here. It tasted of home."

Dora's lips parted with arcane whispers, and two objects coalesced in her hands. One was a dark horn of polished wood, its coiling sea snake murmuring with the ocean's depths. The other, a coin etched in swirling designs, pulsed with a golden light.

"These are mine," Dora said. "I always knew." Her gaze met Tyche's. "I knew you were my mother. I remember Olympus and Hermes taking me away." She looked at Lep. "These were given to me by the tower, Father. They are mine."

Lep's eyes widened in surprise. "Father?" he echoed, his voice rough with emotion. He looked at Tyche, then back at Dora. "She called me father."

Tyche's eyes glistened. "I heard." A smile touched her lips.

Dora tilted her head. "Is it not alright?" she asked. "Do you not wish to be my father?"

Lep knelt beside her. "No, Dora," he murmured. "It is more than alright."

Tyche leaned closer, her hand pressed against her belly. "Lep is the one who found you," she explained. "He brought you to me."

Dora's eyes widened. "I remember it well." She glanced at Lep. "Thank you."

Lep caressed her cheek. "You are welcome, daughter."

"Ikelos," Dora said. "What is he like?"

Tyche hesitated, her gaze shifting to Lep. "He is—complex. He is a god of Nightmares, but—"

"I know his darkness, Mother. I was with you in his nightmare." Dora's brow furrowed. "But I refuse to behave like him."

Her form flickered, then shifted, her features becoming monstrous before returning to normal. "I have his power, too," she said.

Tyche's smile faltered. "Tell us about the watchtower's gifts."

The child glanced at the artifacts in her hands. "This is Aether's Edge, and this is Fate's Weight." She lifted the horn into the light. "Aether's Edge is a branch of the Gorgon's tree. It can whisper warnings or bring forth shadows. It is also a part of Grandfather's primordial waters."

Lep's frown deepened. "The Gorgon's tree?"

The carved snake on the horn slithered across its bell. "The tower gave it to me."

Tyche pressed her hand against her belly. "And Fate's Weight, Dora?"

The child held out the coin. "This is the balance. It can bring fortune or control the shadows. It is a part of you, Mother."

Lep took the coin from her palm and turned it in his fingers. "Control the shadows? What do you mean?"

Before Dora could answer, Tyche gnashed her teeth against her first contraction. "The baby's coming."

Dora's eyes widened. Fate's Weight shimmered in her palm. "Mother! I can help ease the pain."

Tyche shook her head, her face contorted. "No, Dora. I need Hermes."

A sudden gust of wind swept through the chamber, and a thunderous rush of wings grew louder. Hermes descended through a large, circular window at the tower's peak. Pegasus' powerful wings beat against the air as he landed in the room.

"Tyche!" Hermes leapt off the steed's back and knelt beside her. "I sensed your pain and came as soon as I could. I've scouted a hidden spring where Styx and Oceanus' waters flow together. It's the safest place for the birth."

Relief washed over Tyche. "Hermes... how can I ever thank you?"

"Lift her onto Pegasus." Hermes motioned to Lep and Dora. "We must be swift."

With a gentle command from Hermes, Pegasus folded his wings and then knelt, his powerful legs tucking beneath him. He settled Dora onto Pegasus' back, then mounted behind her. Hermes reached out a hand to Tyche and pulled her up as Lep supported her from behind. But as Tyche scaled Pegasus, dark ichor blossomed between her legs, and she cried out. She wrapped her arms around Hermes' back as the contraction ripped through

her. The messenger motioned for Lep to climb on behind Tyche
and hold her secure in his arms.

Hermes clasped Tyche's hands against his chest. "I rescued
you and Dora from Olympus before. I won't fail you now."

"Hold on. You're safe." Lep leaned forward on the horse's
broad back to secure his woman in his arms. "We'll be there
soon."

Pegasus launched from the tower, his wings carrying them
through the airy expanse. The wind became a rushing melody
to accompany the rising crescendo of Tyche's labor. Far below,
the scroll of land unrolled. Silver-threaded rivers wound through
emerald hills, revealing the distance they covered. Tyche's cries
rose with the pain of childbirth. Each bellow tightened Lep's
grip around her. Finally, the shadowed mouth of a cave appeared
before them, growing steadily larger, as Hermes' voice cut
through the wind and Tyche's cries.

"This spring is a source of primordial power—a confluence
of Titan energies hidden from the eyes of Olympus. It predates
even the Great War." Hermes gestured toward the shadowed cave
entrance. "Since the dawn of time, the Titan's Cradle has brewed
the waters of Styx and Oceanus into a single ancient power." His
words grew somber. "This union of waters illuminates the heart,
Tyche. They reflect the desires of those who appear before them
and expose the secrets concealed below the surface."

Tyche groaned and twisted her fingers into Hermes' cloak.

The landscape blurred into a shadowed cave entrance where
Pegasus landed. Trickling water sounded through the damp
cavern, and starlight reflected in the water as images of her sister
and father rose to meet Tyche.

Hermes helped the goddess dismount from Pegasus' back. Her legs trembled, and she clutched her belly.

"The spring is ahead." Hermes gave a sideways nod. "Lep, Dora, quickly."

Inside the cave, the air hummed with energy. Hissing water rushed through the chamber in a perpetual sequence of its shifting energies. Hermes guided them to a deep body of water that shimmered with an otherworldly luminescence.

"This cave, this spring," Hermes waved an arm around the cavern, "is a sanctuary where we, with Titan blood, are welcomed."

Hermes directed Lep to help Tyche into the water. "This convergence creates a barrier against Olympian interference. It is why I brought you here. In this sanctuary, your birth will be shielded from the gods' prying eyes." He paused, his gaze meeting Tyche's. Seeing the sweat beading on her brow, he added, "You will be safe here. Do not fear. We were unable to come here before because Olympus held you within its grasp. It is due to your recent escape that we have this opportunity to bring you here. The gods are in disarray, and their attention is elsewhere, but that will not last. We must deliver this child quickly, before they plot their revenge."

Tyche moaned as Lep sank into the pool behind her and pulled her body into his arms.

Hermes knelt at the spring's edge. "I know the burden of your choice. You have chosen the path of love that demands sacrifice. But I swear to you, I will protect you and your children." He glanced at Lep and Dora. "I will make sure you are not disturbed. Pegasus awaits outside. We will stand guard. If the situation changes, I will return."

With an encouraging nod at Tyche, he stood and stepped back from the spring's bank, then his form faded into the dim light of the cave. The quiet shifting of Pegasus' hooves stirred from beyond as Hermes stood sentinel in the night.

Love's shield births a shadow, as sacrifice questions its worth. Can a mother's heart hold both light and darkness when good and evil contend?

LOVE'S SHIELD BIRTHS A SHADOW

Tyche's screams echoed through the cave and careened off the damp stone. Pain arched her back as she thrashed against creation's twisted parody of the bone-deep contraction. Her agony flickered across the dark water with images of monsters and demons from the depths as the water lapped around her body, then convulsed, twisting in a spiral of turquoise and obsidian. Lep held Tyche close to his chest and wiped the sweat from her face. *Mortality's price? The gods' final, vicious jest?* She screamed the words in her mind.

Lep braced himself against Tyche's back and laced his arms under her shoulders, then leaned close and murmured soothing words against the storm of her cries. "You are strong, woman." He gripped her fingers in his. "Squeeze my hands." Then a sudden surge in the pool shattered the intimacy of Lep's comfort.

Oceanus breached the surface with a convulsion of water. His form rose from the pool in a roaring emerald gyre. Diamond spray scattered from his colossal frame, and the primordial water's thunder pulsed from his substance. Tyche stretched a trembling hand, but the god's focus turned to the water behind him. Across the pool's skin, a frigid exhalation spread, and Styx' midnight shadow unfurled. The threads of her darkness curled together in a drape of night, her silhouette pulsing with an inner cold that enveloped Tyche with a whisper of the underworld's caress.

Dora's hand flew to Fate's Weight, the coin pulsing with a golden light. She glided into the water next to her mother and cupped Tyche's sweat-slicked cheek before pressing the coin against her brow. Tyche groaned in exhaustion and settled against Lep's chest in the momentary reprieve of pain.

"Daughter." Oceanus' voice rumbled against Tyche's ear. "Let my essence ease your suffering. Surrender to its embrace."

She moaned as the water wrapped around her limp body, drawing her deeper into its comforting coolness.

Tyche stirred, then gasped when her stomach clenched with the next contraction. She howled into the pain and clawed at Lep's hands as the pool churned and whipped around her like a storm's tempest.

"Sis-Terrr," Styx' voice rasped. "LeT My sHadoWs shIELd YOu fROm THiS daRKnesS. I WilL takE yOUr PAin aS mY oWn." A dark mist coiled around Tyche in her sister's protective embrace.

Lep braced himself, his hands slick with the pool's dark water, and pulled Tyche's knees back to widen the passage. A hot bolt of pain ripped through her belly, and she stifled a scream.

"Push!" Lep urged as he gripped her legs from behind.

Tyche cried out again and bore down, grunting with the force of the contraction. The baby's head crowned, and a grotesque, alien shape pushed against the stretched flesh. A cloud of black ichor bloomed in the water, then it folded into the mist surrounding her.

Oceanus' foamy hand rested against his daughter's cheek. "Soon the child will be born, and your pain will ease."

Tyche's body shuddered as she leaned back into Lep's arms in a boneless heap.

Styx hissed and drew her waters over Tyche to quell her raging fever. "En-DuRE, Si-SteR. LeT ThE sTREngth OF aNcIEnT bLOoD fLOW tHRough yOU."

"My father and sister are worried for me." Tyche writhed against Lep's chest in her delirium. "Their distress washes over me in the currents."

"Yes, Oceanus and Styx are here with you. Dora and Hermes, too," Lep whispered over her and smoothed the hair back from her face. "One more push."

Tyche clenched her jaw and leaned forward to clasp her knees. Her chin dug into her chest as her muscles contracted into the involuntary desire to push. She drew a shuddering breath and bore down, grunting.

Then, with a final, desperate heave, the child forced its way into the world, its rasping cry stifling Tyche's scream. Lep reached between her legs and lifted the baby from the dark waters of the pool. He held her up, wet and steaming, and placed her on Tyche's quivering stomach. The newborn peered at her through blackened orbs of malignant night. Her slick gray skin vibrated and churned as it transformed.

A wave of disgust hit Tyche, and she backpedaled away from the abomination. "No. Not mine," she cried and pushed it away.

Lep scooped up the child with one hand, then severed the cord with his blade. Styx recoiled when the child's aura unfurled to ensnare her shadows, the water around them roiling in revulsion.

Oceanus pounded his fists of water against the cave's walls and roared.

Dora stood at the water's edge and stared at the baby, her features twisting with a wave of horror as she studied her newborn sister. But fear flickered in Dora's eyes, too, followed by a strange, unsettling recognition.

Can you see it, too? Tyche wondered, gooseflesh rising on her arms. *The same shadow that opposes the light inside you?*

Even as the child drew her first breath, the shadows deepened and darkness recoiled. Tychoneira's taut skin revealed angular muscle and bone, and her flesh rippled in a grotesque dance. Then, her limbs elongated and her spine arched. Coarse, dark fur sprouted from her skin, and a wolfish snout protruded from her face. Her eyes narrowed into predatory slits and glowed with a feral intensity. Just as quickly, the wolfish form dissolved, replaced by a coil of shimmering scales. A forked tongue flicked from her mouth. Then the scales melted, and limbs pushed through her skin to resolve into a disturbingly perfect human child.

Her dark gaze traveled over Tyche's face, then the cave, a new world now revealed to her. Behind her thin-lipped smile, curved fangs gleamed, and black, inky hair writhed on her head. Tyche gasped as Tychoneira dissolved into a slow, sickening ooze.

Lep gulped at the putrid mass in his hand, which had once been the baby. "The child is not human, Tyche, nor god, but something far more sinister." A cry ripped from his throat as he recoiled and flung the creature from him. Tychoneira hit the water, her form shifting again. Scales shimmered across her body, and it slithered from the pool into a dark crevice of the cave wall.

"It's evil." Tyche closed her eyes against the nightmare.

Delirium ravaged her mind, the cave walls blurring, then dissolving. One moment, grand marble columns of Olympus rose around her, the scent of ambrosia thick and sweet. Next, the columns vanished, replaced by rugged peaks of a lost world, wind whipping at her face. Then a crushing pressure pushed against her, and the peaks disappeared, replaced by the ocean's depths swallowing her whole, the silence broken by her panicked gasps. A distant voice, Lep's plea to return, swirled through the chaos. Shadows deepened, shifting, unseen eyes watching. The cave pulsed with a discordant drone as if the stone came alive in Tychoneira's presence.

A sharp screech pierced Tyche's confusion. Her eyes snapped open when the child's form erupted from the crevice in a blur of scales and fury. The creature uncoiled in a whip of dark energy and struck at the air, attempting to leap toward the cave's exit. Tyche gasped, her heart pounding a frantic rhythm against her ribs.

From the depths of the pool, a dark figure of shadow and fire rose. Styx moved with unnatural speed, her form solidifying into a barrier of flames at the cave's entrance, blocking Tychoneira's path. "YoU sEEk pAsSaGe, ChiLD... BuT tHIs tHrEshOlD iS nOt fOr yOU. ThE pRiCe Of eNtRy Is a sUrRenDeR... Of aLL tHat yOU aRE." Her words carried the heat of the forge. "WiLl yOU rELinQuIsH YoUr dIvInE pOwEr AnD bEcOmE... mOrTAl?"

Oceanus lifted his hands to the cave's ceiling, and the pool's waters surged upward, swirling into a protective dome around Tyche, Lep, and Dora. The barrier glimmered with emerald light against the creature's rage. Tyche tightened her grip on Lep and Dora and cried out in fear.

Tychoneira's scales rippled, then dissolved, replaced by the glint of razor-sharp talons. The monstrous bird screeched and snapped its beak at the watery shield. The bird vanished, its form melting into a hulking bear. Red eyes blazed, and a guttural roar shook the cave. The bear's claws raked at the water, leaving deep gouges that shimmered and then reformed. With a final, earth-shattering howl, the bear's form elongated, its fur darkening into midnight. A giant wolf towered over them with teeth bared in a snarl.

Tyche screamed as Dora raised her hand, and Fate's Weight pulsed with light. A wave of calming energy permeated the water shield and settled over Tychoneira, causing the wolf's snarl to falter and its eyes to narrow in confusion and rage.

"NeVEr! I WiLl NOt bE bOUnD!" The wolf-child howled.

A wave of fire erupted from Styx. "YoUr hEArT iS cOnSuMeD By dARkNesS. YoUr sPiRiT bOuNd To mALiCe. YoU cAnNoT PaY ThE toLL. By tHe oAtHs Of ThE gOdS, I... BaR... YoUr... WaY." The cave entrance pulsed with a fiery glow.

Beside Tyche, Dora's hand trembled, but her gaze remained steady. Tyche held her breath in shock as the scene unfolded. *What have I created?* A stab of dread lodged in her chest.

The waters around Tyche twisted in a violent clash of colors and distorted visions, displaying her inner despair. The gods' images rippled in her mind, trapped beneath the pool's surface. Hera's cruel mouth—a crimson gash in the swirling chaos—leered at her, the goddess' words biting like poisoned vipers. The Nekrochim's grotesque form clawed at the edges of her vision, screaming mOthER into the abyss. Then, Ikelos' face of betrayal twisted around her and pulled her deeper into the black mirror of her terror.

But then, a pulse of light cut through her crushing despair. Dora's innocent eyes, wide with trust, coalesced, their edges tempered by the swirling waters. Lep's face emerged on the water's flesh, creased with worry and love. Their tender faces, born of love and hope, rippled outward in blue waves across the surface of the agitated water, calming the tempest within her. The waters of Oceanus hummed with promises of a new beginning and a path to redeem the fragments of her soul.

Tychoneira let out a high-pitched shriek, her eyes twinkling with malicious glee. "Weak, good," she hissed. "iNnoCEnt. PaTHetIC."

"You are wrong." Dora's gaze fixed on Tychoneira with an expression of pity and contempt. "You are the weak one, sister. You are evil."

Enraged, Tychoneira lunged toward Dora, her hands morphing into grasping talons. But Dora raised Fate's Weight, and a wave of opposing energy soothed Tychoneira's rage.

The cave shuddered. Boulders tumbled from the ceiling into the water. Tyche cried out in terror at the display of her daughter's untamed powers.

Tychoneira's glare intensified, her voice dripping with venom. "YoUR viRTuE sICkEnS mE."

The newborn scowled at Dora with simmering hatred, as though she sensed the goodness in her sister, a purity that seemed to repel her. "YoU ArE wEAk, LiKe mOtHEr." Tychoneira's eyes narrowed at Tyche, forked tongue darting across her lips. "DeSPaiR. fEAr. dELiCiouS."

Tyche stared at her baby in disgust, her own flesh and blood, the evil the gods had feared. A damning truth settled over her—they had been right all along. Her daughter, a monster, the kind the gods murdered to prevent, vibrated in her mind. Bile rose to her mouth. Could she love this child? A single word, a haunting refrain from the nightmare, wavered in the silence.

m O tH e R

A mother's choice weaves deception, as love's sacrifice shadows the sting of betrayal. For it is in a heart's farewell that hope may birth, even when darkness claims its kin.

IN THE HEART'S FAREWELL

The cave's dark walls wept into the spring's embrace. The birthing had taken its toll, and Tyche's sickness returned with renewed ferocity. The splashes of sorrow struck the measured beat of Tyche's final hours as she drifted, suspended between two tides—Styx' icy currents and Oceanus' mortal springs—a fragile dam against the wildfire of her fever. An inner blaze burned through her body that consumed her godhood, leaving behind the painful embers of mortality, while within her, a maternal despair settled for the daughters she would leave adrift.

Across the water's skin, swells exposed Lep's rippling visage of anguish. Golden pools of grief, his eyes portrayed the price of her decision, the love between them trembling with heartache as they prepared for their final farewell.

At the spring's edge, Dora stood over her mother's floating form, her hands in rapid dance, constructing a protective barrier of light and shadow. The tender caress of Dora's power spread across Tyche's fevered body. The shield's light beat like a defiant heart against the growing darkness, pushing back the water's shadows and illuminating Tychoneira's cradle with a strange, unsettling light. The infant stirred, and the cave's water drew back in revulsion.

"Your fragile protection changes nothing." Ikelos' voice purred from the infant's mouth. "You are mine, *my love*, as you have always been. You will never be freed from my nightmare."

A trapped moth fluttered against the cage of Tyche's ribs. She recognized she'd been a vessel in Ikelos' sinister plan. The betrayal left a bitter taste in her mouth. "Your grand design crumbles," Tyche rasped. Understanding flayed the flesh of her heart. "Your nightmares did not break me—they built something more powerful within."

"loVE," the baby hissed, Ikelos' voice a venomous snarl. "A worthless frailty. I sought to possess both my daughters in their slumber, but Dora's spirit banished my shadow. Yet, this one..." The baby's black eyes sparked with dark desire. "She welcomed it. Through her, I will claim both realms, mortal and divine."

A wave of fury rippled through the spring as Oceanus roared. "Silence, you vile creature! You have twisted my daughter's love into a weapon, *Nightmare*. You will pay for this treachery." His gaze lingered on the infant before turning to Tyche with a softened gaze. Oceanus rose from the cave's springs, his form a fluid blend of water and flesh. He caressed her brow, his cool waters soothing her fevered body. "Beloved daughter." His murmur, the lament of the sea, crashed against the banks. "To watch you fade..."

"The gods gather," Hermes warned. "They track your fading strength like predators drawn to blood."

Tyche sensed the conflict of Lep's love for her and the threat of Tychoneira's dark power. She drank in the sorrow of his eyes, the longing to comfort her, yet he hesitated, as if fearing his caress would carry the stain of the rising darkness.

"There must be another way," Lep murmured, his words laced with anguish as he turned to Oceanus. His fingers tightened around Tyche's arm in a desperate grip. "We cannot let them have you both."

Oceanus' form shimmered in hidden sorrow. "Your sister's dark waters can conceal your divine nature and lead the gods to believe you have joined her in her realm. I have suffered the loss of one daughter to Olympus' manipulation. I will not yield another."

Through the haze, Tyche grasped the truth—her nightmares, the gods' decree, and Ikelos' warped scheme—all leading her to this moment of desperate decision. "There is a way," Tyche coughed, and the water rippled around her. "We give them what they want to see."

"What do you mean?" Deep creases dug into Lep's brow.

"A deception," Tyche said. "A false death. We make them accept that I am gone, and Tychoneira is lost to them forever."

"But how?" Lep searched Tyche's face. "How do we make them believe it?"

"With the waters of the Titans, mine and those of Styx combined." Oceanus' watery form hovered over his daughter. "We will create an umbra of illusion, a paradox where the fusion of life and death will cloak the truth from the gods' eyes, safeguarding you and Tychoneira."

"A paradox of life and death?" Lep asked, his brow furrowed. "Are you certain of this protection, Oceanus? Or is it a tomb?"

Oceanus' form rippled with ancient power. "Consider it as a ward, Lep, an illusion crafted from our primordial origins. My waters give life, while Styx' reflects the river of finality, of death. When our waters combine, they induce an illusion so powerful, it will deceive even the gods. They shall witness Tyche's end and Tychoneira's departure, though it will remain a mystery they cannot comprehend. The waters of life will conceal the true nature of Tyche's death, while the waters of death will obscure Tychoneira's departure. It is a shield of contradictions they will not unravel."

Tyche reached out and gripped Lep's hand. "And you, my love. You will use the Gorgon's blood to kill and resurrect me. The waters' opposing forces of life and death will protect us from the gods." She raised her palm, filled with the waters of her father and sister. "They'll believe my daughter and I are no more, and we'll be free."

Lep's sorrow burned her heart. Their long gaze mapped the terror of their agreement. "And Tychoneira?" he asked.

Silence enveloped the cave, punctuated by the rhythmic dripdrip of water from the cave's weeping walls.

"I will take her to the depths of my realm." Oceanus pressed a watery hand against his chest. "My waters will hide her from the gods' sight and shield the world from her darkness. She will be safe there."

Tyche shivered, and Lep pulled her close. He started to speak but instead held her, his grip tight as if to keep her from vanishing. He kissed her forehead, then met her gaze with eyes as fierce as a dying sun.

"I'm afraid, beloved," Tyche murmured. "To die and to be reborn is a terrifying thought."

"I will not let you be lost." Lep's words were a desperate vow, but he looked away, betraying his fear.

Her fading divinity called for her to reassure Lep. But even through her pain, she heard the doubt in his voice and looked to Oceanus.

"Father..." Tyche's eyes flickered, hot coals in her sunken face. "Even Styx, with her dark heart, shows concern."

Oceanus grazed her forehead with his lips. "Styx may have accepted power when she chose to side with the Olympians, but she has not forgotten the bond of blood."

"And now, I select love's course," Tyche murmured. "Will you forgive me, as you absolved her?"

"There was no need for pardon then, nor is there now." Oceanus' form trembled. "Yet, it pains me to watch another daughter leave my reach."

The hidden springs throbbed in a rhythm of mournful lament. Hermes stirred in Tyche's periphery, his presence a wordless declaration of the ties resisting Olympus' control. Then the waters flowed above them, interwoven swirls of light and darkness, of life and death, in a display of the grand deception to come.

Tyche turned her mother's tender gaze to Dora. "Daughter," she rasped, "come near, my precious one."

Dora stepped forward and cradled Tyche's cheek in her palm. "Mother, I shall be strong."

"I know you will." Tyche's tears sizzled across her hot skin. "Strength is not enough, my beloved daughter. Be patient, yet bold. Remain true to the light that abides in you. Above all else, protect your beautiful heart."

"I will," Dora vowed. "I shall bring you pride."

"Daughter, you already have." She laid her hand on Dora's and squeezed it. "You are my light, my hope, and my blessing."

Her gaze drifted to Lep, her heart filled with tender sorrow. "Lep..." She breathed his name like a treasured memory. "Hold me close."

Lep waded into the water, and Tyche sighed at his cool touch against her burning flesh. He enfolded her in his arms of refuge. "I am here." His body trembled around her. "I will not release you."

"I feel your love." Tyche's fingers traced the lines of his grief in a silent goodbye. "However, this love exacts a sacrifice."

She looked toward the threat of Tychoneira's cradle in the churning waters. "Even in her darkness, I find a glimmer of hope." She sighed into the fold of his arm. "And the faith she'll find her path to the light."

"And should she not, what happens then?" Lep's rough whisper scrabbled across the water's surface.

"Then we are her light." Tyche held Lep's worried gaze. "We will protect the world until she discovers her way."

Tyche's mind wandered to Lep's failed attempt to heal her with the Gorgon's blood. She understood then that her illness, this metamorphosis, was not of a mortal nature but the shedding of her godhood. Now, the blood was her single hope, her way to a mortal resurrection. Then a vision arose—the frigid splendor of Olympus, the condemning gazes of the gods. *Mortals, rising*, the statues had echoed, dread warping their golden countenances. Her trial's charade of fairness in the great hall had been, in truth, a prison shaped by ornate words. *Chaos, set free.* They feared her child, her defiance, her love. Yet, here, within the Titan's Cradle, she had discovered a love that challenged their might.

As her vitality faded, Tyche saw a radiant glow of trapped starlight gather between Dora's palms. With a tender nudge, the child launched the shards of light, sending them spinning toward her mother. The waters glistened under the constellation of stars and separated, revealing the Wheel of Fortune and the Horn of Plenty.

Tyche's breath stopped short as the Wheel throbbed with a lifeless fire. Its carved symbols flickered and dimmed in their vague contours, while the Horn tipped toward her, its bounty now displaying a solitary white flower. "My children," she sobbed. "You're here to take your leave."

With a final revolution, the Wheel turned to unveil a parting glimpse to its mistress—a sun-kissed meadow, a cottage among wildflowers, Lep and Dora's laughter-filled faces. A lone tear streaked down Tyche's cheek in the bittersweet acceptance of the life she would not live. The Horn's petals floated toward her and brushed against her face in soft remembrance of the abundance she had dispensed to mortals. She considered all the gifts she had granted and the blessings she had conferred, understanding Lep and Dora were her greatest treasures, her most valuable contributions to the world.

"Thank you." Tyche's voice cracked in her sorrow. "Thank you for your service, your might, your beauty. But my journey takes me elsewhere now."

The Wheel and the Horn grew faint and dissolved into the churning waters. A sense of calm descended upon Tyche at the acceptance of her destiny. She had chosen love, and through that election, she had gained a release no god could ever offer.

The vision receded, leaving a soft afterglow in her mind as the edges of her awareness blurred. The chill of Styx' embrace penetrated Tyche's bones with a spreading numbness. Lep held her tightly, his face ashen while his heart beat in time with her waning pulse. Tyche sighed under his touch, his trembling caress on her cooling skin, and sensed his sorrow washing over her.

Tyche acknowledged Lep's panic and knew he was angry that his promise to her of protection and healing had not been fulfilled. She understood his grief, his helplessness as he watched her life fade. Tyche floated in the Titan's Cradle, in the void between life and death. The chill in her limbs increased, and her chest rose with a soft swell. "Lep. Don't... don't mourn."

She watched Lep shake his head, wordless, his eyes locked on her face as though imprinting her image in his mind for safekeeping. The refuge of the cave carried despair's scent and settled over Tyche.

"I love you," Lep gasped through unchecked tears. "More than any words can tell."

Her hand, icy and wet, extended to touch his face. "And I love you," she murmured. "Always."

Tyche relished Lep's frantic touch as he brushed away loose strands of her hair. His words offered hollow comfort that did not match the fear in his eyes. *Don't lie to me.* When her grip slackened, Lep swayed. *No.* His eyes found Hermes in a wordless appeal for solace before his legs buckled. *Don't let him fall, as I can no longer catch him.* Hermes caught the healer in his arms, his own face drawn with anguish.

Through her fading sight, Tyche tracked Lep's trembling form, his face hidden against Hermes' shoulder. *Oh, Lep,* she thought, her heart aching. *Let him borrow your strength, Hermes, for mine is gone.* Hermes clasped him against his chest as his body shuddered. *Your pain ripples through the water and cuts my heart.*

Oceanus' form twisted in his despair as he extended his arms toward Dora. "Come, child." His words hummed through the water. "Join your mother in the spring."

Dora took her grandfather's waiting hand and waded into the pool. With a tender touch, she laid her hands on Tyche's brow and began to sing. A gentle melody lifted and wove with the vitality of Oceanus' life-giving waters.

"Use your gifts, Dora." Oceanus smiled in encouragement. "Use Aether's Edge and Fate's Weight. Give your mother a moment of peace."

Dora looked from her grandfather to the gnarled surface of Aether's Edge. The horn's sea snake coiled around her wrist. In her other hand, Fate's Weight shimmered, its symbols shifting with her emotions. As she sang, a faint warmth flowed through Tyche's limbs, and her body convulsed with breath. The frigid hold of Styx eased its grasp, its inevitable claim momentarily held at bay by Dora's light.

The warmth of love shields the chill of mortality, as the shadow of regret lengthens on farewell's eve. For it is in the surrender of the heart that love's legacy endures, even as fear whispers of the morrow.

31

FAREWELL'S EVE

Tyche shivered as the lingering warmth of the birthing pool dissipated. Lep stirred beside her and gathered Tyche in his arms, lifting her from the water, then settled her onto a soft bed of furs prepared on the cave floor. Tyche's teeth chattered as he pulled her against his bare chest. Soon, his warmth seeped into her skin in a slow, comforting trickle.

Why am I not dead?

She had expected death, even welcomed it, but her joy at finding Lep beside her eclipsed all else. A sharp blade of relief cut through her distorted senses as the rise and fall of her chest defied the silence that should have claimed her—a wonder sustained by her daughter's power. Though she still sensed her hours were few, as long as Lep was next to her, she could face anything.

"You are cold." He breathed against her hair and rubbed her arms vigorously.

Tyche leaned back against him, her thoughts sluggish. "It's different," she whispered. Her unblinking eyes turned inward, to a place of private recollections. "Without the water, without the buffer, I feel everything so intensely. Am I dying? I feel my life emptying into the abyss of my choices and regrets." She pulled his hand to her lips and kissed his palm. "Take my love. Hold it with you forever."

Lep's hand tightened around hers. "Do not talk like that. Dora's power gave you time to prepare for your journey, for us to say our goodbyes," he murmured as he burrowed his cheek into her neck.

Tyche sighed at the tremor of his emotion coursing through her.

"Oh, Tyche. Who am I if I cannot offer you what you need most?" He glanced at the Rod of Asclepius, forgotten near the spring's bank. "What is this foul illness I cannot mend?"

"Hush, beloved. Do you not know? You are all I need. All that I long for." She clutched her chest as a wretched cough brought forth the golden stain of coming death. She wiped her mouth with the back of her hand and wept in the arms of the man she loved.

Lep held her closer and said nothing, but Tyche sensed the despair in his tender touch. He kissed her neck, her shoulder, his lips lingering against her skin. "Do not leave me," he whispered.

Tyche turned in his arms and searched his eyes. "Lep," she breathed, her fingers tracing the lines of his face. "I'm afraid."

Lep's eyes flicked back and forth across her face, her eyes, her nose, her mouth. A sob rose in his throat. "I am, too."

Their desperate kiss was a tender, wordless vow. It held all the courage they had left for the sacrifice to come. They nestled in each other's embrace, and soon, the rise and fall of Lep's worry lulled her into a peaceful sleep.

Time stretched, an eternity of quiet respite. Tyche drifted, her dreams no longer haunted by Ikelos' betrayal. Instead, they were filled with the gentle rhythms of village life, the warmth of Dora's laughter, and the gentle strength of Lep's presence.

Then, with trembling fingers, Lep traced the delicate curve of her cheek. Tyche stirred, her eyelids fluttering open. She awoke to his gaze of quiet reverence. "How are you feeling?"

Tyche managed a faint smile. "Weak, but whole. So perhaps I am not ready for death just yet." She shifted, her gaze falling on the empty cradle beside her. "And Tychoneira?"

"Oceanus has taken her to the deepest part of the spring," Lep said. "He said it is for her safety... and for ours." He smoothed a finger over her creased brow.

"I trust him," she whispered into the space between them, "but it still feels like part of me has died."

"We will see her again," Lep reassured her, though his own eyes held a flicker of doubt. He knew, as she did, that time was a cruel and traitorous god.

"Lep?"

"Hmm, my heart?"

"Once I am dead, what if... what if the Gorgon's blood doesn't bring me back to life? It didn't heal me before at your cottage, at least not permanently. What if I—"

"Do not," Lep interrupted. "Do not think in that way. The blood will perform its duty. It must."

"But if it doesn't," Tyche persisted, "will it... will dying hurt?"

Lep hesitated, and his gaze fell away. "It is a slow process," he admitted. "Like hemlock, it begins in the feet with a creeping chill, then rises—paralyzing—until it reaches the heart."

Tyche's breath hitched, and her body tensed in his arms. "Slow... paralyzing..." she whispered.

Lep exhaled in sadness. "Do not think on such things. Focus on us. On Dora."

"Dora," Tyche murmured against the bulge of his arm. "If I don't come back, you'll protect her, won't you?"

"With my life," Lep vowed.

"She's my rightful successor," Tyche choked on her grief. "Goddess of Fortune and Shadow. It's her birthright. The balance has to be maintained."

"I understand." Lep's hand tightened around hers.

"And Tychoneira," Tyche sobbed. "She's so different from Dora. I pray Dora's goodness can balance her darkness."

A moment of silence fell between them, broken by the soft gurgle of the spring. Tyche's gaze drifted to the cave's entrance, to the world beyond.

"Sometimes..." A faint smile curved her lips. "I wonder if my rebellious nature was worth it. If I hadn't defied the gods, Tychoneira wouldn't exist. But then I wouldn't have known you. Or Dora."

She turned back to Lep, her eyes an ocean of love. "It seems the expense of love is great, but worth the cost."

"Love is always worthy." Lep's nod emphasized his words.

Tyche's expression softened as she stared at Lep. "Do you remember when you taught me how to care for the villagers' wounds? My hands were clumsy, unused to such delicate work."

Lep's smile sparked in his eyes. "And you were so frustrated. You, who could move stars, struggled with a few simple herbs."

"It was a humbling experience." Tyche traced the rough texture of his calloused palm. "But unfamiliar emotions consumed me in those moments, sensations alien to me as a goddess."

She paused, her watery eyes searching his sun-drenched eyes. "When I become mortal tomorrow, will there be this much pain?"

"Yes," Lep answered with a sigh. "You will experience everything. The joy, the pain, the love."

"Then hold me," Tyche pleaded. "As if this moment is all we have."

Lep gathered her in his arms. His lips found hers in a tender kiss of their impending separation.

"I love you, Tyche," he murmured. "More than these simple words. More than life itself."

Please let this moment last forever.

"And I love you, Lep." Her fingers tangled in his hair. "More than any goddess has ever loved a man."

They embraced in the desperate pain of their fleeting love. The warmth of their joined skin burned like a dying flame, their hearts communing before the grip of mortality would soon take hold.

"Tomorrow." Tears shimmered on Tyche's cheeks and burned in the heat of her fire. "Tomorrow I will be mortal. And I will feel everything, as you do. Every joy, every pain, every moment of love."

Lep devoured her with his eyes, passion and grief contending for dominance on his face. "Then let us savor this moment," he said as he turned her body to face his. "Let us fill it with all the love we hold for one another."

Tyche pushed back his advance. "Give me your knife."

Lep hesitated. "Why?"

"Please, give it to me," she pleaded.

Reluctantly, Lep drew his blade and handed it to her. Tyche took it in her trembling fingers and carefully cut a lock of her golden hair. Her lips trembled as she held it out to him, her eyes brimming with unshed tears. "A reminder."

Lep's hand closed around the token of her love. "Tyche—" Lep began, but Tyche pressed a finger to his lips to silence him.

"I despised you at first," she confessed with sorrow. "I allowed my divine arrogance to stand in the way of your pure heart. I regret it. If only—"

"Please... you do not need to explain anything to me. Not now." Lep's eyes closed against her vulnerability.

"I must," Tyche insisted, and pulled his face closer. "And I... I ask forgiveness. For allowing myself to be so easily manipulated by Ikelos. For my part in the destruction of the village. I wonder what will happen to them."

"They will persevere," Lep assured her, tracing the line of her neck. "You have become their emblem of rebellion against the gods."

"And you." Tyche nestled against his chest. "You will be strong, too. Lead them well, my love. Your strength is my legacy. And please... live. Live for us. Live for Dora."

"Speaking of Dora," Lep murmured, "Hermes took her with him to Pikerni. He has gone to find Apollo and explain to him about Tychoneira and our plan to deceive the gods."

Tyche buried her face in Lep's shoulder. "I hope they get there in time."

A growl rumbled outside the cave, and a shiver trickled through Tyche's blood. *Ikelos will never allow me to escape.* Then, Lep's hand tightened around hers, and the quiet promise of his love anchored her.

"We will face whatever comes. Together." He held her tight against his chest. "I am beside you. You will never be alone again."

Tyche closed her eyes, her heart beating with bittersweet love. "Together," she whispered into the void.

Mortals weave a shroud of defiance, as the herbs of grief scent the dawn's regret. Though the gods cast shadows on the humans' chosen fate, mortal love endures in the ritual of the heart.

HERBS SCENT THE DAWN'S REGRET

Morning light sliced across the worn floorboards as Apollo, Dora's hand tucked securely in his, stepped through the open doorway of the lesche. Inside, he sniffed the faint aroma of last night's meal and the earthy fragrance of drying herbs. Bundles of chamomile and asphodel hung from the rafters over the bar and swayed in the morning breeze—Lep's herbs—and Apollo's heart swelled with pride.

Unlike the Olympian gods, who dwelt in the airy heights of Olympus, Titans were born of the earth itself, their essence intertwined with its substance. Lep's gathered herbs reminded Apollo of his primal connection, his forgotten roots, and the conflict between his nature and the divine schemes that brought him here. *Tyche's choice is made.* Apollo's scrutiny swept over the cobblestone square visible beyond the lesche entrance. *We have no choice but to deceive.* A grim resolve hardened his features. *They must believe she's dead.*

The villagers' soft chatter died at Apollo's sudden arrival, and they turned to face him. At the sight of Dora, a collective gasp turned into a sigh of relief.

"Dora!" Kalliope cried. "You're safe!"

They surrounded the child in a sea of relieved embraces, their eyes soft with affection. Dora whimpered and nestled into familiar arms.

"I'm glad to be home." She leaned her head against Kalliope's shoulder, her eyes downcast. "But I miss Althea."

A sharp knife of guilt twisted in Apollo's stomach as he witnessed the reunion. *I took a son from his mother once.* The memory of delivering Lep into Chiron's care pressed against his heart. *Can I ever make amends?*

Christos rose from his seat at the table, his white beard catching Apollo's strange light as he crossed to the bar. Grunting, he drew a *krater* of wine out from behind it and patted the vessel's side. "Protected through the battle's destruction," he said to Apollo as he poured the golden liquid into cups.

"For Lep's father," Christos said, "and for the god who brought Dora back to us." He extended the ale to Apollo. "Your son, Lep—we love him as one of our own. He heals us and protects us. And you, Apollo, have returned a child to her home. For this mercy, we offer what little remains, and with grateful hearts."

Apollo accepted the mug, the weight of it a strange comfort in his hand. *They still find time for kindness, even after all that has been taken. We, the gods, have offered them so little in return.*

"Thank you, Christos." Apollo tilted his chin. "Your goodwill means more than you know."

Christos skirted around the bar to the table, the legs of his chair squealing as he sat.

Apollo joined him and peered at Christos over the mug's rim as he drank. "Dora is an extraordinary child."

Christos eyed Apollo. "She is. Dora was Althea's world. Perhaps, now more than ever, she is the village's daughter."

Christos lifted the cup to his lips. "We have lost so much. Tryfonas, Althea, our homes, but we have also gained. We have seen the strength of our people and the depth of their love. And we have seen your favor." He lifted his eyes to meet the god's.

Apollo's heart wrestled with the sincerity in Christos' words and the deception he was forced to uphold. Hermes' message swirled in his mind—a child born, a sacrifice demanded. Deception was necessary. *The villagers cannot know Tyche's plan.*

"Favor," he said, "is a rare and precious thing. Especially in these times."

He raised his drink, his gaze flitting across the mortal's face. "To your son, Tryfonas. To Tyche. And to the strength of your people."

Christos raised his cup. "To them," he agreed. "And to you, Apollo. May we all find peace."

"Where are Lep and Tyche?" Christos asked. "We haven't seen them since they went to the watchtower."

"Hermes took them to the Titan's Cradle," Apollo explained. "Tyche has given birth. They are there now."

A wave of reassurance rippled through the listening villagers.

Dimitra remained at the cooking fire, her face a sketch of grief. Kalliope's hands moved with a steady rhythm through her herbs, caressing the delicate leaves. *Their quiet strength.* Apollo sensed a stirring in his Titan blood. *These people faced Olympian wrath and survived.* He admired their steady gazes. The silent language of their hands. *The mortals give Lep purpose and show him a life beyond the stony indifference of godhood.*

Apollo's fingers grazed the cup's rough edge. This simple drink held power—human hands, mortal grain, and an honest craft. The ale warmed his throat, tasting of earth's persistence. *Far from Olympian schemes where Zeus bends even family to his will.* He sipped the amber nectar. *Here mortals choose love, as my son has done.*

"The gods destroyed our village," a woman's voice cracked, sharp and brittle. "My children sleep beneath the ruins of their home."

Christos set down his cup, the clay thudding on the rough table. "My son died *defending* this village. Tryfonas understood... He died to secure our right to choose."

Dora stepped away from Melina and stood next to Apollo. She rested her hand on his knee, then tilted her head to look at him with a solemn expression. His heart seized at the quiet gesture, and he smiled at her. Then, as he glanced at Christos, he recognized the grief stamped in the man's bent frame, the unspoken questions of why. Silence clung to the walls of the lesche.

"Why is Dora with you?" Evy spoke into the stale room, breaking the stillness.

Apollo turned to her and then to the people crowded around. "Hermes brought Dora to me when he delivered the message about Tyche's condition. He knew the child would be safe with me and that I would bring her here to you." His gaze swept over the villagers. "Tyche burns with fever in the caves beyond the spring. Each moment draws her closer to mortality."

"Then we prepare for what must come." Dimitra's tears cut tracks through the dust on her cheeks. In response, Kid pressed against her skirts. "We'll ready the springhouse for her final cleansing." Her hands fluttered nervously, as though searching for a task to anchor them.

Christos' hands tightened around his mug. "We'll need a bier to transport her," he said. "Perhaps olive wood from the grove where Tryfonas used to play as a boy." He looked away, his memory lost in the distance.

"The gods will come." Apollo's words fell like the first thunder before a storm. "We must let your sorrow guide our preparations, for that is the truth they will witness." Silence settled over the hall, broken by the soft sniffling of the villagers.

A bitter laugh shattered the silence. "Haven't we given enough to please them?" The grieving woman clutched her shawl tight. "What more do they want?"

"They want to see Tyche dead," Apollo said. "And they will."

Defiant whispers rippled through the lesche. Dimitra reached up to the rafters and pulled down bundles of dried lavender. A sweet fragrance rose to the ceiling and offered a fragile comfort against the weight of sorrow. "We'll honor her," she choked through her tears, "as we have honored those before her for generations. The gods may witness, but these rites are our own."

Kalliope rushed to Dimitra's side, her fingers unbundling the sprigs of the flowers. "I kept her robes," she said, "from that first day she brought Dora home. I wrapped them in silk and stored them away."

"No!" Apollo's light flickered. "Let her go as she lived among you." *Let her go, as Lep loves her,* he thought, the words a vow to his son.

Through the morning, Apollo proceeded to the square as the village hummed in a somber hive of activity. Men labored in the grove, the rhythmic thud of axes ringing as they felled a mature olive tree, its wood destined to become Tyche's bier. The women worked with grim purpose, weaving funeral garlands of lavender, thyme, and asphodel. Apollo frowned to see Dora gathering fallen petals, her lips pursed in concentration.

Christos gripped the rough-hewn edge of a plank as the men worked. Then he turned to Apollo with a weary sadness. "What happens when a goddess... when *they* die?" he whispered. "Is it like our passing?"

Apollo's face darkened. "This is a rare occurrence," he murmured. "I believe it is the first time a goddess has chosen the path to mortality." He paused, his attention drifting toward Dora, then back to Christos. "I would think Tyche's spirit will return to the source, unless she yields her power to another."

Silence fell between them as they turned to regard Dora among the women. As Dora carefully arranged the petals, Apollo's attention lingered on the girl, and his mind drifted to the countless children he had seen perish in wars. *She is like them.* A wave of protectiveness surged through him. *I will not let the gods take her, too.*

Apollo roamed the hilly boundary rising behind the lesche as Evy emerged from the nearby springhouse, her arms laden with white blossoms glistening with dew. She stepped carefully, as though the flowers were tender extensions of her own grief.

"For the bier." The rough edge of unshed tears caught in her throat. "And lavender to ease her passage." She laid the flowers on the ground, her fingers lingering on the dew-kissed petals. Evy caught Dora's eye as she worked, then smiled. "She will be like her mother," she said, glancing up at Apollo, "a protector of this place."

Dimitra nodded absently and continued to weave braids of herbs and flowers as she sat in the square with the other women. "The springhouse..." she began, her words trailing off, her solemn gaze intent on the half-finished garland in her hands. "The ritual cleansing..." She pressed her lips together and wiped tears gathering on her cheeks.

Melina placed a comforting hand on Dimitra's shoulder. "I'll heat the waters," she murmured. She rose and headed to the path leading toward the stone walls of the springhouse.

The outward grief and the gentle touch of the women's hands stirred a strange emotion in Apollo's chest. *Such fragile beauty is the proof of mortality's fleeting nature. A splendor the gods so easily destroy.*

A child's piercing wail cut through the quiet hum of the village. Kalliope's shoulders shook as she pressed her face into her hands. Apollo's gaze flickered toward the sound, and a cord of empathy tightened his chest. *Another heart broken by the shadow of Olympus.*

Christos' calloused fingertips rubbed along the honed steel of his axe as he stepped forward. "Tyche gave herself to protect what she loves. As Tryfonas did." He glared at the blade, its dark stain a horrid tribute to his son's sacrifice. "He understood," he continued with a broken sigh, "that sometimes we must defy the gods... to remain human."

Apollo examined them, his divine light a gentle warmth against the afternoon shadows. *They work together with such purpose.* His eyes swept over the scene. *This is what Lep chose,* he thought, *this delicate beauty, this brutal grief.* He pressed his hand against his chest at the stab of shame to his heart, recognizing the vast chasm between his divine detachment and their bare, human sorrow. *They accept sacrifice in ways the gods have long forgotten. How could Olympus be so blind?* He ached to offer reassurance, to mend the divide between their mortal sorrow and his divine apathy, but the necessary words eluded him, choked by the weight of his complicity.

While the villagers arranged Tyche's ceremony, Apollo sought a means to commemorate Tyche's sacrifice and ease her journey. He turned away, his footsteps light on the rocky ground, and made his way to the rise above the spring. *I can ease her departure.* Apollo stared at the horizon. *For Tyche, for Lep.* He extended his hands, and the earth beneath him shuddered. His power flared from his fingertips, shaping the flesh of the ground.

A monument of pure, white marble rose from the earth, its wheel-shaped form sparking with an eternal radiance. Ancient symbols burned themselves into its surface, images of fate, transformation, and rebellion. *A tribute to her journey,* he thought, his heart aching with a father's sorrow and a god's regret. *This will guide her transformation and help her braid together the mortal with the divine to ease the pain of her passing.*

As he worked, a single tear cut a warm path down his face. Apollo froze, confusion ripping through him. *What is this?* He swiped the wetness from his cheek. He had known sorrow, of course, but the *feeling* of it was different. The human sensation collided with his consciousness, sharp, perplexing, yet familiar. The tear fell, a tiny droplet of light against the thirsty soil, and understanding perched in his soul.

He continued to shape the ground around the monument, forging a deep spiraling foundation. Then the earth parted and swallowed the lower portion of the wheel, anchoring it to its heart. The air shimmered with his power as the earthy scent of turned soil wafted through the stillness. *Tyche.* His heart beat with unexpected reverence. *You chose this. You chose to feel this love and grief, to experience it all. To die.*

Apollo completed the last of the symbols, the monument now rising as a defender against the coming storm. He noticed a presence at the edge of the cliff as he stepped back. Christos stood still, silhouetted against the sun's descent. Apollo observed the old man's slumped shoulders, his stare haunted, as if scouring for his son's ghost in the valley below.

With a sigh, Apollo approached and placed a hesitant hand on Christos' shoulder. The man turned, his eyes filled with an abiding sorrow.

"The *gods*," he muttered. "They take and they take and leave nothing but grief." Deep lines creased his forehead. "You know this well, don't you?"

Apollo's heart ached at the emptiness in Christos' eyes. He knew pain, the gaping hole left by loss that settled in the bones. "I do," he said. "I lost a son, too."

Christos dipped his head, his attention returning to the valley, to the distant, fading sun. "Tryfonas..." he whispered. "He was a good boy. He would have been a strong man."

"He was," Apollo agreed. "Tryfonas fought bravely alongside your people. He knew what was at stake."

Christos stared at the god of the Sun, his eyes searching, probing, as if trying to decipher the secrets hidden in Apollo's gaze. "You gave Lep away." His words were thick with unspoken questions.

Apollo stared into the memory of that day, his confession whispered in the wind. "I gave my son to Chiron, believing it was for the best. I intended to safeguard him. I never knew Lep, nor gave him my love. I made a choice I regret every day."

Silence fell between them, broken by the mournful cawing of the raven. Christos turned back to the valley, a single tear coursing down his cheek. "My son. My Tryfonas," his words a broken groan, "was a good boy."

Apollo squeezed the old man's shoulder, offering comfort. "I know the emptiness. The longing for what was, for what might have been."

Together, Apollo and Christos descended the rise, the village's grim activity drawing them back into its fold. They paused in the village square, where the last rays of the setting sun cast long shadows across the cobblestones. In the distance, the men still worked in the olive grove, shaping Tyche's bier from the wood of the tree where Tryfonas had fallen. Christos' gaze lingered on the copse. "The olive grove," he said in a cracked rumble, "where my son fell. Its wood will bear her well."

Dimitra emerged from the lesche and settled onto a low stone bench in the plateia. A soft rustle of herbs drifted through the quiet as her fingers wove them into a garland. She stopped and sighed, tracing each delicate stem as if memorizing its form.

"The springhouse awaits," she murmured. "Our rites, our ways... our love." Her red-rimmed and swollen eyes held a distant, haunted look.

Melina trotted along the path from the springhouse, resting near the base of the rising hillside, from which a faint steam curled into the evening air. Nearing the edge of the lesche, her foot caught on a loose cobblestone, and the copper basin she held clattered when it slipped from her grasp, scattering sprigs of thyme and rosemary across the stones of the square. The sharp clang shattered the quiet grief, making what lay ahead a jarring reality. Apollo's nostrils flared at the familiar perfume of the herbs as it drifted toward him from the scattered leaves. *They give her every rite, every honor, while the gods demand only sacrifice.*

A sense of foreboding settled over Apollo as the mortals continued their preparations in the open square. His divine light softened as he observed their defiance and grace. He frowned, recognizing a faint tremor in the earth—a sign that the gods were drawing closer. He sighed and crossed the square, then entered the dim interior of the lesche.

Apollo stood still in the doorway, his attention drawn to Dora, who sat near the hearth, her hands carefully arranging the flowers for her mother. *Tyche's legacy is a double-edged sword of sorrow and hope.* He understood now, the way Lep loved Dora, the tender protectiveness in his eyes—a guardian, and with that, a father's love. *He loves her like his daughter,* Apollo contemplated, a warmth spreading through his chest, *so I too will cherish her.* An oath formed in his heart. *I will protect her. I will honor Tyche's sacrifice, and I will be here for Lep, as I should have been.*

"Help Kalliope with the herbs, child," he said. "Your mother would want them to be perfect."

His gaze drifted across the square toward the monument he had created at the spring's edge. The enormous wheel served as a pathway between the mortal and divine, anchoring Tyche's soul to the earth and ensuring her legacy lived on.

A single ray of sunlight pierced the smoke-darkened rafters and illuminated Lep's hanging herbs. Yet, even this light could not dispel the shadows of what was to come. He would be ready.

Mortal hands weave a final rite, as love's choice births a human soul. For it is in the heart's surrender that freedom dawns, even as gods yield to the power of human love.

33

LOVE'S CHOICE BIRTHS A HUMAN SOUL

Pegasus split the morning's orchid glow as he descended toward Pikerni, Tyche cradled against Lep's chest, her fever burning through her thin garments. Hermes urged his mount faster as he clutched a sphere of dark garnet pulsing with a faint, internal light.

They landed near the village springhouse, where Pegasus knelt, allowing Lep to ease Tyche from the winged horse's back. The squat storehouse steamed in the morning air. The stone flesh of its walls bore the carved images of gods whose unblinking eyes seemed to follow their movements. Dimitra, Melina, and Kalliope stood in solemn watch beside the waters of purification, awaiting the goddess' arrival to prepare her for sacrifice. Kid pressed against the stone walls and bleated softly.

With hearts torn between grief and the desperate hope for the village's salvation, the women received Tyche into their care. "Gently now," Dimitra murmured. The goddess' legs trembled as they helped her inside the springhouse.

"Daughter of waters, hear our song." Dimitra's voice cracked as she guided Tyche into the primordial flow. The steam hissed and curled around them, carrying memories of that first day when a stranger had become family.

"As we wash your form with care." Melina's fingers worked the herb-scented oil through Tyche's wavy locks. "Remember love beyond despair."

While they wove herbs and flowers into her damp tresses, their voices joined in the song of lament. "Through strands of fate, we weave our prayer, each bloom a blessing, each petal a tear. Though mortal hands now crown your head, divine grace lingers where we tread."

Kalliope emerged from the spring's storage room, holding a garment that shimmered like captured starlight—Tyche's divine raiment from her first arrival. "Your godly robes, my lady. They've waited here for you since that day."

"No." Tyche's fingers brushed the rough homespun they'd given her months ago. "I choose to die as I lived here—one of you."

"As you wish," Kalliope murmured.

Dimitra and Melina helped Tyche from the cleansing waters. Their final hymn rose as they held the goddess steady while Kalliope dried her with prickly homespun fabric. "With mortal cloth, we wrap your form, though you once wore the stars above. Each thread now binds you to this earth, where you have chosen mortal love."

Steam snaked around them like departing spirits as they dressed her in a simple robe. Outside, the first arrows of sunlight shot the springhouse walls with amber light, and the etched gods moved together in shadow-dance along the walls.

Near the entrance, Lep and Christos waited with the funeral bier, the platform of polished olive wood they had crafted with their love. The women had lined it with fresh herbs and white asphodel, while a cushion stuffed with lavender and thyme lay ready to cradle Tyche's head.

"Slowly now. Be careful," Kalliope murmured as they helped Tyche settle onto the bier.

The wood was cool against her fever-hot skin, and the flowers crushed beneath her weight released their sweet perfume. Kid pressed close to nudge Tyche's dangling fingers as Apollo and Hermes took their positions at the platform's handles.

The procession wound through streets still bearing the gods' wrath. Broken pottery crunched beneath the mourners' feet, and the beams' exposed bones jutted from collapsed homes. Somewhere, a baby's cry pierced the morning chorus of birds, but the mother quickly hushed the distraught child.

Dora trudged beside the bier and held fast to her mother's hand. Behind them, villagers followed with oil lamps lit against the departing night. Their soft prayers of sorrow rose and fell, sacred words of grief carrying on the morning breeze:

"Through shadows deep and waters wide," Evy murmured, her gaze fixed on the distant horizon.

"Guide her soul on morning's tide," Christos choked out as he clutched the platform's side rail.

"Though immortal bonds now fade away," Dora's song wavered. Tears brimmed the hollows of her eyes and carved streaks of anguish on her cheeks. "Love's light guides her final way."

Apollo and Hermes bore Tyche's funeral couch up the rise. Below them, at the spring where her story in Pikerni had begun, the procession of villagers gathered in mournful silence. Above them, the gathering storm clouds churned with a deep growl, and a shaft of light speared the darkness to bathe a descending stone altar in a golden glow. Below, the oil lamps in the mourners' hands flickered, and dread tightened their expressions as they stared at the ornate table settling onto the rise.

A chill traced its way down Tyche's limbs. *A farewell gift from the gods.*

Apollo's gaze lifted to the storm-dark sky with a deep scowl lining his face. He turned to help Hermes gather Tyche's form from the bier and lay her on the altar where Lep waited. Below, at the spring's edge, the marble monument gleamed in the bleeding light, its wheel-shaped form channeling sacred waters.

"You, who claim divine right to rule, hear me now." Tyche's voice carried clearly despite her weakness. "My rejection of your laws is not born of defiance, but of a love that stands unbent before power." Thunder growled a warning, but she continued, her fingers finding Lep's hand. "I choose mortality. I choose *love.*"

The air crackled around Lep as he stood over the altar, the Staff of Asclepius a familiar weight against his spine. The honed edge of his knife caught a sharp glint in the sudden flare of his eyes. He reached back and grasped the writhing rod and slid it over his shoulder. Lep's gaze fell to the snake curled around the Gorgon's branch, and deep lines of sorrow tightened the corners of his mouth. "Gods, grant me strength for what I must do," he rasped into the bright indifference of the sunlit morning.

His gaze flickered to Tyche. Her eyelids fluttered open and found his. A faint smile touched her lips. "You must do this, my beloved," she whispered. "For love."

"I cannot," he whispered. "To kill the one who taught me the meaning of love..."

Apollo stepped to his son and covered Lep's hand on the staff with his own, then settled his other hand on his shoulder. "Sometimes the greatest act of love is letting go," he murmured. "You chose mortality for love once. Now help her do the same."

Lep's hands steadied as ancient words of ending fell from his lips. The incantation called death's essence from his veins, and his skin darkened where the transformed blood pooled. Lep raised his arm and pressed the rod against his left wrist.

"I love you," he sobbed.

Tyche's eyes fluttered open, and a faint breath parted her lips. "And I, you."

The serpent stirred, alive and writhing in his hand. Its fangs sank into Lep's flesh and greedily engorged on the tainted blood. A cry ripped from Lep's throat before he yanked the snake away and unleashed it on Tyche's breast. It slithered upward and pierced her neck to deliver the poison. Tyche cried out and struggled against the serpent's embrace. The snake's body pulsed as it forced the blood into her veins. With a sharp tug, Lep seized the snake by its tail. In a flash, its form solidified back into the staff.

The poison began its work, and a creeping chill clawed at Tyche's feet before creeping higher. "Like winter claiming a pond," she whispered, her voice growing distant. "First the edges freeze... then deeper. My divinity fractures like ice."

Lep gathered her failing body in his arms. His eyes, dark with grief, spoke the lament his lips could not utter.

"My legs... I can't feel them anymore," Tyche murmured. "The mortal world feels... heavy. As if gravity itself is claiming me." Her fingers found Lep's and squeezed them. "The stars. They're so far away now."

As consciousness slipped away, Ikelos' presence slithered through Tyche's fading mind. "Did you think I ever loved you?" His words held mockery and regret. "Each nightmare I sent was carefully crafted—the Nekrochim, your deepest fears—all designed to break your will. I shaped our child in darkness, whispered to her while she slept in your womb. Each terror I created was a seed planted to make her my instrument against Zeus."

"You failed," Tyche murmured. "The nightmares didn't break me as you believed they would, Ikelos. They awakened a mother's rebellion."

"Love," he spat. "What is love? Such a frail thing. I tried to reach both daughters in their dreams, but Dora's light rejected my darkness. Tychoneira though..." His presence coiled tighter. "Through her, I will rule both realms."

A tear slipped down Tyche's cheek, and Oceanus' presence emerged in the ancient wellspring of her grief. "Daughter," he whispered. "Your sister's waters will guard your spirit while you transform. Even Zeus cannot penetrate such depths."

As the waters of life flowed from her eyes, her father's tide of love swept over her. "You chose well," he murmured. "Some sacrifices are worth any price. Do not grieve for Tychoneira—I will keep her safe in the deep where even the gods cannot reach. I love you, my child."

When the poison's chill reached Tyche's heart, it stuttered, and the last traces of divinity shattered and fell away. The final beat rang across the spring—mortal, finite, free.

In the silence that followed, Hermes clutched a crystal amphora, etched with inscriptions of transformation. The vessel thrummed with Styx' power as he gathered Tyche's spirit before it could drift toward Charon's domain. The dark waters within rippled with protection, ensuring Tyche's soul would not cross the final threshold.

Thunder crackled across the stormy sky as Apollo stepped forward. Hermes handed him the sphere of umbral garnet he had brought from the cave. The container's surface glowed with luminescent veins that pulsed with an inner, starlit fire. Within it, Tychoneira writhed, her form caught in a furious confluence of her father's shadow and her mother's light.

"Release her," Zeus commanded from the roiling clouds above. "Let us see what darkness Ikelos has wrought."

The sphere shattered. Tychoneira rose into the air, her infant form writhing with coils of darkness lashing out erratically toward the terrified villagers below and upward to the observing gods. When she spoke, two voices emerged—one childlike, the other familiar. "fINalLy. DId YoU THiNk yOU cOUlD coNTaIn Me? I aM oLDeR tHAn YoUr LaWs AnD deEPer THaN yOuR pOWeR."

A roar of dark energy emanated from the child goddess eager to break free. In the distance, the watchtower where Dora's mortal life had begun crumbled into dust. Black corruption spread through the spring, and the water's smooth surface peeled backward in its revulsion. The villagers fell back in terror as reality itself seemed to warp around the infant.

"You see now why she cannot live," Zeus boomed. "Both mother and child must die."

The spring erupted, and Oceanus rose in a towering column of churning water, his appearance terrible and magnificent. "You will not have her." His voice held the might of the ancient seas. He reached for his granddaughter with hands of living water. The currents surged and created an illusory shroud, obscuring Tychoneira's descent.

On the rise, the ancient stone altar groaned and cracked under the strain of the child's power, and Lep tightened his hold on Tyche's lifeless body.

"Grandfather!" Tychoneira screamed in Ikelos' voice. "I shaped her for this—to break the tyranny of Olympus! Each nightmare was a seed of revolution. Through her, I would rule the cosmos!"

The dark child's power lashed out, fighting against Oceanus' grasp. But her grandfather's waters were inexorable, drawing her down into depths where divine sight could not penetrate.

"No!" The baby's words, laced with Ikelos' rage, split open the sky. A torrent of darkness lashed out. "I a m d i s s o l u t i o n! I a m c h a o s! I a m—" The thrum of dark power intensified as the infant was drawn down toward the churning spring waters. Just before the surface swallowed her, a single, heart-wrenching whisper escaped the innocent mouth.

mOtHeR

Then, the waters closed over her, and she was gone.

Lep cradled Tyche's body, his healer's hands shaking as he smoothed her hair. Apollo stood behind his son, one hand on his shoulder, offering the strength needed to maintain their deception. Below at the spring's edge, Dora stared up toward her mother's body and nodded to Lep, then turned toward the ripples where her sister had disappeared.

The women fell to their knees in the mud, and their sorrow rose to join the birds' song. Kid pressed against the altar, his mournful bleats echoing across the valley.

"Daughter of waters, hear our grief." The villagers' voices rose. "Though divine grace has fled your form, mortal love shall guard your rest."

As the mourners formed a solemn procession, their moans faded to reverent silence as they bore Tyche's body toward the place of her coming transformation.

At the spring's edge, the marble monument towered above the earth. Its massive wheel stretched six times the height of a man. Eight great spokes radiated from its center like the rays of Helios' crown. The visible half reached toward the heavens, while its lower portion plunged deep into the spring's source. Each spoke bore intricate channels that spiraled across its surface, carrying water from rim to hub in a labyrinth of waterways. Between the spokes, symbols of fate were carved deep into the marble—a mother's sacrifice, love's dangerous rebellion, and the choice between power and destiny.

As the mourning litter with Tyche's body drew closer, the wheel stirred. First a tremor, then a deep rumble shook the earth. The channels filled with water, and the great wheel began to turn, grinding stone against stone with Fortune's ancient song. Dora gasped, her small form straightening as her mother's fading power sought her out. Light blazed from Dora's fist as the power of Fate's Weight surged toward the spinning wheel. Darkness and light merged where her power touched the spokes, and the wheel spun faster.

The monument's sunlit face gleamed on polished marble, while below the earth's line, darker channels connected to deeper waters. At its heart, where the spiraling channels of the great wheel converged, a transformation chamber waited, large enough to cradle Tyche's body. Clear springs of liquid sunlight rose through upper passages and mingled with viscous, dark currents that seeped through deeper grooves, entwining the waters of life and death. Driven by Dora's power, the great disc hummed with immortal magic, its energy thrumming through the stone and into the chamber.

The wheel's channels pulsed with swirling light as the procession approached. Solid marble stretched unbroken from earth to sky—no seam, nor visible way to enter the massive structure. Yet, as Lep signaled the bearers to lower their burden and step back, magic stirred. Tyche's form rose from the bier, wrapped in sacred light. The impenetrable stone flowed like liquid marble, creating a passage that had not existed moments before, drawing her into its chamber.

In the darkness of the tomb, time dissolved into water. Tyche drifted in the space between worlds. Mortality dragged at her substance, pulling her deeper into darkness where memory and moment united.

Truth surfaced from the depths. Ikelos' touch burned cold now—his whispers to their unborn child, his seeds of darkness planted in sleep.

"You shaped our daughter for chaos," Tyche spoke into the void. "None of it was real."

Within the waters of life and death, her memories stirred. The village had planted itself in her heart. Images caressed her mind—Lep's gentle touch, Kid curled against her during stormy nights. Each recollection of belonging anchored her to the mortal world she had chosen. Her willing sacrifice had begun the moment she chose her daughter's life over power.

Through the waters, Oceanus' words flowed gentle as the spring rain. "The transformation comes, my child. Let the waters guide you."

"fAtHeR," Styx' words rippled black as the midnight river. "LEt Me sHow HEr." Her sister's waters curled close, dark and knowing. "I cHOse POweR," she whispered. "yoU cHOsE LoVE. EaCh pAtH dEmANds ItS pRiCe."

"The cost of love," Oceanus murmured through his clear springs, "is worth any pain."

Tyche's bones grew heavier. The weightless grace of immortality settled into human substance, tangible and real. She thought of Lep waiting outside, of the life they would build together. She was no longer a goddess looking down from Olympian heights but a woman, a villager, who had chosen her own fate.

"I'm ready," she whispered as the last traces of divinity fell away.

Suspended between worlds, a profound stillness enveloped Tyche. Her body settled into the embrace of the waters' confluence, awaiting a final spark.

At midnight of the second day, Lep approached the monument, and the stone parted at his touch. In the chamber, Tyche lay still as death, cradled where the luminous springs met the slow, dark currents. Power surged through the interconnected channels, ribbons of light weaving through the waters and across Tyche's skin, binding mortal essence with her divine form. The air inside carried the damp earth's musk and a faint odor of charged stone.

Whispers of starlight danced across her skin. As Lep stepped into the chamber, a discordant note jarred his senses before fading back into the regular thrum.

The Gorgon's blood stirred in his veins as Lep knelt beside her. His voice trembled with words of rebirth, each syllable drawing emerald light beneath his skin. Power surged through his blood, separating divine from mortal essence until his veins pulsed with the rhythm of life and death. His healer's hands, steady despite his racing heart, found the precise spot above his wrist.

Lep raised his right arm, the staff gripped in his left. "With this blood," he whispered, "I bring you life anew." The blade flashed, and drops of his blood fell onto the staff. The serpent stirred and drank from the offering. Lep knelt beside Tyche and caressed her as if she were a fragile blossom. He placed the rod against her breast, and the serpent's fangs grazed her skin. A surge of liquid sunlight pulsed through her veins.

"Return to me," Lep whispered and cradled her head. "I choose this path with you, Tyche—mortality, uncertainty, love."

Silence stretched. Then Lep pressed his forehead to hers, his breath warm against her skin. "I love you."

Her heart woke to mortal rhythm, its beat steady against his hand. She gasped and drew a breath that would never taste ambrosia again, but her lungs filled with the scent of Lep's warm presence.

Styx' waters withdrew with a sister's final blessing, while Oceanus' springs bid farewell to his daughter's immortal nature. Power rippled through the chamber one final time, then stilled.

Their first touch was tentative, uncertain—then hunger took hold. When they kissed, it was with a deep and desperate passion after so much restraint. His hands tangled in her hair while hers mapped the strong planes of his chest. The wheel's waters released an eerie cadence of whispers through the stone chamber.

"I chose this," she breathed against his lips. "I chose you."

He pulled her closer, showing her with touch what words couldn't express. Their hearts found the same rhythm, two mortals choosing each other above all else.

Free. The word burned through her blood as she took her first steps from the monument, steadied by Lep's strength. The village could wait until morning. Tonight belonged to them. Tyche had found something greater than immortality—she had found home. Belonging.

A single beam of light sliced through the darkness of the tomb, highlighting the still form of her body. The warmth of Lep's hand grounded her, yet a faint chill lingered at the edges of her awareness.

Nightmares construct a cage of torment, as betrayal's venom poisons the sanctuary of the heart. For it is in the soul's labyrinthine descent, a dream within a dream, that the faintest light may flicker, even as illusions shatter against the cold stone of truth.

DREAM WITHIN A DREAM

The barn came alive with the rustling of the animals and cradled her like a forgotten memory. Warmth pressed against Tyche, solid and real, yet a subtle unease lingered beneath the surface of the sensation, a ghost of cold against her skin. Her eyelids fluttered, and she looked up with a mortal's gaze where her immortal light had once shone. Kid bleated and nudged against her cheek. She pulled his bearded chin closer to look into his questioning rectangular pupils.

A smile softened Lep's features when he leaned over her on an elbow. Tyche's eyes fluttered with a surge of pleasure as his fingers traced the smooth skin of her face.

"Welcome back," he smiled. His hand caressed her hip, then her shoulder, and Tyche closed her eyes to the tremors rippling across her flesh.

Her fingers mapped the contours of his jaw, his lips, the texture of his skin, soft and warm under her touch. "This mortal form feels undeniably real," she whispered into his probing hazel eyes. "Almost too real."

"Do not think such things." The warmth in his face flickered, then returned. "You are here, with me. Everything is fine. You are home now."

After the first day back, her days dissolved into a blissful haze. Tyche and Lep spent mornings tending the garden, afternoons among villagers, and evenings in whispered confessions. Laughter echoed, love bloomed, and the life they thought lost was reborn.

The fire crackled in the stone hearth of the lesche where everyone gathered. Tyche snuggled close to Lep and listened to the villagers' humming discourse as it wrapped around her in its familiar cadence. She sat higher on the bench when she noticed subtle shifts in her friends' appearances. Her hand clamped on Lep's knee, and she leaned forward to study their garish smiles, their synchronized, exaggerated merriment, as though they responded to an unheard cue.

Tyche pulled Lep's arm closer so she could whisper into his ear. "Are you noticing their vacant eyes and hollow laughter? Something's wrong." A feather of anxiety tickled her skin.

"You're being overly sensitive, my love." Lep squeezed her knee a bit too tightly. "They're relieved to have you back. Don't look for shadows where there are none. Everything is fine."

Drawn by the enormous moon, Tyche stepped outside the hall. The bulbous orb swelled and flung its shadowed barbs across the village. In the fractured light, Tyche could make out the steam rising from the springhouse in unnatural waves. The carved gods writhed, and their eyes blinked at her in their hatred.

Then, a mocking whisper slithered along the ground and wrapped Tyche's ankles. "Did you believe you had escaped me?" Ikelos whispered into her ear. "You are mine, my love. Both of you."

The trees encircling the square shuddered and heaved, their trunks expanding and contracting like diseased lungs. Knotted, veined roots burst from the ground and spread across the square to ensnare Tyche's limbs. The vines rustled against her skin, then burrowed into it, their thorny spurs becoming a network of pulsing veins beneath her flesh. Bark withered and fell away to reveal gnashing, tooth-lined jaws, emitting a chorus of inhuman screams. "yOuR sOuL iS oUrS nOw," they groaned in unison. "wE wIlL fEeD oN yOuR fEaR."

"You trapped me!" Tyche screamed in panic, "I'm inside your nightmare!"

"You speak true, princess." Ikelos' dark laughter cut a line of fear across her chest. "This nightmare is your home now."

Tyche spun around to the lesche's open doorway. Through the distorted frame, she saw Lep, his movements slow and disjointed. He sat before the fire and leaned into the flames. "It's just—just—just your imagination." He seemed to speak to the burning coals. "Everything's—fine. Fine, you see?"

Kid bleated loudly, and Tyche turned to his call. The goat reared up on his hind legs and pawed the air. First his hooves, then his limbs and body began to twist and melt, his form pushing against his skin until it split with a sickening tear. His eyes flared with an unholy light, and a guttural cry tore from Zeus' mouth as his flesh and bone rearranged with audible cracks and pops. "You have defied the will of Olympus!"

One by one, the lesche vomited forth the villagers. Christos lurched toward Tyche, his grin a rictus. "The reaping begins," he groaned.

Dimitra followed in jerky movements. Her gaze darted between Tyche and the throbbing moon. "The earth hungers," she hissed.

Evy murmured as she skipped around Tyche. "The roots are thirsty." Her gaze fixed on Tyche's feet.

Melina's smile cracked, revealing teeth too sharp and too numerous. "The blood will flow." Her jaw unhinged into a wide, monstrous grin as blood burst from her mouth and eyes and pooled around Tyche.

The thralls closed the distance, forming a circle around her, their movements a slow, macabre dance of destruction. A low hum emanated from their throats, and their shadows stretched and elongated, merging into a single, writhing mass. Flames erupted from the lesche doorway, and Lep stepped into the courtyard, his form wreathed in fire.

"Tyche, everything is—" he moaned before the villagers lunged.

They descended upon her in a whirlwind of gnashing teeth and grasping claws.

"Such fragile creatures," Ikelos sneered in her mind, "easily bent to my will."

This isn't real. It can't be.

The cobblestones beneath her feet softened and became a yielding, flesh-like surface that breathed with a sickening rhythm. "hE lIfTs YoU uP, hE bRiNgS yOu DoWn," the abominations chanted. Each breath of the earth betrayed her in a mockery of the life she once held. With each inhale of the ground beneath her, Tyche's body was thrust upward. As she was lifted into their waiting claws, their corrupted voices rose in a scream. "hIgH aS gOdS!" *I am falling, falling from grace, from power, from everything I knew.* "iN hIs NiGhTmArE, yOu WiLl DrOwN," Ikelos' demons continued. With each exhale, she was dragged down into the brutal descent of her mortality. She screamed as the claws raked across her skin. *I am nothing. A plaything in Ikelos' cruel game.* Fingers tore at her skin, leaving deep, ragged gashes. Claws raked across her face and carved paths of golden ichor. Teeth bit into her flesh and tore chunks away as she flailed against her captors. Through the chaos, Tyche glimpsed Lep's eyes wide with terror.

Lep, can you hear me?

His body seemed to move against his will—his mouth forming a silent scream trapped within him. Even as his hands tore at her flesh, his eyes held a broken, pleading horror. A chorus of moans filled her ears and drowned out her own cries. *I can't breathe. I can't scream.* Over the discordant hum, a fragmented chorus pushed against her senses. "fLeSh bOnE rIp tEaR sOuL sKiN wE bArE." Tyche reared back and screamed, begging for her end. The coppery tang of blood and the sickening crunch of bone made her retch and gag. As her consciousness faded, she saw Lep, his face streaked with her blood and his eyes filled with a hollow, broken horror.

Then, the moon rolled back, and the earth plunged into a suffocating darkness. A single, harsh beam of light cut through the void and illuminated the village cat. With a disjointed stride, it curled around Tyche's legs. When she bent to pet the animal, its head pulsed in a wild rhythm. She stifled a scream and pulled her hand back. Its head snapped back at an unnatural angle, the skin of its neck stretching and tearing as a second, larger head pushed through. Black ichor oozed from the torn skin of its neck.

"Your punishment is long overdue." Hera's voice hissed through the fanged maw. Her grotesque head protruded from the creature's torn flesh and throbbed with an erratic rhythm. The abomination's four eyes glared at Tyche through narrow slits of malice.

In the distance, the Gorgon's tree groaned and twisted. The red blood of mortals flowed from the snakes' mouths that formed the tips of the branches, staining the cracked ground beneath. A wet, slurping sound drew Tyche closer to the tree. Ikelos' form vibrated in rapid succession—man, wolf, snake—as he coiled around the tree. His distorted voice thundered from the leaves as he swallowed the blood dripping from the snakes' mouths.

"YoUr sUfFeRiNg... hAs oNlY... jUsT bEgUn."

She tried to scream, to warn Lep, but no sound escaped her throat. Her limbs became heavy and unresponsive, as though bound to the cold stone beneath her. The tree extended its roots, thick as pythons, and reached toward them. The earth cracked and groaned beneath their relentless advance.

There is no escape. I am trapped in the tomb of my own nightmare.

Then Tyche's bindings fell from her body. *Ikelos allows it.* "We have to find a way out of the nightmare." She pulled Lep's arm. "This isn't real."

"But Medusa sings me a lullaby," Lep murmured, "and the blood—it's so beautiful."

Tyche's gaze fell on Dora standing before the Gorgon's tree—a *somnium* of horror. *Dora is here, too?* Her daughter stood statue-like, as if hypnotized by Ikelos' partaking of blood from the dripping mouths. Tyche caught the flicker of a dark, gnarled branch in Dora's hands. *Aether's Edge!* But the horn writhed, while the sea snake coiled around it, hissing and snapping as it strained to be reunited with the tree. In Dora's other hand, Fate's Weight spun. Its symbols flashed erratically, and a loud rhythmic clicking emanated from it. The sound of a monstrous tide roared from the horn, and the stench of rotting seaweed wafted over the village in a thick fog. Dora's lips moved, but no sound reached Tyche's ears. Tyche knew Dora was trapped in her own nightmare, fighting her own battles. *Fight him, my daughter!*

Tyche's consciousness flickered, and the nightmarish vision faded to a black, formless void. She grimaced at the rigid stone beneath her. The odor of wet marble mocked the dream's visceral horrors. A heavy, mortal ache pressed her body against the unforgiving stone of her sarcophagus. Her gritty eyes fluttered open to the tomb's oppressive darkness. All vanished—Lep, Dora, the tree, the blood—a cruel trick of the mind.

"No," she whispered into the monument's silence, the word a curse to the hope she had clung to. Her clumsy fingers traced the smooth marble of her grave. The resurrection was never real. Just another device of Ikelos' cruel nightmare. This was her reality now—cold, unforgiving, and eternal.

The stone beneath her groping fingertips persisted, yet the oppressive darkness dissolved, revealing a vast, open sky. Colossal Scales hung suspended in the air. Their pans swayed in the mounting wind. Against the backdrop of churning clouds, Lep balanced on one pan. Stone statues of the gods hovered around the Scales, stern and judgmental in their expressions.

The faces of the carved gods looked on, their silence broken by a thunderous declaration.

"You have defied the laws of Olympus!" A blaze of lightning flashed across the heavens and illuminated Zeus. "By using the Gorgon's blood to resurrect a goddess, a soul already condemned, you have perpetrated an act of unspeakable audacity!"

A bolt of lightning struck the Scales, and Tyche screamed as the pan beneath Lep's feet plummeted. He fell toward the writhing branches of the Gorgon's tree, now revealed in its grotesque glory. The tree formed from Medusa's petrified body pulsed with dark energy, and its rhythmic throb matched the frantic beating of Tyche's heart.

As Lep plunged toward the earth, the tree's serpentine branches lunged upward and wrapped around his limbs, his torso, his neck. *No, Lep!* Tyche's scream burst in her mind. Medusa's arms tightened their hold on Lep in a monstrous caress that made Tyche's stomach churn.

"You sought to understand life and death," Medusa hissed. "Now, you will experience them both—for eternity."

The snakes sank their fangs into Lep's flesh. Their bodies pulsed as they delivered their lethal poison to paralyze his body, stop his heart, and extinguish his breath.

No, no, no! Tyche's mind rebelled.

His healing powers fought the venom in a futile struggle against Ikelos' will. His body convulsed as his bones cracked and reformed, his skin a sickly pallor that soon flushed crimson with fever. His eyes rolled back in his head, then snapped open, wide with the silent plea for release shaped on his warped lips.

Then, as quickly as they killed him, the snakes revived him in a mocking display of mercy. Their hollow fangs discharged a consuming fire, and a surge of poisoned blood pulsed through his veins to his heart. His lungs spasmed in the violent return to life.

But the relief was a brutal deception. The serpents began their cycle of endless torture anew. They bit, they poisoned, they killed. They bit, they revived, they resurrected. Lep screamed in the endless loop of agony, suspended in Medusa's clutches.

Lep's body, a bloody canvas of scars and festering wounds, bore the marks of countless deaths and resurrections, each a fresh wound on Tyche's soul. His cries of defiance now held a broken melody of surrender.

Oh, my love, my hope, please, no more. Tyche pleaded silently as the sole witness to his unending agony.

A dark lullaby from the Gorgon's tree drew the villagers' souls. Their trance-like stares rested on Lep's body, which was bound to the pulsating trunk.

No, not them, too! She lunged forward, attempting to pull them back, but Ikelos' control held her limbs unresponsive. The people's fingertips elongated and twisted into twig-like extensions. Bark-like texture spread across their skin to reveal a dark, woody substance. Pupils shrank to pinpricks, then vanished, leaving knot-like hollows.

Tyche's stomach roiled. *Stop! Please, stop!* Contorted bodies sank into the tree's trunk, Medusa's petrified flesh yielding. Their wooden limbs extended, indistinguishable from the tree's snakelike forms. Wens, formed by the heads of the villagers, thrust themselves from the tree like grotesque pustules, and their woody eyes stared out into the nightmare landscape.

Despair constricted around Tyche's throat as Ikelos compelled her to witness her friends melt into the living hellscape, their bodies grafted into the tree's sinew. A venomous chorus of distorted voices rose from the Gorgon's rustling branches. The tree's lullaby coalesced into a dirge of evil.

I'm so sorry, she sighed into the tomb's cradle.

The burl of Christos' wooden face grimaced as it split and cracked around his words. "wE aRe OnE wiTH tHe SoMNiuM nOW, tYCHe. wE aRE iTs eYEs, iTS EaRs, ItS vOIcE."

Dimitra's twisted arm stretched toward Tyche. A snake hissed, and her whisper issued from its mouth. "Weeee are the rootssshhh... *hissss*... that biiiiind youuuu."

A hot fist of terror clenched Tyche's heart. The peaceful village, the tender moments with Dora and Lep—all illusions and cruel deceits. She was a phantom, neither alive nor dead, immortal nor mortal. Ikelos' form shimmered, and he stood beside Tyche. He swept back his sweaty hair, then winked at her with a golden eye.

"Did you believe you could avoid your fate, princess?" His fangs gleamed in the darkness as his hand gripped her arm, then slid to her waist, pulling her closer. "Asclepius' promise of resurrection was a lie. The Gorgon's blood has no power over a fading star."

His fingers traced her cheek, then moved to her throat, his thumb pressed against her pulse, and he bent to kiss her mouth. Ikelos' lips forced hers open, and his vile tongue invaded her mouth, his predatory gleam fixed on hers. His other hand caressed her chest with a light, dismissive touch. Then, he ripped her burial shroud from her body and howled as he plunged his claws into her, tearing through her flesh and bone. A wet scream escaped Tyche as her body convulsed in agony. Ikelos grinned to see Tyche's fragility and breathed in her torment. With a bloodied hand, he ripped the Wheel and the Horn from her body, blackened and twisted.

"Your essence is mine—therefore, your powers are mine." He pressed his hand over her wound. "I warned you that the mortals would taint your power, your immortality."

Tyche tried to struggle against him, but his laughter held her impotent.

"Yes, my love..." The god of Nightmares splayed his hand over her belly. "You have stolen from me the thing I desired most in the world—our daughter—and now I take matters into my own hands. You have chosen your fate, and it is death."

He lowered his head and licked the gaping wound in her chest. His wolf's venom seeped into her flesh and sealed the wound with a searing, corrupted scar. Tyche's body shuddered. A silent convulsion rippled through her as the venom burned.

"May your name be forgotten, your power turned to dust," she whispered in a broken rasp.

A dark smile played on Ikelos' mouth while he painted patterns of destruction across her limp body, using her own blood as ink. "You are trapped, *mortal*—trapped with *him*."

A cruel conductor of Tyche's horror, Ikelos gestured toward Lep. "He thought to steal you from Hades, to defy the natural order. Now, he pays. And you, my love, will watch."

Lep lifted his head from his chest and strained toward Tyche. "*Goddess of Fortune*," he mocked, "now you are the one who needs a sliver of luck."

Tyche couldn't look away from Lep's tormented suffering, held captive by its cruel display. His screams and convulsions tore at her sanity. "Stop it." Her broken plea rose against Ikelos' laughter. Tyche sobbed and turned away.

"Why should I?" He lightly caressed her arm. "Watch, princess." The Lord of Nightmares grasped Tyche's chin in his claws and forced her to look. "See how he squirms in Medusa's grip. His healing powers become his torment. Look how his suffering is prolonged by each wound he heals and every breath he draws."

Deformed extensions of the Gorgon's tree, the villagers reached for Tyche as the chorus of Ikelos' taunts issued from their warped mouths. Tyche screamed, her mind unraveling in her battle between reality and illusion. She buried her face in her hands to fend off the malevolent whispers that slithered into her consciousness.

"You were always *weak*, princess. Did I not warn you?" Ikelos' venomous caress sang through her veins. "Love over power. Ha! You were a fool to believe you could defy fate. Look at your healer, a plaything, a puppet on my strings."

Tyche watched Lep writhe in the tree's grip, and a flicker of darkness stirred within. Nightmare's wicked grin smeared her mouth. "He deserves it. He deserves to suffer." Ikelos' taunts wrapped her body in poison and sunk their fangs into her mind.

Horror washed over her at her repulsive thoughts. "No," she cried in a desperate plea for sanity. "I don't mean that."

Just as her mind threatened to shatter, a faint, fragile melody drifted through the chaos—a fragment of Dora's lullaby, a tether to the world beyond the nightmare.

"You do," he purred. "Love is weakness. Power is all that matters."

She recoiled in horror as Lep's suffering burned into her vision, and Ikelos, sensing her wavering resolve, pressed his advantage.

"*He* did this, Ty," he whispered into her ear. "*He* stole your divinity and trapped you in this mortal's body." Ikelos' eyes raked across her form, and he shook his head in disgust. "He played *god*, and now his toll is due."

Letting his words sink in, he paused and kissed her forehead. "What did he seek to gain? A moment of happiness? For a love that was always destined to end in death?"

Memories of sacrifices and forced choices stormed through Tyche's reeling mind. Had Lep considered her, or acted out of selfish desire?

Ikelos' insidious hum continued. "He knew the risks, the consequences. Yet, he persisted, dragging you down. He used you, Tyche, as the gods used you before. The little healer thinks only of himself."

"Goddess of Fortune." The villagers' petrified visages contorted as the god of Nightmares' words gushed from their warped mouths. "Ikelos spins your Wheel, and now it crushes you."

A spark of anger ignited the embers of Tyche's dying heart. Had Lep betrayed her trust, dooming them both to eternal suffering?

No! He would never betray me!

"He should have let you die," Ikelos crooned. "He should have allowed you to find peace. Now you are here, and so is he, and you will both suffer for eternity."

You offer me death. Lep brings me life.

Nightmare's poisonous words wormed into her mind, and his horrifying satisfaction bloomed, alien and unwelcome. She observed Lep's suffering and railed at the horror.

"Yes," Ikelos' voice poured from her lips. "Suffer. Suffer as I have." Tyche clenched his deceptive words between her teeth.

You can manipulate me, but you have no power over me.

Her eyes gleamed with a wolven glow, and she turned to the god of Nightmares. *Stop, Ikelos! It's me you want. Leave Lep alone!* But instead, Ikelos' words cascaded from her mouth.

"Show me more. Show me his pain."

No, no! I love Lep!

Ikelos grinned and dismissed her pleas. "As you wish, my queen." His voice caressed her with dark delight. He gestured toward the Gorgon's tree, and its grip tightened on Lep as the snakes burrowed into his flesh.

She cried out in disgust at Ikelos' thrill of Lep's torment as if it were a potent, intoxicating taste on her tongue—the sensation that could only belong to Nightmare—the master of manipulation.

Lep's petrified expression contorted as the horror bled from his mouth. "Tyche... *see me*... please. Am I... lost...?"

The cold hand of his pronouncement pressed Tyche into the slab beneath her, illuminating the fragile boundary between dream and reality. Trapped between worlds, her still form lay in the tomb. The nightmare wrapped around her—a dream within a dream.

Ikelos' laughter vibrated through her. "Did you think it was merely a dream, my love? Asclepius is bound to the Somnium, the heart of my power. His torment is real."

But even as despair settled over Tyche, a flicker of warmth ignited in the scars of her heart—a memory of Dora's laughter, of Lep's love. This darkness would not break her. For Tyche knew, deep within, that love is a dangerous rebellion she would never abandon—a rebellion that burned even in the heart of Ikelos' nightmare.

A solitary figure against the silent stone, Dora wept outside her mother's tomb. "No, Mama, it's not supposed to be like this. You were supposed to live."

The years carve my mother's lasting mark of rebellion into the worn stones. Within the darkened tomb, whispers of her love carry on in a fractured hymn of enduring strength. For it is in the roots of fate that even wounded spirits may discover their path, and love's vigil remains until the dawn of hope breaks.

EPILOGUE
Love's Vigil Endures

Many years later, the village has been reborn as a sanctuary for those who dare to defy the gods. Although the old buildings have been replaced, its heart remains a place of respite for the weary traveler burdened by the torments delivered by the Olympians. This city, born from defiance, measures its fortune in belonging and offers no shiny gold or titles of authority. The roads, as Dora knows, lead to sanctuaries of asylum and to a future yet undiscovered.

Dora sits on a curved stone bench in the old square where the lesche still stands. Over the years, its foundations have been integrated into a wider plaza of marble. The plateia is the city's heart, and from it, wide, newly paved roads stretch outward, like the spokes of a great wheel, each a pathway leading to a sacred site. She turns to gaze along the lines of the spoked roads.

The course to Tyche's monument begins as a wide avenue, lined with flowering trees that bloom in an endless cycle. Dora tilts her ear to the murmur of churning water, the Wheel's spiraling channels spinning with love's dangerous rebellion. A sense of her mother's restless energy emanates from that direction, as if a challenge to resist the old order. She feels her mother's pull, a curiosity about the legacy of mortal choice.

A wistful smile softens the edges of Dora's mouth as her gaze drifts to the road of Apollo's monument. *Grandfather.* The avenue pulses with a steady, amber luminescence, winding through fields where grain bows in waves, their tips catching the daystar's brilliance like tiny, gilded flames. Low in the sky, the monument churns in the appearance of a swirling sun of golden energy. Its shards of light press against her skin with a familiar warmth that pierces through to rim her heart with gold. Apollo's love flares in Dora's chest with his soft assurance—*I am here.* Often, Dora observes pilgrims gather beneath the luminous sun, their gazes tilted toward the sparks of his light in adoration. But the brightness fades as the tether of duty lures her back to the heart of the city.

She sighs and adjusts the shawl on her shoulders, then turns her gaze to Hermes' elusive path. A mercurial flicker of light dances into existence for a moment, hinting at a path toward the village's edge—then vanishes, only to flicker anew in some unforeseen corner. These swift, vanishing pathways turn each footfall into a gamble hinging on Hermes' fleeting favor. Dora deciphers the wind's whispers and the sudden glint in the air to trace these paths. And if the currents align with the subtle grace she has come to recognize, the distant beat of Pegasus' wings confirms her way forward.

Dora turns toward the most somber temple, Styx' Gate—its path paved with dark, polished stones that drink the light, leading to a sanctuary of quiet contemplation. The gate itself, a flat plane of swirling, black water, strikes her with a simultaneous jolt of fascination and dread. Dora often encounters Charon's spectral barge appearing within the gate, awaiting his call to collect Styx' toll.

Tyche's daughter steps on the road toward her grandfather's vast monument. Oceanus' fountain is a journey through a vibrant, ever-changing landscape. The salt-licked air fills her lungs, and a smile touches her lips as Aether's Edge begins to sing of the primordial river. The hum of rushing water grows to a deafening roar as the fountain of her grandfather's oceanic power comes into view. Dora laughs to see children play in the waters of his love.

Finally, the path to Asclepius' monument leads Dora on a winding trail through a grove of ancient, gnarled trees. She inhales the scent of herbs and healing and perks her ear at the vast stillness. Dora stares up at the colossal effigy of the Staff of Asclepius entwined by a living serpent. She watches from afar as the ill come to the Sacred Grove of Asclepius, seeking renewed health with prayer. The snake's tongue, which tastes the air around the sick to sense their heart and intention, always makes her shiver as it judges their virtues. If deemed worthy, the serpent's fangs pierce the offered skin and release a healing venom.

Lep, Father, come back to me.

The ancient barn, where Tyche once slept, connects to the lesche by a smaller, well-tended path. The old structure stands tall to this day and serves as a call to love and willing sacrifice.

Remnants of Tyche's soul linger in the somnium of Ikelos' nightmares. The relentless moans of Lep and those broken shards of Tyche's soul define the god of Nightmare's dangerous power. The rotten roots of the Gorgon's Tree radiate outward to stain the borders of the earthly realm. In the far reaches of Oceanus' depths, Tychoneira stirs. But deep in the crevices of her heart, Dora believes this city possesses the truth necessary to loosen these chains of evil.

In the frayed web of fate, there are times when Dora glimpses traces of her mother's fractured spirit. She accepts that even in defeat, Tyche's memory lives on—discovered in the willingness to choose.

The sun pierces the clouds and casts ominous shadows across Pikerni, extending toward a dawn of promise and peril. In the meantime, Dora keeps the watch, weaving together the strands of fortune to guard those who choose to defy the gods and discover refuge in this city of love and rebellion, and she awaits the day her mother and Lep will find their way back.

Tyche's Compendium

- **Agora** (Ἀγορά), Ah-go-RAH: A marketplace in an ancient Greek city or village.

- **Aioropaia** (Αἰωροπαία), EYE-or-oh-PAY-ah: Kalliope's daughter, meaning "swinging child."

- **Althea** (Ἀλθαία), al-THAY-uh: Dora's adoptive mother in Pikerni.

- **Apollo** (Ἀπόλλων), ah-POL-ohn: god of Music, Arts, Knowledge, Healing, Plague, Prophecy, Poetry, and Archery. Father of Lep and son of Zeus.

- **Artemis** (Ἄρτεμις), AR-teh-miss: goddess of the Hunt, Wilderness, Wild Animals, the Moon, and Chastity.

- **Artemisio** (Αρτεμίσιο), ar-te-MEE-see-o: A prominent mountain range located to the north of the Gortsouli Valley, in the Arcadia region. The village of Pikerni is situated on its lower slopes.

- **Asclepius** (Ἀσκληπιός), ah-sklee-pee-AHS: god of Healing, Medicine, and Physicians, also known as Lep in the village of Pikerni. Son of Apollo and Koronis.

- **Asteria** (Ἀστερία), ah-ster-EE-ah: a Titan goddess of Nocturnal Oracles and Astrology.

- **Astraea** (Ἀστραία), ahs-TRAY-uh: goddess of Justice, Innocence, Purity and Precision. Her constellation is the Scales.

- **Charis** (Χάρις), KHAR-iss: A mortal name adopted by Tyche.

- **Charon** (Χάρων), KHA-ron: The ferryman of the underworld who carries the souls of the newly deceased across the rivers Styx and Acheron.

- **Chiron** (Χείρων), KHEE-ron: A centaur who raised Asclepius (Lep) and taught him the healing arts.

- **Christos** (Χρήστος), KHREE-stos: A villager in Pikerni. Father of Tryfonas and Panos.

- **Dimitra** (Δήμητρα), THEE-mee-trah: A villager in Pikerni.

- **Dora** (Δώρα), THO-rah: A child in the village of Pikerni and Tyche's first-born daughter, whose name means "gift from the gods."

- **Eileithyia** (Εἰλείθυια), eh-LEE-thee-ya: Goddess of childbirth and labor.

- **Ergasterion** (ἐργαστήριον), er-gas-TEE-ree-on: A workshop, laboratory, or place of work where Lep concocts his remedies.

- **Evy** (Εὔη), EV-ee: A villager in Pikerni.

- **Geryon** (Γηρυών), gee-ree-OHN: A three-headed giant from Greek mythology.

- **Gortsouli Valley** (Κοιλάδα Γκορτσούλι), kee-LA-tha gor-TSOO-lee: A fertile agricultural valley that stretches below the village of Pikerni, offering a sweeping panoramic view.

- **Harpy** (Ἅρπυια), HAR-pee-ah: A Greek mythical creature with the head of a woman and the body of a bird.

- **Hera** (Ἥρα), HEH-ruh: Queen of the gods, wife of Zeus, and goddess of Marriage and Childbirth.

- **Hermes** (Ἑρμῆς), EHR-meez: Messenger of the gods, known for his swiftness and cunning.

- **Ikelos** (Ἴκελος), EE-keh-los: god of Nightmares. He possesses the ability to shift forms and to create and manipulate shadows and nightmares. Brother of Morpheus.

- **Kadoi** (Κάδοι), KAH-doy: Earthenware jars, often with handles, used for transporting liquids (such as water, wine, or milk).

- **Kalliope** (Καλλιόπη), Kah-lee-OH-pee: A villager in Pikerni. Mother of Aioropaia.

- **Kykeon** (κυκεών), Kee-keh-OHN: A traditional ancient Greek beverage made primarily from barley, water, and herbs.

- **Koronis** (Κορώνης), ko-RO-nees: Asclepius' (Lep) mother.

- **Krater** (κρατήρ), krah-TEER: A large ceramic vessel used in ancient Greece for mixing wine with water before serving.

- **Lesche** (Λέσχη), LES-khee: A building or hall used for gatherings and conversation.

- **Mainalo Mountains** (Μαίναλο Όρη), MEH-na-lo O-ree: A mountain range surrounding Pikerni.

- **Mantineia** (Μαντινεία), Man-tin-EE-uh: An ancient city in Arcadia, Greece.

- **Medusa** (Μέδουσα), MEH-doo-sah: A Gorgon that provided Asclepius (Lep) with blood.

- **Melina** (Μελίνα), Meh-LEE-nah: The village midwife.

- **Morpheus** (Μορφεύς), mor-FEFS: god of Dreams and the brother of Ikelos.

- **Nekrochim** (Νέκροχειμ), NEK-roh-kheem: A creature of nightmare created by Ikelos to drive Tyche mad. It is a fusion of twisted limbs, torsos, and faces of her children.

- **Nemesis** (Νέμεσις), NEM-eh-sis: goddess of Retribution and Divine Vengeance.

- **Nikothoe** (Νικοθόη), nee-ko-THO-ee: The specific Harpy sent as an instrument of the gods' vengeance.

- **Oceanus** (Ὠκεανός), oh-keh-ah-NOS: The primordial Titan god of the great, earth-encircling River Okeanos, wellspring of all of the earth's fresh water—rivers, wells, springs, and rain clouds. Father of Tyche and Styx.

- **Olympus** (Ὄλυμπος), OH-lim-pos: The mythical home of the Greek gods, located atop Mount Olympus.

- **Panos** (Πάνος), PAH-nos: Christos' youngest son.

- **Pegasus** (Πήγασος), PEE-gah-sos: A winged divine stallion, Hermes' personal mount in this story, serving as his means of swift transport.

- **Pikerni** (Πικέρνι), Pih-KER-nee: A small village situated at the edge of Lyrkio Mountain, within the mountainous region of Arcadia, Greece, near Mantineia.

- **Plateia** (πλατεία), pla-TEE-ah: A public square or open space in a village or town.

- **Selini** (Σελήνη), seh-LEE-nee: goddess of the Moon.

- **Skiamachia** (Σκιαμαχία), skee-ah-mah-KHEE-ah: Training practice dummy.

- **Somnium**: The central nexus and power source of this world; it is the origin and reservoir of the terror and nightmares that sustain Ikelos.

- **Styx** (Στύξ), Steeks: In Greek mythology, the Styx is both a river and a goddess associated with Hate. Known as "the dread river of oath," it serves as the main river in the underworld, separating the living from the dead. Styx is the sister of Tyche and daughter of Oceanus.

- **Tryfonas** (Τρύφωνας), TREE-fo-nas: Christos' oldest son.

- **Tyche** (Τύχη), TEE-khee: goddess of Fortune, Prosperity, and Luck. In Greek mythology, she is the personification of chance and fate. She is the daughter of Oceanus and sister to Styx.

- **Tychoneira** (Τυχονείρα), TEE-kho-NEER-ah: The name Tyche gives to her unborn daughter, meaning "dreams of fortune."

- **Τύχη μήτηρ προστάτης, δύναμίν σοι δίδωμι** (Tyche meter prostatis, dynamin soi didomi): A Greek blessing meaning, "Tyche, protecting mother, I give you strength."

- **Zeus** (Ζεύς), Zefs: King of the gods, Ruler of Olympus, and god of the Sky and Thunder.

About the author

J Demos is the debut author of the dark mythological fantasy novel, *Tyche's Rebellion*. For her, this book transcends the words on the page. It is a love letter to the Greek village of Pikerni, the source of her children's ancestry and the community that closed a family circle long broken. This deep sense of belonging led her to immerse herself in the Greek language, ancient history, and classical mythology.

As a visual artist and writer, J Demos is dedicated to supporting the residents of the dying village of Pikerni. She plans to donate a portion of the novel's proceeds to help fund the village's restoration and support its people. Currently, she resides in North Idaho and is actively working on her next dark mythological saga under the watchful, if occasionally distracting, supervision of her cat, Boots, and a spirited wild squirrel named Arsonist LeafBall.

www.ingramcontent.com/pod-product-compliance
Lightning Source LLC
Chambersburg PA
CBHW030236120726
47903CB00005B/1504